Heresy Alpha

Book I of The Marian Imperium

Richard Warren

UrLit Press

THE MARIAN IMPERIUM
PROCONSULATUS HYPERBORIALIS
PROCONSULATUS BRITANNIA MAIOR
CALEDON
EBORACUM
PROC. ALEMANNIA
PRACAS
PROC. GALLIA
PROC. RAETIA
RAVENNA
THE RESERVATION
OSTIA
PROC. ITALIA
PROC. HISPANIA
COLUMNAE HERCULIS
PROCONSULATUS NUMIDIA
S Q P M

Populo Bohemico

PORTUS IVANEUS
CASTRA KREMLOVSKA
NOVGOROVIA
PROCONSULATUS RUTHENIA
CASTEL NICOLAEUM
CAMPUS MARIAE
MARIAPOL
MYSTRAS
THEBES
THE CALIPHATE

CHAPTER 1

Marcus

The governor looked down upon the hateful city. Rain battered against the grimy windows of his office. Every droplet thumped at his temples. Marcus covered his face with his hands.

'Damned migraine again,' he muttered. He couldn't recall having one before he moved north. Things like migraines just didn't happen on the shores of the Bosphorus.

From the exarchate's thirteenth floor, he could see right across the sooty edifices of the cityscape below. The drab sandstone melded with the dirty windowpane and the long streaks of rain. On this awful day, the whole of Caledon seemed to be clawing its way in.

Hoping that a bit of fresh air might help, he unlatched the window. There was a terrible howl, and it was as if someone had chucked a kalich of ice at his chin. With an effort, he hauled the window shut, cursing in Greek under his breath. How could this be May?

'Barbaric place,' he growled, gripping the windowsill. He oughtn't to complain. Coming to this backwater had been his idea, even if it had been the only way to secure his exarchal promotion. What had he expected? The weather, to say nothing of the locals, were hardly going to be of a mild Hellenic temperament. There was no point getting worked up about it now. Especially not today.

The migraine had been with him even before he'd got to the office that morning. He could still see the hologram of his wife sat opposite him in his study, the neon outline of her chiton oscillating in the Mediterranean breeze of her peristyle veranda. As usual, she'd berated him for some trifle, but he'd understood what she really wanted to say. The same thing she'd been saying for the last year since he'd arrived. *You didn't have to take Caledonia. Such a backward, faraway place. You could have stayed here. But your promotion was more important than me, wasn't it?*

'May I, exarch?' a voice broke in. Marcus started. Why did the local women have such deep voices? He raised his hand, soothingly cool from the windowledge, to his throbbing temple. As ever, his secretary had slipped in unnoticed.

Polite but insistent, Severa was one of those officials whose tone always implied you'd forgotten something, regardless of whether you really had. Her name wasn't actually Severa, of course. It was Siobhan, but learning to pronounce impossible barbaric names was hardly why he'd been sent to the barren outpost. Severa was near enough, and in any case it suited her.

Marcus simply growled in response, the most his migraine would permit. The irascible bluescale of his wife's face, so devoid of any sympathy or understanding, still lingered before him. He'd teach Severa a lesson for coming in unannounced.

She loitered before his desk, her shapely form little obscured by her dun standard-issue tunic and skirt. In fact, its hem was definitely a tad shorter than the office basilika decreed. Her bright blond hair was rather loose too. His anger subsided. Their women certainly were uncouth, less polished and graceful than those of the south, but they weren't entirely without charm. Indeed, sometimes he felt the Mother had made them a little too much in the image of Eve.

The small star-shaped green light, set over the icon of the Virgin above the door, paled to a faint shade of amber. Marcus' eye darted from Severa's skirt to the light, then dropped to the icon. He fingered the ring on his hand.

'Yes, sister adjunct, what is the matter?' Marcus asked, focusing on Severa's forehead. He was annoyed at himself for such unsoldierly behaviour, and it was hardly the first time. The light slowly turned green again.

'Only to remind you, exarch, that your transit to the capital departs in fifteen minutes,' Severa replied. She assumed her official manner, but a smile lingered on the corners of her rosy lips.

The races. Of course. He was expected to be there for those too, not just the main event. How could he have completely forgotten? He'd never have done so in his prime, when he'd been a real soldier. When he'd still been master of his own destiny. The damned migraine wasn't helping either. His wife might have been kinder to him. At least today, of all days.

'*Vero*, yes – yes,' he stammered in Latin, trying to look unsurprised. 'Full dress uniform. And be so kind as to bring some painkillers, will you?' he barked after Severa as she disappeared as noiselessly as she had come.

Fifteen minutes later, Marcus stepped into the parking lot, accompanied by Severa. His white full-length uniform was stifling, with its high collar and heavy red matrician cuffs. The tight-fitting red beret, with its three solid-gold laurels on one side, made it even worse, as if a snake from his native Syria had coiled itself around his brain.

The headlights of his vehicle, the official electric, were already on. Konstantin, his military tribune, held the door open. Well over one-and-a-half passus with close-cropped hair, he too wore the white dress uniform, though in his case without the red cuffs and sporting just a single leaf on his beret. Marcus inwardly thanked the Virgin. There was only so much that could go wrong with the sturdy Novgorovian at one's side.

He nodded as he clambered into the electric, which felt particularly low to the ground today. Mercifully, Severa did not start chattering as she got in beside him. Konstantin was his usual laconic self, mute and motionless in front. Marcus lounged back in the leather seat. This was the last thing he needed today.

Rain lashed the windows of the car as it pulled into the busy streets of Caledon. An awful throng of plebs slipped about on the cobbles, hastening to evade the governor's convoy as it rushed by. It wasn't the usual bustle of traders and slaves today. For today was the twenty-ninth of May, the feast of Our Lady of Battlement, and all the idlers were out looking for a bit of fun. Or trouble.

As the car left the narrow side streets and emerged onto the Imperial Mile, Caledon's magistral, the medieval castle appeared. It looked particularly foreboding today, high up on the hill and half-obscured by storm clouds. Torrents of rainwater rushed from its battlements down its sheer black walls. Marcus didn't like barbarians, but he had to give it to them. Had the walls of Mariapol been built like those five and a half centuries earlier, they'd not have needed the Virgin to save them. Then there'd have been no need of today's celebration, and he might have stayed put.

'*Tenebrae,*' Severa commanded. The windows dimmed. The saluting soldiers lining the Mile became no more than a blur, as did the mass of soaking humanity they held back. The russet heads of the slave children, and the shredded banners with which they had clothed themselves, faded into an unobtrusive bluescale. Marcus thanked the Virgin again. There was quite enough of that to come today. The car left the city and pulled onto the highway. The road sign, '*Eboracum – CC Mille Passus,*' appeared through the windscreen. Two hundred versts to the capital. That was plenty of time for a quick nap.

'Estimated arrival in thirty-two minutes,' Konstantin said. Lulled by the hum of the electric as it accelerated to full speed, Marcus' mind wandered. His window adumbrated the dim forms of the other vehicles, motionless but for the rush of the landscape beyond. Our Lady of Vindolanda flew by on a hilltop, the granite of Her colossal helmet, breastplate, and outstretched gauntlets blackened by centuries of weathering. It was warm. His head nodded.

'Shall I start your briefing, exarch?' Severa's bass cut into Marcus' reverie. He grumbled and sat up, waving his hand.

'*Ad gubernatorem Caledoniae consilium,*' Severa said, requesting the relevant briefing. The dashboard responded, asking for the password. The windscreen dimmed, then lit up with a large white hologram of the letters *S.P.Q.M.*, the seal of the senate and people. Beneath was a double-headed eagle with outspread wings and, above both, the star of the Virgin. The hologram faded, replaced by the title of the requested report.

'*In nomine Matris, et Virginis, et Spiritus Sancti.*' The recording began with the usual invocation, 'In the name of the Mother, the Virgin, and the Holy Spirit.' Marcus bit his lip. Latin spoken in that rough Caledonian accent always grated. Why couldn't his officials learn the language properly? The Hispanians and Numidians he'd commanded before had never struggled. It was deliberate obstinacy.

First up were the military reports from the frontier. The usual trouble in the Highlands. The usual agitators. He strummed on his armrest. He'd heard it all before, and was bored.

'Dispatch the twentieth, no more than two centuries,' he instructed the dashboard. The record cut short, skipping on to the naval report. There was nothing new. Just summaries of radar activity and threat assessments for the Septentrion Sea. Then the killer blow, the publicans' report on the tax take. He leaned against the window, trying to soothe his pulsing temple.

'*Sub rosa consilium,*' the dashboard announced. Marcus bolted upright. Classified reports. That was unusual. Highly unusual. Military intelligence rarely remembered Britannia, let alone Caledonia. And when they did, it was rarely good news.

'*Occulte,*' Marcus ordered. A holographic veil appeared, obscuring him behind a soundproof barrier. At least now he could ogle in peace. Admiring Severa's shapely thighs on the seat next to him, he sighed, then spoke the cryptographic key.

'Classified report. Tier secret. Origin signals intelligence. Named recipients only,' the automated pre-script stated. It then named all the pronconsuls and exarchs of the outer occidental provinces, who could be counted on two hands. It was odd. All very odd.

The briefing started. An intelligence officer speaking Greek. While all other legionary and thematic commands, and the civil consistoria, were obliged to use Latin for official correspondence, military intelligence simply dispensed with that formality altogether. They were barely accountable to anyone, save the empress herself. They were hardly going to be chided for their Latin grammar. He didn't care about that, though. The sound of his native tongue, softly and correctly spoken, was a relief in itself.

'Intercepted enemy communications show heightened concern with seditious activity in southern provinces of the Caliphate,' the report stated. Well, they certainly weren't alone there. He had no end of such trouble himself.

'Reports to Caliphate High Command and Committee of the Whole in recent months indicate increased monitoring of a popular movement in southern Asian provinces. Movement is understood to be of a dissenting religious affiliation.' Must be something their lot had been working up to destabilise the Caliphate. Keeping them busy so they wouldn't bother the Imperium too much. That sort of thing. The usual game.

'The sign of the false prophet has been seen,' the briefing continued. Marcus started. He had been wrong. It was definitely not their lot. They would never take a risk instigating something of that nature. He started paying attention.

'Exact nature of disturbance remains unclear. Decentralised in several locations across Caliphate pashalik of Asia Meridiana. No consistent pattern emerges from intercepts, beyond use in all cases of the sign of the false prophet. Priority mandate to all proconsuls, exarchs, and legionary and thematic commands to report immediately any evidence of contagion. Alert level, heresy alpha.' The report terminated.

The sign of the false prophet. The Alpha Heresy. In an intelligence report. In the Caliphate, of all places. It made him uncomfortable, after what had happened five months earlier. Outside, the Septentrion Sea was collapsing furiously against the cliffs of eastern Anglia. The painkillers hadn't helped. He scowled at Severa through the privacy shield, cradling his bald head. The day was getting more trying by the hour, and they hadn't even arrived yet. Still, orders were orders, and he must carry them out.

'*Finite*,' he said, and the holographic veil disappeared. 'Sovereign mandate to all legates, tribunes, and praetoria. Heresy vigilance level raised to severe.' Severa raised her plucked eyebrows. He ignored her. The electric decelerated and exited the highway. They had reached the provincial capital, Eboracum, and would be at the stadium in a few minutes. Marcus straightened out his uniform, brushing down his already spotless doublet.

The stadium was located just outside the medieval walls. That was typical in the northern provinces. In the period of their ignorance outside the empire, their peoples had forgotten how to build anything but castles or the most primitive temples in honour of their false prophet. Stadia like this had only been put up four centuries ago, after the second reintegration of the west. At least that meant the facilities would be modern unlike everything else up north.

Five storeys high, it towered over the old limestone walls, vying with the skyscrapers of central Eboracum in the distance. Clustered beneath the walls was a servile shanty town, stretching as far as the eye could see. A group of slave children had already spotted the governor's retinue arriving. They ran up to the windows, pointing at their open mouths in a fruitless attempt at an extra ration on the feast day. Marcus averted his eyes.

'Your escort is ready, exarch,' Konstantin said, as the car came to a halt. Marcus eyed the throng of waiting humanity and prayed the Virgin be kind. Even with the electric's soundproofing, a low rumble was audible. It rose and fell like the waves of the Septentrion, beating on his aching temples. He opened the door.

It was as if he'd surfaced above the waves. He was clobbered by the hideous roar of fifty thousand voices and blinded by Eboracum's clear skies. He swayed, but Konstantin steadied him. He was getting too old for this.

His instinctive authority soon returned to him. He surveyed the legionary guard of honour lining the red carpet, examining especially his own Caledonian legionnaires. Interspersed among those of Anglia and Gallia Minor, they stood to attention in the same white doublets, with the red Marian star and golden *S.P.Q.M.* lettering on their epaulettes, but were easily distinguishable by their kilts. Konstantin led on, three more tribunes flanking Marcus on either side. As the defile passed, the legionnaires saluted, hoisting their assault rifles. He touched the laurels on his beret. They were well turned out today. At least something was going well, but this was the easy bit.

Marcus ignored the mass of slaves beyond, most of whom wore frayed tunics or threadbare blouses, but he could not avoid hearing them. The pulsing of the waves had become the tidal chanting of the crowd, as the fortunes of the racers ebbed and flowed within the stadium. While slaves were not, of course, permitted inside, they could follow on the giant holographic screens stuck to its outer walls. All eyes were riveted on these, which glittered with psychedelic colours. Whenever a racer pulled ahead, the wheels of her bike's hologram would bulge larger than life and become gilded, shrinking back to size as soon as she was overtaken.

On the lintel of the main gate, the Greek words, 'Be kind to Our Lady,' were stencilled in large red letters. They entered beneath and ascended the stairwell within. Despite the stadium's otherwise iron-and-glass structure, the proconsular vestibule had been rendered in the late medieval, post-Descension, style. Its broad marble stairs were framed by high squinch arches, reminiscent of the Church of the Holy Wisdom itself. Over the last was a great painted icon of Our Lady of Battlement, descending from heaven as the Demiurge with the star of the Mother above her head. Beneath her feet lay the enemy's hammer and crescent, crushed and bleeding. Marcus bowed his head, touching his rosary to his lips.

When he looked up, a large silhouette at the top of the stairs was framed against the stainless May sky. He didn't need to wait for his eyes to adjust to know who it was. The day was already taking a turn for the worse. His escort drew respectfully aside.

'*Chaire*, my old friend! So good of you to grace us with your presence. I do hope your journey wasn't too arduous? I hear it's rather grim up there. We're all getting on, after all. But needs must!' the silhouette addressed him sarcastically. It spoke Greek, but with a grating Germanic accent. The migraine renewed its assault.

Marcus squinted, shielding his eyes. The silhouette moved down a step. Three golden laurels on a red beret glinted in the sunshine, as the shadow morphed into a well-built man in his late forties with a shock of blond hair. He wore the same dress uniform as Marcus, but towered head-and-shoulders over him, and the stairs weren't helping. The man smiled condescendingly.

Flavian, the governor of Anglia, had never been a favourite of Marcus'. Perhaps it was his being an Alemannian, a people he'd always found ill-mannered. Or maybe it was his being ten years younger that grated. After all, while technically of equivalent rank under the proconsul of Britannia Maior, no one seriously equated being exarch of Anglia with being exarch of Caledonia. Anglia had the provincial capital, and more legions. Flavian was ahead of him in the cursus, and he knew it.

'Had the latest report?' Marcus asked, ignoring Flavian's question and dispensing with the customary salutation. Flavian smiled, implying that of course he had, and had far better understood its meaning than Marcus could ever hope to.

'Oh yes, and it's got all of us in the propraetorium in quite a quandary,' he said. He winked and made a crossing motion on his chest. Marcus glanced about apprehensively, which only increased Flavian's amusement.

'Oh, come on now, my good fellow, lighten up! – I hear it's one of yours today, isn't it?' he asked, laughing. 'If I heard right, claimed to be some kind of chieftain too, didn't he? To think, such effrontery from a pleb, and before such a respected magistrate too!'

Marcus was on the point of retorting that the man had been a nobody, when Flavian gave him a hearty slap on the back. He stumbled into the light.

A sea of fifty thousand agitated faces rose before him, the furious waves of their cries crashing with new violence upon his ears as two racing bikes, one red and one green, vied for top spot on the arena floor. They swerved and skidded around an obstacle course, jumping chasms and negotiating perilously narrow ledges. The fans on opposite sides of the stadium wore red and green tunics, their faces painted in the same national colours. At every turn, they leapt in and out of their seats, shouting the Greek victory cry of '*nika!*', or chanting their team's slogans in Anglian or Gallic whenever their biker got ahead. A smaller number in blue and yellow sat dejectedly in the other corners of the stadium. Two bikes lay in a crushed heap beside one of the jump ramps. The bloodied bodies of two young women in riding gear of the same colours had been dragged to the edge of the arena, where medics were fruitlessly trying to revive them.

The proconsular box was small, intended to accommodate only a limited number of dignitaries. Three stories up, it was designed to be maximally visible. Its marble facade was also revetted in the old style, displaying a large golden star over the carved letters *S.P.Q.M.* Set into its ceiling was another star, this one made of glass and glowing with a lambent pale green light. To either side of the box was a giant holographic projection of a woman in military uniform. Each had enormous wings, whose feathered pinions rustled in the breeze, and huge spears, which they brandished at the sky as they cheered the racers on.

Marcus and Flavian headed to the front row. In the middle was an empty throne with a star carved into it, to either side of which they seated themselves. The seats were wooden with high backs, and rather uncomfortable. Flavian smiled unsubtly at Marcus' discomfort as they sat down.

'*Kalimera*, good day, may the Virgin protect you.' Marcus exchanged the usual greeting in Greek with his neighbours. These were the governors of the other exarchates of Britannia Maior, Gallia Minor in the west, and Thule and the outer islands. Both women in their forties, they too wore the same white uniform with red cuffs. One Greek and the other Italic, both came from old families. There was nothing remarkable in that. Just the usual careerists with the natural head-start afforded by sex and birth. Neither seemed particularly interested in the fate of their teams. Nor in Marcus.

Several senior officials were already seated behind, logothetes and quaestors of the provincial consistoria. All wore grey dalmatic tunics embroidered with a white star, differing only in the quantity of gold laurels on their lapels. A cluster of military legates, strategoi, and tribunes loitered by the stairwell, some holding glasses in their hands. No one seemed much interested in the spectacle below.

The proconsul hadn't arrived yet. She was more of a concern. Argyra Juba, the governor of Britannia Maior, was a Numidian by birth. They had always been a proud people anyway, but to make matters worse Argyra's family, the Jubae, claimed to be one of the oldest in the empire. Like Flavian, she was about ten years his junior. He wasn't sure whether he feared or loathed his boss more. One thing was clear, though. She didn't much like him. To be fair, it was natural enough that any man in a senior office who was getting on should be frowned on. But it wasn't just that. Since the unfortunate events of last year, he'd had the unavoidable sense that he was suspected of something more concrete. At best, he was sure she thought him a dullard who wasn't passing muster. At worst... well, that didn't bear thinking about. Just looking at the empty chair beside him made him itch.

By now the races had ended, but the crowd was still raucous. A lithe young woman was pacing around the perimeter, vaunting beneath the sparkling holograms of the sponsors. Her jersey lapels were crimson, contrasting with the green of her vanquished competitor who sat dejectedly nearby. Red flags waved in the crowd. It was another win for the Angles. There was no surprise there.

One demesman with a red-daubed face unfurled a banner which read, 'not Angles, but Angels!' Seeing two praetorians approaching, he dropped it and bolted. Their white caps showed they belonged to the local heresy praetorium, which was out in full force today. Flavian laughed raucously and winked at Marcus, a sparkle in his eye.

The victorious racer still wore her close-fitting leathers, but now removed her helmet to reveal a cascade of golden hair. She beamed up happily at the cheering crowd of reds. Squatting, she shook her hair round and round in a sort of victory dance, brandishing her helmet in the air. One of the winged holograms beside the box mimicked her. Marcus imagined her blond locks spinning above him on his bed, in a contortion of slender limbs.

He smiled to himself, but the pleasant distraction proved shortlived. A trumpet blared. He bolted upright as his migraine returned with a vengeance. He shifted about in the uncomfortable wooden seat, fingering his doublet cuffs. The proconsul had arrived.

CHAPTER 2

Marcus

At first, the crowd didn't react or seem to notice. Then the winged holograms stood to attention, clutching their spears to their chests. A light flickered on the arena floor, and a low hum enveloped the stadium. Though the crowd was still jeering, all sound evaporated. An army of slaves appeared from the wings and hurriedly cleared the arena. The trumpet blared a second time, now clearly audible in the otherwise silent stadium. The citizenry gradually became aware that the spectacle was over, and faced the box.

A military escort was ascending the stairwell. Everyone rose. The star light in the ceiling deepened from a pale lime to a viscous green. A woman in military uniform, the spear centurion of the sixth legion, stepped into the box. In her hands was an old banner with a painted icon of Our Lady of Battlement. The proconsul followed behind, accompanied by the domesticus of the Britannic legions and the proquaestor, head of the provincial consistorium. The propraetorians, Argyra's personal bodyguard, filed out to all sides. The pick of the sixth Victrix, they wore unmarked black tunics and dark visors instead of military uniforms. One of them looked Marcus up and down perfunctorily, her lip curling. It was a great start. Even his boss's bodyguards disapproved of him.

The spear centurion moved aside, and the proconsul stepped forward. She was dressed in the same uniform as Marcus and the other governors, save that instead of a beret she wore a kamelaukion crown. This was inset with four golden laurels, forming a wreath around a silver Marian star in its centre. Pendilia of pearls hung down to her shoulders on either side of her proud ebony face. With the statuesque limbs of her race, she stood a full head taller than Marcus. She nodded curtly as she brushed past. Flavian, who was beaming at her slavishly, got a smile. The bloody sycophant had already won the day.

Argyra stood before her seat, facing the crowd. Out of the corner of his eye, Marcus could make out her aquiline profile as her dark eyes surveyed the citizenry. She seemed to see all and none of them at once. When she looked at you, her gaze was always somewhere in the middle distance. It always unnerved him. But then, it was said she was a close confidante of the empress. So in a sense, she was already halfway to gnosis herself.

Taking their cue from Argyra, fifty thousand citizens mutely shuffled back into their seats. By now the arena had been completely cleared. The holographic projections had disappeared and no trace of obstacle course or racers, dismembered or otherwise, remained. Everyone waited.

The trumpet sounded a third time. A troupe of dancers and musicians ran out from the wings, leaping about madly and wailing. All wore medieval costume, some of slaves and merchants, and others of princes and patriarchs. Their cries gradually dissolved, harmonising into a chant as the choir formed a single defile.

'*O panymnite Miter!* O, all-glorious Mother!' the chorus rang out, carried to all corners of the stadium by the amplifiers. 'Rejoice, O Bride Unwedded, salvation of the world!' Alongside everyone else, Marcus stood with his right hand on his heart. The familiar hymn fell upon his ears in Greek, though others heard Anglian or Gallic instead.

'The Angel Gabriel marvelled at the beauty of Thy maidenhood, and the bright splendour of Thy chastity,' the choir sang. 'What worthy praise can I bestow upon Thee? And how should I address Thee? At a loss, I do as I was ordained. I call out to Thee. Rejoice, O Maiden full of grace! O champion incomparable, commander-in-chief! We, Thy faithful, dedicate unto Thee the prize of victory, Thou who hast saved us from calamity. In Thy almighty power, free us from all the perils of this world! Rejoice, O Bride Unwedded, salvation of the world!'

At the last word, '*kosmos*,' thunder resounded through the stadium. There was a blinding flash, as if lightning had struck. The floodlights dimmed, and the choir ceased. The entire arena was illuminated by a gigantic holographic projection of a blood-red crescent moon. A distorted call-to-prayer could be heard, followed by cruel laughter. The dancers resumed their wailing. Women and children fled, terror-stricken, in all directions. Men dressed in a colourful array of sashes, turbans and astrakhan caps pursued them in a frenzy, brandishing curved sabres.

A deafening cry of woe arose from the centre of the arena. The dancers drew aside, encircling a man who lay prostrate in their midst. He was old, with a snowy beard, and looked very frail. A heavy jewel-studded crown had fallen from his head. He tried to rise but quickly paled, dropping his golden sword. As he fell back to earth, the call to prayer and laughter sounded again.

There was another crack of thunder, and a white light blazed through the stadium. By the time it faded, a young woman had appeared beside the old man's corpse. She wore a simple white chiton with a silver breastplate on top. Her dark locks were tied back with a purple fillet, and her olive skin and sharp features betrayed her as a Greek. Kneeling beside the old man, she placed her hand on her heart in prayer. She slowly picked up his sword and crown, and rose to her feet. Looking up, she thrust the blade into the sky. A thousand trumpets blared. Now it was those wearing the turbans who were alarmed. They rushed desperately around the woman, raising their hands and imploring mercy, but she was unmoved. Her stern and pitiless face remained riveted on the sky as her golden sword scintillated in the holographic light.

With another flash of light, a great hologram of the moon appeared over the stadium. Its white face at once eclipsed. When it reappeared, it had formed a purpureal halo around a young woman who was enthroned within it, dressed in royal regalia. On her head was an ancient crown, above which shone a silver star. She, too, held a sword in her hand and, like the maiden below, her expression was hard and unforgiving. The moon expanded until it wholly blocked out the sky. All that could be seen through it was the enthroned queen. The turbaned men despaired and, dropping their sabres, fled to all corners of the arena. Only the maiden was left. The queen descended upon her, and the maiden fell to her knees in prayer. In her fright she dropped the crown and sword.

'Take this sword, and avenge the children of the Mother!' an ethereal voice boomed around the stadium. The queen smiled at the maiden kindly, pointing at the sword and crown. Kneeling, the maiden picked them up again. As she rose to her feet, she placed the crown on her head.

'*O Hagia Sophia!* O Holy Wisdom!' the chorus bellowed. 'Rejoice, O Bride Unwedded, salvation of the world! Rejoice, O Maiden full of grace! O beam of light most radiant. O joy of chaste and virgin maids, surpassing all the angels!' The descending moon enveloped the maiden, as if they were becoming one. The entire stadium rose, placing their hands on their hearts.

'All hail the Virgin! And all hail Justinia, Her possessed and chosen!' Argyra cried, as all took up her words. 'Praise be to the Immaculate! Saviour of the City, scourge of the infidel, She who was untouched by man! All hail the Virgin, our Saviour!'

The maiden thrust her sword into the sky again.

There were loud cheers as red, yellow, green and blue flags waved in unison. Not far from the box, an old Gallic woman was weeping. Her green face paint smudged with her tears, as she feebly said, 'Praise be!' On all sides, people raised their hands to heaven, ecstatically repeating the same words. Others bowed their heads in silent prayer. Flavian was already on his knees. Feeling his boss's eyes on him, Marcus hastily kissed his rosary, enunciating the prayer as audibly as possible.

The cries did not let up for some time, but at length the crowd settled down. The floodlights dimmed. When they came back on, the arena had once more been cleared. The sand churned up by the dancers had been entirely covered with a fine metallic gauze. Stretching to all corners of the arena, its film formed a single unbroken sheet of aqueous grey, which glimmered in the floodlights.

The trumpet sounded, followed by another sonic hum. Argyra stood up, raising her arms, but fifty thousand pairs of eyes were already riveted on her expectantly. Some almost looked impatient.

'*Quirites!*' she addressed the citizenry, using their old title. 'We are gathered here today to mark this holy day, the twenty-ninth of May. On this most holy of feast days, we give thanks to the Bride Unwedded, Salvation of the world.' The crowd bowed their heads reverently.

'She, pure Virgin, saved us from the infidel in our hour of need,' the stentorian Argyra continued. 'She, our Champion Incomparable, made Her Holy Descension and came unto us. And in Her infinite wisdom, Our Mother chose Justinia. Justinia, the maiden unsullied, became Her vessel and, in so becoming, she rejuvenated our failing strength. For the patriarchs had grown weak. The masculine lineage of the old kings had become enfeebled with age, exhausting itself through the innate failings of its sex. Misled by the eros of their false prophet, their swords had grown rusty.'

Marcus watched his boss dejectedly. Why couldn't they just get the sorry business over and done with?

'In the lost provinces of the west,' Argyra went on, gesturing at the crowd, 'kings concealed their greying hair with crowns of gold. But those false crowns, placed upon their heads by false prophets, were too much for their masculine strength to bear. And so, six centuries ago, in our hour of need, they came not to our aid. Old alliances were forgotten. Then, shameful to speak of, we lost even the provinces of the east.

'All that remained to us was the City itself, now besieged by every contrivance of the infidel. Meanwhile, the last patriarch slumbered. The marble emperor, so named because his fear and infirmity had lent his skin the pallor of stone. And though he bore the name of the founder, he brought shame to it,' Argyra declaimed, her eagle's nose wrinkling with disgust.

Marcus' eye found his tribune in the corner. The Novgorovian's face was expressionless, his whole body rigid. One of Argyra's propraetorians turned her shades on Marcus. His gaze hastily returned to his boss.

'For such was the decline of men in those days that a king could not even keep the enemy from our gates,' Argyra continued. 'Such is the masculine, whose strength is not renewed, but ever atrophies with time. But then, O Holy Justinia, the Virgin became you! You took up your uncle's sword, and in you we found our strength again. In that hour the glory of the Virgin, the light of the Maiden, so long suppressed by the patriarchs, at last shone forth in all its power. And that light, too bright for the infidel to bear, was his downfall.'

Nearby a boy in blue face paint yawned. His mother slapped him, and he stood up straight. The rest of the crowd was not bored, however. It seemed rather on tenterhooks, as if it knew what was coming, and indeed just then Argyra stopped speaking. The gauze glittered, as if it had woken up. A ripple ran across its sleek surface. At the sight of this, the crowd became ecstatic. The sonic depression meant their chanting was inaudible, but Marcus' chair began to vibrate as the citizens stamped their feet.

'But alas, Quirites, error is ever with us,' Argyra resumed, wagging her finger, 'and so we must be vigilant!'

A pair of large titanium gates at the far end of the arena opened. A ragged man with an overgrown red beard, about the same age as Marcus, appeared. He wore a plain-white divitision tunic, reaching down to his knees. He was handcuffed and flanked by two praetorians.

'In heterogeneity, strength. And in strength, kindness!' Argyra repeated the imperial motto. 'Indeed, but the Virgin descended unto us again for a reason. In her possession of Justinia, the Maiden Unsullied, Our Lady of Battlement reminded us of what we had forgotten. That we must keep the purity of the Bride Unwedded. That chastity alone is the true path to power. That the unchaste and the unbeliever weaken us. That every inchastity, every heresy, is an affront to the Virgin, and must not go unpunished!'

By now, the crowd had reached fever pitch. As it grew more agitated, the gauze flickered and more ripples ran across its surface. The light in the box turned a deep amber. Marcus' chair shook with the stamping of the crowd, vibrating rhythmically with the pulsing of his temples. He groaned and rubbed the side of his head, hoping the day would soon be over. Flavian watched him with a sardonic smile, one of his eyebrows raised.

It was a cruel reminder of what he already knew. That this was one of his. He had seen the prisoner before. Not just seen him, but tried him. Not just for any offence, but for heresy. Heresy was a sin against the Virgin. So too was it an offence against Her possessed embodiment on earth, the empress. Heresy was therefore treason. That had meant trial by a military governor and a full ecclesiastical inquisition. He had presided, and it had been a disaster. A convicted alpha heretic. And an insult to a Vestal to boot. It had all been on his watch, and on his head.

The sonic depression lifted. The roar of the crowd crashed against the box like a tidal breaker of the Septentrion. Many of the citizens could no longer contain themselves, some even jumping up and down like impatient children. Most of the real children in the stadium clambered onto their seats or parents' backs, trying to see what was happening. Beneath the cries of the citizenry, the baying of the slave mass outside could also be heard. With revulsion, Marcus pictured them glued to the giant holographic screens. Countless thousands of dirty people sat in the dust, entranced by the luminous glow of the coming spectacle. A spectacle he had unwittingly provided.

Argyra stared imperiously at the crowd. Her eyes were bloodshot with genuine rage. No sonic depression was needed to quieten her audience now. All hung on her every word. The time had come. This was it.

'This man—' Argyra began. The crowd howled. She raised her hand, and it became still again.

'This man strayed from the path of purity!' Argyra continued, as the crowd cursed. 'Ever are the old masculine frailties reborn. Ever the corruption of the patriarchs threatens to return, to our ruin. But we will be vigilant! We will stay true to Our Lady. We will chastise those who stray from the path She has set before us. In heterogeneity, strength. And in strength, kindness!'

Some of those nearest the perimeter spat at the prisoner.

'Governor exarch of Caledonia,' Argyra addressed Marcus. He jumped to his feet and stepped up beside her. All eyes were upon him.

'Kindly pronounce the sentence rendered unto the culpable by the High Strategic Tribunal of the exarchate of Caledonia,' she commanded. Marcus cleared his throat. Argyra studied his every move, daring him to make one misstep.

'*In nomine Matris, et Virginis et Spiritus Sancti*, in the name of the Mother, the Virgin and the Holy Spirit,' he began, with the Latin invocation required before any judicial act, 'citizen of the name of

Cassian Macleod, it has been proven beyond all reasonable doubt that, in the five-hundred-and-forty-ninth year of Our Lady's Descension, you affirmed your adherence to certain false beliefs outlawed by the *Lex Iustiniana de Proscriptione Magna* of the twenty-ninth year of that event. Having refused to recant and entreat Our Lady's forgiveness before a competent magistrate, you have been found guilty of heresy.'

As he pronounced the last word, '*haeresis*', the crowd picked it up, prolonging its final syllable into a hiss. Some in the front of the stands even managed to hiss and spit at the same time. Every time they did so, the gauze rippled, as if a polychromous viper were sunning itself in the floodlights.

'By the powers invested in me as exarch of Caledonia, and as president of the High Strategic Tribunal—' Marcus continued, but the hissing reached a terrible crescendo. He held up his hand until it relented, glancing down at the prisoner. Despite his fifty thousand accusers, the man made no protest whatsoever, but the blue pinpricks above his copper beard were riveted on the gauze.

'By the powers invested in me, and for the gravity of your crime, citizen...' Marcus said, but faltered as a sharp pain ran through his temples. Argyra's eyes shot in his direction, like the icy wind that had greeted him that morning. He straightened up.

'Citizen Cassian Macleod, for your heretical defilement of the sanctity of the Virgin, in Her name, I, Marcus Comnenus, hereby sentence you to the Supreme Measure—death!' he finally managed to say, and was immediately swamped by the simultaneous hue-and-cry of Angles, Caledonians and Gaels. Everything erupted in a riot of colour and motion, as red, yellow, blue and green bodies shoved at one another, vying to get the best view of the arena. The snake inside his brain curled up a little more tightly as the star light turned blood red.

One of the praetorians pulled a knife out of his fatigues and, seizing Cassian, slit his nose. The prisoner reeled, but before he could react the praetorian had planted his boot into the small of his back. Cassian tottered and fell forward onto the gauze. Lamps at each of its four corners pulsed alternately brighter and dimly lambent as the cries rose and fell in each quadrant of the stands. The ripples intensified and soon transformed into waves. Cassian tried to rise, but tripped as a violent current knocked him off his feet. He flailed, trying to steady himself, but every time he succeeded in rising was immediately thrown onto his back again. He wailed as his body rolled around helplessly. Flavian chuckled.

As the crowd's laughter grew louder and more pitiless, the sentiment lights flashed with ever greater vigour. The gauze became restive. Huge waves emanated from its surface in shards of fine metallic dust. Clouds of that dust soon reached thrice the prisoner's height, increasingly forming into solid masses that kept dispersing and reforming with the rising and collapsing of the waves. Observing this, some in the crowd shouted more distinct words and phrases. The old woman in the green woad crowed, 'Vulture, claws,' but her voice was drowned out by an Angle nearby shouting, 'Wolf, teeth, rip apart!' Similar cries could be heard on all sides, some almost pleading.

The sentiment lights were not deaf to their words. At length, the metallic dust condensed into four indistinct entities, which towered over their victim. While all shared the same steely sheen, it was otherwise hard to say for sure what they were. All resembled animals, though none found in the real world, each being many times greater in size. Two were akin to ostriches, but one had a horrid beak on it for tearing carrion, and the other had heavy, unlifelike claws. Opposite these grotesques was a giant lizard whose oversized tail had a flail at its end as large as a man's head, which it swung around erratically as it lumbered towards the prisoner. Finally, there was a wolf of an unnaturally large hulk. Nor was its face quite that of its natural counterpart, for all of its features were tiny save its gargantuan jaws, for which all else seemed to have been shrunken to make space.

Seeing the horrid work of their creation, the crowd roared its approval, goading the creatures on with cries of 'get him!' and 'take him!' Others were less ambiguous, chanting 'finish him!' One Anglian woman even shouted, 'Cut out his groin, that'll teach him!' As her girlfriends descended into hysterics, the sentiment lights grew incandescent. The stadium was a frenzy of anticipation, as the birds, lizard and wolf closed in on the prisoner.

Marcus stood at the balustrade, watching the beasts advance towards Cassian. He felt dizzy. The faces of the creatures and the crowd became mixed up. The Anglian woman was bent double, spinning her blond hair in a mock victory dance to more peals of laughter from her girlfriends. When she raised her head, her teeth were bared, and she had bloody fangs. As the Gallic woman punched the air, her green sleeve slipped back, revealing a talon where a bony fist should have been.

Marcus swayed, and steadied himself. Argyra frowned. He retreated to his seat. It was scant help, instead sending shockwaves through his entire body. His very head was vibrating now. He lifted his beret and scratched his bald scalp.

'Gee up, old boy, you're missing the show!' Flavian cut in. He was leaning across Argyra's empty throne with an unpleasant smile. His breath stank. His long Alemannian nose seemed to redden and elongate into a beak. Why did he always have to press his face so close?

The wolf was already snapping at the prisoner's heels, as the bird with the giant beak made a dreadful clacking noise. The lizard's tongue flickered in and out, eyeing its prey. By now Cassian was hardly able to stand, turning left and right like an entrapped animal, but finding no escape. Segments of the crowd were crying '*Nika!*', cheering their chosen creatures on to victory as they had their racers that morning. The blue, green and yellow fans, still smarting from their defeat, had taken up the cause of the birds and the lizard with a new fervour, while the Angles were chanting, 'wolf, wolf!' Not just the blonde, but all the reds now had hideously misshapen faces, their paint become blood, with the same hungry jaws. Marcus could hardly bear it any longer. Flavian gave him another slap on the back. He reeled.

Suddenly, everything went quiet. At first he thought he had fainted from the blow, but then he saw Argyra. She had frozen in shock, her thin black arms gripping the balustrade as she stared down at the arena floor. Cassian had fallen to his knees. Something had slipped from his frayed tunic. A small amulet showed against its coarse white cloth, consisting simply of two twigs affixed to one another.

Argyra was not the only one who had noticed. Silence had descended on the crowd, punctuated only by an occasional gasp of astonishment. The sentiment lights dimmed, reflecting the new serenity. The beasts, which had been on the point of tearing the prisoner to shreds, dissolved back into the gauze. Clutching at the amulet on his chest, Cassian quietly moved his lips to the Greek words '*pater hemon*.'

'Heretic!' Argyra said. 'Cut the sound! Cut the sound, damn you!' she screamed at her staff, losing all composure. There was a scrambling in the box as bodyguards, quaestors and logothetes vied to obey her orders. Flavian leapt to his feet. A few seconds later, there was the usual flash of light and low sonic hum. Argyra's dark eyes were bloodshot with rage. Still gripping the balustrade as if her life depended on it, she shook with such anger that her diadem slipped to one side. Its pendilia became knotted, but she was either unaware or no longer cared.

It was too late. The crowd was already jostling to get a better view, trying to hear what Cassian was saying. The sonic depression had failed to silence him. On the contrary, it made his words carry farther. Down on the arena floor, he was beneath its radius. While it had silenced the crowd, it had not silenced him.

'Kill him! Kill him!' Argyra shouted at the praetorians below, who could no longer hear her. Even in the proconsular box itself, chaos reigned. Everyone was shouting, as officers and officials tripped over each other, issuing conflicting orders to no one in particular.

'Our father, who art in heaven,' Cassian's voice cut clearly through the crisp May evening. The crowd became riotous, but whether it was cursing or praising the prisoner was impossible to tell. The only words that could be heard were those emanating from Cassian's bowed head.

'Kill the cretin, damn you!' Argyra said, in her frustration wrenching an assault rifle out of the hands of one of her propraetorians, whom she shoved aside. Rapidly hoisting the weapon, she took aim. Several people gasped. Civilian use of arms on a feast day was illegal.

'Hallowed be Thy name!' Cassian bellowed, as the crowd let out an inaudible gasp. For exactly as he uttered the words, the sentiment lights reignited. A new cloud rose from the gauze. As it settled, a lion could be seen standing before Cassian. Unlike the previous monsters, it was of a normal size and might even have been real, were it not for its metallic hide and great mane glinting like silver in the floodlights.

The crowd was dumbfounded by the new spectacle. Even Argyra was temporarily stunned, her arms drooping and her rifle no longer trained on Cassian. The lion pawed at the gauze, slowly surveying the crowd, taking in every corner of the stadium. Finally, its gaze alighted on the box, and rested there.

'As we forgive those who trespass against us,' Cassian's prayer continued. It was unclear whether the lion was staring at Argyra or Marcus, but it unnerved him. For some reason, he felt guilty. Another bolt of pain shot through his temples.

'Amen!' Cassian finished, looking up. With that word, the spell seemed to break. The lion faced the prisoner. Several kilted men in the yellow stands leapt to their feet and started chanting something.

'Heretic!' Argyra screamed again, raising the rifle and letting fly several rounds in Cassian's direction. Moving with a swiftness beyond that of any real animal, the lion reared on its hind legs, shielding the prisoner as the bullets glanced harmlessly off its metallic hide.

'Die, die, damn you!' Argyra said. 'Why won't the cretin die?' As if in response, the lion looked up at the box again, facing Marcus directly. This time there could be no doubt. Guilt and pain rose up within him. The lion averted its gaze, turning back to Cassian.

The prisoner spread his arms wide. The lion bowed its head, then fell on him with its whole weight, crushing his body. Cassian expired at once, without a single cry. The lion dissolved into the gauze, the sentiment lights extinguished, and the sonic depression ended.

The crowd erupted, screaming hysterically. All the Caledonian fans were on their feet, and a deafening cry of 'Thane!' rose from the yellows. Some men were already descending towards the barrier, trying to reach the arena floor.

'Why didn't you tell me he was their damned chieftain?' Argyra's panic-stricken voice reached Marcus from somewhere far away. His temples thudded. The woad on the citizens' faces was melting, running into their fangs. All had become a pack of wild beasts.

As his head swam, in the midst of the dreadful crowd his eyes lit on one lonely face, that of a young Caledonian girl. One fixed point amid the waves, she alone was unmoved. She was looking right at him. Her pale blue eyes transfixed him, just as the lion's had. His head was burning. He shut his eyes.

When he opened them again, the girl had vanished. The snake in his brain contracted, then everything went black.

CHAPTER 3

Agnes

The river was unusually quiet today. Agnes raised her field glasses to her eyes and scanned the far bank. To north and south, there wasn't a soul in sight.

That was odd. It was already four post-nocturn, and the first rays of the desert sun were rising across the river. By now, the fishermen were usually out in full force, trying to make their day's catch before the real heat came on.

'Anything, Katepana?' Agnes' deputy, who stood beside her, asked, his bright Nubian eyes more eager than afraid. At twenty-seven, he was only a year younger than her, which wasn't bad for second spear.

'Nothing,' Agnes replied, 'but that's just it. Doesn't feel right. Something's up.' She held up her glasses again, but this time her view was blocked by three naked men on the near bank.

'Damn the Osmans!' she cursed. The legionnaires, who had been swimming in the river, now stood on the shore nearby. They hadn't yet bothered to don their desert combats, which lay in a heap close by. Instead, they were fooling around with a young crocodile, which they were goading with a stick.

'Go and sort that out, will you?' she asked. Strabon nodded and swiftly descended the riverbank. Distracted by the crocodile, which despite its tiny size was snapping with unexpected ferocity at the stick, they did not at first notice Strabon and were still laughing raucously. Belatedly realising their predicament, they stood to attention, saluting. One simultaneously tried to cover his groin, reddening as Agnes shot him an angry glance with her cold green eyes.

She was frustrated. As ever, she'd volunteered for this assignment, which the legate had happily given her. She'd volunteered because it mattered. There was no doubt the drugs were being smuggled upriver from here. If someone didn't put a stop to it, the illicit smuggling would go on corrupting the empire. That someone was her.

Still, her century had already been stationed here for six months, across the river from the abandoned city of Thebes. The main body of the twenty-second legion was some fifty versts north, outside Kaine, the first modern city north of the first cataract. Kaine was basically a livable place. Her watch had been glowing all night with epistles from the other centurions, projecting holograms of the girls dancing and singing. She was beginning to wonder if volunteering had been a mistake.

From her lookout point on the riverbank, all fifty tents of he encampment could be seen, set in neat rows beneath the palms of the riverside oasis. Some of her legionnaires were already stirring, readying their arms. Beyond, the desert stretched away into the distance until it reached the mountain ridge. Against its backdrop, the shadows of two giants were already emerging. Seated on their thrones, the colossal statues of the ancient patriarchs loured menacingly over the encampment. Agnes disliked them intensely. Once or twice she even thought she'd heard them scream.

She wasn't just frustrated being stuck out there. She felt guilty too. Strabon had volunteered as well, with his usual eagerness. Like her, he hadn't had an easy start, and had only got where he had through hard work. Also like her, he came from the fringes and had been a slave until his late teens. A cook boy for one of the Nubian drug gangs, it had been his good fortune to be captured by the twenty-second during one of its routine raids to the south. After a few years as an infantryman, he'd made second centurion. When Agnes made spear centurion, the katepana of the first legionary cohort, she'd chosen him as her deputy. There was no denying he knew the Nubian buffer like the back of his hand, but that wasn't why she'd picked him. He was utterly loyal, and such a man was priceless in a tight spot.

Fortune had smiled upon her, too. Serving at table in the exarchate of Carpatia a decade earlier, back in her hometown of Laugaricion, she had met the legate of the seventh legion. Marcus Comnenus had been the first to see her potential and had recommended her to the local exarch for military service. Carpatia was an impoverished backwater, so she'd had nothing to lose. Service in the legions meant no longer being a slave and, besides, a chance to serve the Virgin. After a year as a legionary cadet, the kindly legate secured a place for her at the military school in Chalcedon. A year later, she'd graduated in the first class and volunteered for the first available commission. Marcus had had her transferred to his service as a second centurion in his seventh *legio Anicia* in Near Hispania.

She had served under him for three years, patrolling the Citeriorian coastline and disrupting illicit shipments moving through the Pillars of Hercules. During that time, Marcus had taught her everything she knew about being a soldier. He had been the first to believe in her. The first to believe she could be something more. At twenty-three, he had promoted her to centurion on transfer to the third *legio Iustinia*, across the straits in Numidia. Agnes had quickly proved her worth there, too. Three years ago, after single-handedly obliterating a smugglers' holdout on the west coast, she'd again been transferred, this time eastward to the twenty-second *legio Pulcheria* on the Nubian border. Following a brief secondment to the legate's staff as spatharios on Marcus' recommendation, she had been made spear. It had been the proudest moment of her life.

She fingered the silver spearhead on her beige beret as she watched Strabon taking the spoilt good-for-nothings down a peg. Like most of the century under her command, the men were from the Bithynikon and Phrygikon. All had the Latin blood of the old empire. It showed in their build, slighter than that of the men of her home province, in their handsome faces and dark curly hair, in their fine olive limbs and the well-toned musculature of their torsos, glinting in the first light of dawn. It also showed in their easy manner and lack of discipline. Hailing from the richest provinces of the empire, they naturally expected everything to come their way in life. They were no more than city boys.

'In heterogeneity strength, and in strength, kindness,' Strabon concluded. The soldiers repeated the imperial mantra after him, then quickly dressed and ascended the bank towards the main camp. The red-faced one gave Agnes another sheepish glance.

The river glittered, reflecting the rosy fingers of the dawn. There were still no sails or feluccas in sight. Sunrise was the only thing showing on the east bank. Time was running out. She would have to make the call soon. She tapped her glasses. The electric lens zoomed in on the temple buildings lining the east bank. The giant sandstone columns cast long shadows in the half-light. Beyond them, in the distance, was the hazy outline of the old Caliphate city. Its bombed-out and abandoned towers were no more than ghostly sentinels today, wasting back into the desert. Once upon a time, it had been the last settlement before the buffer. She needed to know that it still was once-upon-a-time. Something didn't feel right, and her instincts never deceived her.

Once they landed, the temple would be their only cover. They had no choice but to go through it. She tapped her glasses again, and a holographic overview of the complex projected before her. Flanked by stone criosphinxes, a neon line leading from the entrance marked the sacral highway that, in the nighttime of their ignorance, the pagans had built to approach their false god. She had only been over there once before, but the recollection made her flinch. The lions with ram's heads. The great barbaric columns decorated with the evil glyphs of the patriarchs. The sordid efflorescence of petals. Everywhere the unbridled excrescence of the masculine. Everywhere erotic suggestion and, worst of all, not a single sign of the Virgin. An unholy and benighted place. She touched the rosary around her neck.

'Katepana?' Strabon asked. He was back at her side, his earnest eyes staring into hers. Agnes read the question there. Across the river, a red halo framed the temple façade. A decision had to be made. She rubbed her forehead, then ran her hand through her long auburn hair.

'We move,' she commanded. '*Iunge*, draw up. Vanguard only,' she added in Latin. Strabon disappeared at once.

Ten minutes later, three small catamarans left the west bank of the river. They moved noiselessly over its surface, each carrying ten soldiers. Agnes lay in the front of the middle boat, her long limbs stretched behind her. The pick of the century lay around her, their assault rifles tucked in beside them. A sniper crouched at either side of the stern. All wore the same beige berets, night goggles and desert camouflage.

The eyes of all were set on the east bank, save those of Agnes. She looked back nervously at the west bank, where the majority of the century had remained. She had given strict orders that if there were any trouble, they were to stay put and hold their position. Under no circumstances were they to attempt the crossing. The west bank had to be defended at all costs. As her boat crested the surf, the statues of the patriarchs rose into view beyond the camp, their sandstone turning scarlet in the first light of dawn. They seemed to be screaming. She shuddered.

A light spray doused her as waves buffeted her boat. They were already approaching the east bank. Now was the time for vigilance. She glanced at the other catamarans. Strabon lay in the front of the left one, scanning the east bank for any sign of movement. She was reassured. She had her best with her. She touched the spear on her beret, then kissed her rosary.

The boats beached gently among the rushes. The snipers leapt out, taking up concealed positions among the long reeds of papyri. Distanced along the riverbank, they had the full temple façade in their sights. Strabon's eyes were on Agnes, awaiting her signal. The quayside ruins loomed up dimly through her night goggles. Twin lines of dilapidated criosphinxes marked out the approach. At their end rose the sheer walls of the temple's first pylon, whose long shadows obscured the entranceway. She zoomed in. There was no sign of any movement. She raised her fist.

The legionnaires disembarked as silently as possible. Agnes led the way, with Strabon following close behind. Nearly the same height as him, she could easily outrun any of the men in her century. Agnes avoided looking at the criosphinxes' unnatural horned heads, with their leering ram's faces, focusing instead on the tumbled masonry all about. Nimbly threading her way through the piles of sandstone and granite, she soon reached the first pylon.

The snipers entered first, filing out to both sides of the forecourt beyond. The other legionnaires followed as rapidly as they could, but the sacral avenue was heavily strewn with rubble. Spying a thousand ambushes in the shaded colonnades, Agnes hastened on, leaping athletically over the stones, but some of the soldiers were already lagging behind. One man tripped. Shards of sandstone went flying, crashing through the silence like a sabre through bronze. Agnes turned angrily, but Strabon hoisted the man back onto his feet. Luckily he was uninjured, and all were soon pressed against the second pylon wall. The sooner they were through, the better, but it was the next segment that worried her most.

A large granite statue guarded the entrance. Twice Agnes' height, the patriarch held his crowned head high, haughtily crossing his arms.

His dwarfish queen stood demurely at his feet. His baleful face leered down at Agnes, concealing a smile. He was laughing at her venture. The darkness of the hypostyle hall and its forest of columns lay beyond. Another thousand recesses. Another thousand ambushes. Her inner voice whispered that something was wrong. She ignored it.

'Your orders, Katepana?' Strabon whispered in her ear, his bald black head covered in sweat. His voice shook, but though his goggles concealed his eyes, she would have found no fear there. He was setting the right example, and so must she. She mustn't give way to fear and superstition. These were her women and men, and this was her mission. Her command. What would Marcus Comnenus have done?

'*Exi!*' she said, thrusting her fist into the air again as she commanded her troops onward. Without hesitation, Strabon dived through the portal. Agnes hung back till last, casting a final glance around the forecourt.

She started and did a double-take, staring at the colonnade. She could have sworn she'd caught a flash of movement in the shadows. She ripped off her goggles, straining her eyes. There was nothing there. There couldn't be. They wouldn't have missed something so obvious. It was just fear and superstition. This was no time for distraction. She spat at the patriarch's feet, and followed inside.

For a moment, she was a little girl again, back home in the shaded woodlands of Carpatia. Like ancient pines, six columns towered to either side, continuing the sacral way. Beyond were at least another hundred columns, outnumbering them on all sides. In the pallid morning light, their faded paintwork came alive, as dog-headed profanities and crocodiles snapped at her. She prayed for the Virgin's protection.

The legionnaires had already spread out through the hypostyle. Rifles in hand, they swung around the columns, checking every hidden recess. Agnes unslung her rifle too and walked slowly up the central aisle. Her eyes flitted nervously from side to side, and up the flutes of the columns resting on their capitals. These bulged obscenely with a bulbous efflorescence, imitating a papyrus plant, and not only that. It was a shameless and disgusting celebration of the masculine.

'Nothing to report, Katepana,' Strabon called out, appearing at the far end of the hall. Agnes exhaled in relief. Where the roof had once been, the last setting of the night sky could just be seen, crowned by the star of the Virgin. She took heart and pressed on, leaving the third pylon wall behind her.

Following the neon lights of her visor, she skirted the ruins of the inner sanctum. With its southern wall to their left, and the sacral lake to their right, they had no choice but to run in a single defile, leaving them completely exposed. Though little more than a ruin, its verges all overgrown with papyri, the lake had formed a stagnant mire as river water pooled there. Its murky surface reflected the sun, which was now fully up, blinding them as they ran. The glare was so strong that it even obscured her night vision, and she could barely make out the blue figures of the hologram at all. She cursed, halting at the corner of the wall, and panting heavily. It was no use. She tore her goggles off.

Something flashed on the lake. Her eyes darted to the far bank, then back along the temple wall. There was nothing there. She stared into the turgid water. Slow ripples passed across its surface, polished knives splaying the morning sun in all directions. One of the snipers gave her a quizzical look. She was imagining things. She must snap out of it. They couldn't dally here any longer.

Strabon arrived with the rearguard. He bent over to catch his breath, then knelt beside Agnes, removing his goggles. He was agitated, but the temple clearly didn't scare him one bit. He only awaited the next event. He reminded her of a wolfhound she'd once looked after, back in Laugaricion. Officially, it had belonged to the exarch, but everyone knew it answered only to her. She smiled, taking heart.

He caught up her smile, taking it as a sign that all was going to plan. Putting his goggles back on, he crept to the edge of the wall. Peering around the corner, he tapped his visor, scanning the temple's eastern approach. Agnes studied his every movement.

'Coast clear. No hostile positions or installations within temple perimeter or immediate vicinity. Clear run to Thebes west,' he announced breathlessly, back at her side. 'Everything ok, Katepana?' he added with a frown. Agnes was watching the lake again.

'It's nothing. *Exi!*' she said, leading them out of the east entrance. She was relieved to be out of the precinct, but they were even more exposed now. It was the riskiest point in the mission. There were a handful of palms and grass patches, but otherwise the open ground was barren for half a verst or so ahead. Everything was covered in a thick concrete dust, blown in from the decaying city beyond. Agnes made a chopping motion, and the legionnaires formed up into two ranks, slowing to a jog.

'*Sta!*' She called a halt, kneeling in the sand about a hundred passus before the first buildings. The first line followed suit, training their rifles on the empty hollows of doors and windows. The second faced backwards, keeping their rear in sight. She cast her eye along the line of buildings, rising like ghosts in the haze of the desert morning. Marking the old boundary of Thebes, they were monoliths of another age, like the temple. Some stretched ten stories in height, while others were much smaller, with no particular order to their layout. It was another of the Caliphate's failed social projects. Chaos and disorder were everywhere. The place had clearly been a dump even before it was abandoned.

It had been at least a few centuries since anyone had lived there. During the wars of religion, the border had been pushed back to Nubia, beyond the sixth cataract. Thebes was never resettled and instead came to mark the start of the buffer. No one came this way now, except the occasional fisherman who as a rule avoided putting in at the east bank at all costs. They feared kidnap by the buffer gangs. Or else it was because of superstition, for the locals never spoke of the temple, or the old city, thinking them cursed.

In the hollowed-out hulks of the edifices no trace was left of glass or wood, or of anything suggesting recent habitation. All had long since been plundered, or else decayed away. All that remained were their great white concrete blocks. A shifting coat of sand kept unveiling the bomb craters and bullet marks in their ashen walls, like some leprous girl failing to hide the patches on her face. It reminded her of the village back in Numidia. The one she'd had no choice but to raze to the ground. She forced the thought from her mind.

The haze of sand and dust was making it difficult to see clearly. Her bright green eyes skipped from one tower block to another. She knew what Marcus would have told her: she had to be sure before she gave the order. But in that concrete graveyard it was impossible to distinguish where one building ended and another began. Or where the main arteries of the town had been. All Caliphate settlements centred on their meschita, but that was all she knew. The ruins of Thebes hadn't been mapped. A decision had to be made. She had no choice. They were going in blind. She signalled forward.

She led an advance party under the first buildings. In their shade was a narrow alleyway between two tavernas. She headed towards it, unslinging her rifle. The legionnaires did likewise, filing in behind her. Strabon led the rest in by another alleyway, a few buildings down. Agnes' route snaked between the faceless edifices, most of which looked like they'd once been insulae tenements. The jetties of their upper stories overhung the passage, providing at least some shade in the growing heat. Agnes eyed the dark entranceways and empty windowpanes, but there were no signs of life. All was deathly quiet.

The alley continued for another verst or so, winding about disorientingly as smaller paths branched off in all directions. The insulae grew taller and denser as they went. Like the temple, it felt oppressive. The heavy concrete massed above, as if it might collapse and crush them at any moment. Once, long ago, people had hidden out in that rubble, desperately trying to escape the bombs falling all around them. Her mind returned to the Numidian village. There, too, people had run for their lives as her century descended upon the drug smugglers. There, too, there'd been civilian collateral. She could never have saved them all. That didn't stop the faces of those she hadn't from haunting her dreams. She shook herself. It was just more distraction.

After another verst or so, the alley unexpectedly ended. They stepped from the shade onto what must once have been a main thoroughfare, wide enough for vehicles to pass in either direction. Though torn up and full of craters, the remains of asphalt could still be seen. Larger tenements, all several stories high, ran along the roadside in a more orderly fashion. The sun, now high in the sky and beating down mercilessly on the road, marked its eastward direction. Agnes was sure it led to the centre.

'No hostiles, Katepana,' Strabon called, emerging from an alleyway opposite. He looked up and down the road as he crossed over to her. The legionnaires formed a guard around Agnes as they trained their assault rifles in both directions and scouted the buildings in the immediate vicinity. Their desert khakis were stained with sweat.

The heat from the ruined asphalt rose through her jackboots' soles. It was beginning to get to all of them. One of her women stumbled as she crossed the dilapidated threshold of a taverna, and her beret fell into the dust. As the legionnaire stooped to pick it up, a mass of dark curls fell across her handsome Greek face. She stood there lazily, her weight poised on one leg as she dusted the sand off her beret, her wet fatigues revealing the shapely limbs typical of the women of the Anatolikon. Agnes frowned. Some of the men were watching too.

'No one's been here for centuries,' she heard Strabon saying beside her. He was smiling, trying to reassure her. That irked her. He seemed to think their work was done. It wasn't. Strabon was gifted, but he was still a man. He still had much to learn.

'*Confirmandum est*,' Agnes replied curtly. 'We need to be sure of that, second.' She spoke Latin, as among officers, not the common Greek of her legionnaires. She didn't want them to hear. That was how Marcus had always done it with her. It was a reprimand, but for him alone. Strabon understood and inclined his head.

The woman's beret was back on her head, making her indistinguishable from the rest once more. The guard stood to attention as Agnes surveyed them. The sweat poured from their young bodies, but all stood erect. None were flagging. She looked at them proudly, regaining her composure, and signalled onwards.

In columns of five, they began marching down the road. Its uneven surface was strewn with bricks and debris, and they had to proceed slowly. Strabon stayed in the rear, keeping watch on the buildings that lined its verges. These grew steadily more uniform in appearance, and it was soon clear they'd left the suburban housing estates. The larger entranceways and cavities of the buildings suggested tavernal bazaars or offices, but the thick layers of sand made it impossible to know for sure.

The road made a sharp turn, broadening into a wide boulevard. It stretched away before them for about a verst, and was flanked by more imposing edifices, likely once municipal buildings. At the end of the magistral was a massive circular structure topped with a white dome. It was greatly dilapidated, and the usual hammer and crescent were missing.

Still, her instincts had been right. They had found the meschita, the centre of Thebes.

CHAPTER 4

Alistair

Birthdays were always a disappointment. The young man looked out across the forecourt of the old basilica and sighed.

There was nobody about. Just the usual army of pigeons, hellbent on expressing their disdain for the ancient edifice in the usual way and, in so doing, adding to the calcifying excrescence that by now entirely coated the ancient stone. Just as their pigeon ancestors had done for centuries before them.

Alistair picked up a stone and threw it at the flock of birds. The silence was momentarily shattered by a desperate flurry of wings. Then, like a shroud, the basilica's habitual stillness settled upon it once more. The sun was just beginning to set. Alistair watched its rosy fingertips clawing at the dilapidated statues on top of the arcade. He felt sad.

This year was a special year, but in his heart, Alistair knew it would be just the same as every other. He wondered whether any of the Poor Friars even remembered that it was his birthday, let alone the year of his majority. Perhaps Father Zosim might, but he'd surely be the only one. That wasn't just because he was so fond of Alistair. Lately, Alistair couldn't help noticing that many of the friars had become terribly forgetful. None were under forty now, after all, and age was beginning to tell on them. Father Zosim, whose wit was still razor sharp, was the exception.

He looked up at the statues of the saints. Many had lost their heads or limbs, but he still knew every one by name. Like old friends, they'd always been there for him on the many long, lonely evenings.

He shifted uncomfortably. He didn't even know how long he'd been sitting there, and chided himself for his forgetfulness. The marble of the plinth had made him numb, and his back ached from leaning against the hard column. He grimaced as he shunted his ungainly frame, trying to shake off his pins and needles. Father Zosim had once told him that the Lord did not smile upon the gluttonous. It was true, of course. Father Zosim never lied. Yet sometimes the truth was an uncomfortable thing.

Something glimmered on the far side of the piazza. A figure was stirring beneath the arcade. It was just one of the Marians doing the evening rounds. Alistair watched the young man, who couldn't have been much older than he was. A handsome young Latin, he was everything Alistair was not and never would be. He watched enviously as the legionnaire loitered beneath the basilica portals, his slender figure and chiselled face thrown into relief by the sienna of the evening sun.

The black baton at the guard's side glowed, but not with the sunset. The red light emanating from within showed that its charge was active. This Latin was one of the new ones, whom he knew only by sight. They were all like that at the start, especially when it was their first military assignment. Serious, exacting and, above all, unfriendly. He remembered the evening curfew, and that he should return to the dormitory soon. Some of the older Marians had grown more relaxed with time, but he wasn't sure about this one. He looked rather bored. He'd best not give him something to think about.

He slid off the high plinth, his oversized feet colliding clumsily with the ground. He staggered as the pins and needles came back on with a vengeance. The soldier glanced across at him. Alistair quickly steadied himself and scuttled across the piazza. He felt the guard's eyes following him as he went, but he didn't look up.

The curfew wasn't the only reason for his haste. Alarmingly, his daydreaming might well have cost him his dinner too. That was unlike him. Mealtimes were the highlight of his day, and it was rare indeed that he missed one. The Poor Friars always took their meals early, and there was no admittance to the refectory if you were late. They were funny like that. They were such kind people, who made allowances for all sorts of things. Truth be told, he wasn't a Poor Friar himself, and wasn't actually sure they were meant to let him share their meals at all. They always did, though, but for some reason insisted that he was never late, and Father Zosim was the fussiest by far. Sometimes Alistair wondered if the kind old man even realised that he wasn't actually a novice. Not that they'd had one of those in a long time.

He ran past the basilica towards the ruins of the apostolica palace, his clumsy frame waddling. While he may not have been the fastest, he did know the Reservation like the back of his hand. Taking a back alley, he skirted the monstrance fountain and passed through the cluster of wooden huts which the Poor Friars for some reason liked to call their dormitory. That had something to do with the old language, which they were awfully fond of using to name pretty much anything they could. Why they had to make life harder for themselves was beyond him. It was just another of their curious oddities that they saw no reason to do away with. He shrugged. They named their food that way too, and it was always good.

In a few minutes, he had reached the refectory, by now quite out of breath. As he approached, he smiled at the Marian who stood guard by the ancient oak doors of the dilapidated little hall. She was one of the older and friendlier ones. The soldier nodded back at him and gesticulated with her thumb at the door, indicating that they were all in there already and that he had better hurry along. The sundial on the ruined temple wall told just before the hour. He was just in time. Glancing back at the Marian, he imagined what it must be like to have a magic watch that could tell you the time whenever you wanted. That was an outsider thing though; such things weren't allowed in the Reservation. Other kids probably got them on their birthdays, but he was an orphan. So there wouldn't have been anyone to give him one anyway.

As he walked through the doors, Alistair reflected that there were a lot of outsider things like magic watches that he didn't understand. He'd been born outside, but couldn't remember where he came from. He'd only been a young child when he left. He only had one memory from that time, of being held in the arms of a woman whose golden hair glinted in the evening sun. There was an icon of the Virgin too, her sorrowful face illuminated by a lamp. The woman was crying and embracing him, but he didn't know why. When he watched the sunsets in the piazza, he hoped their last rays might reveal her again.

One thing he did know was that his birthplace was a long way away and much colder than the Latian homelands. He also knew that it was different outside. Perhaps that was why when outsiders visited, they always thought the Reservation was much bigger than it really was, because of all the old ruins. It must have looked grand to them. They didn't know he and the friars actually lived in just a few ramshackle dachas behind the basilica.

The friars were already seated. They lined two wooden tables facing one another across the cramped hall. At its head was a high table on a raised platform, at which the bishop Father Vigilius and a few of the older friars sat. Beside the bishop was Father Zosim, whose beady green eyes followed Alistair from under his bushy brows as he shuffled along, trying to be as quiet as he could. The old man nodded at the one remaining chair by the door. Alistair slid his large thighs under the table, trying not to scrape the floor with the rickety chair legs.

The old men sat quietly with their hands folded before them on the table, the heavy woollen cloth of their cassocks tucked under the oak board. Most of the tonsured heads were grey. Only the occasional black or blond hair could be seen making a last stand on an otherwise balding pate. The majority looked down at their hands or straight ahead in silent contemplation. If that was indeed what it was. Alistair could never quite be sure. One or two might well have been asleep. Sometimes he thought they more resembled a flock of old birds than the last monastic order of the West.

The rotting timber of the rafters cast long shadows across the refectory. He'd never understood why they couldn't have a little more light at mealtimes. It was entirely windowless in here, and even during the daytime, the heavy oak did an excellent job of blocking out the fierce Mediterranean sun. The candles were always too few, and most were placed on the high table. The bronze crucifix on the wall behind the high table, with the diagonal line of scarlet paint daubed across it, was about the only thing that could be seen clearly. The only actual light in the entire place, and the only techne in the entire Reservation, was a faint dot in one corner of the ceiling, which permanently shone red. Alistair disliked it, and had never understood what the point of it was. When he'd asked Father Zosim about it, he'd just told him that that was the law. Then he'd said something about an emperor, which Alistair hadn't understood.

His stomach rumbled loudly. He looked around in embarrassment, but no one had noticed. There was no sign of the food yet, and the wait was becoming interminable. His foot twitched nervously. He'd never understood why he always had to be on time just to wait in silence like this, before he got to eat. They ought rather to have called it a reflectory than a refectory. In any case, they might at least have spared him the torment on his birthday. Still, as usual, he would just do what everyone else did. Sit there in silence and try to look as serious as he could. He'd no idea why the Poor Friars were so fond of silence, but he certainly wasn't about to incur the bishop's wrath by finding out.

At last the bishop cleared his throat, raising his fine wizened face to the room. Some of the friars stirred. His severe aquiline eyes surveyed the benches before him, his brows contracting as they hovered over Alistair. Father Vigilius was a greybeard too. He was actually younger than Father Zosim, but Alistair couldn't remember him ever being anything other than an austere old man. He was known for his castigations and it was rumoured among the friars that his mortification exceeded anything that had been seen in the Reservation for generations. Alistair had always known, though, that at heart he was a kind man. Like the rest, he'd never once questioned his sharing their meals. On his last birthday, he'd even let him have a drop of mead.

'*In nomine Patris, et Filii et Spiritus Sancti,*' Father Vigilius prayed. He raised his eyes to the crucifix, making a movement in that shape across his chest. The friars followed suit, even one or two that Alistair had been sure were asleep a moment earlier. One of them actually kept his head down and his eyes closed as he crossed himself. Alistair copied the rest. The light on the ceiling blazed a purpureal red like clotted blood, before reverting to its usual crimson.

Two middle-aged friars entered the refectory from a side door. It was their turn to wait at table this evening, and to prepare the meals during the day. All the Poor Friars had to take their turn, unless they were elders. It hadn't taken Alistair long to be able to tell their cooking apart. He had his favourites, but they were all excellent cooks. Sometimes he wondered why they didn't ask him to do his bit, and he'd initially felt bad for not volunteering. When he'd asked Father Zosim, the old man had said something about the discipline and life of the monk, which as usual Alistair didn't really understand. So, after a few years, he'd concluded it was just another friar thing and left it at that. Still, he had a nagging feeling the real reason might be that they didn't much fancy his cooking.

'*Benedic, Domine, nos et haec tua dona,*' Father Vigilius continued, blessing the bread that the friars set on the board before the monks. Alistair's stomach rumbled again, and his mouth watered. The bread was freshly baked with rosemary and garlic, in the Latian style, and the sweet fragrance filled the room. He was seized with a temptation to grab it at once, but he'd learned years ago that he must wait. As a boy, he'd earned himself a stern reprimand from Father Zosim for failing to do so. It was another of the Poor Friars' curiosities, and how he'd first learned what a sin was. Under no circumstances would they partake of any food before they'd pronounced their Latin incantation over it. Even so, the exertion of resistance was nearly making him faint.

Father Vigilius mumbled something else in Latin as the rest of the food was brought out. The ingredients were simple, as befitted the friars' station, but were always well prepared. The soup was hearty and full of beans, and the vegetables were fresh. The monks grew everything themselves, since much of the Reservation was really just a farm. Even the forum of the old patriarchs, with its ruined temples and the big arch with the pictures of the Forsaken People, was no more than a giant allotment. The friars didn't waste an inch of the few paltry hectares that were theirs by ancient law. They couldn't afford to do anything else. The Marians gave them nothing. Not because they were mean. Some of the guards could even be kind on occasion. That was just the way it was. It was illegal.

'*Agimus tibi gratias, omnipotens Deus,*' Father Vigilius concluded, making thanks for the food granted them, '*Amen!*' His last word was taken up by all. Alistair repeated it too, and the light mellowed to a rich burgundy. He didn't know what it meant, just that he had to say it before he could eat. Now he fell on his food like one of the pigeons, snapping at everything all at once. He felt Father Zosim's disapproving eyes on him, but he wasn't going to trouble himself about that. He hadn't waited all this time for nothing.

'*Vita Sancti Cassiani*,' another friar began as Alistair tucked in to a large piece of bread, 'the life of the most venerable Saint Cassian.' It was so dark that Alistair couldn't see who was doing the reading this evening. It sounded like one of the newer friars, if such a word could really be applied to any of them. Someone always read during meals, and they took turns with that too. It was another of those oddities Alistair had become accustomed to over time. He wasn't actually sure any of them even knew what they were listening to, if they were listening at all. It was always something about someone who had died long ago, and it was always so boring. Wasn't the food interesting enough on its own?

'For in those days, in the reign of Julian the Apostate,' the voice droned on, 'the people had turned away from the true faith, and back to the old gods, forgetful of our Lord.' Alistair had already finished his bread, and looked with envy at the untouched piece before his half-dozing neighbour. He caught Father Zosim's eye, who nodded at the bowl of soup in front of him. He could already hear the chastisement that usually accompanied that look. That he ought not to covet that which belonged to others, and that he should rather look to his own and be grateful thereof, and so on. Alistair reluctantly eyed his soup. He began noisily ladling chunks of turnip and carrot into his mouth, splashing the oak board as he did so. Father Zosim frowned.

'But the holy Cassian was not swayed by the unbelief of his fellow men,' the monk continued in his nasal voice, 'for he was strong in his faith, and strayed not from the true path. For the truth had been revealed unto him, and Cassian knew that the Daidalic Hall had long fallen. That Phoebus no longer had his mantic laurel, nor his prophetic spring, and that the speaking waters had been silenced.'

Alistair glumly contemplated his empty bowl. He was finding it hard to follow. He often didn't really get what the readings were about. Their Latin was usually very old as well, which didn't help. He'd no trouble with the Italic spoken in the Reservation, but the old tongue was another matter. It wasn't that they hadn't tried to teach him when he was a kid. Father Zosim had kept at it for many years, and deep down Alistair suspected that even now the old man hadn't entirely given up. That was another of the monk's favourite subjects, that he didn't try hard enough at his Latin. He'd once heard a rumour that the outsiders had some way of magically speaking to each other in their own tongues and being immediately understood. It was like a dream.

'But Julian had foregone the wisdom of his forefathers, and strayed wide of the true path,' the lecture continued as Alistair stifled a yawn and stole another look at his neighbour's untouched bread. 'Alas, ever is it so that the sinner cannot brook the sight of the good man and his good deeds. And so, when it reached the emperor's ear from the venerable Cassian's own pupils that he was teaching the true faith, instead of urging them to take up again with false gods, the emperor was wroth indeed. Julian's retribution was swift and cruel. The emperor decreed that Cassian, the holy martyr, should die at the hands of his very own disciples. Thus, unlike the pagan Socrates, whose students defended him to the last, the holy martyr was instead stoned to death by the very children who ought to have venerated him most.' The red light pulsed lazily at the word 'martyr.'

He had to make haste now, before the final prayer. He stealthily reached across the table and broke off half his neighbour's bread, who in no wise reacted to this involuntary sharing of his dinner. Alistair did not look at the high table, knowing full well that his misdeed would not have escaped the old man's notice. Besides, it was his birthday. If he couldn't have extras today, when could he? He reached over and grabbed the rest of the bread.

The refectory quietened down as the friars finished eating. Alistair stuffed the second chunk of bread into his mouth, glancing half-defiantly at the high table. He just had time to see Father Zosim shaking his head before Father Vigilius pushed back his chair. The bishop made the crossing motion on his chest again, facing the hall in silence. Everyone rose, save those too old or infirm to stand.

'*Pater noster...*' Father Vigilius began with the usual words. Those words, which Alistair had heard repeated every day after every meal for as long as he could remember, were probably the only Latin ones he really knew by heart. He'd once told Father Zosim that, in one of his little abortive acts of defiance. To his surprise, the old monk had replied that to know those words was, in truth, enough. It was at that point that Alistair had realised he was probably never going to understand everything that went on in Father Zosim's head. All the more so because, ever since that peculiar conversation, the monk had gone on trying to drum still more Latin into his brain. It didn't make any sense, but Alistair didn't want to disappoint him. He'd learned over time that the monk had his ways, and it was usually best just to go along with them.

'Forgive us our trespasses, as we forgive those who trespass against us,' the bishop continued, his words echoing in every mouth in the little hut. Alistair mumbled them under his breath, glancing furtively at the high table. Father Zosim was no longer looking at him though, but was instead gravely contemplating his folded hands. Alistair wondered what any of them had to be forgiven. If what was said about the outsiders was true, weren't the friars the ones to be pitied? They weren't known as 'poor' for nothing.

Father Vigilius soon got to the bit about temptation and being delivered from evil. That had always been Alistair's least favourite. He forgot what he had been thinking about, observing the now clear board before him. It was true that perhaps he oughtn't to have taken that extra half of bread. Nor the rest of it, for that matter, but it would have gone to waste otherwise. Besides, it was his birthday. Why had no one remembered or said anything?

'For thine is the kingdom, the power and the glory, for ever and ever. Amen!' the bishop finished, his voice rising with remarkable power.

For a brief moment, his face seemed that of some hale young shepherd astride one of the seven hills of the old city, facing the morning sun. The ceiling light fired, then died. So too Father Vigilius blazed but briefly, before crumpling back into the body of an old man. There was a loud scraping of chairs, but Father Zosim stood up and raised his hand. A flotilla of tonsured heads rotated towards him.

'I would like to take this opportunity to make a brief announcement,' Father Zosim said, 'for it is a special day today for one amongst us. One, it is true, who is not strictly of our order. But one whom we nonetheless all count as our own.' The old man, followed by all the rest, turned to Alistair and smiled. His freckles burned magenta as he shuffled uncomfortably in his chair. He had been sure they'd forgotten. Now that he knew they hadn't, his habitual shyness reasserted itself. Perhaps he ought to have been more careful what he prayed for.

'And while it is not our rule to give gifts to one another, I think an exception can be made for one who is not, strictly speaking, of our order,' Father Zosim continued with a wink at Alistair. He nodded to one of the younger friars who had been serving. The monk stepped out of the shadows, carrying something wrapped in green velvet.

In the dark, it was impossible to tell what it was, but Alistair's heart leapt with excitement. Had the friars somehow induced the Marians to smuggle in one of their devices? Perhaps even a magic watch. There were kinder ones among them, after all. Not the zealous guard in the piazza, for sure, but there were others who were even rather fond of him. Some of the monks were smiling, evidently in on the secret already. Now he thought about it, quite a few of the friars must have been in on it. Perhaps they all were. Getting one of those watches in would have been no mean feat, what with the ancient ban on all techne in the Reservation.

The monk handed Alistair the bundle of green cloth. In his agitation he forgot his embarrassment, grasping at it eagerly. It was hard and surprisingly heavy. That was odd. One of the Marians had once told him that their gadgets were always made to be as light as possible. It had to be some kind of wooden box or small chest. That was it. They'd put the goods in a box. They'd have had to hide it, and hide it well.

Alistair hastily placed the box on the board in front of him, as a group of friars gathered round to watch. A few even brought candles with them to get a better view. Running his hands over the soft velvet, he greedily opened the folds of cloth as if he were unpeeling an orange. Delving into their dark recesses, he became flustered. The velvet had been intricately overlaid in a tight knot, whose unravelling was no small labour. At last he succeeded, standing back and screwing up his eyes in the dark. Gold lettering gradually stood out.

'*Novum Testamentum*,' he slowly read aloud, the words involuntarily spilling from his lips. As his eyes adjusted, the form of a book emerged from the shadows. Not just any book. *The* book. A copy of the book. There was no box. No box, and that meant one thing. There was no treasure. No magic watch. His heart fell.

'So, what does our young friend say?' Father Zosim interrupted the silence. Alistair beheld the fog of smiling faces as if waking out of a heavy sleep. The smiles were not ironic, but expectant. Expectant of gratitude. Were they mad? How on earth could they expect him to be happy with a copy of the book on his eighteenth birthday? And a Latin copy as well. That might be their idea of giving, but it certainly wasn't his.

'Thank... thank you,' he stammered. 'Thank you!' he repeated, forcing himself to smile at all the expectant faces glowing in the candlelight. His eye lit on Father Zosim, one of whose bushy eyebrows had risen. Wrapping the book back in the cloth, he pressed it under his arm and, without another word, ran out of the refectory.

'And may it serve you well!' Father Zosim called out behind, to chuckling from some of the older friars. Alistair barely heard.

Crashing through the wooden doors, he ran past the Marian sentinel without wishing her good night. His tears were already welling up. It was as much as he could do to get out of her sight before he began to sob.

He'd known it, of course. He'd always known it, right from the moment he'd wound up in the Reservation. No one really cared about him or what happened to him. The woman with the golden hair was the only one who'd ever cared, and he wasn't even sure if she was real. The monks were kind, but in truth, the only thing they were bothered about was their prayers. Their interest in him had never extended beyond that. Besides, why should they care about him? He'd reached his majority now, and wore no tonsure. They knew he was never going to be one of them. Perhaps they'd always known. Maybe that was why Father Zosim always chided him for his unhealthy fascination with the outsiders. A book. A stupid Latin book. That was all he meant to anyone.

He was still running, and soon reached the dormitory. He'd long inhabited one of the smaller wooden huts, ordinarily reserved for novices, at the end of the row of dachas the monks called home. Though none were particularly luxurious, their interiors being uniformly spartan, their size depended on the seniority of their inhabitant. As he smashed through the rickety door of his novice's cell, which was no more than a few square passus in size, its dinginess was another cruel reminder of how unimportant he was to everyone.

Tossing the book aside, he threw himself face down on his bed and sobbed uncontrollably into his pillow. He had never felt so alone in all his life, even after so many long, lonely years in the Reservation. There had been no other children to play with. No brothers or sisters. No mother or father. There'd only ever been the monks for company, the pigeons and, on rare occasions, the friendlier ones among the guards. Now, at last, he knew that in truth even that meant nothing.

CHAPTER 5

Marcus

The face of the little girl in the stadium crowd still filled Marcus' vision. He had the dim sensation of falling as his chair slipped from under him. The marble floor of the propraetorian box rose up to meet him. Someone was shouting. He rolled onto his back, trying to reach towards the light, but it was no use.

The vermillion of the ceiling star light clawed weakly at his closing eyelids as everything ceded to night. His head spun ever faster, as if he were hurtling backwards through time and space, until he lost his footing completely. The stadium disappeared, as the feast of Our Lady and the last half-year dissolved into a single moment.

He was standing before the courtroom windows again. They had been large, nearly reaching the ceiling. Through their wide glass panes, he'd been able to take in the full Imperial Mile from one end to the other. It had been a commanding view, and one of near holographic clarity.

He wondered why the curial windows were always spotlessly clean. Those of his own office were always so grimy. No matter how hard he tried, he couldn't get them cleaned. It was no accident. Up in the castle, 'their' castle, it was one rule. Down in his exarchate, it was another. It was sheer obstinacy. He thumped the windowsill.

Out towards the sea, beyond the mighty hill that overshadowed the city, dark clouds gathered in the firth of Bodotria, mustering for a full land assault. One of them had already engulfed the gnostic star atop the decaying medieval steeple that marked the head of the Mile. Soon, Caledon would wrap herself in her habitually sodden cloak, drawing a grey veil over her sallow visage of medieval stone. How was it that the city managed to look even more unlovely during the Saturnal? Right now, even in the depths of winter, the gold leaf covering the broad domes of Mariapol would be glinting in the sunshine. He pictured the great Circus, and the empress' box decked out in resplendent garlands and rosaries. The crowds of fair Hellenic faces smiling in the hibernal sun, and that of his wife when she was young. It was on just such a day that they had met. She had been another woman altogether then, the very image of Justinia herself.

He glowered at the Caledonians thronging the boulevard below, as if it were their fault, and not his wife's, that he was stuck here alone in their province for the feast day. Every so often, yellow ant-like clusters oscillated through the crowd. The local deme. A hoard of drunken racing fans. Sporting their usual lemon face paint, some were already libating the cobbles with the like-coloured contents of their stomachs. Others jostled at one another, their kilts flailing in the wind as the praetorians waved their batons at them. It was a ridiculous sight, and a fitting prelude to the joys of the local Saturnal. No doubt a repeat of the previous year's mayhem was in store.

Marcus frowned and turned away from the window. For all the world, he might well have been standing there alone, it was so quiet. All that could be heard was the howling of the wind around the castle walls and the first droplets of hail rapping against the windowpanes like a harpie's claws. He was not, however, alone. Beside the tribunal, Konstantin stood guard. His tribune was his usual self, his face expressionless as he surveyed the dock, witness box, and empty wooden banks before him. He hardly seemed to breathe.

The prospect of the morning to come was greatly depressing. Nor was there any guarantee they'd be done with proceedings by the meridian. Anywhere else, a run-of-the-mill adultery case like this would never have come up to an exarch from the lower courts. The accused had evidently caused a fuss with the centumviral jury. For whatever reason, the pleb had refused to make the usual confession and supplication to the Virgin for forgiveness, and instead exercised his right of appeal to a higher authority. Why he couldn't have just said the prayer, earned himself a clean acquittal, and been on his way was beyond him. But then, this was Caledon. If the last year had taught him one thing, it was that nothing was ever straightforward with these people. Just try to show them the reasonable way. The easier way. Indeed, what was in their own interests, and what would they do? The exact opposite, unfailingly.

Still, it wasn't only that. He hated the intricacies of religious matters. It was a far cry from the simple life of the soldier, which, for some reason, he'd deluded himself was what he was going to get up north. He studied Konstantin enviously as he stood to attention beside the bench. The tribune wore the ordinary starched black uniform of the Marian legionnaire today, with its single polished star on the lapel. He pictured his protégée Agnes Radomira so dressed, smiling back at him proudly on the day he'd fixed her centurion's epaulettes to her shoulders. If only he'd stayed a plain soldier, as he'd been when they'd served together in Near Hispania. As he'd been in his youth as a tagmarchos in Mariapol.

The doors at the far end of the courtroom opened. Severa bustled in, clutching a tabula to her chest, long legs tottering and hips swaying. Her heels clopping on the marble floor echoed loudly around the curia. She had again failed to observe the advisory basilikon about flat soles. Why was there always something? It wasn't just irritating, it was embarrassing, and he was annoyed at himself for noticing. Still, he reminded himself that he shouldn't expect anything else in the outer provinces. Dress a barbarian however you liked. Make her a legionnaire, a sacerdote, or even a Vestal. A barbarian was still a barbarian.

'The accused is ready, exarch,' Severa said, unconsciously straightening her dress. 'He's had the full preparatory briefing, and is ready for the trial proceeding with your excellency...' She hesitated, her pale fingertips fiddling with the top of the tabula, as if it were a clam shell she was trying to pry apart.

'Yes, yes, sister adjunct, out with it!' he said, as his eyes roved disapprovingly down her sinuous black dress to her high heels. 'Please do get to the point. Aren't your people known for not beating about the bush? Need I remind my secretary that I've a long enough day ahead of me as it is, without her prolonging my pain?' His tone was already more relenting. As usual, his nerves were uncoiling at the sight of her curvaceousness. He chided himself for another unsoldierly lapse.

'Sorry, governor, my apologies,' she stammered. 'The thing is, you see, the prisoner... He is not, ehm, how to put it? He is not wholly civil, as such,' she said, slightly mispronouncing the Latin 'civilis' with her Caledonian inflexion.

'Civil?' Marcus spat. 'Is a governor to expect civility from his prisoner? I care nothing whether he is civil or not. He can be whatever he likes. It's his neck that's on the line. No, I should rather think he should be the one worried about whether I am feeling civil today. What trifles!'

'Yes, your excellency, of course,' Severa replied, but was clearly not done yet. 'Perhaps I did not convey the sentiment sufficiently strongly. I thought your excellency should be aware that, while he has been briefed, the prisoner's disposition is of a protestational nature. The prisoner insists that he is a – how to put it – a chieftain, or local katepano, of sorts... Given the circumstances, I would recommend that, before he is put before your excellency's person, due consideration is given to – to restraint, exarch.' She peered awkwardly at Konstantin. Marcus frowned.

'So, an exarch is to fear his prisoners as well now, is he?' Marcus asked, laughing. 'And, while he's at it, flatter their delusions of grandeur?' He looked at Konstantin, too. The tribune grimaced as he maintained his vigil of the empty courtroom. That was quite right. They were soldiers. They'd nothing to fear from a raving Caledonian drunkard.

Marcus sighed as he collapsed onto his throne, glancing distractedly at the small star-shaped green light on the ceiling. While always so placed in gubernatorial and official buildings, this one was particularly well optimised for its sentential and sentiment analysis. Admittedly, he'd never quite understood the point of that in a courtroom, where evidence could be coerced anyway, but it was a legal requirement. His eyes moved to the contrastingly sub-optimal fresco on the wall behind him. It was the standard depiction of the Descension, but Justinia was much too large for a mortal before her holy gnosis, while the eclipsing moon embowering the Virgin had turned a wan slate with age. Both the legionnaires manning the battlements of the beleaguered Mariapol and the infidel soldiers swarming beneath them looked like children.

'*Inducite reum!*' Marcus barked at the empty courtroom, waving his hand. The far doors opened, and two legionnaires escorted in a handcuffed man. The prisoner, who wore a white smock, was well over a passus-and-a-half tall with bright blue eyes, a bushy ginger beard and long, unkempt red hair. He lumbered up the aisle between the empty benches like some overgrown Caledonian bear. Though he offered no resistance to his guards, no sooner had he caught sight of Severa than he winked at her lasciviously, and his eyes sparkled with a devilish blue fire. Severa shuddered. The light turned amber.

The soldiers brought the prisoner before the tribunal. Though the bench was set on a raised dais, allowing the judge to look down on the accused, he was so tall that he was nearly eye-level with Marcus.

One of the legionnaires was on the point of shoving the prisoner onto his knees when Marcus lazily raised his hand to countermand the order. He slid a notch further down the hard back of his throne. There was plenty of time for that yet. From behind drooping lids, his eyes bored into the Caledonian's face like two burning censers. Severa shifted uncomfortably in his periphery, fussily raising her tabula as she prepared to record the trial proceedings.

'*Civis*,' Marcus addressed the prisoner as a citizen, 'by what name are you kno—?' He stopped short. To his great surprise and annoyance, the prisoner was still staring at his secretary, utterly unabashed. He was quite unused to being ignored so brazenly by a native, not least one whose fate was in his hands. Was the man even aware he was the exarch? Severa nodded to assure him she'd remembered to activate the sonic autotranslation. Of course she had, but there had to be some explanation. Such obstinacy defied belief.

'Citizen!' Marcus repeated, impatiently scrutinising the holographic display embedded in the bench. 'I ask you again – and note it well, for it is the last time I shall deign to ask – by what name are you known?' His icy stare failed to douse the flames in the Caledonian's eyes. The guards' arms twitched spasmodically by their electrobatons.

'Cassian,' the prisoner announced at last, smirking at Marcus just as he was about to rise. 'Cassian Macleod. That's my name. But I'd wager you know that already. So to my mind, what's the bother of asking? What you probably did nay know is that I'm the thane of Caledon. Aye, true by blood. So, governor, this here is my castle. My castle, aye, that it is.' He grinned at Marcus, reiterating his name and title with another wink and half-bow to Severa. There was an audible tightening of leather as Konstantin's glove fastened around his baton.

'Citizen... Cassian,' Marcus continued, forcibly ignoring his impertinence. The screen was now animated by a flickering light. Severa's hand hovered a few digits above the tabula crooked in her elbow. Holographic images jumped out of the bench, moving in time with the dancing of her fingers. Cassian was jostling some praetorians in the rain, trying to evade arrest.

'Aye, I know, it's a strange name, isn't it?' the prisoner asked with a guffaw. 'Not common in these parts, I'd say, more like one of your folk down south. But you see, my ma had her ways, especially with me being the thane and all. She was all for naming us after the blessed fathers of old, and that's as well as may be if you ask me!' Cassian cast about, apparently expecting some confirmation from Severa and the soldiers. Instead, at the word 'blessed', the star light flashed crimson. It reminded Marcus of an angry boil on his chin, which had been threatening to burst all week.

He cautiously fingered the spot, observing the prisoner with displeasure. It was baffling. Such effrontery, to say nothing of such blatant immemory, was beyond anything he'd seen for many years. Not since the slave riots, at least. How could this Caledonian satyr, who was in such legal peril, and moreover of such low station, see fit to lope about before a governor like this and do all in his power to hasten his own condemnation? Was the man even aware that without a repentance, he could have him locked up quicker than he could say 'Saturnal'?

'Citizen of the name Cassian Macleod, or whatever you claim to be,' Marcus resumed, trying as hard as he could to maintain his veneer of boredom, 'please be so kind as to confirm for the benefit of this court that you are the subject correctly identified in the following holorecord.'

Severa waved her hand over her tabula, and a new projection rose from the screen. It was summer and the sun shone on the Imperial Mile. Despite the dull pigmentation of the hologram, it was clear that it was stiflingly hot. The many Caledonians thronging the Mile in their native dress showed that it was a feast day, most likely that of Our Lady of Battlement. Cassian was striding down the Mile in a kilt, watching the procession. Periodically he would smile down at the slave children tugging at his kilt, handing them tidbits of food from his sporran. In his hand was a large bottle, out of which he kept taking swigs. Whenever he did so, tottering slightly, the bottle's contents would spill into his beard, which he would messily wipe with the back of his hand. Marcus pursed his thin Syrian lips.

A throng of Caledonian women and girls were processing down the Mile. In their hands they bore colourful banners emblazoned with the icon of Our Lady of Battlement, sword in hand and wearing a large golden crown. Most of the icons were set over the lettering '*S.P.Q.M.*', while others had Greek legends with the gnostic titles of the Parthena Sophia from the Secret Book. Marcus had never really understood what most of them meant. Nor, for that matter, what most of the Virgin's gnostic mysteries were all about.

The holographic Cassian was similarly uninterested in gnostic proverbs. His eyes were instead fixed on the young women going by, and one in particular. Not much past her majority, like Severa she had the cascade of reddish-blond hair typical of a Caledonian woman. As all the rest, she wore a cherry-coloured tartan skirt and white blouse, across which a red sash with a silver star was slung. Raising her bare arms above her head, she clapped, as together with her fellow marchers she sang the Gospel of Truth:

> 'The Divinity recognised Her Nous, the Mother of Truth, and spoke of the Virgin, who gave birth to the light!'

Cassian jostled the other spectators as he tried to keep pace, his eyes never once leaving the woman as they devoured her russet tresses, milk-white neck, and skirt pulsing rhythmically to the hymn.

The record skipped forward. The sun was dimmer now, but it was still the same day. The scene changed from the Imperial Mile to a courtyard somewhere in the medieval quarter. It was early evening. Cassian was no longer the only reveller with a kalich in his hand. He stood outside a taverna with his confederates, drunkenly singing a Caledonian war song. In the midst of his cups, fire kindled in his wine-sodden eyes, and his grip on his companions' shoulders slackened. The young woman reappeared, flanked by two of her fellow marchers. She still wore her processional outfit, but the sash and star were gone. As she crossed the cobbled forum, she glanced back over her shoulder at Cassian and smiled. One of her companions giggled. The woman slapped her friend's arm playfully but did not stop looking at Cassian, who gazed back at her. One of Cassian's fellow revellers pushed him forward.

Severa's hand performed another pirouette over her tabula. A rapid sequence of medieval alleys skipped by, coming to a stop on a deserted side street whose cobbles were strewn with abandoned kalichs, sashes, and polychromous confetti. The young woman appeared, giggling and tottering slightly. Cassian soon came into view, too. He was by now altogether drunk, but the cobalt fires beneath his bushy red eyebrows were in no wise dimmed. As he pursued the woman down the alleyway, he periodically lunged sideward into a doorway and sang an amorous ditty, causing her to titter and blush. Finally, the recording halted at the end of the alley. Cassian had caught up with his prey, who leant drunkenly against a wooden doorpost as she looked up at him flirtatiously. Catching up an abandoned sash that hung on the post, she slung it over his broad shoulders, and they both collapsed out of sight. The star light shone like a ruby.

'*Satis!*' Marcus exclaimed. 'Are we quite done, or must I first hear the full repertoire of Highland love songs in all their beauty?'

Severa blushed. She quickly reassumed her usual studied seriousness, but he could not help noticing how much the rosy flush became her. He grew angry with himself. It was another slip. Why had he been so mesmerised by the plebeian spectacle anyway? He mustn't let his guard down like that again.

The program terminated and the empty courtroom came back into view. Marcus studied the real Cassian. The satyric gleam in his eyes was gone. Was he, just perhaps, pondering his misdeeds? Might he even repent? Then he remembered that he didn't care. Why was he getting drawn into the detail of all this tiresome nonsense? He was the governor. He still wasn't even sure why the business had come up to him in the first place. He just needed the whole affair wrapped up as quickly as possible. It looked to be getting on for the zenith now, though one could never quite be sure under such baleful northern skies. Cassian's repentance and a prayer to the Virgin for his forgiveness would mean a swift acquittal. Then he could send the drunkard back to the sewers of Caledon where he belonged.

Still, what if for some reason the pleb refused to repent? Then he'd just have to have him locked up until he changed his mind. A year was usually enough for them to give up the game, but exarchal discretion technically allowed for as long as was needed. That was because the absence of a supplication to the Virgin meant the accused's offence was unmitigated in Her eyes. That left only one possible punishment for the unrepentant. Death. To avoid that necessity, as was almost always the case in practice, a bit of mild coaxing by the tagmata and, if needed, public humiliation, might be applied to help the recalcitrant come to their senses. He dearly hoped all that hassle wasn't going to be necessary.

'Citizen Cassian Macleod,' Marcus resumed wearily, as if the holographic interlude had been no more interesting than the latest publicans' report, 'the evidence you have witnessed today, provided to me as judge by the quaestorial prosecution and taken directly from the curial record, attests conclusively to your extramarital intimate relations with another citizen. Do you agree with the accuracy of the evidence that the court has itself provided, and thereby wish to drop your appeal to your centumviral conviction, and supplicate Our Lady here, before the witness of this court, that She forgive you the *nefas* of adulterous *moicheia* by which you have profaned Her, and that She commute your crime to the venial sin of moderated fornication? Or do you wish further to contest the veracity of the evidence?'

'Veracity?' the prisoner replied with a fiendish smile. '*Veritas*, you mean? If I'm nay much mistaken, governor, you're asking me about the truth?' The little blue fires had reignited.

'Answer the question, citizen,' Marcus demanded, still trying to sound bored. 'Do you, or do you not, agree that the evidence demonstrates that your relations with this woman were not as those divinely sanctioned between wife and husband?'

'Divinely sanctioned, you say?' Cassian asked, laughing. 'Now, that's altogether a different question, governor! I cannae answer for what you see as being divinely sanctioned, and by whom. Well, that's a fine phrase your lot have got there. But if you're asking about the truth, I can tell you I'm no liar. What you've got there is the truth and nought else!' The light was already burning Marcus' eyelashes.

'Citizen Cassian,' he said seriously, 'I counsel you to weigh your words very carefully. You have admitted before a competent magistrate to intimate relations exceeding the divinely sanctioned bounds of marriage. I am obliged to remind you of the law, and the punishment that inheres to a crime of this nature. You are aware, are you not, that such relations profane the Holy Mother, and what such *nefas* means?'

'Profanity, is it?' Cassian replied, playing back Marcus' words like some demonic bird. 'What you and your lot mean by that, governor, I cannae tell you. You'll have to tell me what you mean by that yourself, and what that has to do with what a laddie and a lassie get up to in their bedrooms. But I'd wager that's something your lot know rather a lot more about than we do, governor, if I'm nay much mistaken? *Nefas*, ha!' The sonic autotranslation flipped '*nefas*' back into Caledonian with grating consonance. The back of Marcus' neck grew hot.

'Let me spell it out for you then, citizen, if you haven't the wits,' Marcus said, smiling condescendingly. 'Your intimate relations outside the divine sanction of marriage profane the Virgin. By law, left unmitigated, such profanity of Our Lady is nefarious, and thereby also an offence against Her possessed embodiment on earth, Her Imperial Majesty. Perhaps you are unaware that, for this reason, *nefas* is a capital offence, attracting the Supreme Measure? That is the reason why we are sitting here right now, having this polite conversation. Though it appears that this fact has escaped your notice.'

'Aye, death,' Cassian answered, staring with loathing at Konstantin, whose glove tightened a little more. 'I know that's your thing, your lot. Always has been. Unsurprising for them that's got no love for life, I suppose, finding in love nought but sin. Although, if what I hear about what your lot get up to is true, there's a fair bit of *nefas* down your way too...'

'Citizen!' Marcus exclaimed. 'You have already tried my patience quite enough. If you're not quick-witted enough to see how things stand for you, I shall not trouble myself any further on your account. Perhaps you'd like a spell in the castle dungeon to give yourself more time to work things through?' He pointed at the rock beneath the curial floor.

'Aye, it's always the same with your lot, governor, isn't it?' Cassian replied, unphased. 'Why is it one rule for your lot, and another for my people?'

'I am not here to bandy words with you, philosoph, thane, or whatever you claim to be!' Marcus shouted, his neck burning. 'You may pontificate as much as you like in your pothouses with your erudite Caledonian friends. Sing together to your heart's content about your mighty forebears, and all the glorious contributions to civilisation they doubtless made. But I beg you, spare my ears! If I wanted lessons in ethics, I should rather make my way back south to Mystras, and enrol in the university there. As it is, I am a soldier, and this is a military court, and you would do well to remember that!'

Cassian reddened. 'Perhaps, laddie, you'd do yourself a favour if you did make your way down to Mystras, if what they say about your own love life is true!' he said, his eyes catching alight. 'My people may be coarse, governor, but we're not blind. We know hypocrisy when we see it. We've heard about what goes on down south. Nought but *nefas* in your palaces – and universities – if you get my drift!' He burst into hysterical laughter.

Severa glanced furtively at Marcus, who had turned white. The gibe was clear, and it touched him to the core. To have the rumours about his wife Hypatia, the Mystras university dean, aired like this in the public curia was more than he could bear. Not least by such a jumped-up pothouse-dweller of Caledon. Especially when she was the very reason he was stuck out here alone in the first place. He felt as if he'd been stripped naked, for his shame to be paraded cruelly before all. The effrontery was simply unimaginable.

'How dare you speak such calumnies of your betters!' he said furiously. 'Your life is in my hands, and you dare rile me like this? From now on, you will address me as befits a magistrate, and speak only when spoken to. Do I make myself plain?'

Cassian was still laughing like a rabid hyena. One of the guards touched his baton against the prisoner's leg. He fell to one knee but, to Marcus' immense chagrin, continued to howl. Marcus touched his finger to his lips and waved it in an arc across the room.

'Do I make myself plain, citizen?' His voice cut unnaturally through the selective sonic depression, like a knife through ice. A second baton touched Cassian, its black chrome glowing like an incandescent rose. Like a bear stung by bees on both flanks, Cassian collapsed face-down on the floor, but even now his body convulsed with laughter. It was humiliating.

'Right, thane, or whatever you call yourself, prison is clearly too good for you, so I've a better idea!' Marcus exclaimed, pointing at the Imperial Mile below. 'You see that steeple down there? If you don't repent right now, I'll have you strapped to it naked until you change your mind. How would you like that? A perfect chance to glory before your people to your heart's content!' He leaned forward, scrutinising the Caledonian's mass of red hair as it uncoiled like knotted kelp over the polished marble. At length, he chopped the air with his hand, and the silence dissipated. The squeaking of the legionnaires' jackboots and Severa's heels was deafening. Suddenly, two sapphires ignited amid the infernal golden coils.

'Stone,' Cassian mumbled, rising onto his knees. 'Who shall first cast a stone? She that is without sin. Let her first cast a stone. Aye, she that is without sin!' The star light deepened to a rich burgundy. Marcus' nape was white hot. The insult to his wife was clear.

'How dare you, pleb!' he said, his knuckles tightening like lattice bombs as he lost all composure. 'How dare you slander your betters! I will hear no more of this. You will apologise to your lawful governor at once for your insolence, or face the consequences.'

'There is only One who can forgive you your sins,' the Caledonian persisted, fixing Marcus with a look of quiet conviction. 'Only One who can lead you back to the grace from which you are fallen. The saints may plead for you before His Majesty, but they cannot forgive you your trespasses. There is only One who can forgive. Only One Redeemer of man!'

His eyes brightened, as if he were only now becoming conscious of what he was saying. A touch of apprehension entered his face. Marcus was stunned. The man had openly invoked the Alpha Heresy, and not just that. He had done so before the witness of a competent magistrate. The adultery charge was irrelevant now. It was unlike anything Marcus had seen since the slave riots of his youth.

'Very well,' he said. 'You have made your intentions quite plain, citizen. You have not only refused the clemency of Our Lady but also given cause to doubt your adherence to the faith. The charge of adulterous *moicheia* is superseded. This curial hearing is hereby disbanded. Sister adjunct, kindly reconstitute proceedings under the *Lex Iustitinia de Proscriptione Magna*, and convoke an ecclesiastical inquisition to try the accused for the offence – for the offence of – heresy!'

The guards seized Cassian and dragged him from the courtroom. Outside, the storm clouds darkened. As the shadows lengthened, the star light painted the curial floor in blood.

CHAPTER 6

Agnes

The meschita shone in the naked sun, its mass of white concrete like snow amidst the dust. As if some demon had upended the peak of a faraway mountain and transplanted it to the desert. Even from the far end of Thebes' abandoned magistral, the sight inspired Agnes with a profound sense of unease.

She signalled to the legionnaires to fan out, and they advanced in a wide defile, picking their way among the debris. It was no longer just concrete and brick. The whole avenue was strewn with shards of rusted metal. The battle had clearly been hardest fought there. As they neared the meschita's perimeter, overturned vehicles could be seen too, half-covered in sand. It was unclear what or whose they had been, but they looked like late medieval oil-powered trucks. There were rumours that they were still used in some parts of the Caliphate. Others of her legion who'd been stationed in the east even claimed to have driven them, but those were just idle boasts. She'd never met anyone who knew how.

'Headquarters of the religious politburo,' Strabon said, pointing at a crumbling façade nearby, 'always nearest the meschita in Caliphate towns.'

Agnes eyed the bombed-out portal. The vestiges of official-looking Saracene script were visible over the entrance. Beside the illegible lettering was the faint rust-coloured outline of a crescent moon encircling a double-headed hammer.

They drew up beneath the giant orbital walls of the meschita's perimeter. Up close, the illusion of pale stone was replaced by a pockmarked face riddled with bullet holes and blast damage. Twenty passus high and constructed of thick white reinforced concrete, they were easily defended and had surely withstood that last siege for some time. Even today, centuries later, you couldn't have asked for a better spot to hold out.

The midday sun beat down pitilessly overhead. The buildings undulated in the desert heat. The walls offered only the narrowest strip of shade to the officers. The rest of the legionnaires knelt in the sun, the sweat pouring from their berets and dripping from their khakis. They hadn't broken march since they set out. It wouldn't be long before one among the thirty fainted. She had to get them out of the sun soon.

'Scouts have circled perimeter,' Strabon said, as they pressed up against the concrete 'No hostile installations to report.'

'Layout and entrance points?' Agnes asked. Strabon tapped his holowatch. A three-dimensional hologram projected in the shade, rotating with the movement of his fingers. Agnes scrutinised the neon lines as they flitted about like gnats. Orbital walls with a single gateway. Inside, a large colonnaded court surrounding the actual meschita, a two-storey domed rotunda. A crumbling minaret no longer safe to ascend. One way in and one way out, with no oversight position. It was far from ideal.

'Iunge!' she ordered. Rifles in hand, the legionnaires drew up on either side of the dilapidated archway. She stood in its shade, listening. All was quiet, save for the rapid breath of her soldiers on the back of her neck. Her boots baked in the sand piled against the concrete. Not a single bird could be seen in the sky's aquamarine expanse. Even nature seemed to have taken leave of Thebes. As if the archway were a portal

to a place life itself had forsaken. Her heart thumped in her chest. The malaise that had been gnawing at her all day was still with her.

She roused herself. This was unlike her. There was nothing to be afraid of. It was just her old friends, the fear and excitement of the chase. Besides, such weakness didn't befit a centurion. She had to focus. Her green eyes narrowed on Strabon on the other side of the arch. His dark eyes held her gaze. The same question was in them that had been there all morning. The same one her wolfhound had asked her on every childhood expedition. Should they go on?

She knew the answer was yes. That it had to be yes. The meschita was the best defensive position in Thebes, an ideal hideout for the drug smugglers. If she left it unexplored, her mission would be incomplete. It was true that there was only one way in and one way out. True that the risk of ambush was high. True that she was risking the lives of her troops. That she was risking Strabon's life, and her own. But if she couldn't take risks, she'd never have made spear. And for all his caution, even Marcus had told her that a calculated risk was sometimes justified. She had to see it through.

'*O panna Maria*,' Agnes prayed to the Virgin in her native Ruthenian, 'visit upon me in this hour.' She raised her fist and led on in, Strabon at her heels, heading straight for the colonnade encircling the meschita's court. She took the left side, and Strabon the right, each with a detachment of a dozen legionnaires. A few soldiers hung back to guard the entrance.

The sandstone rotunda reared up in the middle of the court like some giant mole burrowing out of the desert. It was clear the entirety of its surface had once been intricately carved with painted arabesques and crescents. In places, traces of faded ochre and turquoise could still be seen. For the briefest moment, Agnes even caught herself admiring the work of such heresy. Yet the unsparing sun also revealed a scene of utter desolation. The carved stonework was cratered on all sides, dappled with bullet holes and shattered from the impact of mortars.

Rusted metal, discarded munitions, and shards of exploded stone littered the court, like a titan's discarded fingernails. Agnes had never seen anything like it and felt a familiar pang of regret. It had to have been some battle. If only she'd been born two centuries earlier, during the third war of religion. Or better yet, in Justinia's day itself. What she wouldn't have given to have been at her side during the Battle of the Red Apple Tree, when the Holy Maiden vanquished the infidel and the shame of Manzikert was undone.

Strabon signalled to her from the colonnade opposite. His group had scouted the other side and, as with her own, there was nothing to report. He motioned to the far end of the court. Agnes nodded and led on under the left wing of the arcade. Strabon did likewise, disappearing behind the rotunda. She flinched. She was always least comfortable without him at her side.

The legionnaires clambered awkwardly over the tumbled masonry, looking about nervously as they went. None had ever seen a battlefield, let alone a battle. The Anatolian woman, smarting in the desert heat, had removed her beret. Catching Agnes' eye, she quickly replaced it. Even Agnes was beginning to feel slightly light-headed. Before her the colonnade receded in a never-ending crescent, whirling in an endless dance like some unholy circus. She kept looking at the meschita, hoping to spy a door in its walls, but its sinuous carvings had neither end nor beginning. The lines became waves. She felt dizzy.

Something glimmered in the colonnade. Up ahead a figure flashed into view before turning aside. The hem of a white skirt lingered beside a column, then vanished. She started, looking back to see if the others had noticed, but there was no one there. She had left her group behind, and the entranceway was out of sight too. There was nothing but the endless recession of the arcade. She felt alone.

'We've found it, Katepana!' Strabon's voice rent the silence as he appeared around a bend ahead and strode up to her, elated. She felt a wave of relief. The others soon caught up too. The ghost of the white skirt faded from her mind. It was just a momentary lapse. Marcus would never have succumbed to such weakness. She couldn't have her legionnaires see it. She was their centurion.

'Lead on!' she commanded. Retracing his steps, Strabon halted a few passus on and pointed at a heap of rubble piled against the wall of the meschita. Stepping out of the shade, Agnes examined the stones. It wasn't clear how it could be an entrance. Her brows furrowed. Strabon simply pointed at the wall. Directly above the stones, in faded red paint, was the outline of a crescent moon and double-headed adze. Clever Strabon. He was right. Someone had deliberately concealed the entrance. She smiled.

'Clear it!' she ordered. Strabon waved his hand. The soldiers began lifting the rubble aside, but despite their number, it was slow work. Most of the stone and concrete blocks were enormous and some took two or three legionnaires to shift. Agnes paced up and down. Whoever had placed them there really meant to deter any intruders. The question was why. She must find out.

Gradually, the upper lintel of a doorway emerged. Strabon hurried the troops along. Beneath the sandstone, steel glinted in the sun. Metallic doors. She grew excited. They were heavy and would definitely need some kind of explosive, but they were only steel. Steel. That was odd. The last religious war had ended two hundred years earlier. How had the Caliphate been able to build like that in those days?

A loud crash interrupted her thoughts, accompanied by a cry of pain. The Anatolian lay beside the door, clutching her leg in anguish. A few legionnaires already knelt beside her. Agnes frowned. The woman must have tripped in her haste.

'I'm sorry, Katepana,' the woman stammered between her sobs. 'I lost my footing.' A large piece of concrete lay beside her. Her leg was badly crushed.

'Bandage her up,' Agnes ordered, pointing to the colonnade. Three legionnaires bore her into the shade. She cursed the useless good-for-nothing. She needed them out of Thebes as soon as they'd checked that meschita. That wouldn't happen now, nor could they beat a quick retreat if they met with the unexpected. She wasn't giving up for the sake of one useless Anatolian, though. It was her mission, and she was going to see it through. She waved at the others to continue.

The rubble was now largely cleared. She marvelled at the great steel portals, picking up her train of thought. There was no way the Caliphate could have built like that centuries ago. Agnes jolted. There was no way. It couldn't have been them, so someone else must have put the stones there. That someone must have come later. Perhaps not even that long ago. She could already hear Marcus urging caution.

'Hold on!' she said. 'Check it first.' Realisation dawned on Strabon's face as the same thought crossed his mind. He motioned to the legionnaires and all stood clear. One of the women stepped forward. In her hands was a dense ball of rubber which looked as if it had been pierced with a hundred tiny pin pricks. Kneeling, she threw it at the centre of the door. It stuck to the burning metal as if glued there.

At first, nothing happened. Then the ball slowly unfurled to reveal a translucent gelatinous mesh, which gradually spread over the entire portal like a giant cobweb. This was so fine that the sunlight continued to reflect off the door beneath, its sheen only slightly dimmed. Agnes marvelled at how such an expanse could be wound into so tiny a device, glancing at the discarded mortar and shrapnel lying in the sand. It was easy to forget how far the empire had come since those days.

The woman tapped her holowatch. Some of the legionnaires withdrew instinctively, but Agnes didn't flinch. The mesh glowed as an electric pulse shot through its surface. Nothing happened.

'Negative, Katepana,' the legionnaire said, 'no ballistic charge detected.' Several of the troops exhaled in relief. Agnes smiled at Strabon.

'Should I take it down?' the woman asked. Agnes glanced at the doors, meschita, and colonnade. The Anatolian woman was still writhing in pain as her leg was bound up. Agnes grimaced. She wasn't about to tell the legate they'd left the meschita unexplored just because of one idiotic kid. The mission must be finished.

'Take it down,' she commanded. The legionnaires retreated beneath the arcade. Agnes knelt behind a column. Strabon took his place at her side.

'Katepana,' he said awkwardly, as he watched the troops taking cover behind the other columns, 'back in the temple... if you saw something, I must know.' For some time, Agnes stared back at him, but at length turned away.

'It was nothing,' she replied, 'just the heat.' Strabon kept looking at her, undeterred. She grew irritable.

'It's this place. The sooner we're out of here, the better. And the sooner the job is done, the sooner we will be,' she added, looking at him pointedly. Strabon took her meaning. Checking for the last time that all were in position, he signalled to the pyrotechnic at the far end of the colonnade, raising his holowatch to his mouth.

'*Tres, duo, unus,*' he counted down, '*incende!*' The woman clapped her hand over her wrist, bowing her head between her knees and covering herself with both arms. The mesh blazed white hot. There was an enormous crash, then a gush of hot air. Even in the desert heat, it was as if an oven had opened on their faces, but in a moment it had passed. Strabon was already back on his feet, peering around the column through his goggles. Tapping his visor, he scrutinised the dusty air. As he raised his holowatch to his lips, his face broadened into a smile.

'All clear!' he said. Agnes and the pyrotechnic followed him back out into the court. The dust gradually settled. Nothing remained whatsoever. All trace of steel had sublimated into thin air. Agnes smirked at the painted hammer and crescent above the lintel. Caliphate or no, whoever had put those doors there hadn't reckoned with her. They hadn't reckoned with her century. She smiled proudly at the pyrotechnic and slapped her on the back.

'Great job, you make Justinia proud,' Agnes praised her with the standard legionary compliment. The woman inclined her head, but Agnes had already turned away, agitated. Until now, her troops might have passed out of Thebes unnoticed, but if the enemy really were there, after that explosion they'd have been left in no doubt. They had to check the meschita and get out as soon as they could. Glancing back at the injured woman, she unslung her rifle and stepped inside.

It was cool, the dry air musty and stale. She reached for her goggles, but the light soon sufficed to make out her surroundings. The building was windowless, the sheer walls of the rotunda stretching up to the dome above. These, and the floor, were entirely revetted in white marble, completely plain but for the single exception, on the far wall opposite, of a giant hammer and crescent. The red stencilling of the double adze and the stars at either end of the crescent moon, stood out dimly in the shadows. She stiffened instinctively.

To either side of the entrance, a narrow stairwell rose to a second-storey gallery beneath the dome. Agnes motioned in their direction, and the snipers ascended. The building seemed larger inside than it had looked from without, belying the unholy trickery the enemy were famed for. Or maybe it was just how spartan everything was, utterly devoid of any decoration save the horrid red crest. She wasn't sure why she was surprised, or what she had expected. She'd heard about meschitas before, but it was still shocking somehow. Not an image of Our Lady in sight. Not a single icon. She shifted uncomfortably, resisting the urge to leave. She must finish the mission.

By now, half the troops were inside. They busily scoured the recesses of the meschita, but there were few, if any, hiding places. If there were any threat she'd have known about it by now, but the lack of hideouts also meant there was no obvious place for a cache of contraband. She strode across to the far wall, pulling on her goggles. A holographic display overlaid the visor. '*Murus Qibla*,' Qibla wall, appeared in green letters. Next to a shallow alcove just in front of her, she read, '*loculamentum Qibla*,' the Qibla niche. Then, beside this, was the word '*mihrab*,' though it wasn't obvious what that referred to. In any case, she didn't understand any of these Saracene words. Nor did she care to. They weren't going to tell her whether the drug smugglers had been there. Nor where they'd hidden the goods.

Beside the hammer and crescent, the words '*sigillum hostium*' glowed red. The arms of the enemy. They'd not been there for centuries, though, and neither had anyone else. She looked back over her shoulder. Some of the others were scanning the wall too, evidently to no avail. Strabon was fruitlessly testing the floor for trap doors with the butt of his rifle. She began to wonder what they were doing there. Breaking in had clearly been a waste of time. The whole expedition had been a waste of time. She ripped off her goggles and marched back towards the entrance.

Many of the legionnaires were already outside. Some had evidently guessed the game was up before being told. A few stood about listlessly, or fussed with their rifles. The sight irritated her. They oughtn't to be wasting time. Her annoyance fast transformed into anger with herself. This was entirely her fault. She was their katepana, and she'd led them there. It was her fault for wasting their time and risking their lives for nothing. She could already see the injured Anatolian beneath the arcade. She felt like a fool. She readied herself to call the retreat.

Strabon looked up as she crossed the floor. He read the look in her eyes and gestured to the remaining troops to move out. Some looked dejected, but all were evidently relieved to be out of the place. Strabon waited for them, then followed out. Agnes, the last to leave, took one final look at the empty meschita, then sighed and turned to the light.

Something glinted in her periphery. She swerved towards the gallery, rifle in hand. Someone was ascending the stairs. She reeled in amazement. Without a moment's hesitation, she bounded after them. Strabon's voice called to her from below, but she couldn't wait.

Dimly, the reflection came to her that there was no way that whoever it was could have slipped into the meschita unnoticed while they were there. Still, how could they have been there before? That was impossible. It didn't matter now. She just had to catch them, whoever they were. She had already reached the top of the stairs, and they were just ahead.

It was immediately clear that they weren't one of hers. They wore no military fatigues and were unarmed. In fact, all they had on them was a simple white shroud, which entirely covered their head and body. She'd seen them before. Or, at least, the hem of their shawl, disappearing from the arcade. She gasped in astonishment. She was following a young girl.

The girl stopped at the far end of the gallery, and did not turn at Agnes' approach. Her face was entirely covered by a veil. Curiously too, she was barefoot. The girl had surely seen her, but she gave no sign. Her heart pounded. She recalled her disorientation in the colonnade, and began to doubt herself.

'*Quis es?*' Agnes asked. 'Who are you?' The girl only stood there, beholding the meschita. As if one of the temple statues had come to life and followed her into Thebes. The cloth on the girl's back was coarse, its hems frayed.

'*Kto si?*' Agnes asked again in her native tongue, without knowing why. The girl shifted. Agnes started, as if she'd stumbled on a desert snake. The girl slowly raised her arm, pointing down at the Qibla wall.

Her lips moved beneath her veil. Agnes bent closer, trying to catch the barely audible words.

'Ai-te-te,' Agnes managed to grasp. 'Ai-te-te?' It didn't make any sense. She repeated it to herself.

'Ai-te-te? *Aiteite*. Ask!' she exclaimed. The girl was speaking Greek. She had no idea why, but that didn't matter. They had a common language. She could reach her.

'Ask? Ask what?' she said in Greek. The girl didn't respond, but continued mumbling the same. Agnes grew impatient.

'I don't understand,' she said. 'What am I supposed to ask?' The meschita was getting hotter as the afternoon drew on. She knelt, drawing right up to the girl's veil. Her lips were clearly visible now.

'*Aiteite kai...* ask and...' Agnes read there. It was like being back at the officers' school in Chalcedon, learning Greek again. She wanted to grab the girl by the shoulders and shake her, but with a great effort, she kept still.

'*Aiteite, kai dothesetai humin,*' the girl said, 'ask and it will be given to you.'

Ask what, though? And what would she be given?

'Ask and it will be given to you,' she repeated, facing Agnes. Her eyes were visible now. Oddly, they were bright blue, more those of Agnes' homeland than of Nubia, and seemed at once faraway and yet transfixing. She wasn't sure the girl really saw her at all. It made her uneasy.

'It will be given to you,' Agnes repeated to herself. As she did so, the girl pointed at the Qibla again, but this time at a specific point on it. Agnes grabbed her goggles. Beside the Qibla niche, illuminated in small green letters, was the word '*mihrab*'. Ask and it will be given to you. She'd found nothing there before. Of course she hadn't. She hadn't expected to.

'Katepana, whom were you talking to?' Strabon asked as he approached, but his voice was far away. She had already rushed past him to the stairs and, in a few swift bounds, was back before the Qibla niche. She pressed hard against the sides of the shallow alcove, but the marble didn't budge. That was too obvious. She put her goggles back on. About a half-passus to the right, '*mihrab*' was displayed on the visor. The reading wasn't precise, and the little green letters kept dancing around. She bit her lip. The clever Osmans. You had to know how such places were built. They weren't going to fool her though.

'The game's up, Katepana,' came Strabon's breathless voice behind her. 'Seriously, we've checked everywhere. The trail's dead. There's nothing here. Shouldn't we best get out while it's still light?' Agnes ignored him. She was so close now. There couldn't be any distractions. Not now.

'*Aiteite, kai dothesetai humin,*' she repeated, running her hand over the marble beneath the spinning letters, 'ask and it will be given to you.' Something slipped beneath her fingertips. She froze, her hand glued to the spot. Her heart thumped in her chest. The low sun flooded in, illuminating the wall. Her hair shone gold as the sweat ran down her auburn locks. With two fingers, she pressed lightly at the marble. It gave way like paper, revealing a small recess concealed within the previously unbroken sheen of white stone.

'Good Justinia!' Strabon gasped. Hearing this, some of the legionnaires re-entered the meschita and gathered around. There was no time to explain. In the meantime, they could deal with the girl. That was all in the background though. Her prize was before her. She moved her hand to the gap in the wall.

'Katepana, shouldn't we first...?' Strabon asked, but was overtaken by his own excitement. Shooing him away, she held her wrist up to the gap. Strabon knelt beside her eagerly, his canine eyes aglow. She smiled happily. The chase was up. She tapped her holowatch to activate the torch.

This time it was her turn to gasp. Inside the vault, a tiny white brick glowed like a luminescent pearl within a shell. Nectar. The smugglers' contraband of choice. Compacted in that little block was enough of the drug to supply a whole city for six months. Half alone would buy a Vestal's palace. That was why they'd walled up the meschita. That was why they didn't want anyone in Thebes. But their secret was out now. Her mission was accomplished. She thrust her hand into the wall.

She just had time to see Strabon flinch, trying to restrain her. Then several things happened at once. There was a deafening crack, a loud puff, and Strabon crying her name. As she snatched her hand away, a force propelled her backwards. Her body felt weightless, as if she were floating. Then she was lying on the floor.

CHAPTER 7

Alistair

Alistair raised his head from his pillow. Even by the standards of his previous birthdays, this one had surely been the worst. He'd waited for his food so patiently, listened to the whole boring lecture about Julian the Apostate and Saint Cassian, and suffered father Zosim's censure just for taking one extra piece of bread. He'd even gone through the whole embarrassing ritual before all the friars, and what for? Had he known what he'd gett, he'd rather have stayed in the piazza with the Latin and missed his dinner.

He looked with hatred at the book lying on the floor. The golden lettering of its binding scintillated in the candlelight. Why were the monks so attached to it anyway? As if it really meant anything, other than their own enslavement. It was the reason they were all stuck in that stupid place, after all. The reason he was stuck there. The reason he was lying in this dank little dacha.

His bleary eyes lit on the tiny window. He rolled off the bed towards it. Even in the daytime, it let in precious little light, but he still enjoyed perching on its sill and looking out at the ruins of the basilica in the distance. Barely anything was visible, but in the last of the fading light, he could just make out the silhouettes of the statues over the piazza. He even fancied he could see the bushy beard of the first patriarch. That one was his favourite, the one the friars called 'the rock.' As a child, he'd long thought it was because the saint was made of stone. Father Zosim had later explained that the name referred to an actual man who had lived long ago, not just to the statue, but Alistair couldn't remember the real reason.

There were a lot of things he couldn't remember. Like how he had originally come to the Reservation, or where he was really from. Or who his parents were. One thing he'd always known for sure, though, was that he had the monks. Even if there was no one else for him to turn to, they at least would always be there. Yet now, he wasn't even sure of that anymore. Still, there was simply nowhere else to go. He couldn't leave even if he wanted to. He was stuck in the Reservation, damned to be alone forever. His eyes watered.

There was a sharp rap at the door. Alistair nearly leapt out of his skin. He was surprised he hadn't heard whoever it was coming. The flimsy pinewood of the novice's shack barely kept out any noise at all. He could usually hear any visitors coming long before they'd even set foot on the steps. Bending down, he picked up the book and hastened to the door, rubbing his sore eyes and trying as best he could to hide his tears.

When he opened it, to his surprise and alarm the young Marian from the piazza was standing there. Alistair stood a full head and shoulders over him, but Alistair instinctively hunched to make himself as small as humanly possible. His eyes darted anxiously to the baton at the legionnaire's side. For some reason, he blushed.

The guard smiled disdainfully, mistaking his bashfulness for fear. He looked him up and down, the corners of his mouth drooping as he surveyed his flabby belly and legs. Alistair's freckles reddened. He crossed his arms, trying to shield himself from view, only then realising he was still holding the book. The soldier's brows contracted. His hand spasmed, and he looked to be on the point of exclaiming something. He seemed to check himself, but his whole body stiffened as he repressed the urge to violence. A tense silence ensued.

'*L'orfano?*' the Latin finally asked in his unexpectedly shrill Italic. 'You are the orphan?' Less a question than a statement, he lingered derisively on the word. It was true that this one was new, but Alistair wasn't deceived. The soldier knew perfectly well who he was. It was just another deliberate insult. He pictured the guard strutting around the piazza, vaunting his athletic body like a trophy. He remembered how he had felt a few minutes earlier, and became angry.

'Yes, I am the orphan, and my name is Alistair,' he replied. He immediately regretted his defiance, but the soldier only smiled again without reaching for his baton. He had to be more careful. You couldn't just go saying what you wanted to these people. They weren't the friars after all and, if what the friars said about them in their unkinder moments was true, crossing a Marian could be a dangerous business.

'You are summoned,' the soldier announced, as all the colour drained from Alistair's face. After a long pause, he added, 'By your – master – the old man who calls himself Zosim,' grinning as he savoured Alistair's alarm. At the sound of Father Zosim's name, Alistair came back to life. He steadied himself against the doorpost. They hadn't come to take him away.

'Yes, yes,' he said, 'I will be along shortly.' The legionnaire remained on the doorstep, giving no sign that he was going anywhere. Alistair was about to remark that he was quite capable of finding his own way to the apostolica. Only in the nick of time did he recall that walking unescorted in the Reservation was technically a privilege and, after curfew, altogether forbidden. In practice, it was a privilege almost always granted. For who cared what a group of frail old doddards were up to? Beholding the legionnaire, however, he saw the answer before him. He did.

Grabbing an old woollen surcoat that hung beside the door, Alistair threw it over his broad shoulders and, furtively depositing the book, made ready to follow. With another smirk at the book, the guard led on. Alistair closed the door, wondering why, for the first time in as long as he could remember, he couldn't go to see Father Zosim on his own. Not that on this particular evening he had wanted to go anyway. Still, it didn't feel quite normal.

With gymnastic strides, the soldier raced back up the sleepy row of dachas, which Alistair had descended half an hour earlier. Despite having longer legs, Alistair struggled to keep up. He was quite sure the Latin was making such haste on purpose. There was a chill in the air now. Annoyingly, his surcoat didn't quite stretch across his full girth. He attempted to pull it tauter, recalling another odd saying of Father Zosim's about the old patriarchs. Apparently, they'd believed the Reservation's climate was the gift of the gods, but found Alistair's birthplace so cold as surely to have been forsaken by them. He wasn't quite sure what any of that meant, but on nights like this he doubted whether the old patriarchs could have been right. The legionnaire appeared at the head of the path, strumming impatiently on his baton. Alistair gave up on his surcoat and hurried on.

Fathers Zosim and Vigilius were the only friars who lived in the apostolica itself, rather than the dormitory shacks. It should really only have been Father Vigilius, as head of the order, but it was also a privilege granted Father Zosim on account of his seniority. No one grudged him it though. For the Poor Friars were not as a rule jealous types. He wasn't sure most of them were even aware of how mean their surroundings were. Or else they didn't care. It was kind of stupid in a way. But then, what kind of privilege was it to live in an old pile like the apostolica anyway?

As he entered under the portal's marble arch, he peered up at the enormous pilasters, whose opulent carvings were bruised by centuries of scuffing and entirely caked in pigeon droppings. Up ahead, one of his winged friends took flight into the rafters, upset by the legionnaire on the stairwell. As the Latin negotiated the uneven stairs, Alistair recalled that the Marians couldn't actually take the place down, much as they would have loved to. It was protected by ancient law. That didn't mean, though, that they were obliged to spend a single solidus to keep it up, and the friars, of course, had nothing. So, like everything else in the Reservation, it was gradually decaying away into dust. He wasn't sure why, but the thought made him sad.

Following the Marian up the stairs, he had as usual to thread his way through the collapsed roof beams and fragments of statuary. It might have been a perilous ordeal in the darkness, had he not known the apostolica like the back of his hand. He noticed with quiet satisfaction that the soldier had his magic light on, but even so was clearly struggling more than he was. He was careful not to smile, though, when the Latin turned back to him at the top of the stairs. Instead, he breathed as audibly as he could and made a show of suffering. The soldier grinned and moved on.

They crossed the landing, passing through to the old chapel beyond. It was the largest hall of such a name that Alistair knew. Despite the moonlight streaming in through the holes in the roof, little could be seen, but he usually came here during the day, and even in the dark, the old pictures on the ruined ceiling were familiar. It was his favourite spot after the piazza, another place he didn't feel so alone. He'd spent hours as a child just gazing up at the decaying frescoes. Many weren't visible anymore, and in some places, where the roof had collapsed in on itself, they'd disappeared entirely. He loved the colours and the men and women in them. He didn't know who they were, other than that they were probably from the old stories in the book, but he knew they were like him. Some were happy and others were sad, and they kept changing all the time, just like he did, moving about in all directions at once. As if they were raging with the life inside them, and just couldn't help themselves. It was all so unlike the rest of the Reservation, and the friars, many of whom seemed more dead than alive.

He stared up at the great picture in the middle of the roof, the one showing the two men touching hands. That one had always been his favourite. Father Zosim had told him the first time he'd visited the chapel that it was the heavenly Father and the first man, though when he was older, Alistair doubted whether Father Zosim could really have known that. The greybeard was full of such old wives' tales. If the Father had ever visited man, as they all thought, it was quite clear He wasn't coming back. Even so, it was nice to think He might have done so, once upon a time.

The soldier stamped his feet impatiently at the far end of the chapel. Alistair had lost track of time, and chided himself again for his forgetfulness in the presence of the zealous Marian. He shuffled on as quickly as he could, dodging the shards of plaster and knee-deep pools of rainwater where the roof had caved in. He looked up nervously as he finally reached the far door, beneath the fresco showing the end of the world, but the crunch of the soldier's boots was already echoing in the corridor beyond.

Alistair hurried after him down the dimly lit passage, which led to the inner chambers of the apostolica. Torches blazed at the end of the dank limestone tunnel, like campfires in a dark forest. Unprompted, his heart lifted. He had always enjoyed coming up here to see the old man. The same rush of warmth washed over him that always did. It wasn't a physical warmth, but something different. Something like the feeling of returning to a place you knew you belonged.

He remembered the book, and his cheeks flushed. Why had he been brought up here at all? Doubtless another lecture was coming, probably about the extra bread. Even on his birthday, and after such a stupid present, the old man was still quite capable of that. He always was. The legionnaire was already standing by the old oak door, tapping his feet irritably. He glowered at Alistair, taking his frown for insolence. Alistair lowered his eyes meekly.

'*Festina, homuncule, festina!*' the soldier told him to get along. Alistair hastily rapped the iron knocker on the rickety oak door. *Homunculus.* Silly little man. The word resounded in his head. Wasn't that a stupid thing to say to someone twice your size? He fantasised about what would happen if he threw his whole weight upon him, smiling at the rebellious thought. Then about what it would feel like to be pressed against those slender limbs, so unlike his own. Against those tight athletic sinews, and the bristle on his olive cheeks.

The door creaked open, awakening Alistair from his uninvited thoughts. Without any acknowledgement, the soldier marched off. Father Zosim emerged in the doorway, his black habit and the candle in his hand illuminated by the fireplace within. The image of the Virgin and the lamp, and the blond woman, flickered briefly before Alistair's eyes. Father Zosim smiled, beckoning him to come in. Already frowning, he brushed past the monk in silence, somewhat more briskly than he had meant to.

The room was as always, with books stacked in untidy piles on the oak table and littering the uncarpeted stone floor. The many gaps in the bookshelves that lined every wall of the little chamber betokened another inquiry on Father Zosim's part. He didn't call it that, preferring the Latin word '*inventio.*' Something about discovering new knowledge. He'd never really got what the point in that was for a monk. Besides, the idea of trying to find something new in old books was inherently rather silly.

Father Zosim gestured to Alistair's usual chair by the stove. Despite his best efforts to refrain from his habitual familiarity, he collapsed into it, making himself at home. He fiddled absentmindedly with the spine of one of the motheaten tomes on the table. On its binding was written, *Codex Triboniani.* Alistair neither knew who Tribonian was, nor what his codex was, nor why father Zosim was reading it. When he looked up, the monk was observing him closely. He shifted uncomfortably, still frowning.

'You were not happy with your birthday present?' Father Zosim asked, his verdant eyes smiling in the candlelight. Despite a lifetime in the Reservation, the old Novgorovian had lost none of the characteristic frankness of his people. As so many times before, his honesty took Alistair off guard, disarming his conceit. He cast about distractedly, his eyes lighting on the row of icons above the fireplace. Most were of long-forgotten saints, but there was also one of the mother, with seven swords pointing at her heart. Her face reminded him of the icon in his memory of the woman with the golden hair.

'Why do you worship her too?' Alistair asked, ignoring the monk's question as he fiddled nonchalantly with Tribonian's codex. 'She's not one of yours really, is she, not like she is for them?' He pictured the Marian's athletic limbs, which had surely carried him all the way back to the piazza by now. Father Zosim smiled, seeing through his attempt to distract him by winding him up.

'We do not worship the holy mother herself, young man, but we hold her blessed for the grace that the Lord bestowed upon her,' Father Zosim explained, without the least semblance that he was answering the same question Alistair had asked since he was a child. He was no longer paying attention though, only pondering how best to contradict the monk.

'Yes, but – but – they worship her,' he said, nodding at the door, 'and that's the reason they keep you all here, isn't it? How can you honour her if she's the reason for what they do to you? It doesn't make any sense! Wouldn't it be better if all those swords actually pierced her heart, and then you'd all be free at last?' He could feel his blood boiling as his words ran away with themselves. He felt guilty, worrying he'd offended the old man, and studied the table sheepishly. He pulled another book towards him, on whose cover was written '*Historia Ecclesiastica*', and started tugging furiously at its frayed tassels.

'The will of man is not the will of the Lord, Alistair, and it may often be that in seeking to do the Lord's will, man achieves the opposite,' Father Zosim answered, apparently not in the least offended. 'The swords that pierce the holy mother's heart symbolise her grief at her loss, and the grief of all mankind. And indeed, there is perhaps no loss so great in this world as that of a mother for her child.' He looked at the icon sadly, then peered into Alistair's eyes as if searching for something. At length, he smiled.

'But I fear, young man, that it is I who has caused you to grieve, for I sense that you were not happy with your present today, despite your words of thanks,' Father Zosim said, raising an eyebrow. Alistair flushed, then grew annoyed at himself for betraying himself so obviously. If only he'd been graced with the olive complexion of a Latin, like the soldier, instead of the pasty freckles of a barbarian. Not for the first time, the old friar had him cornered. There was nowhere left to turn. There was nothing left for it but to own up.

'I guess, no...' he stammered, trying to find the right words. 'It's just that – you know – it's not that I didn't appreciate the thought, I mean it's just that, it was my birthday, and not just that...' He stopped short and, to his own surprise, burst into tears. He tried hiding his face in his palms, but his tears streamed into his tunic cuffs. Laying his head on the oak board, he tried as best he could to disappear entirely. Father Zosim waited patiently until he had finished crying, then put a hand on his shoulder.

'We do not have such things to give you as you want, young man, and I am sorry for that,' the monk said. 'I have always been sorry that we have been unable to give you everything you desire. But, as you know, our lives here are simple, and our wants and needs are few. Still, I fear that we have so much come to see you as one of our own that perhaps we have forgotten that, in truth, you are not.'

Alistair raised his head and looked at him mistrustfully. He rubbed his sore eyes. He felt angry again, though he wasn't sure why.

'But I am one of you!' he protested, his words pouring forth in a torrent. 'At least, this is my home, is it not? I may not be a monk like you and the other friars, but I live here too. And I keep your rule as you do, don't I? I mean, I even eat the same food!' Father Zosim's eyebrow rose again, and he fell into an embarrassed silence.

'Yes, Alistair, this is your home, and you must know that we have – and always will – cherish you among us. And now you are a man!' Father Zosim said, with a smile of such warmth as Alistair could rarely remember. To his surprise, there was pride in the old man's eyes.

'Even so, Alistair, search your heart and you will find that I am right,' he continued. A shade of sadness entered his face as he studied the icon of the Virgin. Alistair reflected that it was true. The old man was right. He was not a monk, and never would be, even if this had been the only place he'd ever called home.

'But Father, I don't mean to say, I mean... I was glad, I was very glad of the present,' Alistair said. As the friar stooped beside the hearth, he looked older than he ever had before. There was something surprising in his face too. Something Alistair had never seen before. A deep, unfathomable sadness. It made him think of the well by the dormitory, from which the monks drew their water. When Father Zosim turned back to him, though, he smiled, and in the flickering of the candlelight the colour of life returned to his face. As Father Vigilius in the refectory, for an instant, the echo of a younger man was reflected there, and he became another shepherd astride the seven hills, smiling at the morning sun.

'Father, I want to ask,' Alistair said, after a pause, 'I mean – if I can – why are you so sad today? You seem to be happy and sad at the same time. Has something happened?' Alistair had always had a frank way of talking to the monk. It had always felt the most natural thing in the world, despite the very great difference in their age. No sooner had he fallen back into his old habit than he completely forgot about the book.

'There are moments in your life, Alistair, that are like the joining or parting of streams,' Father Zosim replied, 'for life is like a great river, and our lives join and part with one another like tributaries of that river. So too at times the river waxes, and at others it wanes. Where today it trickles, like a rivulet over sandbanks, so shallow that the shoals are visible, tomorrow it will flow rich and full. And just as it is for the river, so too for us it may be that unseen junctures lie ahead.'

Alistair did not understand, but listened patiently. After so many years, he was quite used to the monk's parables.

'Such is the will of the Almighty!' he concluded. 'You yourself have just reached a great juncture in the river of your life, which now waxes to its full flow.' His smile was warm, yet tinged with a certain melancholy.

'Father, I believe there is something you wish to tell me,' Alistair said, speaking his thoughts exactly as they came to him. 'Is something going to happen to me?'

Father Zosim looked surprised, but smiled again, as if the question were not wholly unexpected. Over the years, Alistair had grown accustomed to the Novgorovian's ability to hold two thoughts in his head at the same time.

Father Zosim's eyes lingered on the icon of the holy mother, becoming infinitely sad. Alistair, too, looked at the seven swords pointing at her heart. Gazing into her pained eyes, for the briefest moment he too felt as if his heart were being pierced a thousand times. He could almost hear her cries of pain and, as if muffled by an insurmountable distance, the cries of countless other voices he did not recognise. He felt as though he couldn't tear himself away, but eventually managed to do so. The voices ceased, like the shutting of a book. The monk watched him closely. Alistair waited for his answer, even though in his heart he already knew it.

'I think you have always known, Alistair, that one day you would have to leave us,' he at length replied, 'and deep down I have always known that this turn in the river of your life would come some day, though perhaps I have denied that truth even to myself. You must forgive the foibles of an old man!' The monk's eyes had grown bright. Alistair blushed.

'And there are other reasons...' the monk said, seemingly unsure whether to go on. 'There are other reasons, Alistair, why you may need to leave us sooner than I had hoped. I cannot tell you why, but my heart misgives me.' For perhaps the first time in his life, Alistair witnessed something resembling fear pass across the monk's face, like the shadow of a cloud on a hillside.

'For you see, the life of mankind is also like a mighty river,' he continued, 'and so too that river waxes and wanes through the centuries, as it takes its course. It is, alas, the nature of mankind to every once in a while be swept out of its normal channel, and scatter into many streams. When it does, it is difficult to see which winding and treacherous course to take. And it may even, without forewarning, become a waterfall.' He glanced mournfully at the icon.

'We have had many years' peace here in this sanctuary,' he went on, still beholding the mother. 'Yes, very many long years' peace, and happy ones too!'

As the firelight played in the old Novgorovian's eyes, Alistair had the fleeting sense that he was no longer speaking to him but to someone else. To someone very far away.

'Understand, Alistair, that the world is turning again,' he said. 'I do not know how, or why, but it is the will of the Almighty. I feel it in my heart, and I know it to be true. Of late, my dreams have been dark. I seem to hear the crackling of a great fire. And on waking, I feel the heat of that conflagration on my face, as if it were blowing in with the dawn.' The monk's face was grave.

'My hour is past, though, and I shall soon return to the loving embrace of the Father,' he said, his eyes shining like emeralds. 'But your hour is come, young man, and my heart tells me that you will leave this place sooner than you know. Do not be sad, Alistair, for my heart also tells me that it is His will that it should be so!'

Alistair's face fell.

'But remember this, when the time comes,' he said seriously. 'The world outside is not the Reservation. The hearts of men may not always be as they seem, and many that seem fair may be foul. But so too many that seem foul may be fair. Remember, always, that in all men there is goodness, though they may not even know it themselves.' Beneath his wizened brows, his eyes shone like jade in the firelight.

'This is something you have always known, Alistair. So long as you see the goodness that is hidden in all men's hearts, you may reach them. And the one who sees the goodness in men may draw it out, thereby healing their hearts. And in so healing their hearts, he may also unite them. Such was He when He came among us many centuries ago, the great Conciliator of mankind. He who taught us that – as the saying goes in the land of my birth – in times of trouble, brother ought not judge his brother. For where judgment is passed, injustice reigns. Make yourself ready then, young man, for the hour is nearly upon you,' the monk concluded, irradiating one final time before reinhabiting his old self.

All that could be heard was the spitting of the wax candles and the gentle crackling of the hearth, burning low as the evening drew on. Like its embers, Alistair's mind glowed with Father Zosim's words. He could hardly take it all in. Must he really leave the Reservation? How would he get by, and where would he go? He hardly even knew why he had to leave, but something inside told him the friar was right.

There was a soft knock at the door, and the ancient oak creaked open. Whoever it was obviously wasn't about to wait for a response from the half-deaf monk. Alistair turned, fully expecting to see the young Latin, but to his surprise Father Vigilius was standing there, his face sombre.

'*Venit hora*,' he said. The hour had come. The bishop addressed himself only to Father Zosim and did not look at Alistair. Neither receiving nor apparently expecting any reply, he at once turned to leave. Alistair had always thought him brisk and remarkably swift for his years, but he had never seen him in such haste. He glanced back at Alistair. He did not smile, but only nodded curtly to Father Zosim, then left. Alistair stared at Father Zosim, hoping for an explanation, but to his consternation the monk simply sat there in contemplative silence.

'Prepare your bag, Alistair, and do not sleep too heavily this night!' he at length said. 'For the hour has come sooner than any of us expected, and sooner indeed than I myself could ever have imagined. Sufficient unto the day be the evil thereof!' Without another word, he rose to retire.

Alistair moved to the door instinctively, as if this were just another of his overstayed visits, but his head was reeling. He was afraid, though he could not quite say why. He lifted the iron latch, but just as he was closing the door, Father Zosim called after him.

'Alistair,' he said, his beady eyes smiling in the candlelight, 'do not forget your present!'

Alistair nodded hastily and, without looking back, ran out into the passage.

Chapter 8

Marcus

The guards hurled Cassian out, and the courtroom doors slammed behind him. Silence descended on the curia. Marcus looked out. Through a chink in the black armour of the Caledonian firmament, the sun appeared. The zenith. The morning was already past, and the whole sorry business was far from over.

By now, the entire Mile was little more than a saffron mass of drunken demesmen. The barbarians had never been able to hold their drink, least of all during the festive season. He loathed this time of the year. There was always trouble. If he'd had his way, he'd have had done with it all long ago. At least the storm would send them all scuttling home, and the sooner the better. Why the powers that be had reinstated all that nonsense was beyond him. Hadn't the Saturnal originally been a pagan festival anyway?

Pagan. His mind skidded on the word, like a boot slipping in an unsavoury residue on the cobblestones. It quickly yielded to another, still more unhappy, one. A word that woke him brutally from his reverie, recalling him summarily to the cold sterility of the courtroom. A word from his native tongue, yet one whose soft consonance pained him more than any Caledonian grunting ever could. A word he'd desperately hoped to escape in the north. Heresy.

How had it come to this? Perhaps he ought to have just locked Cassian away at once, but it was too late for that now. The fool had invoked the Alpha Heresy, and done so publicly. The law now required a full religious inquisition. The synkellos of the diocese himself would have to be involved for the ecclesiastical cross-examination. Only the heretic's recantation would suffice, followed by his re-indoctrination. That failing, it was the Supreme Measure. Death.

Marcus had never been particularly fond of any priest. They were a patronising bunch at the best of times, and he'd never met one who wasn't in love with the sound of his own voice. Solon Tzimiskes, the high sacerdote of Caledon, was a classic example. The smooth old Greek was a sophist of the first order. A typical eunuch, always playing with words, and as cruel as they came. He dearly wished he could have avoided having anything to do with the priest, or with the *Fides* at all, but Cassian had left him no choice.

There were risks in involving Solon. Those rumours about Hypatia. Where had the gossiping pleb heard them from? They ought to have stayed down south. What if Solon dragged it all out in court? Not that he'd have brought it up at dinner. Such things weren't spoken of in polite society, but the public curia was another matter. If the pleb started rambling again, Solon wouldn't let that opportunity slip. For there was nothing a sacerdote loved more dearly than reminding his temporal lord of his own moral superiority.

'Your excellency?' Severa asked with a polite clop of her heels, as if trying not to wake him from his reverie. He examined her dress again, and frowned.

'*Sacerdos*,' Marcus commanded. 'Summon the priest, Solon Tzimiskes. Get that old Greek in here, and quick about it! I don't care what debauchery he's up to today with his deacons. No excuses, you hear? Even if he's holed himself up in that cathedral of his – I don't care. Drag him out and get him in here.' The star light, which had settled back to a pale green after Cassian left the room, acquired a lemon tinge. He pursed his lips, fingering his rosary. Even unseen, the Caledonian was fraying his nerves.

'Yes, your excellency, of course, but I – I also wondered, exarch, if I may...?' Severa asked, with a strange insistence in her voice. 'I wondered whether your excellency might wish to consider the option of the – of the – Reservation...?'

Marcus stared at her in disbelief. The Reservation. The dispensation available to a senior magistrate to spare the convicted heretic, in favour of life imprisonment in the last reserve of the old law. The injection that put them into a stupor, their transcontinental transfer by armoured lightcraft and, by the time they woke up, electrified admantine walls on all sides. No means of escape. No techne. No contact. No chance of ever infecting anyone outside again. To all intents and purposes, dead to the world. It was extremely rare, and only used when the heretic was so important that application of the Supreme Measure was impossible. Or, rarer still, but not unknown – even if never admitted – were cases where the heretic was in fact no heretic at all, but merely someone whose existence was an inconvenience to the state. Or else to someone powerful. Neither circumstance applied here.

'I would strongly advise an exception is made in this case, governor,' Severa persisted, 'for reasons of a – of a political – consideration. The accused's claim to thanehood—'

'What on Earth is a thane?' he interrupted. 'It is nothing to me what he claims to be! He's a perfect nobody from the gutter. He will recant, or he will burn. Just get the high sacerdote in here, will you? Solon. Kindly summon his eminence, the synkellos, whose presence the exarch requires forthwith for his – for his religious – opinion in a judicial proceeding. Yes, for his religious opinion.'

Severa cantered back across the marble towards the doors, her fingers jabbing sullenly at her tabula as she went.

'*Basilika!*' Marcus grumbled, entranced by the undulation of her skin-tight skirt. Why couldn't she follow the regulations? They were there for a reason. He turned to Konstantin, but the tribune clearly had no interest in what women did or didn't choose to wear. A true soldier, with focus. As he'd once been himself, in better days, when he'd served with Agnes Radomira, the Ruthenian centurion. He was ashamed of losing his former discipline. It was all Hypatia's fault, for making him go to this backwater alone. And now he'd let himself get drawn into this whole sorry business.

Half an hour later the doors opened, and a gaunt man about the same age as Marcus entered the courtroom. His slight build and delicate features, together with his clean-shaven olive cheeks and ultramarine eyes, combined to give him an artificial impression of freshness and youth. This impression was enhanced by his starched dalmatic tunic and overlaying white chlamys, emblazoned with its red star. Their heavy fabric covered the entirety of his emaciated body, while his golden synkellic diadem concealed his baldness. He was flanked by two blond Caledonian youths, both sporting the same dalmatica and condescending smile. Severa followed in their wake.

Marcus glanced up, but did not rise to greet the priest. He was immediately irked by the sight of the man, whose carefree life had told more easily on him than his own. He examined the screen before him, pretending to scrutinise some court records. Out of the corner of his eye, he noted with pleasure that Konstantin made no salute. That was of course correct, since regulation did not require the honour for those of non-military rank. Even if some of the cathedral guards had made the habit of doing so.

He waited until the priest stood before the tribunal, waving his hand over the screen as if perusing a particularly uninteresting report of the publicans. The synkellos needed to know who was in charge from the outset, lest he try anything during the inquisition. At length, Marcus raised his eyes lazily, but Solon retained an oleaginous smile, one which in no way menaced the upper half of his face. The Greek's pale eyes were steely and unkind. Marcus looked him up and down, glancing sidelong at the adolescents and, seeing that the eunuch had been carousing, suppressed the full expression of his disdain. He had most likely been in his cups, and his oily tongue might be even freer than usual.

'*Chaire, agapite file,*' Solon said at last, hailing Marcus as if he were an old friend. 'May the Virgin protect you. Always a pleasure, my dear exarch.' He spoke well, but his aristocratic Greek was unnaturally high-pitched. He inclined his head almost imperceptibly. His presumed familiarity riled Marcus intensely.

'*Chaire, synkelle,*' he replied, nodding still more imperceptibly as he dispensed with the usual formalities. 'I thank you for your attendance at this short notice.'

The corners of Solon's thin lips curled. The priest was actually expecting an apology. He immediately resolved that he would get none.

'The matter is one of only limited consequence,' Marcus continued, resuming his mien of feigned boredom. 'However, as you will no doubt have surmised, it is – unfortunately – one of a judicial competence.'

A conceited smile still painted the eunuch's countenance. He waved his hand imperiously at his attendant deacons, who left the courtroom.

'Pray excuse my ignorance, exarch,' Solon began as soon as the doors closed, 'I do not mean to be importunate, but if the matter is one of a judicial competence, what need has your excellency of the presence of the ministers of Our Lady? Her poor servants surely cannot better our respected governor's knowledge of the laws, nor the quaestorial clerks' understanding of the Codex and the latest amendments thereto?' He looked at Severa and Konstantin with an innocent smile.

Marcus glowered at the sacerdote. Why was he playing the fool? He knew exactly why he was there. There was no reason a synkellos would be called in to court if the issue didn't concern heresy. The diabolical eyes of the Caledonian twinkled before him like sapphires, and his neck grew hot. He loosened the top button of his uniform. Annoyingly, Solon noticed. His eyes glinted.

'Yes, the matter is one of a judicial competence,' Marcus replied, endeavouring to look through him, 'but it is also one which – to use the language of your order – is contingent upon a matter of the *Fides Marianea*.'

Solon's eyes flashed as Marcus formally invoked the name of the Marian faith. 'Then it is perhaps not, after all, a matter altogether without significance? May I ask what charge is laid against the accused?'

'*Haeresis*,' Marcus replied. The priest's jaw fell, and his eyebrows arched. He almost looked afraid. He turned to Severa and Konstantin in feigned perplexity, but his face lost none of its colour. Severa swayed unsteadily on her heels, but Marcus observed with satisfaction that Konstantin was in no way moved by the priest's little act. In fact, the tribune hadn't acknowledged Solon's presence at all since he'd arrived.

'A serious matter indeed!' Solon exclaimed, pretending to recover his composure. 'And, to think, a case of heresy here in our good little province... So far from all the sin and intrigue that alas – though it pains me to admit it – plague the capital today!'

Marcus stared at the eunuch. He knew no one believed him, so why did he insist on carrying on his dramatic prelude? Was he expecting the Apollonian laurel? He ought rather to be flayed.

'But you must excuse me, your excellency, I can get rather carried away!' Solon said. 'I understand why – and, indeed, I am glad that – you have involved the religious authorities at once in a matter of such import. I shall not hesitate to lend my assistance to the gathering of the required evidence ahead of the inquisition.' As he peered meaningfully at Marcus, his mouth twisted into a wry smile. The priest was clearly convinced the exarch needed someone shut up in the Reservation. Someone inconvenient, and likely no heretic at all. The venial eunuch was preparing to name his price for his religious assent.

'Alas, synkellos, such is the seriousness of the matter that I fear it cannot wait even a single day, no, not even a feast day. We must move to an ecclesiastical inquisition at once,' Marcus said. Solon's eyebrow rose. Marcus smiled inwardly. No more cavorting for the old eunuch today.

'But, your excellency – and, again, I must plead your forbearance – for my knowledge of the *Lex Iustiniana* cannot possibly rival your own,' Solon answered, his thin lips curling again, 'is not a preliminary proceeding first needed to establish the evidence before moving to a full religious inquisition?' He smiled politely.

'Your interpretation of the law is quite correct, high sacerdote,' Marcus replied. 'The preliminary proceeding was held this morning. While it is indeed, as you say, a matter of the faith with which we are concerned here, the accusation had – at the outset – only attracted a civil penalty.'

'You have no doubt already sought the recantation by the accused of their false beliefs?' Solon asked.

'The accused has so far shown no inclination to recantation,' Marcus replied. 'I am sure you will appreciate that, if proven, such a charge may attract the highest criminal penalty under the law. That is, *res capitalis*.'

'Why indeed, excellency, that is quite right, as the proscription laws of the *Lex Iustiniana* require – and moreover, I believe I am not much mistaken in understanding that, in this particular case, the accused may also be a figure of a certain local standing?' Solon asked, forgetting the legal ignorance he had pleaded a moment earlier. 'That is, a Caledonian katepano, of sorts? As such, I assume your excellency is also giving due consideration to the Reservation transfer procedure?'

'Yes, that is what the accused claims,' Marcus replied, his eyes lighting angrily on Severa, 'but I have seen no evidence in this case, beyond their own assertions, to justify the finding that they are a figure of any influence or importance. The only circumstances that have been clearly attested are that the accused is of a heretical persuasion, and that he shows no inclination towards recantation of his false beliefs.'

'You mean to say,' Solon said, a genuine shade of doubt entering his eyes, 'that you are persuaded that the accused is a genuine adherent of the – of the – Alpha Heresy?'

'Why yes, high sacerdote,' Marcus said impatiently. 'Why else would I have had recourse to summon your synkellic eminence to attend this hearing on a feast day?'

Solon studied him with alarm, trying to determine whether he was serious. 'But surely, governor, with all due respect,' he stammered, 'you would not take so – so unorthodox – a step as to exclude the dispensation of the Reservation in a capital matter, without first involving the higher authorities...?' His feet twitched, as if he were about to bolt for the door. While neither here nor there to an exarch, for a high sacerdote a convicted heretic in his diocese wasn't a good look. It would leave a black mark on his ecclesiastical cursus. Not much chance of making Grand Synkellos of the City after that.

'As I have said, the accused is of only plebeian standing, and as such I find no political justification for the Reservation procedure in this case,' Marcus said. 'Nonetheless, given the accused's own heretical testimony provided directly to this court, as the competent religious authority in my province, I require your ecclesiastical inquisition of the accused, to ascertain whether a recantation may be elicited.'

Marcus rose, motioning to Severa to begin preparations. They'd do things the proper way, like last time. If Solon couldn't extract a recantation, the insolent heretic could go to the dogs, and the priest's reputation with him. When Marcus looked up, Solon's eyes had paled. The eunuch nodded stiffly and retreated towards the courtroom doors. He was surely already working up some subterfuge. Best not give him the chance.

'Sister adjunct, kindly convene the court to commence ecclesiastical inquisition in one hour,' Marcus ordered before Solon had reached the door. The priest halted. Severa's plucked eyebrows rose. Her lips moved, but Marcus glowered at her. Like a sleek black mare, she trotted towards the doors, overtaking the priest as she hastened to carry out her orders. Momentarily entranced, Marcus shook himself, wroth at himself for yet another lapse.

An hour later, the accused was led back in. Seated on his throne, Marcus still wore his black uniform but now donned the exarchal chain, with its large golden star. Solon sat to his left, still arrayed in his white chlamys. Severa pointed the soldiers towards the dock. Placed beneath the windows, this consisted simply of a wooden seat.

Marcus loured at Cassian as he sat down. In the baleful half-light of the now raging storm, he was pleased to see the Caledonian sullen and taciturn. With a bit of luck, he'd have his recantation and apology by sundown. If not, he'd have him tied naked to the gnostic steeple and see whether spending the Saturnal night on the Mile didn't change his mind.

'*Carcerem claudite!*' Konstantin commanded in his Novgorovian monotone. A thin, semi-liquid film fell from the ceiling around the dock. It briefly oscillated like water, then solidified, becoming as transparent as glass. There was no more than a flicker in the prisoner's dull eyes, who barely seemed to notice his incarceration at all.

'*In nomine Matris, et Virginis et Spiritus Sancti...*' Marcus commenced with the usual formula, but left off as the doors re-opened. A slightly-built young woman in a long pale-green dress entered, accompanied by two handmaidens. Her face was covered with a cerulean veil, through which nothing of her features could be discerned. The viridescent spectre said nothing and made no sign of greeting to anyone, but as she glided past them, the guards knelt. Solon sprang sycophantically to his feet, like a cork popping from an amphora.

Marcus hastened to shut his gaping mouth, praying the Virgin be kind. His hand trembled as he pulled out the chair to his right. The resident Vestal of Britannia Maior. She was of the highest dynatorial stock on her father's side, from a Bohemian family reaching back the empire's full six centuries, and not just that. Her mother was Princess Amalasuntha, the younger sister of the empress. She was a royal. Her very presence was petrifying.

How had she heard? His eyes found Solon. Of course. It was his doing. Referring the matter up to a Vestal to get the accused sent to the Reservation and thereby salvage his own reputation. The damned eunuch knew there was no way a mere governor could gainsay a Vestal. He had outwitted him.

'*In nomine Matris, et Virginis et Spiritus Sancti,*' Marcus repeated shakily, 'I call this court to order. This ecclesiastical inquisition is convoked to try matters pertaining to the *Fides Marianea*, under the *Lex Iustiniana de Proscriptione Magna*.' He turned to his right.

'I thank my lady of the *Ordo Vestalis* for the cathedra of Britannia Maior, Her Royal Highness of the House of Premyslid, and the synkellos, high sacerdote of Caledonia, for their attendance,' he continued, bowing low to the woman, then nodding curtly to Solon. The Vestal sat serenely, apparently unmoved by the sight of either the unkempt prisoner or of anything else around her.

'Citizen Cassian Macleod,' Marcus began, 'you stand accused of *haeresis*. As an offence under the Justinian laws of religious proscription, you do not have the right to legal representation. As required by those laws, I ask you, before the witnesses of their Vestal and synkellic eminences, whether you wish to recant of your heresy?'

The Vestal shifted at his last word, raising a hand to her veil. It made him uncomfortable. She was perhaps a third his age, but for him, as for any other mortal, the prospect of a Vestal's pronouncement was terrifying.

By contrast, Cassian had neither acknowledged her nor any of the proceedings taking place around him. He completely ignored Marcus' question, and a tense silence ensued. Everyone, save Cassian and the Vestal, was affected by it. Even the guards, young men endeavouring to look the picture of severity, exchanged a nervous glance through the liquid glass. Severa's fingers performed a full circus over her tabula. Evidently, none had ever seen such a thing before.

'So be it, then,' Marcus said at last, no longer daring to employ the lazy drawl he had that morning. 'Citizen Cassian Macleod, in the absence of a recantation, you must submit to sacerdotal cross-examination to determine whether the charge be found valid. I call to witness the synkellos of Caledonia, to whose diocese you belong, and who will therefore lead this inquisition.'

Solon rose, touching the red star on his chlamys and straightening his crown. Comporting himself with as much solemnity as he could, the priest descended the tribunal and sauntered towards the dock.

Marcus sank back into his throne, studying the Vestal out of the corner of his eye. The whole business had gotten much riskier with her arrival. Besides, there was still the matter of his wife. The sooner it was through with, the better. He no longer cared how. He just needed shot of Cassian as soon as possible. Outside, the sky had briefly divested its stormy raiment. Such barbarians were as unpredictable as their weather. Perhaps he should have had him shut up in prison at once, where he couldn't cause any trouble, but it was too late for that. The proscriptorial inquisition was out of his hands now.

'Ahem, *in nomine Matris, et Virginis, et Spiritus Sancti*, I bless you, my child, you who are *sine fide*,' Solon began. He glanced apprehensively at the Vestal as he gave the sacerdote's customary benediction, which had nonetheless to be bestowed on anyone not yet condemned for heresy. The Vestal shifted again and laid one of her pale wrists, sheathed in green silk, across her lap. Marcus tried not to admire her delicate freckled hands, nor her silver ring emblazoned with a crowned white lion.

'Let me begin by asking you, citizen, whether you are familiar with the tenets of the faith?' Solon asked, fast regaining the habitual sanctimony of a preacher. 'For it may be that, in the poverty of your ignorance, you have never even encountered the Holy Wisdom of Our Lady, nor perhaps even heard of the Gnosis of the Virgin?'

Cassian ignored him. His eyes were so dull, and his body so motionless, that it was as if he had been ossified into one of the bearded ghosts of the patriarchs, like some destituted icon from the past.

'But this is scarcely believable!' Solon exclaimed, his eyebrows raising nearly to the rim of his diadem. 'For the creed of the Hagia Sophia is known throughout the empire. Indeed, for five-and-a-half centuries there hasn't been a soul from the Pillars of Hercules to the Kremlovskan Camp – and, yes, even here in farthest Caledon – who hasn't heard of the Descension of Our Lady, and of our salvation through Her Gnosis!' As his words bore him to a squeaky crescendo, drops of spittle flew from his mouth and collided with the liquid glass. He struck Marcus as more resembling an amphitheatrical actor than a provincial synkellos. Or else some small-town lector, chiding one of his wayward pupils. How had he, a soldier, ended up having to listen to the old fool's sermonising? His mind drifted back to the Circus in Mariapol, and he remembered Hypatia. He straightened up, watching Cassian nervously.

'Yet it seems, citizen, that you do not bear witness to that Gnosis through which the Virgin became flesh many centuries ago?' Solon asked, with a rhetorical flourish of his hand. He stepped up to the dock. As he peered into Cassian's vacant eyes, he pressed his lips so thinly that they were hardly visible. Marcus pondered whether the eunuch looked at his Caledonian boys like that during his nocturnal games, but suppressed the disgusting thought.

'I am even informed,' Solon said, 'that not only do you fail to accept the truth of the Descension, but you do not even accept the destitution of the eros of the false prophet.' His last words slipped from his lips almost as an afterthought, but they acted on Cassian like an electro-baton. The Caledonian's eyes swept the priest's emaciated frame, as a broad grin spread across his face. Solon withdrew a step.

'You claim...' Solon repeated, but his voice wobbled.

'*Lapis!*' Cassian said, leaping to his feet and slamming his hands on the glass, causing the Vestal to start. '*Lapis, lapis, lapis!*' The priest flinched, scanning the glass uneasily.

'I am afraid I fail to understand what you mean by 'stone', citizen,' Solon said, turning to the bench as he slowly regained his composure. 'Do you, or do you not, recognise the destitution of that theurgist and son of the spirit of lie that gave himself out to be a god?'

Cassian shut his eyes, as if the words had stung him like a nettle.

'Answer the question, citizen!' Solon said. 'It is my view that you do not have any intention of recanting your false beliefs, and entreating the clemency of Our Lady for your bodily salvation in this life. Which being so, you are placed in great peril. Yes, in great peril indeed!' He shot a meaningful glance at the Vestal.

'Who shall cast the first stone?' Cassian asked, opening his cobalt eyes. As they scanned the eunuch's synkellic robe, red star and dainty golden crown, they seemed to be burning.

'I am the one asking the questions here!' Solon exclaimed. 'I remind you, citizen, that it is you who are on trial.'

'I saw a great white throne, and Him that sat on it.' Cassian said. 'From whose face the earth and the heaven fled away, and there was no place found for them. And the dead were judged according to their works.'

Solon's face turned white. The Vestal touched her brow, as if she were in pain. Marcus was alarmed. The heretic didn't care a jot what he said, not even with a Vestal in the room. And not just a Vestal, but a princess. A princess who was, at that very moment, under his exarchal protection.

'How dare you, you vile dog!' Solon screamed. 'How dare you speak such profanities here, here in the presence of her holy eminence! Retract these profanities at once, or I shall have no choice but to request – to entreat her eminence – to take the necessary measures to ensure your forcible—' He stopped in mid-flow. The Vestal had risen from her seat.

Marcus pushed back his chair, but she was already descending the steps. Like a dryad borne by the waves, she glided across the curial floor, the jade silk of her dress rippling around her like an ancient marble. Solon bowed, retreating to the wings. The Vestal approached the dock and stood before the glass. Everyone waited on her word. Even the storm had relented.

For some time she remained so, as if she really were the mute and sea-girt apparition of a goddess. Then she signalled to the guards to open the dock. They looked in confusion at Konstantin, who turned to Marcus. He was horrified. Was the princess even in her right mind? Heaven forfend that anything should happen to her royal person on his watch. That would assuredly be his end. There was nothing for it, though. The command of a Vestal maiden of Our Lady was sacrosanct. He nodded to Konstantin.

'*Carcerem aperite!*' Konstantin commanded. The glass quivered and became translucent as droplets ran down its surface. Finally, the entire pane collapsed into a small puddle, which drained away through a grille. The legionnaires' hands hovered over their batons, but Cassian remained still. It was the princess who moved first, drawing back her veil to reveal a strikingly beautiful face. Marcus had only seen the resident Vestal of the proconsulate on feast days, and always veiled.

Now that he saw her properly for the first time, he realised how young she was. She was barely past her majority. Cassian grinned and, quite unexpectedly, the Vestal smiled back at him, her emerald eyes and delicate Bohemian features lighting up with a radiance unlike anything Marcus had seen for many years.

'I am Anastasia Premyslovna, of the *Ordo Vestalis*. What is your name, my friend?' she asked.

'My name's Cassian Macleod, thane of the Caledonians, for my sins,' he replied. He addressed the Vestal simply, as if he had not been in a courtroom, or his life had not been in her hands. Marcus was stunned by his presumption. The idea that the pleb would address a Vestal and a royal thus, using his pretended title, defied belief. As if he were trying to impress any other commonplace wench from a Caledonian pothouse. He covered his mouth, masking the quaking of his jaw.

'I am glad to meet you, Cassian Macleod,' the Vestal said with a smile, 'although I am sorry to meet in such fashion, for it is indeed, alas, your sins that we are here to speak of today.' Her smile faded, and her eyebrows contracted sadly. Her wide, earnest eyes were almost tearful.

'Do you know what my name means?' she asked unexpectedly. 'No, of course not. I am sorry, there is no reason why you should. "*Ana-stasia*" refers to the Ascension. Of a rising up, away from the sins of our besmirched world, to the unsullied heights of heaven.' She almost looked apologetic, as if she worried she were taxing Cassian unduly, but he was listening intently.

'I think you know whose ascent back to heaven we are referring to?' Anastasia asked after a pause, her eyes shining beatifically. In the clear features of her face, over which a few of her tied-back locks had fallen like spun gold, Marcus could almost see the visage of the Virgin Herself as She ascended. He suppressed the blasphemous thought, but the light still showed a steady green.

'I'm thinking you mean the holy Mary?' Cassian answered. 'If that's who your name honours, milady, then you're blessed to have such a name as that. Aye, that you are.' Something like recognition glimmered in her eyes.

'It is kind of you to say so,' she said, though a hint of sadness had already entered her smile. 'For what is this life, indeed what is the life of woman, and of man, at all, if it is lived without kindness? Our heterogeneity is our strength, yes – but what is that strength truly worth without kindness?' Turning away pensively, Anastasia failed to notice how Cassian's brows knitted, as if one of Caledon's sullen clouds had come to rest there. Marcus exchanged a nervous glance with Solon despite himself.

'For many are our acts of unkindness, especially in our weaker moments,' she continued, her bright eyes almost pleading as they fixed on Cassian. 'Woman is weak, and man weaker still. It is so easy for us to stray from the true path illuminated by the Trinity. But if nothing else, we must always remember to be kind to Our Lady in what we say and in what we do—'

'Sorry lassie, what did you say your name was again – Assumpta, wasn't it?' Cassian interrupted. 'That's the name we use in these parts. Assumpta. Aye, that's a fine name indeed, milady!'

Anastasia, who no longer faced Cassian, froze at the strange address. Marcus eyed the golden halo of her head with dread. The curia was completely silent, save for the slight rustling of Solon's chlamys.

'Yes, above all else, we must never forget to return the kindness of the Mother, who forgives us our sins, though we so little deserve it,' she said as if Cassian hadn't spoken at all. 'Though we are weak, we must all strive to be worthy of the kindness of the Mother. For so beneficent is She, the Virgin Unsullied, that She pardons even those who insult and defile Her virtue. For all mortalkind are weak, and among mortals no frailty is so great as that of the masculine, which was not made in Her image. But the Holy Trinity illumines the path of righteousness, and for the sinner, the three lights of the Mother, the Virgin and the

Holy Spirit are as bright stars that lead the repentant back to chastity. So then, my friend, search your heart and ask yourself, truly. Have you earned the kindness of the Mother by your actions?'

'Assumpta, was it?' the prisoner repeated, a devilish light in his eyes. Marcus had the unpleasant sense of no longer listening to a conversation, but two coincidental monologues. He ought to have intervened, but that was impossible. Only a madman interrupted a Vestal, let alone a royal.

'*Haeresis!*' a squeaky voice broke in. 'How dare you! How dare you profane her eminence with your disgusting blasphemies? You are trying to be clever, yes, like your false prophet, but I see through your sophistries. You mean to suggest that Our Lady did not ascend to heaven of Her own accord, but was taken up – assumed to heaven, *Assumpta*, as your lot say – by your false deity.' Solon's face was white with rage. Marcus glared at him. The sacerdote pressed his lips, containing himself only with difficulty. Then his face reddened as he realised his error. He lowered his eyes demurely, placing his hand on his chlamys star, but Anastasia only smiled at him forgivingly.

'You are mistaken, my friend,' the Vestal said, closing her eyes, 'for my name is not Assumpta, but Anastasia...' For the first time, there was a slight tremor in her voice. Marcus touched the back of his neck. He was sweating. Things were going from bad to worse. What if the princess's dynatorial kin complained? It might even reach the imperial court. At the very least, his boss would hear of it. It was extremely rare that a Vestal, let alone a royal, should have dealings with anyone outside her class, to say nothing of a homunculus like Cassian.

'Begging your pardon, milady,' Cassian replied, a lambent sparkle in his eyes. 'I must have misheard your grace. Did you nay say that your name was about the Mother going up to heaven and all?'

Solon was back on his feet, but Marcus glowered at him and he sat back down. Why had the old clown had to go and involve a Vestal?

'Yes, my friend,' she said patiently. 'My name, Anastasia, refers to how the Virgin twice ascended. For, many centuries ago, in the days of the old patriarchs, the Maiden of Galilee was possessed by the Mother, who thereby became flesh and dwelt among us. But alas, the men of those days were blind to her Holy Gnosis, and were misled by the deceiver and the eros of his false prophet. And so, blighted in their immemory, the new patriarchs led us far astray. The innate weakness of men ran its natural course until, in those dark days five-and-a-half centuries ago, the infidel encamped before the very walls of the City itself! But the Virgin did not forsake us. For She descended unto us again, in the very hour of our direst need. In Her possession of the virgin Justinia, She laid Her divine strength upon the saintly maiden, who set right the faith and destituted the tyranny of the false prophet. Thus, the frailty of man was tempered. By the true faith alone was the empire reunited, and the Holy Wisdom of the Virgin, as foretold long ago by the venerable Egeria, at last made manifest. Then, Her work done, the Mother ascended a second—'

'It's a pretty tale that, lassie,' Cassian broke in. 'That it is. But there's only one ascension that I know of. There's only One who ascended to heaven. There's only One who rose of their own power, and it was nay the holy mother!' The star light became burgundy.

'That is unkind of you,' Anastasia said uncertainly. 'I do not believe you know what you say. Yet in speaking so, my friend, you do Our Mother a great unkindness. For what I say is simply the truth, long known to all. The Mother twice ascended. In your heart, you surely know that this is—'

'Unkind?' Cassian interrupted again, his eyes blazing with a new fire. 'You see, lassie, I hate to say it, but I can nay make out what you mean by that. Thing is, I look around me here, and I see a lot of unkindness to my people. And last time I checked, it's your lot who are in charge here, are you nay?' He waved derisorily at the tribunal, then at the city below. Sweat ran down the back of Marcus' tunic in a torrent. Cassian had insulted a royal. It was too late to shut him up in the Reservation now. The pleb would have to be made an example of, and publicly. The palace would insist on that. That meant his own neck was on the line, too.

'You do Our Mother a great unkindness,' Anastasia stammered, almost to herself. 'Yes, what you say is unkind. For Our Lady was not assumed to heaven, for the simple reason that She alone is the Queen of Heaven, and there is none other than Her that reigns there—'

'That may be your truth, lassie, but I can tell you, it's no truth of mine!' Cassian said, flecks of foam gathering in his red beard. 'And it ne'er will be! Kindness? What's kind about your lady, if she lets so many go without, and even lets the slave bairns starve in the streets while your lot sit here talking about your lady? No kindness in that, aye, lassie. The thane would nay brook it!'

'Am I to understand by your words,' Anastasia asked very slowly, 'that you do not hold with the doctrine of the One-and-Only Queen of Heaven?'

With horror, Marcus noted how all the colour had left her face. She really had hoped to save Cassian, after all. He locked his hands together, trying to stop their violent trembling. The room grew still. Outside, even the storm gods held their breath.

The brazen smile deserted Cassian's face. Instead, some new feeling worked there. Something serious, heretofore unseen, was contending with his innate brashness. Like the burning pediment of a temple, his eyebrows arched, and for the briefest moment, he seemed afraid. Then, as if some martial god had lain his gauntlet upon the temple, resolution flattened them again. He stared at Anastasia defiantly, almost with hatred.

'Aye, little girl, that I don't!' he said. 'For our holy mother sits in heaven, arrayed in splendour among all the saints and the heavenly host, besides the throne of Our—'

'Blasphemy!' Solon squealed. 'Heresy! How dare you profane Her name? My lady, I urge you most humbly, for the sanctity of Our Lady, and the honour of your royal person, to confine this heretic at once—'

Marcus was on his feet, about to shout him down, but Cassian beat him to it.

'I'm perfectly in my right mind, you old hypocrite, and I mean what I say!' he yelled. 'Beat me as much as you like, but don't even think of packing me off to your prison. I willnae go there, even if you force me. The thane would rather die than suffer that disgrace. Aye, that he would!' His words beat Solon backwards, and he tripped over his bench.

Anastasia's face was completely white, her distress and confusion plain to all. Marcus was sweating like a pig. The princess had definitely meant to save Cassian, be it by recantation or the Reservation. That could not happen now. Understanding dawned upon him. Cassian had resolved to die for his beliefs; he even desired it. It made Marcus uneasy. Perhaps he oughtn't to have ruled out the Reservation so quickly. Had the Caledonian planned his martyrdom all along? He did not know, but one thing was clear. By insulting a royal, Cassian meant to take the exarch down with him.

'*Heu mihi miserae*,' Anastasia said, pitying her own misfortune. 'Then you are lost, alas!' A look of genuine dejection spread across her handsome face, and her eyes grew bright. Marcus' cheeks were numb with terror.

'I am left with no choice,' she said despondently. 'For I see that you are lost to the faith, irretrievably lost. Those outside the *Fides* are lost to the Mother, and shall not return to Her.' An expression of intense pity entered her face, more melancholy than anything he had ever seen. As if she herself were being condemned, rather than Cassian. So too for Marcus, her words were edged with a steel sharper than any Saracene sabre. He clutched his side, as his old wound from the slave riots burned.

'The Virgin has offered you Her clemency, Cassian Macleod, but in return you have shown Her only unkindness. Many times, citizen, you have been offered the chance to recant, but you have rejected Her grace,' Anastasia said. Her eyes were faraway, as if she were speaking under compulsion, possessed by a voice not her own. The star light flared, painting the room bloodred in the half-night of the storm.

'*Iudicio Matris, Virginis et Spiritus Sancti*, by the authority of the Mother, Virgin and the Holy Spirit, vested in me,' the Vestal continued without enthusiasm, 'I proscribe you, citizen, as anathema, you who are outside the *Fides Marianea*.'

Marcus blanched. This was not how it was supposed to happen. His wound seared again, as if the slave who had dealt the blow had come back to life to finish the job.

'*Et te excommunicatum et anathematizatum esse decerno*, I declare you excommunicate and anathema,' Anastasia managed to say, almost inaudibly. '*Et damnatum cum fraudatore in ignem aeternum iudico*, I judge you damned with the deceiver to the eternal fire.' Her face was utterly cheerless, for all the world as if she had just committed herself to the everlasting flames. She replaced her veil. Konstantin gave the command and glass once more dripped from the ceiling.

'*Quae sine peccato est vestrum primum lapidem mittat*,' Cassian said as the liquid solidified around him, 'she that is without sin among you, let her first cast a stone!'

Anastasia paused, already halfway up the tribunal steps. Then she hastily re-took her place at Marcus' side, her sylphlike grace abandoning her. Her whole body was as stiff as a marble herm, and a muffled sob emanated from her veil. The truth stood before him, as clear as the Propontine Sea. There was only one sentence left for him to pass. Nor was it just Cassian who was being condemned today. He was condemning himself too.

'*In nomine Matris, et Virginis, et Spiritus Sancti*,' he said, ignoring the pain in his side as he rose to his feet, 'citizen Cassian Macleod, from the evidence set before this court and your own testimony, I find you guilty of the crime of heresy, under the *Lex Iustiniana de Proscriptione Magna*, of the twenty-ninth year of Our Lady's Descension.' Solon skulked in a corner, trying to make himself scarce. Who could blame him? As for himself, there was nowhere left to hide. An insult to a royal. On his watch. He was done for.

'As the penalty prescribed by the law for your crime, for one duly declared anathema,' he pronounced, 'I, Marcus Comnenus, exarch of Caledonia, and president of the High Strategic Tribunal of the province, hereby sentence you to the Supreme Measure.'

'*Carcerem aperite!*' Konstantin said, as for a final time the glass melted away. Seizing Cassian by the shoulders, the legionnaires yanked him to his feet. He tried to resist, but was not fast enough, crying out as an electric shock ran through him. The batons touched him a second time, and he collapsed. The guards dragged him away as if he were already a corpse, but he managed to raise his bleary eyes to the tribunal.

'Damning me, are you?' Cassian called back at Marcus, writhing as he slid across the marble. 'Aye, it's one rule for your lot, and another for us, isn't it?'

The Vestal shuddered. Marcus' face turned pink. He did his best to pretend he hadn't heard, trying not to picture Hypatia. Nor what she was up to while he was stuck out here alone on her account, his reputation in tatters.

'I know what your wife is up to, governor,' Cassian said, swatting away one of the guards. 'Hypocrites! Look to your own, look to your own first, you hear?'

Marcus looked out the window, desperately trying to ignore the diabolical voice. The sky over Caledon was altogether pitch now, as the night came on. Pain shot through his side, and the black clouds danced in a charybdian swirl.

'That's right, you heard what I said,' the condemned man persisted, as the guards heaved him with a final, titanic, effort through the curial doors. 'Look to your own house first, before you go condemning others. Look to the lady Hypatia. *Quae sine peccato est.* She who is without sin!'

There was another bolt of pain, and the storm became a hurricane. 'Silence, heretic!' he said, losing control. 'How dare you...' His words died in his mouth. He clutched his side. Anastasia flinched. Lightning illuminated the courtroom, extinguishing the red light as the chair slipped from beneath him. His eyes rose to the pewter sky. The courtroom disappeared, and the hurricane dissolved into the mist on the Bosphorus.

He gasped for air. His throat was raw, and he felt sick. Someone was pressing on his chest. Soft hair brushed against his face. It was a pleasant feeling. He opened his eyes. Blond hair and the generous proportions of a woman's chest came into view, rising and falling above him. A familiar voice was calling him.

'Excellency?' Severa asked, shaking his shoulders. 'Are you ok?'

Marcus sat up, brushing her aside. A tall man in a white uniform stood over him. His tribune's face came into focus, framed against the vernal evening sky. The star of the Virgin shone over the stadium.

The proconsular box was empty. The legates and officials had all disappeared. Down below, the last of the demes were leaving the stands, their yellow and green scarves trailing behind them. There was no sign of Flavian, nor of any of the other governors. No sign of Argyra, nor her entourage. He was finished.

He tried to rise, but his hand slipped on his matrician cuffs and he fell back with a thud.

CHAPTER 9

Vadim

Like the snow on the palace roofs outside, fast melting in the morning sun, the girl's shift slid effortlessly onto the bedsheets. Vadim had hardly to pass his hand down her back and her brassiere fell away too.

He lay back in the soft cushions and sighed. Above him was an incomparable vision of loveliness. The soft northern light streamed through his chamber window, igniting a thousand stars in Ganna's long golden tresses. As if its gilded rays were tipped with charcoal, it seemed intentionally to have shaded her chest so as to give it the impression of sculpted marble. He ran his hand across its contours, stiffening beneath the sheets. Her azure eyes were as clear as the Euxeinic Sea. Not for the first time, he wondered how he would describe the beauty of Cossack women to one who knew only that of the south. Had not the Virgin made them in Her own stainless image?

With a selkie's grace, Ganna slipped out of her undergarments. Vadim's hands descended the gentle undulation of her back to her slender waist, resting on the arc of her alabaster thighs as they locked themselves about him. Her mouth creased as she gripped him. A flush spread across her chest, like the crimson dawn over the mighty river outside. Her panting was like its incessant waves, rolling over him. He wanted to lose himself in that river, to drown himself forever in the golden lap of her embrace. To forget the world and himself. His hands caressed her white arms and the rose crowns of her chest, sliding down to her buttocks. She moaned as her fingers squeezed his broad shoulders, her flaxen hair brushing his face as her torrid body rose and fell against his. He pulled her closer, descending into oblivion as he sank into the gilded waves. Her soft lips kissed his ears.

'*Moy korol,*' Ganna whispered in Novgorovian. 'My king.'

Her words ran through him like ice. He awoke from his reverie, as if the river had spat him out upon its cold shore. His whole body went numb as her grip on him loosened. Her wide eyes looked down at him in alarm.

'Argh!' Vadim said, shoving her aside. In a single bound, he leapt from the bed. He shook himself, running his hand through his jet-black hair as he moved to the window.

'My prince, I did not mean to—' Ganna said, but Vadim raised his hand. Still undressed, she sat mournfully on the edge of the four-poster bed, her blond braids hanging down over her penitent face, but the sight of all her pearly nakedness now left him cold. How carefree he had been but a moment before.

His green eyes roved nervously over the medieval carving of the windowsill. Outside, the gilded domes of the trinity churches sparkled like luminescent balloons, as the last of the snow ran down their sides. By now, the sun had risen over the forked red castellations of the palace wall. The red berets of the royal guard were on their morning round, patrolling the parapet. They bobbed along beside the crenellations like candles on a cake, their white uniforms and polished rifles candescent in the dawn light. Beyond, on the far riverbank, the morning traffic glinted on the electrohighway. The city was coming to life, joyfully greeting the new day. If only he could share in that joy, but that could not be. Today was not a day for celebration, not for him. Ganna should have known better.

'Never call me that,' Vadim said. 'You know how much I hate all that is false, Ganna.' She raised her doe's eyes, which were wet with tears. How fair those Cossack eyes were, even in melancholy.

'But you know you are my lord, my dear one,' she said, 'and today is a great day for you.' He scowled, and she dropped her eyes demurely.

'You know today is not a happy day for me, Ganna,' he said. She tied back her hair, exposing the dimpled peaks of her snowy chest. Catching Vadim admiring her, she smiled coyly, but a flash of light reflecting off the river distracted him. A lightcraft disappeared into the ether high above as its metallic shell shot up into the stratosphere, its ion fins already spreading like a giant diaphanous web. It was most likely heading south to the capital. He pictured the domes of Mariapol and tugged angrily at his long black hair.

'What use is there in being a stupid priest, Ganna? Is that all I am worth? Is that all you think of me, even you?' He eyed the soldiers on the rampart with envy. If only he could be one of them. To wear a uniform instead of an unmanly chlamys, and carry a rifle instead of a worthless sceptre.

'I am only a servant, my lord, and I do not know much of such things,' she said, looking at her hands, 'but I know that it is your father's wish, and he will be proud of you today. Your father is a great man, and one day you will be too, my prince.'

Vadim laughed bitterly, shaking his head. Ganna blushed.

'My father? My father wants me to be a priest, yes, a useless sacerdote like him. What are they all even for? I mean, it's all just ceremony, just a sham, isn't it? And that's what my ordination will be today. A stupid sham. What's the point in pretending otherwise?' He let off, seeing the alarm in Ganna's eyes.

'Oh, don't worry, Ganna,' he said, moving back to the bed. 'I'm not going to do anything stupid. You know very well that I'll go through with it, as Father wishes. Even Mother wants me to do my duty. She thinks it'll advance me, the Virgin knows how.' Her cornflower eyes made him forget what he had been saying. Kissing her rubicund lips, he slipped his hand into her cleavage, as her supple hands crept up his thigh. He threw her down onto the bed, lifting her legs against his chest as he entered her. He was soon drifting back into the river's golden embrace.

There was a loud knock at the chamber door. Vadim cursed, rudely surfacing above the waves. Ganna looked up at him in terror, as if she thought the sparks from his eyes might catch in the wooden posters and set fire to the bed. He roared at the oak door, demanding to know who it was.

'*Yeto ya*, Dnilo, it is I,' a sheepish voice replied in Novgorovian from the other side. 'I am very sorry, *moy gospodin*, I would not have disturbed you, only that Her Highness the Princess Eudoxia Cassimirovna has requested the honour of your presence.'

Vadim's face fell. Ganna hastily gathered her clothes.

'*Vkhodit.*' He commanded his valet to enter, already pulling on his hose. A gaunt man in his early sixties entered, bowing respectfully. He had a white beard, and wore a red tunic emblazoned with a crowned double-headed silver eagle. He waved furtively at Ganna, who pulled on her shift and slipped out a door behind one of the tapestries. Its silken weave and gilt '*A.U.R. DXXX*' banner oscillated as the door closed, as if the Virgin's robe on Mariapol's walls and the magical tempest engulfing the Rus ships had come to life. Dnilo watched nervously as it settled back over the hatch.

'What on earth does Mother want, old man?' Vadim asked, a stray black curl falling across his forehead as he shook his head angrily. '*I pryamo*, tell me straight please. You know how she is. What's she up to? The ceremony isn't for a few hours yet. Why does she need to see me now?'

'*Moy prints*, you know that your presence is always a delight to your mother,' Dnilo said with another bow. 'Her Highness, the Lady

Eudoxia, is ehm – how to put it – Her Highness is concerned at your lack of enthusiasm for today's—'

'Yes, yes, Dnilo, I know Mother isn't best-pleased, but it's hardly news to her, and anyway she knows I'll do what Father wants…' he said, but paused, noticing his valet studying the floor. 'Wait, there's something else, isn't there? Come on, *moy dorogoy chelovek*, spit it out, what's Mother up to?'

'*Moy gospodin*, you know,' Dnilo said, peeking at the tapestry, 'Her Highness, your mother, she does not, ahem – in view of the vow you are to take today – she does not approve of your, of your liaison, with your…' He desisted. An angry flush was suffusing his master's neck, like rose petals in milk.

'*Chert!*' Vadim swore. 'Isn't it bad enough that I have to go through with this stupid ordination as it is? Is Mother determined to spoil my happiness entirely?' He slammed his large fists into the wardrobe, and one of its hinges snapped. Dnilo continued to study the floorboards.

By now, the sky was dappled with the diaphanous fins of several other lightcraft, floating like giant jellyfish on the surface of the sea. The red berets jested as they patrolled the parapet. He yearned to be free. Their mothers hardly told them which women they could have. He was a prince, but what was that worth when he wasn't even his own master?

'Tell Mother I am coming,' he said at last, shaking his head in resignation. Dnilo bowed his head and turned to leave.

'And Dnilo, if you'd be so kind,' he added, as the floorboards creaked beneath his valet's feet, 'not a word about this to Mother, please?' He waved his hand at the shipwreck tapestry. Dnilo bowed again and slipped out the door.

Half an hour later, Vadim stepped into a high-ceilinged room on the other side of the palace, two servants in the same livery as Dnilo bowing as he entered. His hair was lacquered in a side parting, and in place of his night robe, he wore a black tunic embroidered with a golden double-headed eagle and star. On his finger was a silver ring with the same eagle, but topped instead with a crown. A tall blond middle-aged woman stood on the far side of the long gallery, gazing out of a high window. She wore a dappled black-and-gold kirtle dress with a high ruff neck. On her head was a small diadem, from whose sides ivory beads hung down to her shoulders. Behind her, the city spires sparkled like glass baubles in the matinal sun.

Gold, stucco and Nubian ivory covered the entire gallery, depicting double-headed eagles, crowns and stars. Spanning the ceiling was a giant map divided into four quadrants, each marked by a heraldic shield with the legends, '*Eboracum, Caput Boreale*', '*Ravenna, Caput Occidentale*', '*Castra Kremlovska, Caput Orientale*', and '*Urbs Sancta, Caput Australe*', the last animated by an iridescent light. A vast mosaic on the right-hand wall showed a medieval army kneeling in a yellow field, beneath a wide blue sky. The heads of all were bowed, their hands placed solemnly on their chests. Their swords and spears lay before them, glittering in the aestival sun like a great moonlit lake. In the centre was a young woman in a chiton on a rearing white steed, her cascading black curls framed in a solar halo as she smiled down at the men. Before her horse's hooves, a man in a purple robe and an astrakhan fur cap knelt as he offered up a golden crown with both hands. Over the mosaic was the inscription, '*Anno Descensionis XXV Princeps Ivanus in campo Marianeo coronam reddit.*'

'Upon the field of Mary, Grand Prince Ivan gave back his crown,' Vadim read aloud. The woman turned, breaking into a broad smile as her keen green eyes surveyed Vadim from head to toe. He inclined his head.

'I have always thought you had his eyes,' she said. 'You have your father's hair, but that is all. Otherwise, you have always been one of us, the very image of our sire.' She glanced up at the kneeling man in the mosaic, then greedily took in Vadim's face.

'My son,' the woman said, offering her hand as Vadim approached. He knelt and kissed the silver ring on her finger, which bore the same insignia as his own. She embraced him tightly, then held him at arm's length as she looked solicitously into his eyes. For some time, they stood together in silence, looking out at the colossal towers of Castra Kremlovska in the distance. Its glass facades rose to the sky like icicles, as if threatening to melt in the sharp northern light, while thousands of little lights flitted about at their feet like fireflies on a summer night.

Vadim's eyes dropped to the red brick of the ramparts below, where his quarters were. Ganna would already be down there somewhere in the servants' quarters, doubtless being riled by the other girls. The thought irritated him, and he grimaced. His mother gave him a sidelong glance, and the corners of her handsome mouth turned down.

'Today is a special day for you, Vadim. Your father and I are very proud of you. I do hope you know that?' she asked. Vadim did not return her gaze, but went on studying the palace wall. He could just make out the smart crimson berets lining the parapet below. He fingered his ring irritably.

'It is a great honour to take the orders,' she continued. 'You know what that means to your father, and to me. And, as is your due, you will take them in our most holy Church of the Ascension. In that church which is, perhaps, most hallowed of all among our people, beneath our most beloved image of the Mother of Casan. You know, Vadim, we have been waiting for this day since you were born—'

'Why do you say these things, Mother?' Vadim said, his cheeks flushing. 'I know it matters to you, but you know how I feel about it. Does that even come into it?' His eyes rested for a moment on Grand Prince Ivan, and he pressed his ring again.

'Besides, I am no eunuch priest, Mother,' he added, looking bitterly at his quarters below. 'You know Our Lady didn't make me that way.'

Eudoxia's eyes followed his. Her shapely lips became pursed, and her hands moved to her slender hips.

'And you, Vadim, know what I feel about – about this – though it pains me to say it...' she said, waving her hand at the window. 'About this, this – cavorting about. And not just that – but cavorting with such a lowborn—!'

'Mother!' Vadim said. 'I am not a child. Why must you insist on treating me like one? If I really must go through with all this ceremony, may I not at least have some life of my own? And am I not a prince? May I not do as I please with my own servants?'

'*U printsa yest obyazannosti,*' she said, switching from Greek to Novgorovian. 'A prince has responsibilities, Vadim. For Justinia's sake, you are the empress' nephew, have you forgotten that? And not just that, you are my only son. The heir to the Novgorovian line. You will do your duty, my son, because you must.' She straightened up, adjusting her diadem.

'You know I will do my duty, Mother,' Vadim replied, 'but I am my own man too, as the men of our family have always been. Would you have me otherwise?' His wroth abated, his eyes almost pleading now. For a long time, Eudoxia only stared at Castra Kremlovska's skyline in silence. To his surprise, when she faced him again there were tears in her eyes. A radiant smile rose to her high cheekbones.

'No, Vadim, I would have you as you are,' she said, gazing into his eyes. 'I know you will do your duty, but I also know you are one of us. You always have been. You know, you are so much the image of your grandfather.' She cupped his alabaster cheeks with her long hands. Vadim smiled weakly.

'You know I only wish you happiness, my son,' Eudoxia continued. 'A sacerdote needn't be a eunuch, after all, even if some do choose that dedication to Our Lady. But he must at least remain chaste until he marries, as you will – and soon, if you so wish. Besides, Vadim, you are a royal. Your reputation – our reputation – matters.'

The cleft between Vadim's brows reappeared. He tried to twist free, but Eudoxia held him firmly.

'So I shall say nothing further about this Cossack girl...' she said, looking at him meaningfully. 'And, if I hear nothing more about it, then I shall rest assured no one else has. All I ask is that you remember who you are, and that in time you must wed. I do not wish you to get hurt.' She broke away and moved to a large mahogany table beneath the mosaic. The hem of her black kirtle swept the marble floor, its golden threads glistering like Ganna's hair.

'You must understand, Vadim, that our fortunes are not what they were,' she said, distractedly tracing the silver corunal inlay of the table. 'Yes, the dignity of our house is not what it once was, and can no longer be taken for granted. We do not enjoy the offices we once did, and our voice no longer carries at the Sublime Port as it did in your grandfather's day. We must protect it however we can. We, my son, must guard our house's honour. It is up to us.'

'But then why do you insist on my joining the sacerdotal order?' he said, his dark eyebrows arching. 'I do not understand what good I can do for us as a sacerdote. Is that really an honour worthy of our house? Look at what happened to cousin Anastasia.'

'You are right, Vadim, what happened to your cousin at the Saturnal was a disgrace,' Eudoxia said, her jade eyes glowing with ire. 'To think, a Vestal treated so shamelessly by a pleb. It would never have happened in your grandfather's day. Your aunt raised it with the empress at the time. That useless little Syrian ought never to have been made a governor, even in a backwater like Caledon.'

'And am I not to expect similar – or worse – contempt, once I am a sacerdote?' Vadim said. 'By the advantage of her sex, cousin Anastasia holds the high Vestal office, with its attendant privilege, but I shall be a mere priest. Honestly, Mother, what can I expect but to face still greater dishonour? Shall I not be defenceless then to protect us?'

'Listen, Vadim,' Eudoxia said, returning to his side and placing her hand on his shoulder, 'no son of mine shall ever face such dishonour. No, we are the House of Novgorod, and we look after our own. Nor does an insult to the imperial family ever go unpunished. You will see. Anastasia's shame shall not be unavenged. But this is also the reason why you must do your duty. The sacerdotal office advances you in the eyes of Our Lady, and so too in the royal esteem. And it is by that esteem alone, by the grace of your aunt, Her Imperial Majesty Theadosia, that our house shall retain honour. Do you understand, Vadim?'

'Yes, Mother,' he replied slowly, 'I understand.' Eudoxia's bejewelled fingers gripped him tightly by both shoulders, scrying his features like runes. Unable to escape, he averted his eyes. She pressed him to her chest, stroking his hair.

A clop of heels resounded around the long walls. They looked up. A footman in red-and-gold livery stood in the doorway.

'*Moya koroleva, moy prints*, it is time,' the man said, bowing low. Eudoxia nodded and the servant withdrew, walking backwards. A shiver ran down Vadim's spine. He disengaged from Eudoxia's embrace, eyeing the mosaic. She only smiled and, placing her palm on his back, gestured him towards the door.

Chapter 10

Alistair

The ships came in to port, their black sails fluttering in the hot morning breeze. He lent out the palace window, trying to get a better look.

Something was wrong. There was something else on board. Something the Alexandrian sailors hadn't meant to bring with them. Planks rattled as men rolled casks off the ships and carried amphorae onto the quayside. A large shadow leapt from one of the wine jars and dashed across the cobbles, like a bolt of black lightning.

'No!' he said, but the sailors couldn't hear him. Instead, they continued to unload more casks and amphorae. More shadows leapt out of the barrels and jars and scuttled off into the city in all directions. He cried out in despair, but it was no use. More ships piled into the port. Soon their great black sails filled the harbour. He waved his hands frantically, but none of the sailors could see him up in the palace.

Across the strait, the entire channel was filling up with the awful sails. They swelled with a sultry wind from the south, and there was a stench on that wind. A sweet, foul stench. It was the stench of death. Down on the quayside, one of the sailors collapsed right before the palace gate. His fellows looked about nervously but, seeing the harsh morning sun, only shook their heads.

Behind them, unnoticed by anyone, shadows darted off the ships in ever greater numbers. Soon they poured onto the cobblestones like a tide of black gore, seeping under doors, into houses, churches and temples. He screamed at the sailors, but still they did not hear him. Another man fell. Then another. Men fell overboard as they tried to alight from the ships, or else were struck dead before their ships even came to port. Black blotches sprouted like mushrooms all over their olive skin, as their eyes became like cloudy glass. Corpses clawed at the living. The barrels floated back out to sea. The amphorae smashed and the wine ran into the dry stones, staining them the colour of blood.

The foul meridianal wind blew hotter on his face as the morning sun turned the channel crimson. He gripped the mosaic tiles of the windowsill. The wall of black sails was so thick that he could no longer see his dromon galleons. How could the western provinces be retaken now? The barbarians would surely recapture the old city, so hard won by Belisar. Was this the punishment of the Almighty?

He looked down at his arms. The wool of his imperial toga melted away like a wax candle. Soon he was entirely naked. Sores burgeoned on his pallid skin, spreading over his body like black ink on blotting paper. Rats ran up his arms and down his back. He tried to catch at them, but they kept getting away. A vermillion haze rose from the Bosphorus, bleeding into the blackened stones of the quayside. His vision blurred. He looked up at the sun, pleading mercy for his hubris.

'If this is Thy will, then strike me down, but spare me this torment!' he tried to cry out, but his voice choked in his throat. His tears came in a flood.

Alistair tasted salt on his damp pillow and awoke with a start. One of the rats was gnawing at his shoulder. He knocked it away, and slowly opened his bleary eyes. The charcoal sails and blood-red sky evaporated. The blotches on his arms were gone. It was dark. Someone was gripping his shoulder, shaking him. That was odd. He didn't share his cabin. He bolted upright, shoving the disembodied arm away. A shadow stumbled backwards in the darkness.

'Master Alistair?' a voice whispered. 'It is I, Brother Lucas, please do not be alarmed.' The young friar who had handed him his present the evening before staggered back to Alistair's bedside.

'But what is the meaning of—?' Alistair said, but the friar raised a finger to his lips. Most of the monks were normally quite content to listen to him prattling on without saying a word themselves. Indeed, he was usually quite frustrated that they said so little. He wasn't sure he could recall ever being asked to shut up. Not least by someone who'd entered his cell uninvited.

He opened his mouth, but something in the Poor Friar's eyes gave him pause. It was written all over his face, unmistakable even in the shadows. Fear. The man was afraid, but of what? He looked out the window, still half expecting to see black sails. It wasn't even first light yet, and the basilica couldn't be seen.

'Please, Master Alistair,' Lucas said, 'I bear a message from Father Zosim who, as you know, cares dearly for you.' The monk wasn't carrying a candle, nor had he lit one when he arrived, but his eyes shone strangely.

'The venerable father says that you are to leave, and that you must leave now,' the friar whispered. 'Don't even wait for first light. Nor are you to look for him.'

Alistair's brows knitted. 'Why...?' he asked, but again Lucas raised his finger to his lips. The monk squeezed his shoulder. He was trembling all over, and his hand was clammy with sweat. Alistair made to reply, but Lucas was already at the door.

'Go now, young master, do not delay, I implore you,' he said on the threshold. 'Your life may depend upon it.' He nodded at the satchel that Alistair had left beside the door the night before. His wide eyes beheld him one last time then, without another word, he disappeared into the night.

Alistair sat motionless on his bed. His mind ran in rapid circles around the cabin, but his limbs felt as leaden as the apostolica roof. Lucas' horrid eyes still stared back at him from the shadows. There were muffled voices from somewhere without. Father Zosim's face appeared, disembodied and floating in the half-light of the dawn. 'Do not sleep too heavily this night,' his words thundered through the silence. *Violentia.*

He leapt from the bed and grabbed his satchel. Throwing an old surcoat over his shoulders, he shoved his feet into his boots and hurtled to the door. Hardly knowing what he was doing, he leaned out into the dewy Latian morning, brushing the cobwebs from his eyes. He looked up the path, but immediately yanked his head back inside. At its summit were a cluster of Marians. There couldn't have been fewer than twenty of them, easily twice the number he had ever seen in the Reservation.

'Go now, master, your life may depend upon it!' Lucas called from the darkness. His heart pounded as he lent against the doorframe. Another voice was screaming deafeningly inside his own head. Go now. Go now!

He bounded out the door and down the path, rushing headlong like a wild boar. His pack clattered on his back, but he didn't look back. He had to get away. Away from the dormitory. Away from the basilica. Away from the Reservation. Away from the Reservation? The question nearly tripped him as he ran.

He bowled around the corner of the last dacha. Up ahead, the track that ran around the back of the dormitory was all clear. He leant against the back of the hut, gasping for breath. His back was damp with sweat, and he could already feel a stitch coming on. He peered back up the path. The Marians were fanning out among the dachas at the far end. They had magic torches in their hands, and their white berets glinted in the light they gave off. White, not the usual black. That was odd.

'Go now!' the inner voice screamed again, and he hurtled on down the track. Beyond the last row of shacks was a walled orchard, in the midst of the allotment where the friars grew their vegetables. He made for the door in the stone wall. Raising its iron latch as quietly as he could, he pulled it ajar and slipped inside. There was no one about, just the silent ranks of the apple trees. The cotton of their blossoms shone in the first light of dawn, the same colour as the Marians' berets. Why were they white today?

The morning erupted in a cacophonous din of shouting and wailing, as doors crashed open. *Violentia*. He pushed off the wall and ran into the trees. The cries grew louder as he bounded towards the far wall, ducking beneath the apple boughs and tearing through the overgrown grass. Nettles snapped at his calves like serpents, but he hardly noticed the pain. Like the apostolica, he knew the orchards and allotments well, and even in the semi-darkness soon reached the far wall. He lifted the door bolt and slipped through, but as he did so another bolt clanked behind. They were after him.

Petrified, he ran down the old garden path beyond the orchard. Less a garden now than an overgrown knot of weeds, its unpaved track was still just about discernible from the dilapidated statues that once marked its way. He threaded through the ancient plinths, endeavouring not to trip over the shards of marble limbs and fragmentary wings that lay all about. Most were angels described in the book, but in the half-light their hollow eye sockets and lopsided jaws leered at him like demons. Others were altogether headless, their torsos casting long shadows like corn stalks in the dawn. He hardly knew where he was going, except away from the dormitory. It was the way westward, the way out to the perimeter. To the Pomerium.

Pomerium. The word chilled him to the bones. The old city limit that marked the end of the Reservation. The end of the old law. He had never actually seen it. Still, if what the monks said was true, it was heavily guarded, and not just that. It was said to be threaded through with some kind of invisible fire. Like some magical fleece which, once you were wrapped in, you couldn't get out of, and which burned you to cinders. How had he hoped to get beyond it? What had he been thinking? It had been madness to try and run away.

There was a noise behind. He hastily concealed himself beneath the plinth of the last statue. He could just make out the solitary figure of a soldier, framed in relief against the travertine of the orchard wall like one of the Forsaken People on the old patriarchs' arch. Ahead, the path dissolved completely, disappearing into a thicket of cypresses. In terror he launched himself into their midst, praying that he hadn't been seen. Like a bear pursued by an ancient hero, he bounded through the trees, borne along by his own weight. He had never come this far before and had no idea where he was going, but some instinct told him he was leaving the old palace precinct. The ground sloped downwards, as the cypresses grew denser and became intermixed with poplars and pines. The undergrowth thickened too and his feet kept getting tangled in the weeds. Water trickled somewhere below. Soon there were stagnant pools on all sides.

There was more rustling behind. The soldier must have seen him, or guessed he'd come this way. Alistair's brow was damp with sweat, and his feet were wet too. He must have waded into a shallow swamp without noticing. Something moved among the dark poplars ahead, where the bank rose again. There were more of them. He was caught in a ditch, surrounded on both sides. He flailed about in terror, but there was no way out.

'*Huc! Huc!*' Disembodied cries resounded around the ditch as the soldiers called each other to the spot. Two white berets glinted among the poplars. At the same time a thrashing noise came from behind, as someone tore through the undergrowth. He dived into the bushes, crawling on all fours to where the cover was densest. At first, his hands and knees splashed noisily in the muddy water, but soon the pool deepened as the stream coursed along his flanks. The shouting ceased.

Footsteps shuffled about somewhere nearby. He kept as still as he could, straining his ears as he tried not to breathe.

'*Quo fugit?*' a gruff voice asked where he had disappeared to. Someone said something in reply. The words were too quiet to make out, but the voice was familiar. The gruff one shouted something angrily, then there was thrashing in the bushes close by. Alistair looked about in alarm. Something glistened ahead amidst the wicker canvas of moss and weeds. Flattening his body, he slid across the mud towards it, feeling like a sea triton from the old stories. If only he hadn't been such an oaf, and more like the Marian. The legionnaire would have slipped through the undergrowth like a fish. The plashing grew louder until it drowned out all else, and water soon splashed his face and chest. Between its jets, the shard of light gradually took the form of a rusty grille. Water spewed from its iron lattice, which was slightly ajar. Beyond was a dark tunnel.

'*Quo fugit, puer?*' the gruff one repeated, addressing the second as a boy. His reply was inaudible, but an angry stamping of feet followed, which made Alistair's blood run cold. If they found him, he was surely done for. He was right up against the grille now. The water rushed out in a torrent, submersing his head and soaking the pack on his back. His hair was full of leaves, and his surcoat completely caked in mud.

'*Huc! Huc!*' a voice said nearby. Gripping the grille, Alistair peered into the darkness. It was now or never. With a last desperate effort, he prized it open and thrust himself inside. The tunnel was narrow and the cold stone scraped painfully against his back as the water ran up his nostrils. No sooner had he squeezed himself in, there was a loud crash hard by, as leaves and branches fell into the water. He lowered himself into the water, keeping his nose and eyes just above the surface. Raised voices floated into the tunnel.

'*Hic erat sed fugit, homuncule, nonne?*' the harsh voice berated the other for letting Alistair escape. 'You legionnaires think you're the gift of Our Lady, but the truth is you're just a bunch of useless idiots.

The kid was right under your nose, but you let him get away, didn't you?' Another branch was torn asunder nearby, and two white berets came into view between the trees. A black beret appeared opposite. It was the Latin. One of the white berets came up to him. A man of gargantuan proportions, he stood a full head-and-shoulders over the legionnaire.

'It's like I always say,' the giant continued, switching to Italic as he addressed the other white beret, 'if you want something done, don't leave it to a legionnaire. Leave the serious business to the grown-ups. Leave it to the praetorians, otherwise you can rest assured this lot will bugger it up.' He jabbed at the Latin's chest, as the other smiled sardonically. The praetorian was hideous to behold, with a jutting brow and pockmarked cheeks like the face of the moon, as if some long-forgotten titan buried beneath the Latian soil had broken his chains and resurfaced on earth. Despite the legionnaire's proud mien, his whole figure cowered before the ancient brute.

'That's right, if this fancy boy had spent less time preening himself, we'd have caught the fat one by now,' the titan said. 'In Justinia's name, to think, they call themselves soldiers and they can't even catch a bunch of old men and one kid. Come on, let's not waste any more time with this idiot, the kid's obviously gone.' As he concluded his harangue, he prodded his index finger into the legionnaire's jerkin so hard that he lost his balance and stumbled backwards into the undergrowth. The praetorian slapped his comrade on the back as they walked away, laughing raucously as he pointed at the Latin's black beret, which had rolled off his head into the mud.

For some time, the legionnaire lay in the bushes without stirring, as the laughter receded. At length he sat up, reaching for his beret. He tried unsuccessfully to dust off the black felt, then brushed down his leather hose. As he made to rise, he put his hand down in the wet leaves. He looked down at his dripping fingers, then gradually turned to the grille. Alistair withdrew into the tunnel, but it was too late. Jackboots splashed nearby. His heart pounded underwater, like a clammy frog thumping against his frozen chest. There was no way he could make a break for it now. A twig cracked beside the entrance.

The Latin's handsome face appeared, framed by the circular opening like a tondo from the apostolica. Alistair froze so stiffly that he might have been one of the piazza statues. The legionnaire peered under the keystone arch, his face obscured by shadow but clearly still smarting from the praetorian's insult. His dark eyes roved over the iron lattice and weathered limestone of the tunnel walls, smoothed by centuries of effluence, before lighting on the shadows where Alistair lay. He lay as still as he could, but the frog's jumping became frantic. The Latin drew his head back into the light. His feline eyes narrowed, squinting at him in the darkness. He had seen him.

The cat's eyes fixed on its prey, its mouth compressing into a cruel smile. Leather creaked as a black glove fastened around the grille. Alistair was trembling all over. Perhaps he'd better drown himself then and there and be done with it, a fate more merciful than the fires that surely awaited him. The Latin leaned under the arch, making ready to seize him.

'*Nonne perfecisti, homuncule?*' a voice said outside, asking whether he wasn't done yet. The soldier froze. There was more cackling. Alistair paled, his blood as cold as the water on his damp cheeks. Their eyes met.

For a few moments the Latin's face was entirely expressionless, as if he were looking through him into the fathomless darkness beyond. The merciless laughter wafted into the tunnel, drowning out the stream. The soldier's lip quivered. His brow furrowed and unfurrowed itself as his eyes widened. Pride, shame, and anger were all written there at once, like ripples blown by opposing winds across a lake. Then, as quickly as they had appeared, they disappeared, swept away like flowers before the plough. His lips stretched into a taut smile, but this time something was different. He was smiling with his eyes.

'*Homuncule*,' the legionnaire said. Something showed in his eyes that Alistair did not understand, but which reminded him of Brother Lucas' earnest face in the candlelight. Alistair opened his mouth, but the soldier had already vanished. The grille slammed shut. There was a rustling and a pile of leaves fell across the entrance, completely obscuring it.

CHAPTER 11

Agnes

There was a faint ringing in Agnes' ears. Her whole body felt sore. She tried to open her eyes, but their lids were heavy and dry. Her fingertips touched the ground. It was cool and smooth. The image of a white wall rose before her. Its marble revetting unfolded like the petals of a rose, revealing a tiny block of snow within.

'Nectar!' she said, sitting up, but was at once seized with a fit of coughing. She forced her eyes open. Everything was white, as if she were in the midst of a thick fog. A chalky dust hung in the air, so dense that it was impossible to make out anything.

The ringing gradually receded. Nearby, someone else was coughing. The noise grew louder until it was all around her. Yet at the same time, it remained strangely distant. The only things that felt real were the soreness in her limbs and someone gripping her arm. She had the vague sensation of being pulled onto her feet. Her legs bore her along mechanically. There was a light. The fog thinned, and the grip on her arm loosened.

'Trapped,' someone said, as she bent double, coughing. They patted her on her back. Agnes straightened up, rubbing her sore eyes. All was deafeningly bright. Strabon came into focus.

'They had it trapped,' he repeated, looking Agnes up and down. 'You ok, katepana? No explosives, thank the Virgin, just a calefactive pulse, but they'd wired the prize against tampering. Went up in smoke the moment you touched it. Still some traces of the stuff about, but most of it's gone, I'm afraid.'

'*Parchanti!*' Agnes cursed in Ruthenian, rubbing her aching back. They were standing beside the entrance to the meschita. Several other legionnaires were bent over, coughing loudly. Many were covered in nectar dust too. One woman was even being sick. The rest had been outside, and now stood watching the embarrassing spectacle. How stupid she looked. What would Marcus have said? Her impatience had got the better of her. She should have known they'd have had it trapped. Why had she been in such haste?

'Did you get everyone out?' Agnes asked. 'All unharmed?' Strabon nodded. That was at least something. It was embarrassing, but it could have been much worse. Besides, she'd found the smugglers' hideout, even if she'd failed to retrieve the cache. They must keep a sample as evidence. Anticipating her order, Strabon summoned two legionnaires and clambered back over the rubble towards the doorway. As she inspected the powder on her fingertips, she recalled a white shawl and veil.

'And the girl?' she called after Strabon. He halted, raising his dark eyebrows. As the other legionnaires stood there awkwardly, trying to pretend they hadn't heard, they seemed to be dancing. She felt light-headed, disorientated by the rosy glow of the vesperine sky. It was all rent with crimson streaks, as if some dying god had dragged their bloody fingers across it.

'*Quid...?*' the question formed on Strabon's lips, but he stopped in mid-flow. Something had distracted him. He looked at the walls of the court, then up at the sky, straining his ears. One of the women's faces turned white.

Now Agnes heard it too. A low rumbling in the distance. Engines. It was unmistakable. The thoughts came in quick succession, as the adrenaline put her giddiness to flight. Had the legion deployed south?

No, that was impossible. None of their vehicles were that loud. If they weren't theirs, though, then whose were they? She too paled. What had she done?

Someone was calling her. She knew it, but they were far away. Too far away to hear. Her head swam. Soldiers stood around her, but all had the faces of animals. Of small fowl, rabbits, and hares. Prey animals with fright in their eyes. All turned to her. One of them was stretched beneath the colonnade. Caught in a trap.

'Katepana, your orders?' the voice asked. There was the same firm grip on her arm, steadying her. Strabon. The animals evaporated, replaced by the familiar faces of her century. All stood in mute expectation. The dull rumble of the engines struck her anew, as if, at first only disturbing her dreams, a child's cries had finally awoken her. She sprang into action.

'*Iunge, iunge!*' she called to her troops to form up. Cursed Gehenna, another voice replied inside. They had to get out of Thebes as fast as they could, but what about the evidence? They couldn't leave without it. Otherwise, it would all have been in vain. And what about the girl?

The troops scrambled, grabbing their rifles as they formed into tight ranks, their movements as frenetic as Agnes' broken voice. Her eyes met Strabon's. She glanced at the meschita. He nodded to the colonnade, where the Anatolian woman was being lifted off her stretcher. They both knew there was only one answer.

'There's little time...' he said. 'We'll catch you up at the river. We won't be long.' She opened her mouth to wish him the Virgin's blessing, but he had already turned away. He summoned two legionnaires to join him, and directed a few more to the injured Anatolian, before disappearing inside the meschita. Her insides contracted. The brave soldier hadn't even asked.

Soon they were running back across the court. The sun was beginning to set now. Strewn about the sand, the jagged edges of the discarded munitions glowed in the scarlet-tinted light like the savaged carcasses of animals. The legionnaires moved as quickly as they could, but their boots already dragged in the sand. She knew they were tired, but there was no time to rest now. She had to get them out. As they rejoined the watch beneath the arch, the sentinels morphed into hares in the lengthening shadows, their long ears erect as they scented danger. She blinked and they became soldiers again.

'No sign of the enemy, Katepana,' one of them said, but his words were immediately belied by a loud rumbling nearby. They could hardly be more than a verst away. There was no way they were getting out without a fight, but she must at least get them out of the blind labyrinth of Thebes. She considered calling for legionary reinforcement, but dismissed the idea. The rest of the century had to hold the west bank, and the first cohort at Kaine was too far downriver. Besides, what would the legate say? This was her command, and her mess. She would clean it up. They were the first century. What had she, the spear, to fear from a few criminals? They wouldn't have a chance against them in a fair fight. They'd soon take the smugglers, and their racket would be exposed for what it was. She touched the spearhead on her beret.

'*Exi!*' she said. They filed out the archway, running back up the boulevard. The diurnal desert heat was fast dissipating. The low sun coated the ivory faces of the bombed-out buildings in rust. As the crimson lintels raced by, their ochre scripts wound and unwound before her like the meschita arabesques, rearranging themselves into Greek. 'All men are equal in the eyes of the Lord,' one read. 'Mercy in labour, not in wealth,' another proclaimed. She shuddered, horrorstruck at her strange thoughts.

They had already reached the head of the magistral when there was a deafening explosion, followed by a titanic crash. At the far end of the avenue a huge cloud of sand and dust rose into the air, completely obscuring the meschita. When it cleared, there was nothing but open sky where the minaret had been. A mountain of sandstone was piled before the walls, and the archway was no longer visible. She felt a dull pain inside. Strabon. She couldn't go back.

Gunfire and shouting erupted on all sides. Several shadows appeared before the meschita. A bullet whistled by. Her instincts kicked in, and she bounded into a side alley, launching herself into a doorway. Her heart pounded as the adrenaline coursed through her veins. They had to get to open ground at all costs. To get out of Thebes' narrow streets. There was still just enough time.

'*Reverte!*' she cried to her troops, commanding them to return the way they'd come. They raced headlong through the maze of winding streets. A black-scarved figure loomed into view behind, brandishing an automatic rifle as he called back to a comrade. There was another explosion. Grenades. They were already on them.

'*Reverte!*' she repeated. '*Ordinem servate!* Hold the line. Do not give battle!' She led them on, hardly knowing where they were heading. It was already dusk. Thick shadows transformed the alleyways into cocoons of night. The adrenaline kept her alert, but everything was still strangely dreamlike. Renewed gunfire brought her to her senses, as bullets kicked around them. There was a cry of pain, and one of her men stumbled to his knees. Her hawk-like eyes shot about. They were being fired at from a passage to their right. She made a chopping motion, and a legionnaire hurled a grenade down the alley. The black disk irradiated a neon green, then exploded. The firing ceased.

'*Ordinem servate!*' Agnes said. 'To the plain!' The injured man was pulled onto his feet by a comrade, as blood gushed from his calf. She couldn't hold the rest up on his account. They had to get out of Thebes. Only there would they have the advantage of arms. They turned a corner, and there was a rush of cool air. The shadowy hulk of the temple rose up on the horizon. They had reached open ground at last. Still, they mustn't stop now. She motioned to her troops, and they advanced in a single defile as fast as they could.

They had not gone half a verst before cries arose behind them. Masked men filed out from the buildings, gesturing chaotically at the Marian line. Some bore assault rifles, while others already knelt in the sand, directing mortars at her troops. Not that it would avail them. Her troops were already out of range of their Caliphate weapons. She had the advantage. She kissed her rosary.

'*Ad fulcon!*' she commanded. Her troops drew themselves up into two semi-circular ranks, facing the enemy. Ten legionnaires knelt in front, pulling cylindrical extenders from their packs and fitting them to their assault rifles. In the inner circle, the rest set small black boxes on the ground before them. The activation keys of the auto-guided drones they contained were soon ready. Agnes placed her right hand on her chest. All bowed their heads.

'O Lady Unsullied, look kindly upon us this day,' Agnes said, raising her shining eyes to the sky. 'Supreme ruler, Holy Mother, bless Thy servant entering battle, and my comrades who are with me, with Justinia's valour.' Many of the young faces already burned with expectation at the familiar words of the battle prayer.

'Wrap them in cloud, and with Thy divine hail protect them,' she continued. 'Holy Virgin, defend me, Thy slave, and my comrades, on all four sides. Suffer not the evil to shoot, nor to pierce with spear, nor to strike nor smite with axe, nor with sword to fell, nor with knife to stab, whether old or young, brown or black, heretic or theurgist.'

Some of the soldiers pulled nervously at the tails of their dark locks, or scratched their olive cheeks, but for Agnes the words rang like a bell in her heart, exalting her to the fray.

'Grant us victory over the infidel!' she finished. The legionnaires stirred, crying, '*Maria victor! Maria victor!*' Agnes reviewed her line. All their weaponry was prepared and all had assumed night-combat readiness, their visors down. She was pleased. Through the infra-vision of her goggles, she surveyed the enemy. She tapped the side, and a number range appeared in green in her periphery. Between thirty and forty. They were outnumbered perhaps two-to-one, but that didn't matter. Their imperial weaponry had the advantage.

Even so, it was curious that the enemy weren't trying to advance. She reviewed her line again. Ten troops in the first rank, and eight in the second. She started. Eight? The number burned in her mind like a hot brand. It should have been ten in each line. Two were missing. In an instant, she was back in the alleyway. Blood gushed from someone's leg. Another dragged them along. She cursed. The enemy line stirred. Laughter floated across the plain.

'Katepana?' one of her legionnaires said, pointing at the enemy's centre. Two naked and blindfolded men were led out in front of the line, flanked by four bandits whose faces were covered by bandanas, but their dark skin and stature betrayed them as Nubians. They shoved their rifle butts into the prisoners' backs, one of whom fell. He clutched at his leg as the unkindness of ravens cackled all around.

'Katepana, what should we do?' the legionnaire asked, but her voice was far away. Agnes' head spun. She was sure he was one of the Bithynians. Perhaps the very one Strabon had chided on the riverbank that morning. She paled.

'*Dobry vecher!*' a voice hailed her from the other line. Agnes reeled. Who was wishing her a good evening in her native tongue? Some of the legionnaires lowered their rifles in surprise. She hadn't imagined it.

'*Dobry vecher, kenturion,*' the greeting repeated, with evident sarcasm. It seemed to come from a telesonum somewhere in the enemy line. Ruthenian. How on Earth could the bandits have known where she came from? She tapped her visor, but was met only with a palisade of black bandanas.

'*Agapite file,* my dear friend.' The voice switched to Greek, as if it had never been speaking anything else. 'I do admire you. You command a fine century. So very loyal. I'm sure they would fight for you to the last.'

Agnes was stunned. The voice not only spoke Greek, but spoke it well. Almost dynatorially. It had been many years since she'd heard the high speech of the capital, not since Chalcedon, but it was unmistakable. Yet here, among bandits? That was even stranger than the Ruthenian. None of it made any sense.

'One must admire such valour,' it continued, and for the briefest moment the sarcasm vanished. 'Yes indeed, one must. But I'm sure, like you, our brave soldiers realise they're out of their depth. Our Leander has lost her way, I fear, and must soon drown.' The voice broke into a guffaw. This was followed, at some delay, by the more forced laughter of the other bandits. Blood suffused Agnes' cheeks. She felt the insult. They were right. She was all at sea, directionless, and would surely drown. If only Strabon were at her side, but he was not. She didn't even know if he was still alive.

'But seriously now, to business,' the speaker said. 'I will give you a choice, centurion. And let me say, I think it's rather a fair one. Let us examine your predicament. You are no fool. You're outnumbered and outgunned.' One of the bandits kicked the prostrate prisoner in his stomach, to peals of laughter. The legionnaire curled up into a ball. As the enemy jostled one another for a better view, she finally glimpsed the speaker. A tall man in combat fatigues, he too had a black cloth across his mouth. In the last light of dusk it was hard to tell, but his face seemed a shade paler than those of the rest.

'So, centurion,' he continued, 'lay down your arms. Give back what you've stolen. Forget what you ever saw here. And I will let you and your little companions go.' A bandit struck the second prisoner over the head with the butt of their rifle, and he too collapsed. The Marian line stirred. She raised her hand, commanding order.

'Otherwise, I will kill them,' the man said, gesturing at the two men on the ground, 'and then I will kill every last one of you. So, what do you say, centurion?' Silence ensued, unbroken save for the gentle lapping of the river far off. Agnes stood motionless in the cool desert air, facing her enemy. It was as if her limbs were encased in ice, as lifeless as the temple statues. She could neither advance nor retreat, but she must act. All waited on her word.

'*Tak cho poviete, kenturion?*' He repeated his question in Ruthenian, with clear menace. She could feel his eyes on her, as if there weren't half a verst, two battle lines and a mass of weaponry between them. Spellbound, she stood rooted to the spot, unable to reply.

Without warning, the man strode out of the enemy's ranks and up to the wounded prisoner. In an instant, he had pulled a pistol out of his fatigues and pointed it at the Bithynian's head. The soldier just had time to look up at his assailant before a crack rang out and his head fell back. A cry of woe arose from the legionary line, but to Agnes it all seemed to be happening in a dream. Like some nightmare she couldn't wake up from.

'Centurion!' the executioner said. He already stood by the other prisoner, his pistol raised as he took fatal aim once more. She had to act, and act now. Her troops looked to her alone. There was no one else. She tried desperately to think of what Marcus would have done, but it was no use. She was frozen. She couldn't move, couldn't speak. How was this happening? She was the spear. Had she really lost one of her men?

Another shot rang out. An instant later, everything descended into confusion. The enemy's left flank collapsed in disarray, and there was gunfire beyond. The bandits' leader was bundled away, the unharmed prisoner abandoned where he lay. Legionnaires had emerged behind the enemy line. They had already formed up and were loosing into the enemy's flank, felling several of the bandits. The odds were already more even.

She smiled. Strabon had made it. She was no longer alone.

CHAPTER 12

Zeno

Zeno frowned at the empty desk opposite. Not for the first time, he asked himself why Maurice found it so hard to be in on time. He scratched his sweaty bald head irritably. It had been a hot summer already, even by the standards of the north of the Italikon. Without doubt the hottest of the three since he'd left Numidia, and it wasn't even June yet.

He cast about the musty office, examining the open cupboards and the green star light on the ceiling. Even from across the room, it was obvious that the icon above the door was covered in a thick layer of grime. The Virgin's face was barely visible. The dusty air was already floating in majestically through the open window, to the accompaniment of the dulcet tones of the morning traffic.

Maurice's desk was still littered with the breadcrumbs of yesterday's focaccia. Stranded in their midst, an island in a marsh of debris, was his deputy's badge. Its brass was so smudged that its legend of *Praetorium Urbis Ravennae* was hardly legible. Why did his division think summer was an excuse to let everything go to pot? The whole place could really do with a proper clean-up.

Zeno scrutinised the faded navy uniforms and unpolished black boots of the other praetorians, keeping tally as they streamed into the office. He was proud of being an early bird and was always in before his team. So he always knew who arrived when. Maurice was always in last, but even by his standards, this was getting embarrassing. He squinted at his holowatch. It was nearly two antemeridian. Where on earth was he?

As if the Mother had answered, a large man lumbered through the doorway. Ducking as he entered, Maurice tilted sideward, as if unsure whether his ample girth would fit through. Zeno leaned back in his chair, his eyes narrowing on his deputy as he shuffled towards his desk like an overgrown sloth. He was clearly struggling with the weight of the bags he carried in his hand.

Maurice sighed loudly as he slumped into his chair, his bags causing a spray of breadcrumbs to fly up from his desk. Zeno tapped his foot as he watched the crumbs gently coming to rest on his own, spotless, desk. He wondered how he'd ended up encumbered with the great Lombard in the first place. If Maurice's father hadn't been an excubator of the Blachernae palace, there was no way he'd have got the job.

Lazily, as if it were in his way, Maurice picked up his praetorian's badge. He pinned it to his blue lapel so carelessly that he didn't even notice how the brass obscured the white star sewn into it. Zeno grunted with annoyance and, as if on cue, another of the buttons on Maurice's taut uniform burst open. His deputy was so busy unpacking his brunch that he didn't even notice. Zeno rapped his black knuckles on the desk.

'Want a slice, Katepano?' Maurice asked, pushing a bag towards him. Zeno stared at him in amazement. The oaf of a Lombard had no idea he was even in trouble. The traffic became more noticeable as the office grew quiet. A siren blared as an electric issued from the garage below.

'What time do you call this, Maurice?' Zeno asked, leaning forward in his chair and tapping his holowatch. 'I don't know if you've noticed, but this is the serious crime division. Serious crime. You call this serious, Maurice?' He gesticulated at the bags and Maurice's open tunic. Another siren blared, before receding into the distance to a chorus of horns.

'Oh, I'm sorry, Katepano,' Maurice replied, 'just with it being summer and all, I thought, you know, it might be nice. For morale, and all.' He waved at the bags, glancing around the office. His eyes already glinted at the sight of the bread. He licked his lips. A Gallic woman in the corner, one of Zeno's better officers, smiled.

'Summer's no excuse to let things slip!' he said, raising his voice so all could hear. 'The Ravenna demes don't stop their usual crap just because we fancy a break.' He gestured at a board on the wall. Holographic lights darted across its surface, the faces of wanted outlaws alternating with maps of city blocks overlaid with neon annotations. Maurice was already crunching through a piece of focaccia. Zeno nearly grabbed it out of his mouth.

'Maurice,' he tried to whisper, but hissed instead. 'My office, now!' He nodded to the back of the room, marching straight to the glass door. Maurice's heavy footsteps followed more slowly behind.

'*Tenebrae!*' Zeno said, as the door closed behind them. An ochre tincture spread across the glass walls, like paint in a jar of water. Unlike the cluttered office without, it was spotless. Just the usual portrait behind the desk of the old lady, clad in white and with a golden kamelaukion, her face blotched out by the holy mandylion. Beneath was the legend '*Theadosia III Imperatorix*'. The room was otherwise completely bare, save for two memorial holograms on the desk, one showing his wife and son, and the other his home village back in Numidia. The greyscale faces of his dead family smiled out at him across the room.

That was how he tried to remember them. As they'd been before the dreadful events of three years ago. He'd put the portrait there so he didn't keep remembering them as they actually died, their faces contorted in terror as they stared at him from the burning building in which they were trapped. So he didn't have to see the cruel face of the young centurion who had bundled him away before he could save them. The Ruthenian woman with the long hair, the one who'd raided his village. That hateful soldier who, when the drug smugglers hiding there didn't surrender, had her century burn his village to the ground.

As Maurice trundled in, he wondered if that was why he rarely used his office. So he didn't have to remember what he had lost. Or else waste away with anger at the centurion, whom he'd surely never find again. Sometimes it was better to work. To work and forget. In any case, he was a man of action and preferred to sit with his officers, even if on occasion it was useful to have an office. This was such an occasion.

'Maurice, let's cut to the chase,' he said as Maurice took a seat uninvited. 'You need to buck up. No, *we* need to buck up. The crime stats for the last few months have been bad, and they're only going to get worse this summer. The exarch's been on at the atamana about it, and she's breathing down my neck.' Maurice's eyes were already beginning to glaze over. Zeno grew wrathful.

'For Justinia's sake, Maurice, will you pay attention?' he said, slamming his hand on the table. Maurice jolted upright, nodding furiously. Zeno shook his head. What on Earth would it take to make the sluggish Lombard bestir himself?

'Look, you're setting a bad example,' he said as patiently as he could. 'Discipline's slipping. We've got to set the tone, Maurice, and you're not doing that right now. From now on, I want you in here before the rest. And I want to see energy, Maurice. Energy! Otherwise Our Lady knows we're never going to fix up this dump.'

Maurice shook his head, his eyes threatening to close. Too late, Zeno recalled that Ravenna was Maurice's home town.

'With all due respect, Katepano, you ain't never going to fix this town,' Maurice replied with something like the manner of a wise elder, even though both were little over forty. 'It's like I been telling you since you got here. Take it from one who knows, Katepano. Latins is Latins.

They ain't never going to change, been like it since the old empire. It ain't no Numidia here, no sir!' He shook his head mournfully. The sight of the fat Lombard lounging in his chair as he shared this unsolicited wisdom nearly drove Zeno spare. His eyes grew bloodshot as he pressed his clenched fists against the table.

'In the name of the—' he said, as the light above Theadosia's portrait became encrusted with amber, but was interrupted by a knock at the door. Zeno looked around angrily. The Gallic woman was outlined against the dull glass. Taking a deep breath, he straightened out his uniform.

'*Intrate,*' he shouted. The door slid open, and the woman stepped in, squinting at Maurice. There was a note of condescension in her look, even of insubordination. Maurice hadn't even noticed. That was exactly the problem. Zeno looked at her impatiently.

'Very sorry for the interruption, Katepano,' she said, 'but I thought you should be aware. There's been an incident at the port. First responders are already on the ground. Triple homicide. Motive unestablished, but likely the demes.' As the officer uttered the last word, her eyes rested on Maurice.

'Any witnesses?' Zeno asked, already moving to the door. He waved his hand at the glass, which became clear.

'Just one, Katepano,' the woman replied. 'A slave. Male. Mid-sixties. On the scene when first response arrived. Unidentified. If there were any other demesmen, they'd fled before the callout.'

'Hold him for questioning,' Zeno said, 'and I want our people down there. *Prompte,* you hear? This one is ours. I don't want the port authority lot on this, ok? That useless bunch of cretins will just get in the way.'

The woman turned to the door.

'On second thoughts,' Zeno said, 'I'll come myself. If it's the demes, I want them to know I'm on to them. And keep the slave for me. I want to question him myself.' He stopped by the door, as if he'd just remembered something.

'Cap and star, Maurice,' he said, 'you're coming with me. To the port. Guard and forensics. Five should suffice.' He smiled, pleased to have an opportunity to shift the sluggard. Maurice sat up, his eyes wide. He even looked a little afraid.

'Look sharp, Maurice! I haven't got all day,' Zeno added and clapped his hands. His deputy bumbled to his feet and, looking harassed, waddled towards the door. Zeno held it open, watching impatiently as the Lombard plodded out into the main office, which already hummed as the praetorians prepared to deploy. His eye lingered on the greyscale features of his wife and son, then he slammed the door.

A few minutes later, their electric hurtled out of the praetorium into the streets of the city. Zeno sat in the back. He rolled his eyes over the dusty pavements and dilapidated buildings as they flew by like frozen holographic stills, their crumbling ochre facades sgraffitoed with medieval icons of the Virgin and gnostic saints. Street peddlers and starving slave children, pointing hungrily at their mouths, leapt out of the vehicles' way. The irascible eyes of a bearded Ravennite peered in through the tinted glass, shaking his fist. The signs of crime were everywhere. Or of criminal intent, at least.

The electric left the central precinct of Ravenna, and soon the orange brick of the city was behind them. They pulled onto a quattrovial highway. He grumbled at the scratches on the windows and the worn-out leather of the seats. The fleet really needed an upgrade, but no matter how much he complained to the atamana, she was never willing to spend a single solidus on it. The old engine rattled, and his stomach lurched as the vehicle pulled forward elastically. The Doric portico of the exarchate bobbed briefly above the passing vehicles, before the colours blended like paint and the palace vanished.

Five minutes later, the electric decelerated and left the highway. Maurice sat beside him, his face pale as he held his stomach with both hands. Zeno frowned. Was the man actually going to retch, for Justinia's sake? His bright idea of bringing his deputy along was already looking less inspired. By the time their car pulled into the docks, his face had acquired a lime palour. Zeno looked out frustratedly. A few first response officers stood beside an electric cordon. One of them waved her hand over a metal post, which illuminated with a neon light. The air beside it vibrated, then became still again. Zeno saluted as the electric hummed past.

The vehicle wound through an endless labyrinth of storehouses. He scanned the red-brick walls and high windows. Their grimy panes adumbrated the towering stacks within, some as high as insulae tenements. Up ahead, the access road came to an abrupt halt before a weathered stone pillar crowned by a double-headed eagle. Beyond, the green waters shimmered in the late matinal sun. On the far side of the docks, freightmen bustled about as a swarm of carrier drones buzzed up and down ships' hulls in concert with their hands.

In contrast, the near quay was completely deserted. The electric parked beside the freight-loading entrance to a warehouse. Its shutters were up, even though there was no ship in port. He donned his navy cap and opened the door. The hot sun splayed on the chalky stones. There was an urgent patter of footsteps. An officious-looking fat man appeared behind Maurice, who swayed slightly as he disembarked the car. The port authority. It was just what he needed.

'What, may I ask, are you doing here?' the man asked, dispensing with the bother of any kind of address. He spoke Italic, but with a Hispanian lilt. Zeno ignored him and, straightening his cap, walked to the hangar entrance. Unsurprisingly, the man was a Mediterranean, like most of his fellow mariners, with all the good breeding that went with it.

'Excuse me, officer!' the Hispanian said, his little feet pottering after Zeno as he struggled to keep up with the praetorian's great strides. 'The port authority has jurisdiction over all maritime affairs, *mari atque terra*. On land as at sea. I am afraid I must therefore politely ask that you desist from your investigation of this matter, which falls to the port authority, and in doing so, I am obliged to notify you that your officers have treated our authority most shamefully, cordoning off the entire precinct without authorisation, and even forcibly denying us entrance to the crime scene.'

Zeno continued to ignore him, smiling at a praetorian guarding the warehouse entrance. He halted.

'The last I heard, the jurisdiction of the *P.U.R.* encompasses all of the exarchate of Ravenna,' he said, looking down his ebony nose at the little Hispanian. 'Apologies if I am much mistaken, but is this not Ravenna?' He looked around at the port. Maurice chuckled and mopped his brow, which had by now recovered its usual rosy tincture.

'Well I never, such flagrant effrontery!' the Hispanian said, his face resembling a plum. 'I, I – you shan't, I assure you – the exarch shall hear of this...!' Shaking his fist, he scuttled off, disappearing around the corner of the warehouse. Zeno grinned as he watched him go, then ducked under the half-open shutter.

Immediately inside the hangar was an open space. It was darker than he had expected, but soon the dim forms of freight containers came into view. Piled up in high aisles, they stretched away into the dark recesses of the building like a church nave. Inactive carrier drones floated in the rafters above, the silence broken only by the soft whir of their idling engines. Three male corpses were strewn about the floor. A few first-response officers milled about beside the bodies, waving conical devices tipped with blue lights over them, and consulting the tabulae in their hands.

Zeno headed straight for the nearest corpse, but stopped as he heard a loud crash behind him. Maurice was struggling to manoeuvre his ungainly frame under the hangar door. The corrugated metal rattled as he scraped his back against it. Everyone watched as he smiled placatingly, and bent down to pick up his cap. Zeno bit his lip. He was right. He oughtn't to have brought him.

'Sitrep, officer?' Zeno asked a praetorian kneeling beside the body. The woman touched her finger to the white star on her blue cap, then pointed at the corpse's bloodied head and chest.

'Situational evidence suggestive of homicide, Katepano,' the woman said, pinching her small Latin nose but otherwise indifferent to the gory spectacle before her. 'Double gunshot wound to the head, and one punctured lung.'

Maurice finally arrived. He squirmed, but before he could open his mouth Zeno had moved on to the next corpse. That, and the following, were similarly mangled, each more bloody than the one before. He examined the face of the last. The features of a bearded male in his fifties were just discernible. From his paler skin and freckled face, he was evidently from out of town, doubtless some northerner.

'Examined this one yet, officer?' Zeno asked another praetorian. 'Any identification?' The man shook his head. Maurice's heavy tread soon pursued behind. He peered wide-eyed at the corpse's face.

'Not from round here, Katepano,' he said, scratching his nose pensively in an attempt to mask his fright. 'No sir, that there's an outsider. I'd wager come in on one of the freighters, and got into a fight over something or other with these demesmen.' He jabbed his thumb at the other two corpses.

'Thank you, Maurice, very insightful,' Zeno said. 'And now, for some real work. You take a look at this one, and I'll get on to the others. Look sharp, Maurice!'

His face fell. Zeno walked off, grinning to himself.

Within a few minutes, he had finished his search of the other two bodies. Their firearms had already been taken off them. There was nothing else on the corpses save a few solidi, bearing the usual crowned and faceless head of the empress. He scratched his bald head in perplexity as he examined the high aisles, receding into the heavy shadows of the empty hangar. A triple homicide was unusual, even in Ravenna. What had happened there, and why? His eyes rested on Maurice, who still knelt beside the last corpse, huffing loudly as he fumbled with its heavy limbs.

'Where on Earth is the bloody witness?' Zeno said to no one in particular. 'Will someone kindly go and fetch him?' All were silent, glancing nervously at one another. He raised his eyebrows.

'Ehm – you see, Katepano,' one of them began. 'Port authority's got him – they'd already taken him by the time we got here, and won't hand him over...'

Zeno was already back at to the entrance. As he wrenched the shutter aside, Maurice said something behind. Zeno did not wait for him, but marched out onto the bright quayside.

A door stood ajar in the warehouse opposite. Above its lintel was a metal plaque with the Latin, '*Auctoritas Portus Exarchatus Ravennae*'. He strode up to it, cursing loudly, as Maurice continued calling after him. The noisome little Hispanian would soon find out what happened to those who obstructed the course of justice. How dare he hold his key witness? He entered without knocking and found himself in a ramshackle waiting room. On the right, two men and a woman in green uniforms stewed in the heat beneath a rattling old fan. He walked straight on through towards a closed door on which '*Caput Portus*' was engraved.

'Excuse me!' one of the men said, barring Zeno's way. 'You cannot simply—'

Zeno gave him a violent shove. His eyebrows arched in surprise as he lost his balance and tumbled backwards, sending the fan and chairs flying. The others leapt to their feet indignantly, but Zeno had already opened the door. Maurice barred the way with his copious frame.

'Cursed Osman!' the port authority chief exclaimed, rising from his desk. Zeno barely heeded him. Instead, his bloodshot eyes darted to the corner of the room, where a small ragged-looking old man with a beard sat. He looked up at Zeno fearfully.

'Hand over the witness,' Zeno commanded, thumping the chief's desk as he brought his face right up to him. 'You have no authority to hold him here, and are obstructing discharge of due process by the exarchal praetorium.'

The Hispanian's rotund face was defiant, but he shrank as he eyed Maurice, who smiled stupidly in the doorway. The old man cackled, revealing a completely toothless grin. Zeno turned on him angrily, grabbing him by the back of his collar. The greybeard squealed as he was shunted from the room.

'You have no authority!' the chief said in a final abortive show of defiance. He peered up anxiously at Zeno as he manhandled the witness from his office, as if terrified he were about to suffer the same fate. Zeno only glowered back at him, and slammed the door. In the waiting room, the chief's secretary was back on his feet. He looked red-facedly at Zeno with mute resentment, but Maurice interposed his huge bulk and the man retreated.

'Katepano, you should know, the body, I...' Maurice said, failing to keep up as they crossed the quayside. Zeno hurried on without waiting, and was soon manoeuvring his quarry under the hangar door. A praetorian ran up with a chair, and Zeno pointed at it impatiently. The old man hastily seated himself, watching the other praetorians apprehensively. His eyes lit on the corpses, and he looked panic stricken at Zeno.

'Right, you may have noticed that I am not a patient man,' Zeno said, pulling up another chair and placing it right before the witness. 'So let's cut to the chase. I know that you were here and, as you can see, I've got three corpses on my hands. That doesn't look good for you. So I'd advise you to answer me straight. What's your name, slave?'

'Sim... Sime...' the man tried to say, his voice shaking with terror as he beheld the bodies. 'Simeon. I am Simeon, sir. Slave of the fifth municipal district, a janitor. Publicly-owned.' He spoke in a monotone, as if reciting by heart.

'Good, Simeon,' Zeno said, looking at him encouragingly. 'Now, why don't you tell us what you saw?'

Simeon broke into a sweat. 'I, I wasn't, it wasn't meant to – I didn't mean to be...' he said, but started wailing at sight of the mangled face of the nearest corpse. He tried to rise, but Zeno thrust him back into his seat. The slave tottered and nearly fell. When he had managed to steady himself, he sat in silence, covering his face with his hands.

'Let's try that again, shall we?' Zeno said. 'What did you see here? And – in case I wasn't clear – I mean everything.'

'I was here, yes, *domine*. We had a meeting of the...' he began, but caught himself as a new look of alarm entered his face. 'I mean – we, our friends, that is – we met here...'

Zeno's nose wrinkled dangerously. 'We? Who is we? What friends? An unauthorised slave meeting, you mean? Don't dare lie to me, greybeard. Out with it at once!'

'Enter in by the straight gate, Simeon,' he whispered to himself, no longer looking at Zeno. 'Yes, Simeon, yes, by the straight gate must you go in. By the straight gate alone can you enter.' His fingers fiddled nervously with his tunic collar under his beard.

'What?' Zeno exclaimed. 'What rubbish is this? Answer the question, slave. Perhaps you did not hear me when I told you I was not a patient man!' He gave Simeon's chair a thunderous kick, shunting him backwards a full passus.

'It was – it was meant to be all quiet down here,' Simeon cried in terror, his servile vowels slurring, 'but when we got here, there were some of the – some of them – you know, the demes, they don't usually come down here. I swear to you, *domine*, I didn't know about the – about the – shooting.'

'Right,' Zeno roared. 'For the last time, slave, what were you and your confederates up to down here?' Simeon's frail old body curled up like a hedgehog, as if he were trying to disappear entirely.

'I, we—' he answered, but his voice was drowned out by the rattling of the shutter behind. Zeno turned angrily to his breathless deputy, who had finally caught up. His face dropped.

'What in Gehenna's name!' he said, running up with the other praetorians. From Maurice's hand swung a small pendant, two pieces of driftwood stuck across one another.

Chapter 13

Agnes

The enemy's left flank had completely disintegrated, but their right was already reforming. Strabon had acted boldly, but he was in peril now. She must come to his aid. It was now or never.

'*Dirige frontem!*' Agnes called to her troops, springing into action. She hardly needed to issue the command. Spurred on by the sight of their comrades, the first line was already presenting. Green laser lights flitted across the bandits' chests.

'*Mitte!*' she roared. There was a high-pitched whistling on all sides. Five more of the enemy collapsed. Still under fire from Strabon's legionnaires, some of the bandits lost their nerve and retreated into the buildings. Agnes smiled. They were no match for her century. Still, their right flank had held, and a few had their mortars ready.

'*Parati!*' Agnes said, signalling to the second line. The eight legionnaires knelt in the sand, their hands on the little boxes beside them. Like the petals of a black rose, their sealing unfurled to reveal tiny metallic balls, illuminated by a ghostly jade light.

A low clunk, a vacuum of air, and a whizz sounded in quick succession from the enemy line. Something exploded nearby, and a cry of pain went up from her line. A shell had landed in the midst of her right flank. Several legionnaires had fallen, and some of the drones had been destroyed. The clunking continued relentlessly. Another shell exploded just before her first line. How had the cursed Osmans achieved such precision with their old weapons?

'*Iacula!*' she said to the second line. Six spheres catapulted into the air, like green shooting stars. They cut noiselessly through the desert night, hovering above the enemy line. Noticing this, some of the bandits raised their assault rifles and fired at the drones.

'*Mitte!*' Agnes called to her first line again. Another volley took out several of the bandits before a third shell exploded close by. She was thrown backwards by its force, but quickly scrambled back to her feet. A woman of the first line lay prostrate nearby. One of her shins was missing, and all the sand around was dark with blood. She wailed piteously, but her cries were drowned out by a crash from above, as one of the drones fell limply from the sky. The mangled carcass of the metallic ball, its propellers riddled with bullets and twisted out of shape, landed in the sand not far from the first line. The night sky pulsed with the enemy's fire, but the other drones were as yet untouched. There was no time to lose.

'Self-identification of targets complete, Katepana,' a voice hailed her from the second line. '*Pluvia dolorosa* ready to launch.' Agnes smiled. Pain rain, as it was affectionately known among the legions. That would do for them. She nodded. The legionnaires all tapped their wrists at once. The drones shone a luminous green over the enemy, some of whom re-doubled their fire. Others lost their nerve and ran for the cover of the buildings.

A light spray issued from tiny pores all over the surface of the drones. Like sea foam, it was so weightless that it might have been no more than a dampness in the night air, but as the droplets fell they quickly reacted with it and ignited. The mist transformed into a blanket of flame that descended on the enemy line. Like some infernal glue, the little fires stuck to cloth and flesh. Cries went up on all sides. A vehicle burst into flame. Some of the bandits rolled around in the sand in a vain attempt to put out the fire engulfing them. Others ripped the flaming cloth from their bodies, but it was no use. Their front transformed into a scarlet banner in the desert night.

'*Primi, dirige frontem!*' Agnes shouted at the first line. It was time to put the *parchanti* out of their misery. The troops raised their rifles. Lasers danced across the burning torsos. She watched with pride as the bandits flailed about helplessly. They were no match for her century. No match for the spear.

'*Mitte!*' she said. A deafening crack rang out in answer. Several bandits fell to the ground, but the sound was louder than she'd expected. To her horror, many of her own line had also fallen. Two of her men lay nearby in pools of blood. One was bleeding out, his chest dappled with bullet holes. The other lay lifelessly beside him. Nothing remained of where his head had been but a crimson beret.

Red lasers danced across the bodies of her remaining troops. A light flashed on her own chest. She slammed herself to earth. There was a rush of air as three more legionnaires collapsed onto the sand, their lungs punctured. Her brain was on fire. Caliphate weapons didn't have that range, and precision rifles like that couldn't be bought in Nubia. Not for any money. Only imperial weapons had such range, but such heresy was impossible.

Engines rumbled in the distance. Beyond the fire, vehicles emerged between the buildings, out of which bandits leapt in droves. The reinforcements advanced across the open ground towards the Marian line. Every so often, one would stop, kneel and take aim at them. A rush of air would follow as a bullet flew by. One of the black ants paused beside the remaining captive, who still struggled on the sand. There was a dull crack, and his naked body grew still. Agnes shuddered. It was fast becoming a rout.

'*Suscipe!*' she ordered the remnant of the first line to fall back to the second. She surveyed what was left of her company. Amid the bleeding bodies of the wounded, there were others unharmed who, like her, had hit the ground in time.

'*Sponte!*' she said, commanding them to fire at will. Another volley resounded along her line. The braver among her wounded rose to their knees and fired too, but were soon met with an answering hail of shot. Troops dropped like flies on both sides. By now she had lost nearly half her company while, like a relentless tide, the accursed wave came on inexorably. Her legionnaires fought bravely, but they were outnumbered and outgunned. There was no sign of Strabon and, to make matters worse, those bandits who had escaped the fire now joined their new comrades.

The enemy's vanguard was less than a quarter verst away. Know the odds, and recognise when you need support. That was what Marcus would have said. She had to call for aerial backup from the legion. There was no other way. She swallowed her pride. Raising her wrist in the dust, she commanded her holowatch to open a line back to her century on the west bank.

The screen merely flashed red. She shouted at it to dial the legion at Kaine, but again it flashed red. All communications were down. She had never heard of such a thing. She rose unsteadily to her feet. Her body ached and her head swam. None of it made any sense. She was aware of the bullets kicking around her, and the desperate cries of her troops, but everything was dim somehow, as if she were underwater. All was a blur of dancing lights in the desert night, accompanied only by muffled shouting and the dull thud of shrapnel and bodies hitting the earth.

'Katepana!' a cry called her back above water. A soldier limped up, her dark hair matted with sweat and sand. Though contorted with pain, Agnes was struck by her elegant Anatolian features, so out-of-place in that bloodbath.

'Should we not call for—?' the legionnaire asked, but her voice was drowned out by an explosion so deafening that it submerged the entire battle. So great was its sonic force that the soldier lost her balance and fell. Agnes too staggered, shielding her ears. It had come from behind the Marian line. She spun around in confusion, making no move to help the woman, but there was no enemy in sight. Just her eight surviving legionnaires, collapsed back into a single rank, their teeth chattering with the clanking of their assault rifles as they sprayed the enemy in a last act of defiance. Bloodied corpses lay all around. *Smrt,* the word rose to her lips in her native tongue. Death. All was lost. No help was coming. They would die there.

'*Cede!*' Agnes commanded the retreat. The legionnaires obeyed at once. The enemy was close at hand now, and it was plain to all that they would be annihilated. Even so, a frown darkened the brows of one of the men. He was right. The shame was terrible. The Marian line never retreated. Such cravenness was extremely rare. And for a first century, unheard of. The man leant down in an attempt to assist one of his fallen comrades, as more shells exploded to left and right, cratering the sand. There wasn't even time to save their wounded, let alone bury the dead. She had to save what remained of her company.

'*Cede!*' she said again, glaring at the man as he tore his arm from his dying companion. Unprompted, the legends of the old patriarch commanders who had fallen on their swords rose to her mind. Would the Virgin forgive her cowardice? She began to run. The shadow of the temple loomed ahead. Her gut lurched within her. The last thing she wanted was to get entrapped there, but it was also their only way through. Their only hope of survival. If they could just reach the river, they might yet rejoin the century, their salvation. She gestured at the temple, but the bandits marked their flight, and the sight emboldened them further. Their line, already chaotic, fractured as some broke ranks in headlong pursuit.

Their lights extinguished, three of the drones still idled noiselessly like black pearls in the desert night, forgotten by the enemy. In their eagerness, several had now reached the original position of the Marian line. Their main body followed behind, passing right under the drones. Agnes saw her chance. She had to do anything she could to buy them time. She hailed a legionnaire, lifting her eyes to the sky.

'*Finis pluviae!*' the soldier commanded her holowatch, ending the programme. The drones fluoresced green, like fireworks in the night sky. Then their lights died, their propellers retracted, and the little spheres fell to earth like lead, their metallic casing falling away like eggshells. The liquid inside immediately came alight as it reacted with the air. Three giant fireballs exploded in the midst of the enemy's ranks, as the sticky substance spewed in all directions. The hostile fire ceased.

'*Ad templum cede!*' Agnes said to her seven remaining troops. Taking advantage of the confusion, they managed to put the enemy behind them again, and crossed the temple forecourt. Back by the sacred lake, she reviewed what was left of her company. All were uniformly ragged, and most had lost their berets. Some bled from wounds on their arms and legs. The man who had tried to help his comrade wept as he slumped against a wall, but his sobs were drowned out by an engine nearby. Agnes pulled him back to his feet. There was no time for weakness.

'*Exi!*' she commanded, as they retraced the way they had come that morning. They moved as silently as they could, but the clanking of their weapons and the dragging feet of the wounded echoed mercilessly around the lakeside, as if the hateful stone wanted to give them away. It was too loud a silence. How could they pass unnoticed? Unnoticed by whom, though? The enemy already knew they were there. The nectar had clearly addled her mind.

At the end of the inner sanctum, the third pylon reared up frightfully like a gargantuan night watchman. In its midst was the entrance to the hypostyle, its shadowy hollow the maw of some hound of hell. In the darkness, her troops became a pack of frightened animals once more, their startled eyes pleading with her, or else mournfully examining their torn and bloodied hides. The despoiled corpses of those she'd left behind rose before her, like dead creatures on the roadside, then the shades of the Numidian villagers, and the charred faces of the woman and child. Something lurched inside. There was another rumble of engines. She raced up to the wall, and dived headlong into its jaws.

Once more she was back in the forests of her homeland, but a forest by night was an altogether different place. She'd once lost her way in the woods as a child, and it had been well after nightfall before she'd gotten out. For hours, she'd wandered aimlessly in a place she thought she knew. The wondrous hues of the barks had all turned a uniform black, their dark hulks transformed from friendly guides to watchful fiends. The cool shade of the trees had become the lair of wild beasts, waiting to spring her in a trap. As they filed back up the sacral highway, the bulging columns too seemed taller in the darkness. Deep inscrutable shadows draped between them, like a heavy velvet shroud. There was no time to scout, and they were in any case too few. The enemy had vanished, but it didn't mean they weren't still being stalked like prey animals.

Something moved ahead on the sacral way. She pressed against a column, her troops following suit. She scanned the way ahead with her night visor. They were already halfway through the hypostyle, and the open court was visible beyond. There was nothing there. She signalled to the column to move on, but they had hardly taken a few steps before something again moved ahead. This time, she looked with her own eyes. A lone figure walked away from them up the sacral way. Even at a distance, from their size it was obvious they weren't one of the bandits. Nor were they one of hers. A white shawl and bare feet. She gasped in astonishment. It was the girl.

'Katepana, what is it?' a legionnaire addressed her in a trembling voice. Agnes did not answer, but halted a stone's throw from the second pylon, transfixed by the silhouette of the girl. It was impossible. How could she have made it there from Thebes? There was no way she could have passed unscathed through the hell of such a battle. Agnes looked vaguely into her subordinate's face. She too was really no more than a little girl. Her features morphed into those of a frightened mouse.

Rubber scuffed on stone as gunfire crashed through the silence of the hall. A group of bandits emerged from a row of columns to their right. A bullet whizzed past Agnes' temple, and the legionnaire fell back with a cry. Agnes dived behind a column. Chips of sandstone and granite flew off the columns as the enemy sprayed bullets in all directions. Up ahead, the girl was gone.

The other six legionnaires had taken cover. One crept around the base of a column, taking pot shots at the enemy. Another had dragged the mouselike woman to shelter, but she was already bleeding out. It was impossible to know in the confusion of that dark forest, but some instinct told her the bandits were only an advance party. She eyed the legionnaire opposite. It was the same man who'd been reluctant to retreat before. She caught his eye, pounding her palm. He nodded, pulling a grenade from his fatigues.

The bandits moved up a side aisle towards them in an undisciplined band. Periodically firing at the legionnaires, they would take cover before advancing and firing again. Two of them had incautiously run on ahead, and were only a few columns away now, so close that the red crescents on their scarves were visible. She fired at them as they came on. They leapt behind a column. She signalled to the legionnaire, who squeezed his grenade. As it flashed green, he swung his arm at the column.

The disk skimmed across the sand like a coin across a pond, coming to rest beside the column just as the bandits emerged. No sooner had they raised their rifles and trained her in their sights than there was an explosion of stone and sand. Blood stained the columns as shreds of cloth and burnt metal flew through the air. Agnes nodded approvingly to the legionnaire. They'd got the damned Osmans.

There was shouting outside the hall. The explosion had given them away. They leapt to their feet, racing towards the forecourt. There were only seven of them left, including her. She was dazed and exhausted, but the adrenaline kept her moving. If she could just reach the west bank, she could get word back to the legion. Up ahead, two wounded legionnaires limped towards the hypostyle exit. Their torn fatigues morphed into animal pelts, all bloodied and shredded by merciless claws.

One of them had already reached the second pylon, when they collapsed under a hail of fire. There was barely time to take cover. The legionnaires were forced to retreat, sheltering beneath the columns beside the wall, as bullets exploded into pillar and pedestal. It was the rest of the group that had attacked them before, having crept up on them unawares. They were two fewer than her remaining six, but they'd sprung them in a trap and had the advantage. Her troops were cornered and in disarray. None paid her any heed, but cowered before the rain of fire. There wasn't even time to issue orders. The bandits were already on them. They were lambs for the slaughter. This was it.

She closed her eyes, praying to Our Lady of Battlement for the gnosis of her soul, but just as she was about to rise, one of the bandits unexpectedly cried out. A second later, another fell. The remaining pair looked around in confusion, but weren't fast enough. The air sang as two more shots took them down as well.

The firing stopped. She touched her face, unsure whether she was still alive. The gunfire had come from behind the enemy. Cautiously, she crept out of the column's shadow. On the far side of the pylon stood a solitary figure. The bandit lowered his gun and ran towards her, without raising it again. Startled, she raised her rifle, but some instinct stopped her from firing. Another legionnaire made ready too, but she raised her hand.

The man halted before them. Still he did not raise his weapon, though they had him in their sights. He had the dark skin and black fatigues of the bandits, and had a gash on his shin. He had clearly been in the battle too. She peered into his face, as she trained her rifle on him. His nose and mouth were covered with a bandana, but she could still see his eyes. They were the clear dark eyes of a Nubian. Of a Nubian, yes, but not a bandit. They filled her with warmth and longing. Unconsciously, she lowered her gun. The man's eyes smiled. Her companion turned to her in alarm, but the man only raised his hand and pulled off his bandana.

'Strabon!' Agnes said as, forgetful of her dignity, she threw herself upon him. '*Ye to zazrak*, a miracle! But how in Justinia's name did you manage to escape?'

'Praise be!' Strabon exclaimed. 'We only got out of the meschita in the nick of time. Had a scuffle with the first lot under the walls. When they came on in force, we hid out in the old city, and they overtook us unnoticed. After we attacked from behind, they pursued us back into Thebes. Our lot got divided. In the end, I only got out by taking the clothes off a hostile, after I did for him.' He looked down sheepishly at his outfit. Then, beholding the meagre remnant of their company, his face dropped. She didn't need to ask about the others. He simply shook his head sadly.

'Katepana,' Strabon said in an undertone, 'there's more. Their weapons, and that man, the one who was leading them—' He was interrupted by a roar of vehicles outside. They weren't out of the woods yet. Whoever was after them was determined they take the truth to the grave.

No command was needed. The last seven legionnaires ran with all the strength left in them. Dashing out of the hall, they raced across the court beyond. The outer wall of the first pylon loomed before them. They were halfway there when cries erupted behind as bandits filled the arcades. Bullets whizzed past. Strabon threw a grenade, there was a mighty crash of stone, and they just managed to slip out.

The shadowy hulks of the boats appeared on the shore, but first to greet them were the twin ranks of criosphinxes, obstructing them like some demonic host. Agnes cursed the unholy images as gunfire resumed behind them. Stone horns shattered as bullets kicked about the statues. A ram's head exploded altogether, and she very nearly suffered the same fate, but by cowering and scrambling, they at last reached the riverbank. Strabon and another legionnaire threw themselves down in the papyri, returning fire as the enemy came on. Agnes and the rest dived into one of the catamarans. Seconds later, its engine whirred as they pushed out onto the waves. Strabon and his companion leapt into another boat.

They lay flat, their rifles trained on the shore as the self-guiding vessels sped them back to the safety of the west bank. Soon the riverbank was lined with silhouettes, like a host of black candles. Yet strangely, the bandits did not present. Nor did they board the remaining boat in pursuit. She didn't understand. Her troops were still in range, but wouldn't be for much longer. She looked across the water at Strabon. He was thinking the same. On the east shore, a gaunt shadow stepped from the crowd. Despite the distance, she knew it was him. The man with the cruel laugh. The one who spoke her tongue. The one who had decimated her century.

The moment passed. They were out of range. The candles became no more than a black ribbon on the horizon, undulating like a desert snake in the night. The legionnaire beside her exhaled in relief, but no one said a word. The catamaran whirred softly, rocking her like a cradle. Her head was light. It was so warm. She could almost fall asleep.

It was more than warm now. It was hot. She wiped her brow. The cool of the desert night was altogether gone. It was getting hotter too, the further they went. The legionnaire's eyes were closed as he sobbed in mute exhaustion, but his tanned cheeks were drenched with sweat. Droplets clung to the end of his beard. It wasn't just her.

There was something else in the background. Something more than just the silence of the desert night, broken only by the gentle lapping of the waves against the stern. A low crackling sound. It soon grew louder, rising into a storm. She touched her collar. Her neck was completely soaked in sweat. She sniffed the air and caught the whiff of pitch. Smoke. Fire.

'Fire!' she exclaimed, facing the west bank. Her eyes opened wide, turning opalescent with the dancing of the flames. The entire west bank was gilded with a vast crimson band. On all sides, a mighty conflagration rose into the desert night, painting its black canvas red and gold as huge chimneys of smoke blotted out the stars. In the distance, explosions could be heard, punctuated by the occasional scream. The entire camp was alight.

'My century...' she said, completely aghast. The words sounded unnatural, as if they hadn't come from her. As if some terrible oracle were pronouncing her doom. Heedless of her safety, she staggered to her feet. The others' surprise was overtaken by their horror. Her mouth hung open in sheer terror. The explosion. It was impossible. The enemy didn't have such weapons.

'*Smrt*.' The word rose unbeckoned to her lips. Death. She looked downriver at Strabon's boat. He too had risen and was staring at the fire. Feeling her gaze, he turned, his face illuminated by the unholy light from the shore. His bright Nubian eyes bored into hers. She looked at him with a sorrow she couldn't explain, and in his eyes something answered her. A kindness that filled her with a warmth unlike that of the terrible fire. An infinite forgiveness. He smiled. As he did so, there was a great explosion. His boat lifted into the air, and he disappeared.

'No!' Agnes said in horror. All around her were only the terror-stricken faces of prey. The twin patriarchs smirked at her from the shore, their sandstone coloured to blood by the flames. There was another mighty bang, and the ground slipped from beneath her. She submerged into the water, and all went dark.

CHAPTER 14

Vadim

Vadim stood beneath the portals of the Church of the Holy Gnosis, gazing dully at the alabaster of the old citadel court. He was dressed in a plain dalmatic tunic and white chlamys, his black locks tied back with golden laurel. The meridianal sun was melting the last snow on the three golden domes of the church opposite. He could hardly believe he was actually going through with the ordination.

His mother had said she'd turn a blind eye to Ganna, but how long was that likely to last? After today, he would be a priest, and he'd have the watchful eyes of the synkelloi on him at all times. He might not be free now, but soon he'd be even less so. He looked irritably at the two blond boys in white beside him. Both stared resolutely at the bronze standards in their hands, afraid to meet his eyes. He scrutinised his own robe, which barely covered the bulk of his shoulders. He felt like a ridiculous overgrown scarecrow. His fingers were numb, but it was not the morning chill. He hadn't seen Ganna since he'd left his mother. She'd made sure of that.

Instead, the last hour had passed in a rapid succession of theatrical sanctimony. First up had been the palace chaplain, for his initial blessing and instruction, all of which he had already forgotten. Next had been his father's man-in-waiting, who had reminded him of all of the royal observances, as if he hadn't known them his whole life.

Finally, and worst of all, the ceremonial robing, presided over by their ageing house sacerdote, the synkellos of Novgorod. Under the lascivious eyes of the old bore, he had been obliged to part with all his clothes, in an ignominious trade for this dalmatica and sprig of laurel.

Across the court, the gilded doors beneath the pale arches of the Church of the Ascension were still closed. The vast mosaic of the Virgin over the entranceway stared back at him mournfully. He was already bored. He had always hated waiting around, being more accustomed to others waiting on him. If there was one person he had always had to wait on, though, it was his father.

He tried to pull his chlamys more tautly over his shoulders, but the cloth bunched up like icing on a cake. He patted it down irritably. Did his father really care about his ordination at all? It was of course one of the seven mysteria, the holy sacraments of the church, but, religious as he undoubtedly was, his father had always been more inscrutable than his mother. You could never quite be sure what the old Greek was thinking, or whether he truly cared about anything but his own glory.

His musings were interrupted by the tolling of a bell. At the same time, the church doors on the far side of the court opened. A chorus of voices poured forth from the dark shadows within, mingling with the bell. The boys stepped forward, hoisting their standards as high as their little arms could manage.

'Rejoice, o Bride Unwedded, salvation of the world!' the a cappella choir sang, their words redounding off the white stone walls of the piazza's other two churches. His stomach dropped. This was it. There was no going back now.

'Rejoice, Unblemished One, fiery throne and Sovereign of all. Rejoice, o Lady, restoration of Adam and mortification of Gehenna. I shall open my mouth and it shall be filled with the Spirit. Glory, glory to the Mother, the Virgin and the Holy Spirit,' the song continued, growing louder.

A procession of sacerdotes in white and deacons in black filed out the church doors. Swinging censers and bowing their heads, they formed an aisle across the court right up to where Vadim stood. They were of all ages, some old men and others only boys. None met Vadim's eye, not even his young cousins, who stood stiffly in the crisp air trying to pretend they weren't cold. He donned his most expressionless countenance. He'd been practising this for months, but hadn't counted on the incense. By now the numerous censers had filled the entire court with the awful stench, which was already irritating his fine nostrils. He had always loathed the musty smell. It was going to be all he could do not to sneeze through the whole service.

'Rejoice, o heavenly stairs by which the Mother descended. Rejoice, o faith of silent beseechers, o dawn that illumines the minds of believers. Rejoice, o Bride Unwedded,' the hymn spilled into the incense-laden air. The deacons stepped forward in unison, clacking their bronze standards on the paving stones. Vadim flinched, trying not to sneeze. His ill-fitting dalmatica was uncomfortable and the laurel's desiccated edges pricked at his temples.

He processed across the court behind the boys, ignoring the motionless defile of sacerdotes and deacons. The mosaic of the Virgin leered down at him as he passed beneath the white lintels of the Ascension Church portal. His ignored Her, eyeing instead the white uniforms and red berets of the palace tagmata by the doors. How ridiculous he looked beside them in his smock. There was no turning back now, though. The boys were already inside. Gulping down a last breath of air, he stepped into the church.

'O Bride Unwedded. O abundance of grace, safe harbour for our souls. O expiation of the world, goodwill of the Mother,' the choir resumed as soon as he crossed the threshold. Incense suffocated his nostrils and mouth. With an inhuman effort, he managed not to choke. At first, nothing was visible at all in the dimly lit church, but gradually the forms of its high gilt walls and four tall columns appeared before him. At the base of the farthest were two great wooden thrones, set just beside the marble altar. Leading up to them, lining either side of the aisle, was a choir of young Novgorovian boys. A crowd of women and men stood behind in the pews, attired in long white dresses and military uniforms emblazoned with red stars. All eyes were riveted upon him.

Vadim moved up the aisle towards the altar, pursuing his diminutive standard bearers. His father's copious frame filled the larger righthand throne. Beneath his bejeweled maniakion collar, his embroidered pontifical loros robe trailed from his arms onto the floor. On his dark curly hair was a golden kamelaukion crown, its two high arches spanning cushions of quilted red velvet. To the left sat Princess Eudoxia in a shimmering white and gold silk dress. She too wore a maniakion on her breast, studded with silver gems, and a kamelaukion on her head. Her smiling eyes were upon her son. In contrast, the prince's dark eyes under heavy brows rested on him with their usual expressionlessness. His large hands clasped a solid silver sceptre, the jade eyes of whose double-headed eagle pommel seemed to be watching Vadim too.

Beside his mother's throne stood a strikingly beautiful young woman, arrayed in a green silk dress. She also had a silver kamelaukion on her head but, unlike those of his parents, it bore the crest of a crowned and rampant lion. From its sides hung pendilia of pearls, threaded into her flaxen hair like a nebula of stars. The maiden smiled sheepishly as he approached, but he did not return her smile. Instead, his eyes fixed irritably on her diadem. It seemed his cousin Anastasia had come all the way from Bohemia to bear witness to his shame.

At last, he reached the altar. The boys stepped aside and the choir fell silent. He dropped to his knees before his father's feet, bowing his head. The old prince extended his right hand, on which he wore a white-gold ring. Set within it was a large moonstone in the shape of a Marian star, emanating a faint iridescence. He took his father's hand and kissed the ring.

'O most Holy Virgin, save us!' the choir sang, taking up the Greek hymn once more. 'Rejoice, o Lady, endless font of living waters. Rejoice, luminous morning, dwelling place of light. Rejoice, dispeller of darkness, You who have destroyed utterly the demons of night. Glory to the Mother, the Virgin, and the Holy Spirit.'

His father slowly rose and moved behind the altar, the boys taking up the snowy train of his royal loros.

'Glory to Prince Theadoric Eugenianus Cassimir, man most beloved of Our Lady,' a herald proclaimed somewhere in the pews. 'Grand Protosynkellos, Pontifex Maximus, Grand Prince of Novgorod, Metropolitan of the Crimea, Hetman of the Cossacks, Man Yet Unstained, most beloved of Our Lady.'

Still on his knees, Vadim shuffled across the hard marble towards the altar. There he prostrated himself, laying his palms upon the steps. His nose was soon numb. The palace churches were always so cold. Like the Novgorovian spring, and his father, they never quite seemed to thaw out. He shuffled his legs. How ridiculous he must look lying there, like some frozen ghost. Doubtless his cousin was secretly laughing at him. He longed to be back in his bed, pressed against Ganna's warm body.

'*O panymnite Miter.* O all-glorious Mother,' his father's Greek baritone sounded above, its weakness masked by the dutiful echo of the crowd. 'Send down Thy Holy Spirit upon us. Forgive us our sins, and bless us our earthly bodies, that we may be pure.'

Vadim murmured the words half-heartedly into the cold floor. Even his loins were numb now. Perhaps they would always be so from now on, like his father's. The old prince could surely not always have been so. He had fathered him, after all. He imagined his own white chlamys hardening into a cloak of marble, imprisoning his manhood and stultifying him into a scarecrow forever. He shuddered.

'Bless us, o Lady, that we may be pure, by the example of Thy Gnosis, through which Thy Sophia, Thy Holy Wisdom, Thy sacred Demiurge, became flesh. And lead us not into the temptation of Gehenna. Lead us not into the ways of the deceiver, and the eros of his false prophet, by whose slander you were evilly demeaned. O Virgin Unsullied, save us from our sins,' Theadoric rasped. His father seemed to be having another bad spell.

'Upon this most holy feast day, besides Thy Descension upon the holy Justinia, we also honour Thy visitation of Matrona the Elect, the maiden of Casan, in the one hundred and twenty-sixth year of that event,' Theadoric addressed the crowd. He touched the red star on his chest, gesturing feebly at a great icon of the Virgin above the altar. Its face was so black that its features could hardly be made out at all. The bright pearls that studded the outline of the Mother's head, her veil encrusted with sapphire, emerald and silver gems, and the icon's solid gold frame all increased the impression that her face had fallen into shadow. Yet her tiny eyes, no more than dark pinpricks in her dun face, bored mercilessly into him, as if she were about to speak some chastisement. As if she were about to judge him.

'We stand in the presence of Thy Holy Image, by which Thy Grace unto the maiden Matrona is preserved to our memory,' Theadoric continued. 'By the light of that Holy Image, I call upon Thy triform Grace to witness this hour, o gracious Mother, Virgin and Holy Spirit.'

Vadim's heart thumped loudly against the stone floor. The ceremony felt interminable, but what would he be when it did eventually end? Would he even be himself anymore? Would he be a man at all?

'By the light of your Holy Image, by which all other images of the iconodule are proven false, I call Thee to witness this most holy of the seven mysteria of Thy ecclesia. To witness the passage of our most sanctified mysterion, the most ancient rite of Thy church, by which

Thy earthly representatives are chosen. The most holy mysterion of that church whose shepherd Thou hast made me, of that church which is the earthly shadow of Thy kingdom,' Theadoric said in his faltering voice. The dynatorial ladies, lords and synkelloi in the pews placed their palms on their chests and bowed their heads.

'For today, my firstborn by Thy Grace, has elected to show unto Thee the ultimate kindness,' Theadoric said, facing the Casan icon. 'My very own son, and heir to the House of Novgorod, Prince Vadim Theadorovich Cassimir, assumes the holy orders of Thy ecclesia on earth. Humbly, o Mother, I beseech Thee to find him worthy. Arise, my son.'

Vadim could hardly breathe. His limbs felt like lead, and the incense choked him, but at length he managed to rise. His eyes met his father's. The tremor of something resembling a smile flitted across Theadoric's lips, like a fracture on the surface of an icy pond. Vadim's hands shook. How deathly cold they were now, yet how warm they had been on Ganna's chest.

'Rejoice, dawn of the mystic day. Rejoice, Thou who hast extinguished the furnace of eros!' his father exclaimed, raising his emaciated hands to the crowd, as the whole church took up his words. Vadim became fascinated by how pallid and drawn they were. His father was surely ill.

'Rejoice, deposer of the mortal tyrant, redeemer from the pagan mire,' Theadoric chanted. 'Rejoice, Thou who enlightens initiates of the Trinity. I beseech Thy Grace to accept unto the embrace of Thy holy ecclesia Thy chaste son, Vadim.' His voice quivered over the word 'chaste'. Vadim straightened up in his over-tight dalmatica.

Theadoric fell into a pious silence, bowing his head. The two boys placed a small oat cake upon the altar and next to it a large book. The tome's battered leather binding was faded, its gilded Cyrillic lettering no longer legible. Vadim stared at it in horror.

'O Bride Unwedded, Thou who free us, Thy faithful, from the flames of earthly passion,' Theadoric said, laying his right hand upon the book, 'lead us unto chastity, that shriven of the sins of man we may enter into Thy kingdom. Shrive Thy son of his sins, I beseech Thee, o Lady, that he may become Thy minister. Man Yet Unstained, I beseech Thee, o Holy Mother, that Thou shrive Thy son of the inborn stain of the masculine, that he may look, chaste, upon Thy Holy Mandylion.' He put the oat cake to Vadim's lips. Its saline taste reminded him of Ganna's skin. Her handsome form rose up before him in all the splendour of its nakedness.

Touching his chest, Theadoric bowed before the Lady of Casan. The icon peered down at Vadim unforgivingly. It made him feel unworthy. To his annoyance, his mother also watched him intensely, scrutinising his every move. He shot an angry glance at his cousin Anastasia, demurely radiant behind Eudoxia's throne. Her diadem was as majestically opalescent as the icon's gems. Why did Anastasia get to have everything her way in life, while he was stood there dressed like some pale effigy? It simply wasn't fair, and he hated her for it. His mother frowned.

His burning eyes took in the ancient oak of the tsaritsa's throne, then travelled up the brightly painted column above. The hateful images crowded the old stone walls of the church, depicting the visitations of the Virgin and the lives of the gnostic saints. Eve, Egeria, Anicia Juliana, Theadora, Pulcheria, Matrona, Kassia, even Justinia, all alike received the gnosis of the Mother caked in lapis, scarlet and gold. It was all a stupid gaudy parade, just like this was. What was it all for?

'O Bride Unwedded, I humbly beseech Thee,' Theadoric continued, with an effort straightening his heavy crown. 'Shrive Thy son, Vadim, of his sins, Shrive him of the infirmity of the masculine, that he may enter cleansed into Thy holy ecclesia, whose shepherd on earth Thou has deemed me worthy to be. That he may be Thy minister, from this day unto that upon which Thou honour him to return unto the motherly embrace of Thy Gnosis.'

Embrace. The word rang in his head like an incessant bell, clanging discordantly as it swung between his itching temples. He bowed his head, prepared to receive the sacrament of priesthood. The consecration of his emasculation. The crowning glory of his humiliation. His hands shook as he clasped them together.

Embrace. It was the cold embrace of the Mother, of the frozen marble of Her church. Of the cold embrace of his own mother, for whom only his princely reputation seemed to matter. He thought of Ganna's warm embrace. How the hot blood had coursed through his veins as they wrestled that morning. Of the great life-force throbbing and swelling through the river without. It was his life-force, and it was about to be snuffed out.

He beheld his father's emaciated figure, so poorly masked by his regal loros. The lesions in his cheeks, where the disease had eaten away at his skin, and his large pale hands. The greying curls on his temples, and his fast-thinning beard. He could hardly bear it. Soon he too would be embalmed, and this ceremony was his entombment. His father's crown detached itself from his head, and appeared in Prince Ivan's outstretched hands.

'Know now, my son, the mysterion of priesthood, by the gnostic grace of Our Lady!' his father exclaimed, briefly recovering his strength. Vadim flinched, and the dried laurel cut painfully into his temples. He glowered at Anastasia as he held out his palms before him. His father raised his hands over his head to make the blessing. This was it. The day of his burial.

All was silent in the church. The boys stepped up to the altar, lifting their sacerdotal standards over Vadim's head. His hands shook visibly now. He tried to stop, but it was no use. A wrinkle creased his father's brow, like a rain cloud grazing a mountain peak. Vadim bowed his head.

'Do you, my son,' Theadoric asked, so quietly that Vadim was sure only he could hear, 'accept this great honour that is conferred upon you?'

He blanched, and could do no more than stand there like a mute. 'I, I...' he stammered. A demonic carousel of images flashed through his mind in quick succession. His frowning father. His disappointed mother. The hateful white lion on Anastasia's diadem. Prince Ivan in the field of wheat. Ganna in her silken nudity. Finally, most prominent of all, his father's dreadful lifeless hands. The cloud on Theadoric's brow darkened, threatening to burst.

'Do you, Prince Vadim Theadorovich, accept this great honour?' his father repeated, the irritation in his voice unmistakable now. He spoke deliberately, as if he wanted everyone to hear. Yet to Vadim, his voice was far away. He saw himself standing before the altar in his ridiculous white robe, as if he had been one of the spectators, not himself.

'I...' he said, peering up into his father's face. An interminable silence ensued. A bead of sweat trickled from beneath the velvet of his father's crown. Theadoric's brow arched, as the storm cloud burst between the mountain ravines. One of the boys faltered, and his brass staff grazed Vadim's head. Vadim glared at him with hatred, then looked with disgust at his own effete robe.

'No!' he said, staring defiantly at his father.

Theadoric's face dropped, all trace of anger erased by his surprise. His mouth fell open, as if he were a sibyl about to utter some dread prophecy. There was a gasp from the pews.

A moment later, Theadoric's face had recomposed itself. An expression of haughty disdain was written there, as if it had become that of the eagle on his sceptre. His thick lips curled into a grimace as his eyes surveyed Vadim's girlish curls and broad young shoulders. Vadim flushed with shame and anger.

A deathly silence reigned, as if everyone were holding their breath. Theadoric opened his mouth, but Vadim did not wait. Turning away, he tore the laurel from his head and threw it on the floor. Then he ran back down the aisle towards the doors.

His mother's voice pursued him, but he did not heed her. Anastasia's sad eyes flew by, lowered beneath her diadem. Everywhere, red berets and white ruffs turned. The eyes of all were upon him, but he didn't care. It didn't matter anymore. All he wanted was Ganna.

Chapter 15

Alistair

Alistair lay low in the water, pressing himself against the tunnel's cold stone as the Latin's jackboots receded into the distance. The praetorians' laughter gradually faded too, until all that could be heard was the gushing of the stream from the grille. A bird chirped in the grove above.

The water was cold against his skin, and his limbs were numb from the hard stone. Cautiously, he felt his stomach. It was very sore. He didn't understand what had just happened. Why had the Marian let him go? There was no time to think now. He had to get out. But how, and where could he go? If he left the tunnel, the white caps would surely catch him in no time.

He slowly raised himself on his aching arms, shaking his legs in the water. With difficulty, he sat up in the stream like a seal, staring at the grille. Only a few paltry emissaries of the Latian morning found their way in, like fingers clawing under the pile of twigs and muddy brown leaves. Barely anything was visible in the darkness, save the arch and stone roof above. He stared fearfully into the velvet canvas of the tunnel's depths. He was beginning to feel throughly chilled. He had to get out of the water. He shut his eyes and tried to think. Ahead, the stream echoed. It must surely get bigger that way. On all fours, he began to shuffle through the water.

The tunnel darkened. Every time he looked back, the light of the grille was smaller, until it was no more than a little glass marble. As he propelled himself along on his hands, the straps of his satchel pulled painfully at his shoulders. His palms and knees were terribly sore, and were soon completely numb. Surprisingly, though, the stone beneath his feet was smooth. It was a strange drain.

The shaft ascended. It was pitch black now, even darker than the Reservation well. His ears sharpened. The stream quietened, but its echo increased. He rolled back onto his knees, stretching his arms up to the tunnel roof. There was nothing there. Tottering on weak knees, he staggered to his feet. His damp tunic and surcoat clung uncomfortably to his skin like seaweed. He reached above his head, but still there was nothing. To his sides, too, his arms met only empty space. He must have looked ridiculous stood there, flapping his arms about blindly like one of the pigeons. What would Father Zosim have said?

Father Zosim. His name stung him like a Marian's baton. What had happened to him? And to Father Vigilius, Brother Lucas and the rest? Why had he only thought of them now? Guilt overcame him. Like some craven, he'd thought only of saving his own skin. He had to go back for them. His feet already turning in the stream, he looked for the grille. It was no longer there. He tried to think what Father Zosim would have said, but no sooner had he asked the question than the horrible truth impressed itself upon him. There was no going back. He'd seen the white caps himself. There'd been so many of them at the dormitory. They must have had the whole thing planned from the start. How could any of the Poor Friars have gotten away? It was only because Brother Lucas had warned him that he got out in time, and that was a miracle in itself.

His large feet froze as he dragged them through the water. His head hung heavily as tears welled in his eyes. He remembered the book in his sack. How selfish he had been the night before. Hadn't he had everything he needed then? Now he had nothing, not a friend in the world. Not even a home. Perhaps all of this was his fault. If only he had been what Father Zosim had wanted him to be, perhaps none of this would have happened. If only he had been better to them all.

As he sobbed, the colours blurred before his eyes, the little lights dancing like the people in the chapel paintings. He caught himself. Lights. How could there be any lights in this labyrinth? He rubbed his eyes dry. There was a small dot in the distance. He splashed towards it as fast as he could. As he drew nearer, the dot became a pyramid. The cloak of night receded, like the rising of a stage curtain. Ancient stone arches appeared above him. The broad stream now ran no higher than his ankles. The dark cavern stretched ahead like the mighty vault of some lost subterranean chapel. He gasped in wonder. How naive he'd been to think he knew all the Reservation's secrets.

The pyramid grew into a shaft of light. Day was prying its way in from a chink in the roof above. His heart filled with hope. There might be another way out. He screwed up his eyes in the blinding light. High above, a drain opened, but it was too far to reach. He fell back dejectedly against the tunnel wall. He pressed his hands against its concave stone, but it was as smooth as that of a chapel, without a foothold in sight. As he peered at the light, it occurred to him that the white caps would surely still be looking for him. What if the Latin had changed his mind and told them where he was? They might easily spy him out down the drain.

Alarmed, he hurried on into the darkness. Another pin prick appeared ahead. His heart leapt. This one was further away. The slope inclined more steeply, and he grew out of breath. As the tide of night receded, the air became less dank. There was a strange noise, too. A sort of low buzzing whir above the gentle rush of the stream.

The opening was just another drain. It was again too high, but by its light he could see that ahead, the sewer forked. One, smaller, way turned sharply upwards, water cascading out of it. As the stream flowed downwards it ran back the way he'd come, but also poured into another larger tunnel running underground. Both were as black as the Styx, but the water had to be coming down from somewhere above. He leant into the smaller tunnel. The air smelt fresher, and was warmer on his face. There was the same low buzzing, as if there were bees up there. The other, meanwhile, was cold and silent. He took the first.

It darkened as he ascended, the walls closing in around him. The echo diminished. His head bumped against the stone above, and he was forced back onto all-fours. The cold water ran into his garments, soaking him to the skin. He sneezed and spat water from his mouth, feeling like an overgrown mole drowned in a drain. The buzzing noise became louder and transformed into a steady whir. He'd never heard anything like it before. In his distraction his hand slipped in the water and, with a splash, he fell flat in the stream.

Cursing, he rose, wiping his face. The water had stilled. Nor was the tunnel ascending any longer. His outstretched arms met only with air. There was another dot of light ahead. The walls of a long chamber emerged around him. He was no longer in a tunnel at all. He ran towards the light, his feet splashing through a pool.

The whirring grew louder still. Details began to populate the chamber walls, as if some artist were gradually adding them to his canvas. Shallow alcoves appeared. All were uniformly small, as if someone had put them there to store treasure chests. There were neither chest nor treasure, however. Instead, white forms materialised within. At first he couldn't make out what they were, but soon piles of white sticks emerged. They grew bigger and more distinct, filling every last one of the alcoves.

The hollow eye sockets of a skull peered out at him. He wailed in terror, dashing for the light. Water splashed the walls as he crashed through the pool. He tried not to look, but couldn't help himself. The walls were covered in strange symbols and leering faces. Stencilled onto one was a donkey on a cross. Then an enormous candlestick with a hundred candles, a man stabbing a giant bull, and so many other bizarre and unimaginable things. He cried out again and ran on as fast as his feet could carry him.

The chamber narrowed. The alcoves, bones and pictures all disappeared. A little grille, just like the one he'd come in by, appeared ahead. The whirring noise became deafening. He grabbed desperately at the rusted iron bars. They didn't budge. He howled, rattling them like a madman. He was so close now. He could smell the free air above. The skull rose before him. With a mighty cry, and one last desperate effort, he threw his whole weight against the grille. There was a crash of metal, and everything went dark.

All was still. His eyelids felt warm, like the embrace of the woman with the golden hair. It had to be morning already. He shuffled onto his back, but his bed was strangely uncomfortable. Why had Brother Lucas had to wake him so early this morning anyway? Lucas. Alistair sat up with a start. He cried out, but something drowned out his voice. Something loud. Something louder than anything he'd ever heard before. So loud he could barely hear himself think. There was pain too. His shoulder ached. He opened his eyes.

At first there were only bright blots, dancing before him like the torches in the apostolica. Then the blots dispersed, and damp leaves appeared all around. He was sitting in the mire of a pond. He squirmed as mud seeped into his undergarments. The grille lay wide open, leading back the way he'd come. He recalled the dark tunnel and the dead people's bones. He leapt to his feet, but tottered and fell forward into a pile of leaves.

He lay motionless, trying to remember where he was. A white beret flashed through his mind. He nearly screamed, but clasped his hand over his mouth. There was still a terrible ringing in his ears. He rubbed them, but the noise did not go away. He was sitting beside the pond, which was thickly overgrown and overhung by poplars. Water trickled out of the pool into the grille. Like a bear rising from a stream, he shook the mud and water from his limbs. His shoulder blades ached, as if someone were pressing needles into them. His arm was all grazed on one side too, and his clothes and satchel plastered with leaves.

He looked up at the trees. It was just the same as where he had gone down into the sewer. Had he gone around in a circle and returned to the same place? He pictured the pockmarked titan in the white cap stepping out from behind a tree trunk. He scrambled hurriedly up the slope, sweat streaming from his cheeks. It was hot, and must be nearing the meridian already.

There was no one else in the grove, just the deafeningly loud hum, intermittently punctuated by a sort of whooshing noise. As if a whole flock of pigeons had taken off from the piazza, only to be followed by another flock a few seconds later, and then another, and another. It wasn't clear where it was coming from. There was nothing but the trees and the pond. He really hadn't any idea where he was. Wherever he was though, he couldn't stay there. It was surely only a matter of time before the white caps would find him. He had to get away, or find somewhere to hide. He reached the top of the bank. The trees gave way.

For a moment, he forgot to breathe. It was as if someone had thumped him on the chest and knocked the air out of his lungs. His eyes opened so wide that they hurt. He rubbed them, unsure whether he was still awake, but when he reopened them it was still there. A vast treeless plain stretched away into the distance. Far away on the horizon was a giant emerald band, as if someone had remixed the lapis paint on the chapel walls and drawn a fine line beneath the broad canvas of the Mediterranean sky. It had to be the sea.

Yet it wasn't this that had stupefied him. Extending out from under the hill where he stood, all the way to the sea, was a paved track. It was unlike anything he had ever seen before. Twice as wide as the old piazza, it ran dead straight right up to the horizon. As if by magic, small carts darted along its smooth surface, so fast that they were barely visible at all. Every time one passed, there was a deafening whoosh and a rush of air. He nearly fainted, steadying himself against a poplar's bark.

'*Via Ostia*,' Alistair read aloud from a rusty sign nearby. The Ostian Way. Beneath were listed the names of places he didn't know. The meridianal sun beat down on the scorched plain. Another cart zoomed by, and a tremor ran through the trees. He covered his ears, watching the carts fearfully as he tried to see if there was some other way. He turned back eastward, and nearly leapt out of his skin.

Towering over the trees behind him was a gargantuan metal wall. Shining like a brass shield, its glare momentarily blinded him. Its mirror-like surface was at least as high as the tower of the old basilica. On its summit was a great tangled knot of metal, as dense as the weeds of the pool below, and pulsing with a magic light like fire.

As he stood there aghast, something moved on top of the wall. He ducked behind the trees, squinting up at the brazen palisade. Several black berets moved along the wall. His whole body went numb with fear. Marians.

Then it dawned on him. This was it. The Pomerium. He had reached the boundary. The end of the Reservation. The end of the old law. Nor had he just reached it, he had crossed it. He was out. He had escaped.

CHAPTER 16

Vadim

Vadim bolted out of the church doors, ignoring his mother's cries and the anxious eyes of the onlookers. He shoved past the guards and ran blindly across the forecourt. He was angry with himself for ever having agreed to go through with the sham of the ordination in the first place. He should never have set foot in the church, and would certainly never set foot in one again. His parents could keep their stupid ceremonies. No doubt Anastasia and the rest were laughing at him already, but he cared not. At least he was free now.

Seeking the nearest refuge, he dove into a passage behind the church opposite. Only once the pallid stone of all three Trinity churches was behind him did he halt. Skulking in the shadows, he shut his eyes, breathing hard. There was no one around. The red brick of the keep towered above him like a cliff. Clustered in its shade were the grey outhouses of the servants' quarters. He made for the nearest door.

It was dark and airless inside the windowless corridor, but he knew his way around like the back of his hand. He walked to its end. Servants withdrew in stunned silence at his approach, bowing or courtesying. He ignored them, descending an iron stairwell. At its foot was a long corridor, off which several rickety doors led. He approached one of them and knocked loudly. No one answered. He knocked a second time, more insistently. He knocked a third time then, without waiting, pushed the door open. There was no lock, and it yielded at once.

'Cursed deceiver!' he said. Ganna's room was empty. She was doubtless on some menial duty. His mother would certainly have made sure there was no way he'd find her today. He stared in mute fury at the room, his black brows brooding over the simple furnishings. He'd been there before, of course, many times, and yet only now was he struck by how simple and mean everything was, as if he were seeing them for the first time. The tiny wooden desk in the corner of the spartan cell. The plain little bed with its threadbare coverlet, clearly not enough to keep anyone warm during a Novgorovian night.

There was a wooden icon of the Mother above the desk. A subscript in Novgorovian beneath read, 'Immemory was engendered because the Mother was not known. Once the Mother was known, immemory was no more.' Vadim glared at the Cyrillic lettering. The faded title of the Gospel of Truth appeared before him, and his father's pallid hand upon its battered cover. He felt the lascivious hands of the house sacerdote on his shoulders again, as he girt him in his priestly shroud, and the brass staff banging his head. His ears rang with all the imbecilic songs. Then his mother calling after him desperately, as if he were a condemned man. His eyes rose to the icon. The Mother's crown became Anastasia's diadem.

He brought his fist down onto the desk like a hammer, and the flimsy board smashed in two. He stormed out, slamming the door behind him. He descended another staircase into a cellar. The air was dank and it was nearly completely dark, but that was no obstacle. He knew just how many turns to take before one came to a rusted iron door. A door that was always supposed to be locked, but which was often not. His hand soon found the cold handle. Metal grated against stone as the door swung open. There was a rush of cold air. He stood at the head of a narrow stone tunnel. Water rumbled overhead. He ran to the far end, and soon reached the supply trapdoor. He gave it a sharp shove with his elbow, and it swung open. He gripped its sides and pulled himself up.

There was a loud whoosh and a gust of wind. He was standing beside a road. Beyond, the river sparkled in the early afternoon sun like a band of stars. Above it the walls of the red keep rose like the velvet of his father's crown, its high towers jutting into the air like a palisade of spears. Vadim smiled. He was out.

Through the silvery birchwood beside the road, the outline of the insulae tenements of the city's plebeian quarter reared up in the distance. Beyond, the glass icicles of the gubernatorial district jutted into the sky. Vadim started walking through the wood towards the city. Images appeared before him in quick succession, weaving like ghosts between the pale bark of the trees. His father's snarling eyes. His mother's pursed and vigilant lips. His cousin Anastasia's fine blond eyebrows. The stupid icon above Ganna's desk. In the silence of the wood, the shame of it all overtook him. There was no question of going back now. He had to get away. He didn't know where, but it didn't matter. He just had to.

A twig cracked in the wood behind him. He scanned the trees angrily, but there was no one there. He was already at the edge of the wood. In his rage, he had reached the plebeian quarter without even noticing. On all sides, the white brick of the tenements rose like the vast hulks of decommissioned freighters, casting long shadows across the tarmac. He marvelled at the silent ranks of twenty-storeyed buildings, and the crowded rows of windows on every level. Each panel of their plastered brick facing bore a giant stencilled icon of the Virgin in blue with the words, 'Be kind to Our Lady.' He had seen them from afar, but never up close. How could people actually live like that?

At first, no one was around, just occasional movement in some of the insulae windows. At length, a few passers-by appeared on the street, steadily increasing as he went on. A few of them, virtually all plebs or slaves, gawked at his strange garments, but he paid them no heed. He must have walked for an hour or so before the tenements dwindled. The light was lengthening now, as the afternoon drew on. Its golden hues illuminated the Cyrillic lettering of shopfronts, which appeared increasingly frequently. A few blocks further on, the hum of vehicles and voices wafted to his ears.

He was in the centre of the plebeian quarter now. The pavements grew busier. Soon, he was just another faceless member of the crowd. Some still remarked his outfit as they passed, but most of those that did clearly took him for a sacerdote or deacon. For the most part, hardly anyone paid him any attention. For the very first time in his life, he felt anonymous. It was a strange sensation, but he liked it.

As the May evening dwindled, some of the shopfronts sparkled with neon. On a nearby stall, the Cyrillic letters of the word '*vino*' danced in glittering maroon and jade around a holographic amphora. The jar spun around as if it were on a potter's wheel, as virtual droplets of wine spilled out in all directions. His legs felt like lead. He sat down on a step in the doorway of a small kafeneion. Greek music drifted from within, intermingling with Cossack songs from the other side of the street as shrill words floated across the ulitsa.

> A bloodied cart raced on by, a Cossack lay upon it,
> Shot through his breast, stabbed to the heart, a spear
> was in his hands.
> From its tip the blood was trickling, a stream of blood
> was flowing.
> A plane tree stood above the river, and above the tree
> a raven croaked.
> The mother weeps for the Cossack. Weep not,
> mother, do not grieve,
> For your son is married. He chose a lady for his bride.
> A mound of earth in the bare fields!

Vadim leant his head against the doorpost of the kafeneion and listened drowsily to the soporific mix of kithar and fiddle. He shut his eyes.

He was in a great field of wheat. It was summertime. The sun beat down on the earth, glinting on the soldiers' armour and spears like a thousand tiny diamonds. All knelt, looking up at the sun expectantly. He alone stood. He shielded his eyes from the glare, straining to look over the shoulders of the crowd. He searched for Prince Ivan at the front, but he was nowhere to be seen. Neither was there any sign of the holy maiden, nor her ivory steed. Instead, where they should have been was a plane tree, standing alone in the middle of the field. The sun moved behind the tree, and its shadow fell over the entire army.

Beneath the tree was a wooden cart on which a man lay prostrate. He was dressed in a long white loros. An eagle-headed silver sceptre hung limply from his hand. As it drooped down beside the cart, blood oozed from its pommel, staining the wheat sheaves like streaks of purple seaweed on the sand. An old woman stood beside the cart. Her body shook with sobs. Although half-hidden in the shade of the tree, Vadim was sure he recognised her face.

He moved closer, straining to get a better look. He was sure it was his mother. He began to run, tripping over the genuflecting soldiers. The woman's sobs grew louder, and she raised her arms towards him. He rushed to her. Three times he tried to embrace her, but every time he slipped through her arms, as if she were a ghost. The last time he lost his balance, and fell onto the corpse in the white loros. A terrible stench filled his nostrils.

As he recoiled in disgust, he saw that the bloodstained robe was that of a young sacerdote. Then, for the first time, he looked at the man's face. Horrorstruck, he realised it was his own. He looked in terror at the woman. Instead of his mother, it was Ganna. Yet she was old, her sallow face horribly contorted as if withered by centuries of age. He cried out in despair.

'Droop not, plane tree, for still art thou green,' the refrain continued, as Vadim awoke with a start. 'Fret not, little Cossack, for still art thou young.'

Night had settled. The music still played, more loudly than ever. The entire ulitsa was iridescent with holographic lights. Feeling a chill on his skin, he examined the spare cloth of his chlamys and was surprised to see no blood. How had he managed to fall asleep in the middle of the street?

A doorman loitered in the vestibule of the kafeneion, eyeing him suspiciously. Drunken cries emanated from within, a chaotic blend of Greek, Novgorovian and Ruthenian, mixing cacophonously with the Cossack songs. Across the ulitsa, the holographic displays of the shopfronts danced in the night. Beside the pirouetting amphorae and spinning wine kalichs were also scantily clad women. Gyrating in time to the music blaring from the kafeneia below, they vied with the drinks for the attention of the passers-by.

'Aren't you a bit handsome for a priest?' a voice addressed him from the street. A young woman stood below the steps, smiling up at him flirtatiously. Despite the coolness of the May evening, her outfit closely resembled that of her holographic counterparts, her translucent chiton and short skirt little concealing her burgeoning chest and buttocks. She had the local women's statuesque build and fair skin, but her dark hair and eyes suggested she was most likely a Zaporizhzhian slave of the Hetmannia. The chill evaporated from his skin.

'Little green periwinkle, twine lower to me,' the Cossack song drifted across the street as Vadim made to move on, 'and you, dear one of the black brow, come nearer to me!' He paused on the steps. The woman morphed into the spectre of the ancient Ganna. He rubbed his forehead, trying to wipe away the last residue of his nightmare. She smiled.

'You're not from round here, are you?' she persisted, fixing him with her dark eyes. 'Why don't you come with me? I'll show you around.' She placed her foot on the first step. The opalescent folds of her skirt fell back, revealing a shapely thigh.

'The sun is low, the evening's nigh,' the song went on relentlessly. 'Come out to me, my little heart.'

Vadim stepped into the bright light of the street. He again made to move on, but hesitated. It struck him that she had no idea who he was. He felt again the anonymity he had never known until that day. He smiled back at her.

CHAPTER 17

Zeno

'I wanted to tell you before, Katepano,' Maurice said, as Zeno seized the little pendant out of his hand, 'but you were in such a rush about the witness. Then, when we got into that scuffle with the port authority, I thought it best to wait. Besides, I wasn't sure they ought to know about it. Not their jurisdiction, is it?'

The other praetorians crowded round the hangar entrance. Zeno squinted at the strange pendant in the half-light, bending under the shutter to get a better view. The crossed driftwood shone in the Mediterranean sun. The light gouged letters into its surface. Four letters. There could be no doubt. It was a talisman. A heretical talisman. He looked up at Maurice in perplexity.

'The corpse, Katepano, the one from out of town... I found it on—' he continued, but his words were drowned out by an almighty crash from within the hangar, followed by a cry. Zeno dived under the shutter. He took in the overturned chair and Simeon's distant figure, evanescing into the shadows of one of the warehouse aisles. The idiots had left the witness unguarded.

'Damn the Osman!' he said to the praetorians as Maurice crashed through behind him. He hurtled down the aisle, which receded before him like an unending forest avenue. The old man was nowhere to be seen. There was a scraping of rusty metal. Zeno rushed towards the sound. In the far wall, a small door stood ajar.

Bounding through, he found himself in a narrow stairwell. Through the wrought iron beneath his feet, the grey head of the doulos bobbed like a buoy in the darkness below. Zeno descended the steps as fast as he could. His blood was hot. He cursed himself for letting his only witness get away. How could he have been so remiss? He shouldn't have let himself be so easily distracted. Besides, Maurice should have told him about the talisman straightaway. And the guard ought to have kept watch on the witness. Rank indiscipline and negligence. There was no more to it than that.

When he finally reached the bottom, he found himself in a narrow tunnel. He could barely see a thing, but it only led in one direction. Footsteps echoed ahead. Another door slammed. In a few seconds he was on it, a small cavity in the wall to his right, but not a door. A wooden trapdoor. He wrenched it open. Maurice's voice called from the stairwell behind, but there was no time to wait. He threw himself inside.

It was another, even narrower tunnel, and he was forced onto all fours as he groped his way along. Steel grazed his palms. A ventilation shaft. Doubtless leading to a smugglers' hideout. That must be where the criminals had been stowing their contraband. If Simeon knew about it, he had to be mixed up with the whole business. He had to catch him.

The shaft clanged ahead as Simeon left an awful stench in his wake. How hard was it to catch one old man? He should have had him by now, but Simeon was faster than he'd expected. He cursed and scrambled on, soon discovering another opening where a metal grille had been knocked out. He stuck his head through. In amazement, he beheld a large subterranean warehouse beneath him. Down in the darkness, Simeon was alighting from the foot of a ladder.

'Stop where you are, you bastard of a doulos!' Zeno swore. The slave looked up at him fearfully, eyes darting to the far end of the warehouse. He hesitated, then he limped as fast as he could away from the ladder.

With difficulty, Zeno squeezed himself out of the shaft, trying not to look down. He had always hated heights. Steeling himself, he gingerly clasped the iron rungs of the ladder, swinging his feet down. He was sweating. He chided himself for his cravenness. He was letting his witness get away. Without looking down, he cautiously descended.

His feet wobbled as they touched the damp warehouse floor. There was barely any light, save the flickering of one old lamp in the rafters above, and not a single freight drone in sight. It had surely to be some kind of abandoned storage facility. So this was where the criminals had been hiding out. The faint outline of a closing door materialised in the darkness ahead. He'd got the damned doulos at last. He hurtled towards the door, but in his excitement slipped in a pool of water, lost his footing and crashed through.

He slowly stood up, rubbing his leg as he looked about. Had he fallen through some magic portal into another world? All around were marble walls, flickering ivory in the candlelight. Above stretched a domed terracotta roof on high squinch arches, with exedra to either side. In one of these was a mosaic with several winged men in white robes flanking another in brown, who sat atop a globe, a ring encircling his head. Beneath were two more mosaics showing an ancient king and queen. The rest of the walls were completely covered in fantastical images of men and beasts.

'Holy Anicia!' Zeno exclaimed. The strange building was full of people. There couldn't have been less than a hundred of them, men, and many women too, all girt in rags. All faced away from him, motionless and mute in the half-light, holding candles in their hands. None reacted to his presence. Slaves. A giant slave gathering. He rubbed his eyes, unnerved by the curious spectacle.

Something moved at the back of the crowd. Simeon was trying to slip unnoticed into the servile throng. His panicked eyes met Zeno's. Zeno straightened his cap and barged into the crowd in silent pursuit. Some of the slaves turned, but none said a word. The greybeard kept appearing and disappearing between their rags like a night fox. The crafty doulos was getting away. He grew hot.

There was a voice now. Zeno halted, peering over the unwashed crowns of hair. At the far end, a bearded man in an ash-coloured smock stood in an alcove beneath the mosaic of the winged men. He faced the slaves, addressing them from a raised dais. The words were too faint to make out, but it sounded like some kind of low Italic. Simeon was nowhere to be seen. He cursed. He had to find the damned slave at all costs.

He began shoving at random people, grabbing them by their shoulders. The surprised eyes of countless faceless slaves, mainly women and old men, stared back at him fearfully. Some became alarmed at the sight of Zeno's navy cap and uniform, and bolted for the door, but most were so transfixed by the unknown orator that they did not even notice him. He ought to have disrupted the unauthorised gathering, but they were too many. There was still no sign of Maurice. It would have to wait until he found Simeon.

'For this people's heart is waxed gross,' the speaker's words floated towards him as he pushed through the crowd. 'Their ears are dull of hearing, and their eyes they have closed. But blessed are your eyes, for they see, and your ears, for they hear! But when ye shall hear of wars and rumours of wars, be ye not troubled. For such things must needs be, but the end shall not be yet. For nation shall rise against nation, and kingdom against kingdom, and there shall be earthquakes in divers places, and there shall be famines and troubles. These are the beginnings of sorrows.'

'What in Justinia's name...?' Zeno said, eyeing the speaker with amazement. His eyes flitted to the mosaic above his head. Maurice's pendant flashed before him. Heretics. Not just a slave gathering, but a heretical one. He grasped at the nearest slave. The same pendant fell from a woman's hand. He stooped, but something glinted in the crowd nearby. It was Simeon's terrified eyes. Zeno shoved after him, shouting his name. More faces turned, and the ranks closed. He swore loudly, no longer caring whom who pushed aside, man, woman or child.

'The children of wrath!' the orator said, his voice echoing around the dome above. Everything had fallen silent. Zeno halted. The douloi had drawn aside, watching him in terror. Between them, a few passus away, the speaker stood pointing directly at Zeno. There was fury in his eyes.

'After thy hardness and impenitent heart, treasurest up unto thyself wrath,' the man declaimed, as spittle flew from his mouth. 'For ye are like whited sepulchres, which indeed appear beautiful outward, but are within full of dead men's bones, and of all uncleanness. Even so ye also outwardly appear righteous unto men, but within ye are full of hypocrisy and iniquity!'

'Right, slave!' Zeno shouted, marching to the front of the crowd. 'Explain yourself. What is the meaning of this unauthorised gathering?' He reached for his baton, but the man showed no fear.

'For then shall be great tribulation, such as was not seen since the beginning of the world to this time, no, nor ever shall be,' he continued, still pointing madly at Zeno. 'And thou, Capernaum, which art exalted to heaven, shalt be thrust down to hell.' He pointed at the mosaic of the king in the exedrum above him. Flanked by his strategoi and logothetes, all of whom were clad in white togas, the patriarch wore a golden jewel-studded crown. Like the man with the angels in the other mosaic, he too had a crimson circle around his head.

'He hath scattered the proud in the imagination of their hearts,' the man went on. 'He hath put down the mighty from their seats, and exalted them of low degree. Put up again thy sword into his place, child of wrath, for all they that take the sword shall perish with the sword.' He indicated another mosaic, in which a greybeard in a toga sat on a rock, his head also encircled by a disk. On his lap was an open book with words in an unintelligible language. The old man gestured at a lion with bloodshot eyes and bared maw. In the flickering of the candlelight, the red eyes came alive, as if stalking their prey. Zeno shuddered.

'Alright, enough of this rubbish, old man,' he said, annoyed at himself for letting the madman lead him on. 'I'm placing you under arrest, *auctoritate Praetorii Urbis Ravennae*—' He broke off. Simeon had emerged from the fog of rags. The slave made a dash for one of the far apses. At the same time, there was a crash as the door flung open, and a red-faced Maurice appeared.

'Katepano!' Maurice exclaimed, then fell silent as he stared wide-eyed at the throng of slaves. Seeing him, the crowd panicked and began running frantically in all directions.

'In the deceiver's name!' Zeno cursed, letting go of the heretic as he hurtled after Simeon. He waved at Maurice to follow, but the praetorian only stood there in a daze, his eyes moving between the slaves, high arches and dome. Zeno bowled through the crowd like a cannon ball. A child wailed somewhere, but there was no time to stop. In a corner of the apse where Simeon had disappeared was another trapdoor. He launched himself at it.

He cried out as he lost his balance, tumbling head-over-heels in the dark as he was propelled relentlessly forwards. His shins grazed painfully against stone as he slid downwards. His body decelerated, and tumbled again. His hands tried to grab at the walls, but they were no longer there. He screamed as he rolled into thin air. Then, with a dull thud, he landed on something soft.

He lay on his back, unsure whether he was still alive. In the dim light, what looked like a lightcraft's translucent ion fin appeared above him. Something buzzed about softly within the enormous iridescent wing, like an insect trying to free itself from a spider's web. He rubbed his eyes. The ion fin dissolved into a fibreglass canvas, stretching across the entire ceiling. The insect mutated into a carrier drone. He flung out his aching arm but, instead of the cold floor of a hangar, it met with some kind of textile.

He sat up, patting the floor. He gasped. He was sitting in the middle of an enormous underground silo. In the neon half-light its walls stretched away in all directions, forming a giant opalescent dome. Something hovered beneath it. He strained his eyes. Hundreds of drones darted about the subterranean firmament, like bees gathering pollen. Beneath him were what looked like a pile of white cushions. Hundreds, perhaps thousands, of little cushions. Each the same uniform white block, piled up in neat stacks all around him. Beneath the vast sapphire dome, the strange pollen stretched as far as the eye could see. He hesitated. Not pollen.

'Good Matrona the Elect—!' Zeno exclaimed. With a crash of stone, a leg flashed into view above. Not a moment too soon, he lunged aside, as a man tumbled out of the shaft and landed where he had been sitting.

Maurice lay there in a daze, his crumpled blue cap beside him. Zeno shook him briskly by the shoulders, calling his name. Maurice looked up at him. For a few seconds he simply moved his lips, but no sound came out. Then he noticed the dome. He sat up with a start. As his eyes took in the white parcels all around, his mouth fell open in tacit wonder. A word formed on his lips.

'Nectar!' Zeno said, saving him the trouble.

Chapter 18

Agnes

Agnes was running through a great forest. Ahead, the foliage was growing denser, the path between the trees ever narrower. Night was hard on her heels, billowing like smoke from beneath the black canopy of fir. Eyes opened in the dark, baleful little fires no one had lit. They were watching her, but she kept running. She had to get out of the wood.

The fires caught in the dry fern. Soon the forest was burning, as trunks went up in flame on all sides. Smoke filled the wood. It had nowhere to escape. It was filling her lungs. She began to choke. A giant burning log fell across her path. There was no way out.

A woman was calling to her. Somewhere a child was crying. Its mother beckoned to her from the trees, holding her young son's hand. They knew another way out. She ran desperately towards them. As she drew closer, she saw that the woman was not Carpathian, but had the dark skin of a Numidian. The kindly woman was waving at her. She wanted to save her.

Just as Agnes reached for her hand, a huge flaming branch crashed on top of the woman and child. She cried out in horror as they disappeared beneath it. She searched frantically amid the burning ruin, but it was no use. All had dissolved into a single conflagration.

Through the burning pines, another Numidian face appeared. It was a man's face, rent with pain and fury. He stared at the inferno with abject terror. At last his eyes came to rest upon her, and they were filled with an unimaginable sorrow. Then they blurred into those of Strabon as his boat was blown from under him. What had she done?

Agnes opened her mouth to scream, but choked instead. Turning onto her side, she retched into the mud. Pitch filled her nostrils. Her body ached, and her clothes were damp. She could still hear the burning forest, but the earth was moist beneath her. She tried to rise, but her hand slipped in the mud and she fell back with a thud.

She opened her eyes. It was still nighttime, but the canopy was gone. In its place was an enormous black cloud obscuring the sky. She coughed violently and touched her side. Pain shot through her leg. She flailed around in the mud, reaching for her rifle. It wasn't there.

She panicked, sitting up and looking around. Why did she need her rifle in the forest? It was many centuries since the last wolves had been hunted out of Carpatia. There were only harmless fowl today. She pictured a frightened hare, then a human face, the face of a soldier. Strabon's face.

'*Cave!*' her legate said, warning her of danger. It all came back in a flash. The temple. Thebes. The battle. Her women and men. Strabon. All were gone. Her uniform was torn and bloodied. She touched her singed hair. Her temples were wet with blood.

She tried to think. The boats. The river. The explosion. She was alive. How was she alive? She cast about in the half-light. Waves lapped somewhere below. She was lying on a riverbank, beneath the papyri. There were voices.

'*Cave,*' Marcus repeated more insistently inside her head. Light was rapidly illuminating the dawn sky over the far bank. It had to be nearly four post-nocturn.

The voices grew louder. They were men's voices. She touched her neck. Miraculously, her rosary was still there. Silently, she prayed to the Virgin for her salvation. The pain subsided. Her mind stirred. The enemy. Her camp. They had been attacked. Her heart filled with anger. How had the Osmans gotten across the river? It must all have been a trap, but how, and why? There was no time to think now. She had to get away from the river. To get away somewhere, anywhere, out of danger.

Words drifted down from above. She rolled over, trying to make as little noise as she could. Slowly, she dragged her body up the bank. It was hard going. Her limbs ached and the plants kept grazing her skin on the patches where her uniform had torn. Eventually, she managed to crawl to the verge of the papyri.

She lay still, straining her ears. Above the low crackle of the fire were other sounds. Rubber soles scuffing against the desert sand. Raucous laughter, and several deep voices. One stood out, more authoritative than the rest. Its words were muffled, but they sounded Greek. She tried to get a better view, but fragments of ash kept getting in her eyes. She rubbed them clear.

Gradually the forms of the camp emerged between the reeds. She gasped. Of the fifty tents on the plain the previous morning, not a single one remained. In their place was a gigantic smouldering mass of burning plastic and metal. Everywhere burnt-out trucks and overturned vehicles lay about, some of their electrics still on fire. Titanic billows of black smoke rose from the plain, spreading like plague blotches across the bloody morning sky. The screaming stone patriarchs reared their evil heads above, surveying the ruin of her camp. Not a single one of her soldiers was to be seen. They had been replaced by a swarming hive of bandits. The black ants couldn't have been fewer than a hundred, at least enough to match her entire century.

A little way upstream was a fire where her lookout post had been. To her good fortune, she had washed ashore to the north, downstream from the main force of the enemy. Still, she was right under the nose of a small contingent of bandits stationed a few passus ahead, some kind of scouts posted at the edge of the camp. They couldn't have been more than three or four at most, and were milling about a small green tent, laughing loudly at some jest. All were Nubians, and wore the same black fatigues.

It was one of her own tents. They had surely stolen it when they raided the camp. What had happened to its occupants? She flushed with anger, reaching for her rifle, but there was nothing on her back. Just her torn uniform, and the frayed red star on her epaulettes. She slammed her fist into the mud.

She kissed her rosary, trying to calm herself. If the Mother had kept her alive, it had been for a reason. Even if she didn't yet know what that reason was. As the beads ran through her fingers, she prayed to Our Lady of Battlement for the gnosis of her comrades' souls. For Strabon's soul. A tear ran down her bloodstained cheek, but she wiped it away.

She couldn't stay here long before they would find her, and there was no doubt in her mind what that would mean. Yet there was no hope of escape downriver. She hadn't the strength to swim, and even if she could get hold of a catamaran somewhere, it wouldn't be long before she was sighted by the enemy's sentinels. How could she hope to escape?

Her mind expanded like a floodplain, irrigated by the rushing tide of her thoughts. The enemy must have had landing craft to have come upriver like that and surprised the camp. Where had they got them from, though? There was no way they could have crossed from the other bank unnoticed, right under the eyes of her century. It defied belief. And where had the rest of the legion been? Where in Gehenna were they now?

She caught herself. She was losing focus. The only thing that mattered right now was getting away. She must hold firm, and time and patience would reveal all. That's what Marcus would have told her. The spectre of the tall man speaking her native tongue rose before her. He would surely come after her as soon as he realised her body was missing. Besides, if she was the only survivor, shameful as that was, it was still her duty to get back to the legion and warn them of the impending danger. To do that, she had to survive, and she had only herself to rely on now.

With a shuffling of jackboots, two of the bandits walked away from the tent towards the river. She lay among the papyri, keeping her body as still as she could. Her heart thumped, and she scarcely dared to breathe. For an interminable moment, everything was quiet. Agnes readied herself.

Suddenly, there was a deafening roar nearby. Agnes nearly leapt up in fright. A strong, unfamiliar smell filled her nostrils. The vehicle could not have been more than a couple of passus away. Rubber skidded in the dust and a cloud went up as it accelerated away. It was all she could to stifle her coughing.

It had to have been a Caliphate truck, like the ones on the far bank. There hadn't been any oil-powered ones in the empire for centuries. So the bandits must have stolen them south of the buffer, somewhere in the Caliphate's Aethiopic provinces. How had they gotten them across the river? Her century wouldn't have missed that. They had to have surprised them by coming upriver on landing craft. Still, what kind of hovercraft were large enough to carry old vehicles like that, yet light enough to negotiate the rapids? The Caliphate didn't have that kind of techne.

The voices were fewer now. Between the reeds, the desert sun silhouetted two figures against the mountain ridge. One of the men looked round, a rifle slung on his shoulder. Agnes ducked beneath the papyri, but he only yawned. Pulling open the tent canvas, he disappeared inside. The other lounged in a chair outside, his gun across his lap. The bandit was facing downriver, away from her. Nothing stirred inside the tent.

This was her chance. Perhaps her only chance. He was only a stone's throw away. She just had to cover the ground without being seen. If she could dispense with them, she'd have a fighting chance at escape. She looked down at her empty hands. She had no gun, but even if she'd had one she couldn't have used it. The bandit's long limbs slouched ever lower in his chair. It was now or never. She kissed her rosary, praying the Mother grant her strength. She raised herself into a crouching position.

The next few seconds flew by like a feverish dream. She crashed out of the reeds, hurtling towards the tent like a hare. Sand and sky flashed before her eyes. The Nubian started, but she was already on him, pouncing like a harpy. His bald head turned, but her hands were already around his neck. The whites of his eyes fired and his hand moved to his gun, but he was too slow. She gripped his head and, throwing her full weight behind her, wrenched it back. There was a loud crack and his body fell back with a thud.

Her heart thumped as adrenaline coursed through her veins. There was stirring in the tent. She yanked the gun out of the dying man's twitching fingers. In two strides, she reached the tent, spinning the rifle about in her hands. The other bandit stepped out, looking around in confusion. With one swing of her arms, Agnes brought the rifle butt down on his head. There was another crack, and his lifeless corpse crumpled back onto the tent. Blood spattered the canvas as he fell, staining the orange sand.

She hid behind the tent, but all around was silent. Horror nearly overtook her at the sight of her victim's crushed skull. She wrenched the canvas shut. She examined the gory rifle in her bloodstained hands. Surprise displaced her horror. Its barrel had a laser sight. It was of imperial issue. She remembered the enemy's laser-guided weapons. Her terror as the red lights danced across her troops' uniforms. How they fell like no more than a row of paper soldiers.

She looked down at the dead bandit lying in the sand. His bandana still covered his face. She grabbed it and wrapped it over her head, concealing her fair hair, then dragged the black khakis off his body. They were heavy and made for a man. She was tall, though, and as she pulled them over the tattered remnants of her uniform, found they fitted well. They were hot. The stench of sweat was almost more than she could bear, but at least she would no longer stand out. There was now even a remote chance she might pass through the camp unnoticed.

She hauled the corpses inside the tent. There wasn't much inside, just a few sachets of dried camp food and some bottles. In the corner was a small cache of weapons, many evidently stolen from the camp. She rummaged through it, tossing aside a few low-grade Caliphate pistols. At the bottom were a rifle, some ammunition, and a hunting knife of imperial make. She stowed them inside her fatigues and slung the rifle over her shoulder.

She crept back outside, keeping as low as she could. There was still no one about, just the burning camp in the distance. She kicked sand over the bloodstains, pulled the canvas closed, and stood the plastic chair upright. Shielding her eyes, she squinted at the mountain ridge, then examined her bare wrist. It had to be at least a verst away. If she could just get there, she could hide out until the legion came.

There was no way she could skirt the camp unnoticed. There was only one way, and that was through.

Chapter 19

Vadim

The Hetmannian woman did not wait, but seized Vadim's hand. She ran down the ulitsa, pulling him along with her. Vadim trotted behind, only half-aware of what he was doing and mesmerised by the long strides of her supple legs. Her body seemed to gyrate in time with the dancing lights of the taverna fronts.

'I know a great place, *paidi kalo*,' she said. 'I'm cold. Let's go there and you can buy me a drink. What do you say?' Vadim nodded. Her shimmering chiton and the iridescent sparkle of her skirt blurred with the neon of the holographic lights, which were growing ever brighter as they headed further downtown into Kremlovska.

A few drunks gawked at them as they passed, but nobody said anything. Apparently, the sight of a sacerdote with a woman was not as rare as he would have imagined. The thought amused him. He pictured his father shrivelled up on his cold throne, and laughed. Catching up his laughter, the girl flashed her dark Zaporizhzhian eyes at him like a shooting star, and put her arm around his shoulder.

She pulled him abruptly into a doorway. The lights of the ulitsa were snuffed out like candles as they entered an unlit vestibule. The air was dank and smelled of alcohol. Without warning, the woman pressed Vadim up against the wall and kissed him full on the mouth. It was a long, hungry kiss, unlike anything he had ever experienced before. He was overpowered by a sweet stench of perfume mingled with sweat, as she wrapped her bare arms around his neck. He twitched as her delicate knee rose up the inside of his thigh. Ganna passed fleetingly before his eyes. He wondered whether he oughtn't to feel guilty, but there was nothing.

Just as unexpectedly, she disengaged. Giggling, she touched him playfully on his chest and, turning away, pulled him down the hallway. As Vadim's eyes adjusted, a velvet curtain emerged from the darkness, from behind which came the strains of loud music. A shadow loomed beside it, then took the form of a man in a long overcoat. The black titan drew the curtain aside slightly, and the hallway flooded with a purpureal neon light. The doorman's toothless grin expressed a mixture of puzzled condescension and amusement. He was on the point of stopping them, but the woman nodded to him with an air of authority and put her arm around Vadim. Without protest, the bouncer pulled the curtain wide, and they stepped through.

After the dim vestibule, the glare was blinding. A Novgorovian song blared out to the pounding accompaniment of a Crimean kithar. At the far end of the salon, a man stood on a stage, clasping a sonic amplifier. The kitharists sat on stools beside him, tapping their feet to the music. The walls and ceiling were covered in the same velvet as the curtain. Its exact colour was impossible to make out in the iridescence of the holographic lightshow that filled the room, but seemed to be a heavy burgundy.

In all corners of the salon, naked women were dancing on little platforms. Men sat around them, holding drinks as they ogled them. As their serpentine bodies writhed to the rhythm, holographic lights in shades of violet and sapphire played around them like rain in the sunshine. Glancing off their youthful bodies, the lights arrayed them in an ever-changing multiplicity of fantastical translucent outfits, as they read and projected the desires of the spectators. One moment the

women donned the red-and-gold wings of a firebird, while the next
they rose Aphrodisian from the sea foam.

Despite the splendour of its ornamentation, the lightshow scarcely
concealed the dancers' bodies at all. Entranced by their rippling thighs,
Vadim stood stultified in wide-eyed amazement. He had never seen
anything like it. Noticing this, his companion gave a high-pitched
laugh. Slapping him on the chest again, she drew him by the arm into
a corner of the salon. There she pushed him into a booth, whose seats
were upholstered in the same suffocating, cheap-looking velvet.

A waiter in a maroon doublet and hose appeared and, without
asking, set two kalichs before them. The woman's eyes sparkled
greedily as she unceremoniously took a swig from hers. Vadim
examined his glass, wondering what it was. The clear blue liquid
shimmered with a ghostly white light.

'So, priest-boy,' she began flirtatiously, running her hand through
his hair, 'how does someone like you end up here? Don't pretend, I
know you're a posh boy, you aren't going to fool me.' She knocked
her knees against him playfully. Vadim looked at her with alarm.

'Hey, *muzhik*, no sweat,' she said with a reassuring smile. 'I don't
know who you are, and I don't need to. You can be whoever you want
to be with me tonight. And I, my holy boy, can be whoever you want
me to be. Only, be a good boy and drink your nectar, won't you?' She
fixed him lasciviously with her gorgon eyes, raising his drink to his lips.
Clawing at his nape, she ran her other hand up his thigh beneath the
table.

Vadim gazed back at her, obediently sipping the sickly-sweet liquor.
He was unable to tear himself away. She nuzzled his neck, and the
heady scent of her perfume flooded his nostrils. His head felt strangely
light. The dancers, the singer and the burgundy of the decor all
blurred into the background. As if they were all just part of one hazy
neon tapestry, whose only vanishing point was this mysterious young
woman. Immemory. The word from the Gospel of Truth rose up

unexpectedly. It felt good. He wanted it. To live, unlike his father. Unlike some stupid priest. He seized her waist with both hands.

The woman grinned with pleasure and sidled onto his lap, but then something strange flickered in her dark eyes. Her gaze left him and moved above his head. Like ice falling from a glacier, her face dropped, and her eyes grew wide with fear. Her smile died. The violet play of the hololights dimmed as two large shadows fell across the booth. Two men stood over them, leering down at the woman.

'Hey, get out of here, will you?' she said, trying to sound confident, but still looking terrified. Her words had no effect. Instead, the foremost of the men broke into a broad grin. Vadim recoiled in disgust. The man, who was at least as tall as he was, had barely any teeth, and those he had were the flaxen of rotting straw. Temporarily illuminated by the magenta light, his threadbare leather jerkin seemed vaguely reminiscent of a tagmatic or legionary uniform.

'*Slyshish*? Hear that?' he addressed the other in Novgorovian. 'Our little sparrow's found herself a new chick! Let's see, what do we have here?' Uninvited, the man slid himself into the booth beside the woman. The other propped himself drunkenly on the table, blocking the way out. His seated confederate leaned across towards Vadim. The stench of stale liquor wafted to his nostrils, and he withdrew involuntarily.

'Don't be afraid,' he slurred. 'No need to take fright, my chick. Just seeing what our sparrow has dug up this time. Oh! Oh my, what do we have here? A little priest-boy!' His companion guffawed.

Vadim glared at the thug's flushed cheeks and stupid toothless grin. His head swam. In the play of the hololights, the man's bald head seemed to grow long ears. His eyebrows thickened, and a scraggly caprine beard appeared beneath his chin. Belatedly realising that the man was pawing at the white fabric of his chlamys, Vadim struck his hand away.

'Whoa, priest-boy,' the man said in mock alarm. '*Davay!* The chert has a temper, and might get himself in a scuffle if he doesn't watch out. Well, let's see what the little devil is made of.' He grabbed the woman by the scruff of the neck. Rising to his feet, he wrenched her out of the booth and threw her onto the dancefloor. The woman tried to scramble to her feet, but the other held her down. Vadim leapt to his feet and made to launch himself at the thug, but everything was hazy, and he felt strangely unsteady. To his surprise, he staggered.

'Not so fast, my little chick,' the thug said, smiling sardonically as he gave Vadim a shove. Losing his balance, he fell back into the booth. Collapsing beneath the table, he watched helplessly as, with a single swipe off his hand, the thug's companion ripped the flimsy chiton off the girl's chest, before yanking off her skirt. Completely naked, she tried to curl up into a ball, but the men pulled her legs apart.

'*Davay!*' the toothless thug said. 'We'll teach our sparrow not to go flying off with pretty priest-boys.' Vadim tried to crawl out from under the table, but the men grabbed him and threw him down beside the girl, who was sobbing into her hands.

'Seems our priest-boy hasn't had enough instruction in the church-house and would like some more?' the thug said, but then hesitated. By now, some of the other punters were watching. Their drugged eyes observed the scene with disinterest, reluctantly distracted from the dancing nudes.

'But house rules, eh?' he added, with a glance at Vadim's effervescent kalich. 'My house, so my rules. I'm a fair man. The boy hasn't paid for his drink. Perhaps he might like to pay up, and be on his way? What shall we settle on, say a hundred solidi? I'd say that's a fair price for a holy boy, wouldn't you?'

It was an extortionate price.

'I don't...' Vadim began, but tripped on his words. They came uneasily, as if from far away. The man grinned at his comrade, nodding meaningfully at Vadim's kalich. Without warning, he kicked him in the stomach. Vadim bent double, yet somehow the pain, too, was far away. He rolled onto his back, glaring up at the thug defiantly.

'I don't carry money,' he finally managed to say. His assailant cackled uproariously, as the other thug descended into drunken hysterics. Meanwhile the girl, who had uncovered her face, was not laughing. Instead, her tearstained eyes beheld Vadim with wonder.

'Priest-boy doesn't carry money!' the thug said, waving his palm at the onlookers in disbelief. 'Doesn't carry money? Well, I never. Never heard of such a thing. But I'm afraid you don't get off that lightly, my little chick.' He kicked Vadim again and grabbed at the girl's legs. Twisting, Vadim tried to kick back at him but, enfeebled, only managed to tap his knee. The man guffawed mercilessly.

'Not had enough of a lesson, have you, holy boy?' he said as he kicked him a third time. 'Well, if you don't carry money, I guess you can pay in kind.' Vadim tried to protect himself, but it was no use. The other held him still as the man pummelled him in the chest and face. He tasted blood.

'Well, well, well, *khoroshiy*, what do we have here?' the thug's delighted voice came from afar as the blows ceased. The man was inspecting Vadim's right hand, a toothless grin spreading across his face. His eyes sparkled with a new lustre as he grabbed at Vadim's hand, tugging at his finger.

'Matrona be Blessed!' he said. 'A ring. And solid silver, if I'm not mistaken. Never seen the like.' His eyes glowed with delight, as his chert's ears and satyric beard lengthened in the hololights. His companion leaned over to get a better look.

'Doesn't carry money, well that's quite alright, *khoroshiy*,' he muttered to himself. 'This will do nicely. But why, *davay*, what's this, an eagle? A silver eagle. A silver eagle with... with... two heads...' His voice died in his throat as all the colour ran out of his face. The chert evaporated. He looked down at Vadim, horrorstruck. He fell to his knees, his head bowed.

'Why, what in Gehenna's got into you?' his companion said, laughing, but at that moment there was a rush of cold air. On the far side of the salon, the velvet curtain had been thrust back. An old man in a red-and-gold doublet was standing in its shadow, pointing in their direction. A hololight flickered on his beard. It was Dnilo.

'What in the deceiver's name...?' the drunk exclaimed, as four masked shadows appeared behind Dnilo. One of them raised a dark barrel, and the air rent with cracks. The thug looked as if he were dancing ecstatically, then blood poured from his mouth. He collapsed to the floor. The girl screamed.

'On the floor, all of you, you scum!' the tagmata said as they fanned out across the room with rifles raised. The music died. The naked girls dived off their podia. The singer dropped his amplifier and hid behind the stage curtains. Stools went flying as the tagmata kicked them out from under any punters who were too drunk or drugged to know what was happening. Soon all lay prostrate with their hands flat on the dancefloor. Only the toothless thug still knelt, abasing himself. Meanwhile the hololights continued vainly decorating the empty space with opalescent feathers and seashells.

'*Moy gospodin*, my lord, mercy, mercy! *Ya ne znal,* I, I didn't know, I didn't...' the thug stammered like a terrified child, speaking a mixture of Novgorovian and broken Greek, as a gargantuan bat appeared behind him. The tagma lifted the man bodily from the ground by the neck, as easily as if he had indeed been a child. He squealed in fear and alarm as the masked soldier thrust him against a wall. Dnilo rushed to Vadim's side, paying no attention to the squealing man. Another tagma knelt down, examining Vadim's bloodied face.

'*Moy prints*!' Dnilo cried in alarm. 'Can you hear me? Say something! Good Mother, how on earth...? How glad I am I followed you.'

Vadim waved him away, sitting up with difficulty and spitting blood. 'It's nothing, old man, just a few scratches—' he heard himself say, but his voice was drowned out by the increasingly desperate gasps of the thug, whose cheeks were now turning purple. The spectacle of the expiring thug, kicking fruitlessly in the dim lilac of the hololights, was strangely fascinating. The image mingled with that of a bleeding sceptre as, like a bear stirring in the undergrowth, something awoke inside.

'Highness,' the tagma addressed Vadim, 'permission to dispose of this scum, *Vashe Vysochestvo?*'

Vadim observed the pathetic thug, so recently his tormentor. His eyes might for all the world have been those of an innocent child. Nor were they the only ones pleading with him, for the Zaporizhzhian girl, her bare torso striated with lilac on the dancefloor, was watching him too. She glanced sorrowfully at the thug then, for some reason, burst into tears. In an instant, Vadim understood. It was a trick. It had all been a dirty trick.

From behind his mask, the tagma watched him intently, loyally. The soldier awaited only his word to decide the brute's fate, as his titanic fist closed like a vice, gradually asphyxiating his enemy. As Vadim looked back at him, the tagmata multiplied, no longer just a handful but ten thousand, all standing in a field of wheat. The bloodied corpse on the cart stood up, and all knelt before him.

'Please, my lord, mercy!' the girl said. 'In the name of the Mother, please spare him.' Tears streamed down her face, smudging the henna of her eyelashes. She looked risible, like some baba yaga stripped of her magic guise of youth. His mouth creased into a grin.

'*Ultimam manum,*' Vadim said, as if he were issuing a military command. The soldier clenched his fist around the thug's throat, then smashed his head into the wall. His lifeless body crumpled to the floor like a black antheap. The woman screamed.

'And this one, strategos?' the tagma asked, unwittingly addressing Vadim as his thematic commander as he pointed at the girl. Vadim smiled at the compliment. The girl's tears dried up as she looked from the soldier to him in abject terror.

'Take her,' Vadim commanded as the tagma stretched out his arm and helped him onto his feet. 'I think we can find a suitable place in the palace castra for her, can't we?' A cruel smile spread across his face.

'*Certe*, strategos,' the tagma replied affirmatively, his eyes smiling back at Vadim from behind his mask. The soldier swept up the girl and carried her weeping from the salon.

'*Moy gospodin*, if I may?' Dnilo asked, as the other tagma doused the scratches on Vadim's face. The old man stared at him intently, evidently trying not to look at the festering antheap, which Vadim was still half-smiling at.

'Now is not the right time, but it is the reason I followed you. I thought you should know, Prince Vadim,' the old retainer addressed Vadim, as he never did, by his first name, a stray ray of violet illuminating his face. Dnilo's resolve seemed to break, and he peered furtively at the thug's corpse. He blanched and swallowed hard.

'It's your father, *moy prints*,' he said at last, straightening up. 'His Royal Highness, Prince Theadoric Eugenianus, is dying'.

The smile deserted Vadim's face.

Chapter 20

Anastasia

Anastasia lay despondently on her bed. Try as she may, she couldn't get up.

It was something she'd always struggled with. She'd always been slothful. She didn't deny that, but it was something else this time. Something that wasn't getting any better.

At the end of the four-poster bed, Bobina, her pet dog, was curled up on the floor beneath the tapestry of the Dea Nutrix. Feeling her gaze upon her, the wolfhound sat up, sticking out her tongue excitedly.

'*Ne*, Bobina, not now,' she mumbled as the dog jumped onto the bed uninvited. Shooing her away, Anastasia rolled listlessly onto her other side, pulling the sheets up to her neck. Bobina slumped down beside her disappointedly, her head on her paws.

Anastasia's pale green eyes lingered sadly on the windowpane. Outside, beyond the palace balustrade, a little hill rose in the mist of the Moravian morning. From its peak, the chapel's funereal white tower jutted like an ancient stele, silhouetted by the dawn. The sight made her feel lonely.

Anastasia stroked Bobina's head absentmindedly. The dog raised its snout expectantly. As she ran her fingers through its thick black hair, dark locks straying across a pale brow appeared before her. She shoved the dog away. Taking her cue at last, the hound leapt off the bed, sullenly resuming her habitual abode beneath the tapestry.

She could barely remember how they'd got back yesterday. It was as if her mind, like the chapel on the hill, had been embalmed in mist ever since. All she could remember was that when their lightcraft took off from Castra Kremlovska, the weight of her love felt so great that it would drag her back down to the palace, to the white church in the cold stone courtyard. To its mirthless portals, through which he'd disappeared without a single word, nor even a kind look.

The sight of the verdant plains below, the nebulous majesty of the Carpatia, even the dear forests and rivers of her homeland, had all left her cold as they sped by. Her father had noticed, of course. He always did and, just as surely, her mother did not. Princess Amalasuntha was only in a rage at her nephew for his stupidity the whole way back. She didn't care what Anastasia felt.

She faced into her pillow. A tear ran down her cheek as she thought of her cousin. She didn't care whether he was a priest or not. She even understood why he didn't want to be. After all, in truth it was only because of her mother that she had been invested as a Vestal. It was true that she had wanted to serve the Virgin, but it was also the reason she had been sent to that dreadful faraway land the year before.

Her family had brought her back from Britannia straightaway. There was no way her father was going to let her stay after the incident with the heretic she had tried to save half a year earlier. She had tried so hard not to think about it, but his terrible face still haunted her dreams every night. His cruel words about the Virgin, and the awful pronouncement she had had to make herself, were ever with her. She wasn't sure whether the sentence of the Supreme Measure had been carried out yet. It didn't bear thinking about. Taking the orders had been her choice, as her mother was so fond of reminding her. Yet, for one of her position, had it really been? After Caledon, she wouldn't wish these vows on anyone, least of all those she loved most dearly.

She thought of her cousin's dear face. Of his handsome Greek eyes, burning with anger as he beheld her the day before. Why did he hate her so? It was terrible. She pulled the cover over her head and shut her eyes. She knew she must resist. That the thought was nefarious. That a Vestal's body and mind were impolluble. She tried to drive his image from her mind, but it was no use. Instead he stood before her again, his diaphanous chlamys clinging to his manly shoulders beneath his alabaster neck. Unable to help herself, she imagined what it would be like to have him beside her in her bed.

As she lay beneath the sheets, she could feel the heat of her breath on her face. She imagined it was his breath, rather than her own. That it was his limbs beneath the silk, rather than her own. Her pulse thickened, and she slipped her hand between her thighs. It was not her hand, but his. His ire had relented, and despite his fire he was touching her gently, his only love. Not roughly, in the way he handled his slave girls, but softly, for his princess. His strong hands brushed her nipples as he kissed her neck. Her fingertips grew moist.

He was descending her body, his sacred temple. She gave him a thousand kisses, another hundred, then a thousand more, and soon she no longer cared what anyone thought. His hair tickled her stomach as he sank into the sweet embrace of her thighs. Her fingers cloyed to one another between her legs as his smooth boyish cheeks rubbed against them.

When he had brought her to her joy, he took her. Not coarsely, like his palace whores, but like a prince with a princess. His soft lips were on her nape as she lay upon her side. Again and again, he drove her to bliss. Her legs quaked uncontrollably, clamping about her soaking hand. With her other, she squeezed her pillow, suppressing a muffled cry of pleasure.

Anastasia opened her eyes. Her joy receded. The dour oak of the ancient bed posts loured down at her. The wan grey of the early morning hung about them like a conclave of ghosts, as if the mist had floated down the hillside, through her window and into her room. As if it were conspiring with her ancestors, the castle ghosts, to wrap her in its shroud, embalm her, and bury her in her guilt and longing once and for all.

In the ruffled folds of the damp sheet beside her was a great cavity, as if someone had lain there. He was not there though, and never had been. Nor could he have been, even if he had wanted her. For profaning a Vestal's body was sacrilege. An unvenial crime that would mean death for them both. A terrible weight was sinking upon her, as if the mist were growing heavier.

Through the window, the hilltop was beginning to clear as the sun at last burnt through. She was overcome by a desperate desire to be up there, to rise above the grey oppression. With a sudden impulse, she leapt from the bed, swinging her delicate limbs to the floor. Overjoyed, Bobina ran to the door and sat there wagging her tail, watching Anastasia impatiently as she dressed.

A few minutes later, she strode out the castle gate, Bobina running happily before her. Grabbing the nearest thing that came to hand, she had dressed in her regnal riding doublet, dark red and emblazoned with a white lion with a golden crown. Her white sleeves and hose shone in the bright May morning. Her loose blond hair, which in her haste she had not even arranged, rippled behind her like sheaves of wheat in a summer breeze. Yet a winter clouded the angelic features of her face, which were steadfastly downcast.

The castle servants drew back reverently as she passed, inclining their heads or curtseying. Anastasia nodded glumly to one or two of them without stopping. Furtively eyeing her with wonder and seeing her riding gear, one of the stable boys stepped forward, but the castle guards shoved him back. Anastasia descended the flight of cobbled white stones leading to Castel Nicolaeum's forum. Two of the palace tagmata fell in behind her, touching their red berets as they gripped the electro-batons which hung at their sides, pulsing with a rosy light.

The tagmata stepped up beside her as she crossed the forum, looking around suspiciously at the bowed heads of the passers-by. Her father was always so fussy about her going out alone when she was at their summer palace. She hastened on to the far side of the little square, admiring the pretty medieval buildings as she went. She had always liked the handsome shopfronts, their upper stories sgraffitoed with scenes from the lives of the gnostic saints. Then the plain Doric lines of the Marian column, crowned by a star. The whole of Castel Nicolaeum was little more than an extension of the castle. Most of the inhabitants were its servants and slaves, with barely a pleb among them. There were always one or two hostile glances, of course, but growing up as a royal she had become accustomed to that. Her father could sometimes be so terribly overprotective.

Already knowing where they were going, Bobina raced ahead down an alleyway that led to the hillside. Anastasia ran after, her feet skimming across the cobbles. Cutting a slightly ridiculous figure, the tagmata jogged behind, gripping their red berets and batons. At the end of the alley, the buildings gave way and the little green hill rose before her. Bobina was already ascending the winding path that led to its summit. Anastasia pursued. The path was rocky, overgrown by the beech and elm that grew densely on its verges, but like Bobina she was used to the way and climbed quickly. Twigs cracked and stones tumbled as the tagmata lost their footing trying to keep pace with her.

The foliage thickened. The damp air hung heavily from the branches of the trees. Despite the freshness of the May air, it felt oppressive. The grey dawn still clung to her, weighing her down. She had to rise above the mist, to emerge on the surface. To breathe freely again. She quickened her pace. The path took a sharp turn, and the tagmata disappeared behind her.

The first station of the Descension appeared, a painted marble in a chalkstone alcove beside the path. Anastasia kissed her rosary. The expressionless Mother was enthroned in an eclipsing moon, about to descend to earth. The receptacle's weathered pilasters were like heavy bed posters, the crumpled texture of their pale stone that of empty sheets. She quickly moved on and, turning another corner, spied Bobina up ahead. The dog had halted at the head of the path, her tongue hanging out impatiently as she awaited her mistress.

She scrambled past another station of the Descension. This one showed the dying Palaeologus at Justinia's feet. The pigmentation had long since faded from the patriarch's face. The prostrate marble stared up at her like some horrid shade, the emaciated lines of its aged countenance drawn in agony. Her uncle's sallow face rose unbeckoned before her, scowling at her love. She scrambled over another rock. The foliage cleared, ceding to open sky.

Bobina was barking joyously somewhere up ahead. The mossy crown of the hill rose before her, covered with violets like a quilt of tiny sapphire stars. Below, the castle rose above the red roofs of the town, the twin flags of the white lion and blue Marian star fluttering from its battlements. Behind was a vast green plain punctuated by lakes, and in the distance a line of hills. Beyond, no more than a hazy speck on the horizon, were the towers of Vindobona. She closed her eyes, greedily gulping the fresh morning air.

The tagmata were still lagging behind. She did not wait, but hurried on to the summit after Bobina. The cheerless facade of the chapel reared up before her, its sombre white steeple rising into the cloudless matinal sky. The sight was no more gladdening than the stations of the Descension had been, but perhaps up here, the Mother might hear her prayer. It was only one prayer, after all.

Entirely open to the elements, the chapel was always cold. Today it smelt strangely stale, but a fresh breeze soon blew in through the Doric portals, dissipating the dankness and drowning out Bobina's barking outside. The diminutive nave was bare, save for a simple stone altar at its far end. On the wall behind was a marble engraving of the last station of the Descension, the apotheasis of Justinia. The Virgin, now ascended back to heaven, was clothing the dying Justinia in the holy mandylion as she enfolded her in an eclipsing moon.

Anastasia approached the altar. She kissed her rosary, saying the usual prayer for the gnosis of the holy maiden's soul and its gathering to the Mother. She knelt on the steps and closed her eyes. The Mother, of course, saw all. She saw right into her soul. She knew her secret shame already. She knew all the terrible depth of her longing. Yet still the words of her confession came only with difficulty. Was that not because, in truth, it was no confession at all? It was rather a supplication. A supplication for mercy.

'*O panymnite Miter!* O all-glorious Mother,' she began, as the circus of the winds rose to the chapel roof. 'May the Mother, the Virgin and Holy Spirit guide me in my despair.' She reached for the icon of Justinia, but the face of Our Lady of Casan appeared instead. He was there, standing before it. Before an altar just like this.

'*O Zoodouchos-Pege*, Lady of the Life-giving Spring, Holy Mother of the Moravians—' She broke off. There was a shuffling nearby. The stale smell filled her nostrils. Then a large hand clasped over her mouth from behind. She tried to scream. All that came forth was a muffled groan, which was immediately washed away in the wind like running water. She twisted, trying to break free, but the hands were too strong. Cold steel touched her neck.

'*Klid*, bitch!' a man's voice whispered in her ear in Bohemian. 'Quiet, or I'll do for you.'

Anastasia became still. Her heart was beating fast, and she could only just breathe through her nostrils. The stench of sweat and filth was sickening.

'So, *princezno*, what do we have here?' her invisible assailant addressed her, as he roughly fondled her breasts and buttocks. She nearly swooned. It was the first time a man had ever touched her. How could this be happening, before the very eyes of the Mother? Was she dreaming? The blade against her throat recalled her to reality. It wasn't a dream.

'If any woman desire to be first,' he rasped in her ear, 'the same shall be last of all, and servant of all.' He bent her against the altar, but a second later roared with pain. The knife clanged against the altar steps. Bobina was barking loudly as she tore at the man's calves, from which blood gushed forth. With a violent swing of his leg, he kicked the dog aside. Anastasia stamped hard on his shins and he staggered backwards.

'*Fena!*' he cursed. 'I'll teach you, you royal bitch!' He tumbled unsteadily towards her, his heavy brows contracted with rage. She tried to evade him, but he struck her across the face and she fell backwards. She cowered on the altar steps, surprised at the man's fair skin, red cheeks, and large green eyes seething with fury. He was local, and might even have been a castle retainer if his dirty rags hadn't betrayed him as a slave. There was no doubt that if he couldn't have her, he would finish her.

The slave grabbed the knife. Anastasia screamed, clinging desperately to the altar as she invoked the protection of the Mother. This seemed to amuse him, and he laughed cruelly. He lunged at her, but froze in mid-flight, dropping the blade. His face contorted and his eyeballs rolled, like those of the dying Palaeologus. As he fell to his knees, white gloves seized him by the shoulders. The tagmata struck him mercilessly as electric shocks ran through his entire body. Anastasia recoiled in horror as the whites of his eyes stared blindly back at her.

'Stop,' she said weakly, but the tagmata did not hear her. The slave writhed and groaned. One of the soldiers struck him violently on the back. Breathing heavily, he collapsed before the altar. Anastasia screamed again and began to cry.

'Stop,' she said through her tears, but still the soldiers did not hear. As they kicked the slave, his body was tossed this way and that as if it had been no more than a twig rolled by a child. He tried feebly to fend away the blows, but it was no use.

'Stop!' she shrieked, her voice rising to the chapel roof. The guards looked up in surprise, slowly lowering their batons. Covered in blood, the slave lay on the floor emitting a low groan. Bobina limped up to Anastasia's side, whining. She threw her arms around the dog, sobbing uncontrollably as she plunged her face into her thick black hair.

'Your Highness, are you hurt?' one of the tagmata asked, kneeling by her side. He solicitously inspected the blood on her lip as his glove examined the bruises beneath her doublet sleeves. It was the same taut white leather that had been administering such terrible pain but a moment before. She recoiled, knocking the hand away. The blade chafed her palm. She seized it up, and flew out of the chapel.

'My lady!' the soldier said, but she did not heed him. She ran back down the path as fast as she could, Bobina at her heels. Her fair hair hung loose to her shoulders, rippling like a wreath of snakes. By now the mist had yielded to a beautiful May morning, but she did not see it. Instead, the slave's face, burning with hatred and lust, was still before her. She gripped the knife tightly, as if it were an ivy staff rather than a blade. The cold steel cut into her hand. It appeared again, glistering against the stone of the altar as the slave prepared to strike her. Then the slave morphed into the Caledonian heretic, angrily assailing her. Finally, Cassian's glowering eyes dissolved into those of her love, staring at her with the same loathing. The same masculine fury. She cried out to the Virgin for mercy. What had she done to deserve such a cruel fate?

The dying Palaeologus flew by. His marble torso became that of the slave, twitching convulsively on the floor as the tagmata beat him nearly to death. Then his fearful face became that of the young tagma, terrified at his own failure to protect her. It was terrible. It was all so terrible. She wanted to shut herself away from the world. She dashed across the forum, ignoring the surprised onlookers. An unescorted

The youth smiled flirtatiously. He approached, towering head-and-shoulders over her. This one wasn't going to be so easy to get rid of. Still, another few minutes wouldn't harm anyone. She bent her knees. Her mouth closed around his manhood as she abandoned herself again. He did not last long this time.

'*Dea Nutrix!*' he blasphemed, groaning with pleasure as he called her his mother goddess. Hypatia awoke from her abandonment. Her mouth grew moist and saline as he spent himself within her. She was disgusted at herself. She felt old, like some ancient Graea. She shoved him away.

'Get out!' she said to the dumbfounded youth, hardly knowing what she was saying. 'Get out! Don't you ever—don't you ever dare come here again—you disgusting man!'

The youth stared at her in confusion, half-smiling as he tried to work out whether she was joking. When he realised she was in earnest, a look of abject terror entered his face. He grabbed his clothes and ran for the door.

Hypatia jumped as the door slammed. Wiping her mouth, she leant against her dressing table. She was shaking. She ran her trembling hand through her dark curls, matted with sweat. She raised her eyes to the mirror. A slender, still-attractive woman in her mid-forties looked back at her. Her olive skin glistened like the hale brown earth of the Peloponnesian hills without. *Carbonopsina.* Eyes like coal. She smiled. That was what her husband used to call her when they first met.

Her mood soured at the thought. The clouds moved across the Spartan hills, and the room darkened. As if a magic veil had been torn away, the woman changed. The ebony lustre of her eyes was no more, and the earthy sheen of her skin turned to mud. Her nipples darkened and slackened, and the skin hung off her thighs. Seizing up her shawl, she covered her body.

The sun reappeared over the valley, and the room illuminated. She shut her eyes, feeling the warmth on her eyelids. It was good, like the

royal was a rare sight, not least one carrying a knife, but she no longer cared. The guards hailed her as she approached the castle gate, but she shoved past them in silence.

Bounding up the stairs, within a minute she had reached her bedroom. Slamming the door behind her, she threw herself weeping onto her bed. She did not even bother to remove her disheveled doublet and frayed hose. She ought to remove all evidence of her defilement, but could not bring herself to do so.

Bobina lay down beside her, whining piteously. She nuzzled into her fur. The dog was warm. She was slowly submersing, sinking into a tepid spring. She shut her eyes.

Chapter 21

Hypatia

Her eyelids were warm when she awoke. Hypatia lay on her back and opened her eyes. Sunlight streamed through her bedroom window. Its rosy rays fell across the bed like fingers caressing her body.

Another May morning. They were always beautiful in Mystras. There was no place quite like it, the quiet university town nestled in the flower-strewn hills of the Morea, especially at this time of the year.

She propped herself on one elbow, smiling at the great torso beside her. The sheets had wrapped themselves about its Adonine form like the drapery of an ancient marble. The young man was breathing lightly. He was still asleep, but she was not.

She ran her hands through her black curls, sliding her limbs towards him. Brushing his face with her tresses, she kissed his cheeks, neck and shoulders, peeling back the sheets like the skin of a ripe orange. The youth stirred, smiling in his sleep. She touched the firm muscles of his chest, kissing his ears, then ran her hand down his stomach towards his groin. A quiver ran through him. She moved beneath the sheet.

As she drew her head downwards, the hairs on his young chest stood on end, bristling against her cheeks. She kissed his stomach. He stirred. Rolling him onto his back, she prostrated herself on his torso. He gripped her head in his hands, kissing her fingers as his manhood swelled beneath her chest. Her moist lips encircled him,

and he slid into her gorge. He clutched at her hair, pressing her c[...] him. She surrendered herself to his sweet, youthful groans. She wa[...] his, entirely his. His slave, to do with as he pleased. Everyone else[...] without, far away.

She gasped for air as he lifted her, her body thrilling with pleas[...] as she landed upon him. Beads of sweat ran down her sun-kissed ba[...] as he thrust violently into her. She threw her head back, clawing at [...] chest and rocking uncontrollably. She moaned, then screamed. In h[...] strong arms, she was no longer old. His lust had rejuvenated her. Sh[...] was a maiden in her first bloom again, taken by her Endymion, woke[...] from his blessed sleep. He cried out as she furiously pounded him on[...] last time, then collapsed on top of him.

Hypatia lay there in silence, inhaling the salty scent of his skin[...] as his broad chest rose beneath her. At length she looked up at the[...] young man's face. She tried to remember which one it was this time[...] She could recall the first few glasses of the previous evening, but th[...] later night was a blur. Other than how they'd made love, just like th[...] morning.

She had picked him out from one of her dialogues, of course. Th[...] were always a few who stood out in each year. It was the old way. [...] best way. She was a Greek, after all. Pederasty was tradition.

She rose from the bed and walked over to the window, her[...] limbs glistening in the morning light. On the hillside belov[...] university buildings baked in the sunshine. Beyond were the vast[...] valley and the bright mountains of the Taygetos rising on the h[...]

'You should go,' she said. He watched her lazily, showing no[...] an imminent departure. That was problematic. It didn't do to[...] with a lover too often. Not that the act itself was frowned upo[...] only that one of her status had to protect her reputation.

'I mean it, *paidi mou*,' she said, putting her hands on h[...] hips. 'It's time for you to go.'

caress of some god. She was overcome by a desire to fly out her window, high above the pine hills of the Morea, high above the clouds. To embrace the sun itself. To lie prone between his hot lethaean thighs. To forget the world and herself. To burn away all sin. To be young again, and forever.

Hypatia opened her eyes, remembering herself. Such irreligious thoughts. What was happening to her? She touched her forehead. Was she going mad? She glanced at the clock on her bedside table. Half an hour until her dialogue. There was still time to visit the university chapel and be shriven.

She moved to her wardrobe, but was halted by the holographic portrait on her dressing table. A bald man in his forties with sharp Syrian features, dressed in a red and white uniform, smiled out at her as he stretched his arm around a younger image of herself. Her holographic counterpart wore a lissom black dress with a ruff neck. She was also beaming. The real Hypatia did not smile, but turned away, flattening the frame on the table.

Ten minutes later, she entered under the stone arch of a small chapel at the end of the university gardens. She had always been fond of the church of Saint Sophia of the Holy Wisdom. Out of the way of the main complex, it was all in the late pre-Descension style, its square bell tower elegantly adorned with slight Romanesque arches. The taciturn mountain rose behind, crowned by the patriarchs' fort and overhanging the university like an eagle's outspread wings. The chapel was probably the only truly quiet place in the entire university. Mainly because the tutees rarely, if ever, found their way down here.

As she awaited the nun beneath the main adze, she admired the yellow brick and red tiles of the arches over the plain Doric capitals. The imperial porphyry of the tesserae, set into the floor in concentric circles, was cool beneath her bare soles. Maybe what they said about the last patriarch being crowned there was true, and that it should be shunned as a cursed place. As a place of misfortune. But what was that to her? There was nowhere she felt the peace of the Mother more. A white and gold fresco in one of the apses showed Her, as Thea, in heaven above, and the Virgin as her gnostic Demiurge below, descending in a silver cloud. Between two angels on the arch above was the older, imperceptibly faint, outline of a seated man. She grimaced, quite sure none of her tutees would have noticed it.

A polite cough interrupted her reflections. The old abbess stood before her in her white dalmatic robe and hood, supporting her shrunken body on a wooden staff with a star-shaped pommel. She was already bent double, but no sooner had their eyes met than she inclined her back still further, attempting to courtesy. Hypatia watched her irritably. Such bowing and scraping had always annoyed her, but since she had married Marcus, and thereby acquired matrician rank, normal people had treated her differently. Why did religious folk always care so much about caste? Granted, a Vestal was different, but matrikios, pleb or slave, weren't all souls supposed to be equal in the eyes of the Mother?

'My dear dean, it is always such a pleasure to see you,' the abbess said with genuine warmth, gesturing to one of side apses. Hypatia followed her in silence as she hobbled towards the confessional. As she slid in, her sore buttocks chafed painfully against the hard mahogany, and she placed her hands beneath them.

'Good Mother, I have sinned,' she began as soon as the nun had drawn the curtain. 'I have joined with men, and that beyond the dispensation granted me by Our Lady. I have adulterated my lawful wedlock, and done so sinfully, even—unnaturally—'

The abbess raised her hand. Even she found it too revolting to listen to, and who could blame her?

'You know what you must do to expiate your sin, my child. The Mother forgives all who earnestly seek Her mercy. With open heart, therefore, supplicate Her for Her forgiveness, that She may remit your sin of *moicheia*, and commute it to moderated fornication,' she said, pointing to the rosary in Hypatia's hand.

'*O panymnite Miter*, all-glorious Mother,' Hypatia recited the familiar Greek prayer, 'I confess unto Thee my sins. Misled by the deceiver, and by the rootlessness of his eros, I have fallen. By the light of Thy Holy Trinity, lead me once more, I beseech Thee, unto Thy grace. Shrive me of the false vesture of the deceiver, and be his immemory undone.'

'Be shriven of thy sin, and go in peace,' the old woman said, closing her eyes as she touched the red star on her dalmatica. Hypatia did not wait, but stepped at once from the confessional. Her backside was numb and her mouth dry, with a still lingering taste of salt. Stooping in the porch, she hastily grabbed up her shoes and stole out into the sunshine.

Descending the sunbaked steps, she greedily inhaled the fresh spring air as its floral fragrance wafted up from the green ocean of the Spartan plain below. As usual, she felt better for being shriven. Not that it really meant anything. Not that she wouldn't do it all again. It was just that there was something cathartic about confessing oneself to the Mother, even if it had to be through the medium of those sexless old nuns of the Order of the Hagia Sophia. Or perhaps it was just being reminded that the Mother had made her the way she was. And if that was Her will, who was she, or anyone else, to gainsay it?

She ascended the garden path towards the fountain, admiring the busts of Mystras' alumnae lining its verges, their marbles shining in the bright Lacedaemonian morning. The university's bearded founder, Gemistos Plethon, Justinia's religious mentor and First Logothete, smiled down at her as he brandished a Platonic dialogue. Eve and the gnostic saints, Leo the Mathematician, and her own namesake, followed. The eagle fountain's twin heads were merrily drenching the blue-and-white bunting with which its ledges were still strewn after yesterday's feast of Our Lady of Battlement. Disheveled blue flags with white stars fluttered from the cypress branches. She squirmed as she recalled the beastly ravages of the night before, already catching the tutees' chatter as they gathered beneath the arcade, awaiting her dialogue. She closed her eyes, trying one last time to imbibe as much of the flower-scented morning as she could. Tomorrow was the last of May. Soon, spring's delicate beauty, like her own, would be downtrodden by the ruder summer.

When Hypatia opened her eyes, someone was walking towards her. A statuesque blonde about her own age was heading towards the church. To her surprise, Hypatia did not recognise her. Mystras was a small place. Outsiders were unusual, especially unexpected ones. As the woman passed, she smiled coyly and flashed her eyes at Hypatia. Dazzled by their azure sheen, Hypatia returned her smile, and something dropped in the pit of her stomach. Brushing back her hair, she admired the beautiful stranger as she disappeared down the path. Her white chiton and golden hair, demurely tied back with a red fillet, glowed candescent in the bright morning. Everything about her was radiant, as if she were possessed by Our Lady Herself. Hypatia blinked, wondering whether she were a figment of her imagination, but the woman was still there. She smiled back at Hypatia again, before vanishing behind the fountain's aquiline wings.

The tutees were growing louder. Hypatia sighed. *Ergasia*. Work. To each the work of Our Lady, whose work was unending. So she too must to work. She could see yesterday's boy skulking beneath the coppery stone of the colonnade. She groaned and walked on, the bright form of the mysterious woman still before her like the stainless glare of the sun.

CHAPTER 22

Marcus

Marcus sat at his desk with his head in his hands. The windows of his office rattled in the wind. Back in Caledon, there was no sign of yesterday's sun.

The migraine, at least, was gone. He still felt slightly faint, and his hand shook as he reached for his drink. He could hardly remember anything of the journey back north, other than that the starry skies over Anglia had ceded to slate as soon as they'd crossed the Adrianic Line. The rest was a blur, beyond Severa mopping his brow, his tribune guiding him down the stadium stairs, and the soporific warmth of the electric. During the heavy, fitful night which followed, Argyra's aquiline nose and Flavian's sardonic smile had greeted him at every turn.

It had been a complete, unmitigated disaster, and that after the debacle of the trial itself. At least a clean execution might have put an end to the matter. An inconvenient entry on his cursus file, no doubt, assured by Anastasia's family. Preventing his further advancement, for sure, but no worse than that. With a bit of luck, the episode might even have been forgotten after a few years, or passed off as a slip-up, one not wholly his fault.

This was different. What could possibly have gone wrong that hadn't? A heretic, an *alpha* heretic, vaunting in front of the whole proconsulate. The botched execution. Argyra obliged to break the lex. The Caledonian demes breaching the arena. Then, worst of all, his fainting so embarrassingly. And not just that, but doing so before all the other exarchs, legates, and logothetes. Before all of Britannia Maior, in short. Perhaps it would be better if he just disappeared. Yes, he had better crawl into some Caledonian hovel in the Highlands and never come out.

Then why, on top of it all, that lingering and misplaced sense of guilt? The lion. What had it all been about? The man had been a fanatic with pretensions of grandeur, that was all. He had deserved what he got. He glanced at the holoportrait of Hypatia on his desk. It was the one of her in her black dress, taken not long after their marriage. The more he looked at it, the more her smile seemed to conceal a frown. Had she been unhappy even then? He looked distractedly at the other picture beside it, that of his legionary command from Hispania. Agnes Radomira's face beamed out at him from the row of centurions. He hoped fortune was being kinder to her.

He raised his drink to his lips but, just as he was about to take a sip, the bell rang. Severa stepped in without waiting for a summons, as usual. She was less radiant today. There was a hint of ash in her cheeks and she, too, looked tired. There was something else, though. He stared at her in silence, swiping over the screen in his desk as he pretended to be busy with something.

'Your excellency, I'm, I'm sorry for the intrusion, but the proconsul...' she began, as Marcus bolted upright in alarm. 'Conference aula four. The proconsul requests your presence, ehm, immediately.'

He dashed into the corridor, quaestorial clerks leaping out of his way.

'Exarch, might I...?' a legionary attaché called urgently after him, but he simply marched past in silence. His mind was spinning, faster than the wheels of the racers in the stadium. And, as surely as one of their riders, he was about to be obliterated.

Perhaps there was a chance he'd just get the usual drubbing down. Surely Argyra wouldn't go all the way? Surely even she wouldn't do that. The untruth of the reassurance jangled discordantly in his head, like an untuned kithar. *Clementia* did not feature in Argyra's vocabulary and, besides, what reason had she to be merciful?

'*Tenebrae!*' he shouted at the walls as he stepped into the conference aula. The glass dimmed to a rich ochre. He was trembling. Was he even an exarch at all? Or just some ridiculous legionary cadet, facing his centurion for the first time?

It was no use. As he seated himself at a corner of the long table, he was still shaking. He felt sheepish. He cast dejectedly about the room, which was completely bare save for the usual faceless holographic etching of the empress. There was nowhere left to hide. He thought of Hypatia. This was all her fault, at the end of the day. Cassian could never have riled him as he had if not for her. She had cost him his peace of mind, and now his job. And where was she now?

He drummed his fingers nervously on the table as he looked blankly at its inset screen. It was a lifeless grey, displaying nothing but a white double-headed eagle and star, with the subscript '*S.P.Q.M*'. How long was she going to keep him waiting? He might have finished his drink.

All of a sudden, the screen pulsed with a pearly light. At the top were the illuminated words, '*Voxprocul – Propraetorium Eboracum*'. Marcus blanched and sat up, moving his unsteady hand to a box below, where '*accipite*' was written. The green letters shone blithely, as if entertaining the delusion that he had a choice. He swiped his hand over them.

There was a muted flash of blue light, and Argyra's statuesque figure appeared at the other end of the room. Just visible behind her were the neon outlines of two of her propraetorian bodyguards. Gone were her dress uniform and diadem of the day before, in favour of a dark gown and ruff-necked blouse. Marcus leapt to his feet. She glanced perfunctorily in his direction as her cyan shadow seated itself at the head of the table, immediately folding its hands before it without offering any greeting. The translucent bodyguards retreated to the wall, their expressionless visors surveying the room. Like slush sliding off a Caledonian rooftop, Marcus slumped crestfallen into his chair.

'*Exarche*,' Argyra began in Greek, not deigning to address Marcus by name, 'let's cut to the chase. Your performance lately has been substandard. No, I choose my words too leniently.' She still did not look at him. Marcus studied his clasped hands, hunching as much as humanly possible.

'From a gubernatorial perspective, your performance has been poor. No, shambolic,' the holovoice continued, resonating through the silent aula. Marcus opened his mouth, but Argyra raised her hand.

'And that is just the start of the matter,' she continued her tirade. 'From an ecclesiastical perspective, frankly, the events of the last Saturnal had already given me cause to doubt your kindness to Our Lady. An affront to a Vestal. A daughter of the Premyslid House, no less. A royal. I'm not going to rehash what I said at the time, exarch. Nor how your – your indiscretion – on that matter even reached the Sublime Port.'

Marcus opened his mouth again, but once more she raised her hand.

'Even so, that was before the events of yesterday. Remind me, exarch, of what I said to you after last year's episode?' Argyra asked. Only now the proconsul's neon shade looked up, fixing Marcus with her aquiline eyes. The bluish light of her ruff oscillated with her rising fury.

'I, I...' Marcus began, desperately trying to recall his boss' words at that last painful interview five months earlier. If only Severa was by his side. One of the propraetorians shifted behind Argyra's chair.

'No, I didn't think so,' she said, looking back at her folded hands. 'I'll confess for a moment I had thought that even your eminently masculine wits might have sufficed to recall my advice. But I see I was mistaken.' Marcus tried to shrink a little more.

'So, let me remind you, exarch,' Argyra continued. 'I said that even you could surely appreciate that there are only so many times I can intercede on your behalf, and now, you will – I am sure – appreciate the delicate position you have put me in. And all this, simply because you have failed to perform your most basic of exarchal duties, to keep order in your province!'

'But, propraetor, you must admit that Cassian Macleod was a delirious fanatic... I promise you, excellency, had I known the alpha would perform like that yesterday, I would have recommended – I mean – there hasn't been such a case in years, in years!' Marcus said, but immediately regretted it.

'Had you known?' the neon ghost exploded. 'Had you known! What on earth is that supposed to mean? Good Matrona the Elect, I always knew you were the doddering male, but not this dim-witted. Were you even awake during the religious inquisition, Marcus, to say nothing of presiding? Nor have I ever heard a satisfactory explanation from you as to why you didn't follow the usual procedure. Why on earth didn't you just lock the troublemaker up at once? You almost make me think you've turned the zealot!' It was the first time in Marcus' living memory that Argyra had used his name.

'I, I was quite apprised of the facts, propraetor,' he tried to explain. 'I assure you, the man–'

'Apprised of the facts?' Argyra said. 'Apprised of the facts, were you? How about the minor detail of his being a barbarian katepano? Did it not occur to you, exarch, that with innumerable members of your province congregated in the stadium, they might, perhaps, pose a threat to public order? You're probably not even aware, are you, that the proconsular praetorium had no end of trouble with those

Caledonian louts afterwards? And that's before we even come to the matter of the public and heretical display of that–'

'Honestly, propraetor,' Marcus stammered, 'there was no way I could have guessed that the alpha would smuggle in a … a … talisman like that to the execution, and the lion, I–'

'No way?' Argyra roared, slamming her knuckles into the virtual table as she leapt to her feet. 'No way? Perhaps, exarch, if you had been paying more attention to the proceedings of the trial itself, and not been so distracted, you might have noticed that you had an alpha heretic on your hands!'

'I'm sorry, but what is that supposed to mean?' Marcus asked, his neck flushing. 'With all due respect, I mean, propraetor.' Thankfully his sanguine pigmentation exceeded the blue-scale of the holocall, but he could not stop himself squirming.

'You know, exarch, exactly what I mean,' Argyra said, crossing her arms. 'Don't make me spell it out. Your moral readings have been going from bad to worse lately. I have your latest report on my desk. Disgusting!'

The thought of a mare's sable hind passed through his mind. He had been wrong. It was definitely a good thing Severa was not here. He looked at Argyra almost pleadingly, but there was no mercy in her eyes. The propraetorians fidgeted in the background. This was it. He was done for.

Argyra opened her mouth, but the holoscreen in the table started flashing violently. Above the double-headed eagle the small Latin words, '*status periculosus,*' glowed red against the dun grey background. A state of emergency.

'Holy maiden of Casan!' Marcus said. A second later, three more words, '*ordo periculi alpha*', appeared unobtrusively next to the first two, which were rapidly turning maroon.

'Excuse me?' Argyra said. 'Such effrontery, even from you, Marcus! After all this, are you honestly telling me that you contest the integrity of your moral reading?'

The aula door flung open, as Konstantin burst in.

'Exarch?' the tribune said, nodding at the door. The ordinarily passive lines of his face were drawn with unwonted agitation. It was clear at once that it was serious.

'Exarch, are you even paying attention, or have your masculine wits at last got the better of you?' Argyra's shade said. One of the propraetorians stepped forward and whispered something in her ear. Her face dropped.

'I, er, my apologies, propraetor, I...' Marcus said, waving his hand at the screen as he rose. As the hologram dissolved, the frozen neon of Argyra's astonished eyes and gaping mouth lingered, ogling him like a gorgon on an old vase.

'Sitrep, tribune?' Marcus asked, as he staggered unsteadily into the corridor. His legs bore him along, just about keeping pace with his tribune's long strides, but he felt as if his head were still there in the aula, pathetically propped on the conference table, staring at the pitiless hologram of Argyra as it awaited the pronouncement of its fate. And what fate was that? No, there could be no doubt now. *Revocatio*. Recall.

'Threat level alpha, exarch,' Konstantin briefed as they strode down the corridor, his voice betraying none of his evident agitation. 'Fires set by unknown assailants in Caledon north and east. Sporadic demonstrations and seditious activity in all urban sectors. Greatest concentration in Caledon centre, southeast of Imperial Mile.'

Marcus' mind raced, as if the spinning wheels of the bike might come loose and fly off at any moment. Riots throughout Caledon. Fire. The day after the feast as well. What did it all mean? He had no idea, but it was bad. This would surely be the nail in the coffin. The word rose to his lips. *Revocatio*.

'Exarch?' Konstantin broke into his thoughts. 'I suggest you receive a full briefing in the operations room. Shall we–?'

'No, you can brief me en route, tribune,' Marcus ordered. 'There's no time. Get me down there at once. Prepare the armoured convoy.'

For the briefest moment, Konstantin looked at him quizzically. Then, as if doubt had never entered his mind, he nodded. As the tribune marched off down the corridor, Marcus recalled his dour face as he watched Cassian during the trial. Cassian. The name rose up and slapped him. This was the same nonsense. He'd soon put an end to it.

'*Quid spectatis*?' he barked at the anxious officials leaning out of their offices, asking what they were looking at. '*Barbaroi*, what do you expect? Just a group of ruffians. I'll soon put an end to this nonsense. You're all so young and inexperienced. Back to work!'

As he descended to the garage, he reminded himself that he'd been here before. He'd already put down one slave revolt, and done so before half these infants were even born. What were all those Flavians worth, after all? They were just weaklings of the court. That was all they'd ever known. Flavian and his lot hadn't even been in a homeland theme, let alone a legion of the outer provinces. They weren't soldiers like he was. Maybe Argyra had him marked for recall, but he certainly wasn't going without showing them all what he was made of.

He strode up to the armoured convoy, where Konstantin already stood rifle in hand. He smiled proudly as his eyes travelled along the line of vehicles, serenely arrayed like a squadron of black swans. Even so, the division of twenty heavy tagmata beside them made him nervous. All donned black body armour, balaclavas, and automatic assault rifles. Surely that was overkill in a backwater like Caledon?

'May I, Excellency?' one of the faceless tagmata asked. The man held a light tunic in his hand, whose lissom black fabric rippled like silk. Marcus nodded, and the man threw the cloth over his shoulders. The tunic fell loosely about his muscles, before stiffening like metal plate. Konstantin tapped the electric, and its heavy door swung open.

Marcus slipped as he mounted the high step, shooing his tribune away as he tried to help him. He wasn't that old yet.

'Fires now reported in sectors west and south,' Konstantin said, handing Marcus a riot helmet. His fingers trembled as they gripped the titanium, examining its sleek chrome.

'Instigators?' he asked, as the electric swung out of the compound into the streets of Caledon. To his surprise, the entire exarchate was surrounded by a further division of tagmata.

'No confirmed information at this stage, exarch. Praetorian intelligence identifies a majority servile presence, with high likelihood of primary instigation by a minority civilian element,' Konstantin replied, then paused. 'I strongly advise transfer of exarchal seat to secure fallback location until full sitrep can be completed, with legionary deployment by twentieth if required.'

'Epicentre?' Marcus asked, ignoring his recommendation. Outside, the citizens and slaves were in unusual haste, jostling one another on the cobblestones. A woman's frightened blue eyes peered in as they shot past.

'Preliminary indications of independent concentration of sedition in all sectors, exarch,' Konstantin said, waving at the windscreen, which illuminated with a dense overlay of tiny green lights like lattice on a cake. To the left, right and centre of the holographic map, the tranquil green was interrupted by pulsing spots of red. The amorphous globules constantly changed shape as they throbbed, expanding to cover municipal fora, and bleeding out into side alleys. Every so often, a new one would appear somewhere else.

'Critical path to fallback location remains unaffected,' Konstantin said, pointing towards the east of the map and the firth of Bodotria, which was still largely green. A dark turquoise line appeared, cutting through the lattice to a pulsing blue dot beside the Bodotria.

Marcus was no longer listening. Instead, he was staring at a lime-coloured oval at the centre of the windscreen. While itself outlined with a thick emerald border, to all sides were large blotches of red. The rusty patches swelled like irritable sores, some visibly darkening like boils about to burst. It was the castle. The bloody barbarians were trying to encircle the castle. He clapped his hands angrily.

'*Nemo demittat!*' he said to the dashboard, broadcasting to the entire convoy. 'No fallback. *Ad arcem*, to the castle! The sedition will be put down at source. Gubernatorial command to all units. Priority alpha.' The windscreen illuminated with his last words, as a dark amber-red line from their current location to the castle appeared beneath. Crimson dots sparkled to either side.

'Exarch, with all due respect, I feel it is my duty to counsel you against this course of action,' Konstantin said, but Marcus only dismissed his words with a wave of his hand. The armoured car swerved into a side street, growling as it rapidly accelerated over the cobbles.

'*Barbaroi,*' Marcus grumbled. The thought of Argyra was making him nauseous. He looked out, hoping it would settle his stomach. The narrow windows and sallow stone of the medieval quarter's houses flew by, their overhanging jetties blocking out the paltry light of the Caledonian morning. The crowds grew steadily denser on all sides, and more faces glared blindly into the car. They were angry faces, and getting angrier. Marcus scowled as a group of barefoot slave children leapt out of the electric's way, dropping the food they had evidently just looted from a nearby shop.

All of a sudden, the sky brightened through the tinted glass as the car cleared an alleyway and pulled out onto the Imperial Mile. The jagged black walls of the castle appeared above, as if the storm god had used a giant flint to gouge a hole in the irascible sky. The sight irritated Marcus. Their bloody castle. It had to be the bloody castle.

'Exarch?' Konstantin asked. In his distraction, Marcus had failed to notice the electric slowing. It had now come to a complete stop. They were already right under the rock, not far from the main guardhouse.

'What is it, tribune? Why have we stopped? Onward! Up to the castle, I say! What's the delay…?' His voice trailed off.

Konstantin pointed out the windscreen. The vehicles at the front of the convoy had all stopped, too. A vast crowd of people blocked the way ahead.

'Sitrep, tagmarchos?' Konstantin asked the dashboard. One of the tagmata beside the vehicle in front raised his wrist to his masked face. The dashboard responded, describing a roadblock ahead and detailing the number of protesters. The sentinels of the compound's laser fence glinted above the crowd, but it was pressed so densely against the invisible barrier that nothing could be seen beyond.

'Exarch, I strongly recommend that we extract from this location at the earliest possible opportunity,' Konstantin said. 'Tagmata judge crowd population unstable, and may increase further. We should remove and deploy legionary support before we proceed further. Your personal security must be–'

'My personal security?' he exclaimed, puffing out his chest. 'Do you think I am afraid, tribune? Have you forgotten I am a soldier too? I'll have you know I've dealt with far worse in my time than this bunch of halfwit *barbaroi*.' Before Konstantin could stop him, he shouted '*aperite*', and the door dutifully swung open.

Misjudging the higher clearance of the armoured vehicle, he nearly fell as he dismounted. Despite the weak Caledonian morning, his eyes took a moment to adjust, but he had the distinct sense of innumerable heads turning in his direction. Several black shadows descended upon him, and in a moment he was surrounded by a dozen tagmata. That annoyed him. Did they really think him so old that he couldn't fend off a few louts? He was no wimp. No Flavian. The Alemannian would have been long gone by now.

'What in the name of Her Imperial Majesty is the meaning of this?' he said at the top of his voice, striding up to the fence. At first, no one reacted, but soon more of the russet heads turned. He was met with a sea of confused pale faces, the frayed tunics of most betraying them as slaves.

'In the name of Her Majesty, I demand to know the meaning of this illegal gathering,' he repeated. A few tagmata stepped up beside him, and several of the slaves shrank back. That was good. There was no harm in reminding the rabble who was boss. His eyes travelled along the uneven row of scraggy redheads as it oscillated like wind through autumn leaves. There were children too, sheltering under their mothers' arms. A group of excitable slaves, nothing more.

Suddenly there was a sound like choking from one end of the servile line. Marcus' eyes roved furiously over the crowd. It was laughter. A pair of blue eyes gleamed back at him from amidst the rags, then vanished.

'Who was that?' he asked. 'Who was that? How dare you!' He looked from face to face, seeking out the familiar eyes. He knew that devilish glint. Where was the damned Caledonian? The bloody heretic was surely behind the whole nonsense. He was somewhere in the crowd.

Marcus caught himself. A chill ran through him. A lion flickered before his eyes, the metallic sheen of its mane sparkling in the floodlights. He touched his face. No, it couldn't be. The man was dead.

'*Times*, laddie?' came a string of broken Latin from the crowd. 'Are you so afraid of us that you cannae even take off your helmet?'

Marcus flinched. A man's voice. A familiar voice. His hand moved to his head. Cursed Gehenna. He'd completely forgotten he was still wearing it.

'I wonder, laddie, who's afraid of whom?' the voice asked, followed by laughter. It caught like plague in the crowd, sticking to those around the speaker, then spreading along the whole line. Faces that had been timorous but a moment earlier relaxed. Arms crossed and chins jutted out. Marcus ripped off his helmet and threw it to the ground.

'I am not afraid of you, outlaw! I command you to show yourself,' Marcus spat at the nameless sea of ruddy faces, stepping forward. Unordered, two tagmata knelt on the cobbles beside him, training their assault rifles on the crowd. A few of the slaves withdrew a pace.

'Nor we of you, laddie,' the voice replied, as its owner surfaced at last. The man was stocky, with lambent blue eyes and bright red hair hanging to his neck in untidy locks. Marcus nearly fainted. Other than his height, he was a spitting image of the one he'd condemned five months earlier. The one whose execution he had witnessed the day before.

'We're good people, and we ain't afraid of murderers,' he said. His last word was picked up and shouted by several of the crowd. Some of the slaves started banging on the castle perimeter. Marcus became unnerved.

'What rubbish,' he protested. 'What murderers? I command you, outlaws, to disband at once and return to your places of–' His voice was drowned out by chants of 'murderer' and '*nex*'. Like shades appearing from a tomb, several heavies emerged from the servile throng. The tagmata raised their weapons.

'Thing is, laddie,' the little Caledonian continued, the riling azure of his eyes not leaving Marcus for a second, 'from where I'm standing, I'd say you got more reason to fear us than we got to fear you.' Another gust blew through the line of slaves, some of whom shook their fists at Marcus and the tagmata. The banging on the laser fence intensified.

'So, I've got an idea for you, laddie,' the man said, pointing at the convoy. 'Why don't you and your whole bunch of Hromaian bastards go back where you came from?'

There was a click as one of the tagmata released the safety catch on his rifle.

'That's right, you heard me, your lot can go back to your city, and I'll tell you something else,' he went on undaunted. 'You can take your bloody lady with you!' He spat at Marcus, who froze in amazement.

'How dare… how dare you!' he said, but his voice was again drowned out by the slaves. They were chanting 'Cassian', followed by 'thane'. Like a slowly rising tide, the crowd crept forward towards the convoy.

'Exarch, I must again urge you to consider retreat,' Konstantin said, near Marcus' ear. 'The douloi here are too numerous for us to neutralise alone. Permission to command tagmata retreat and request immediate legionary reinforcement, exarch?'

Marcus heard the Latin, but did not respond. He could not respond. He was frozen, like a deer encircled by a pack of wolves. Entrapped by a sea of furious freckled faces and ghostly pale eyes, all crying 'murderer' at him as they drew ever nearer. They hated him. They wanted to seize him. To lay hands on him. To annihilate him. He needed to get out, but he could not.

A sharp pain roused him. He raised his hand to his face and felt blood. A stone had grazed his cheek. There was another click. A gunshot rang out. A child slave, not far from the ringleader, collapsed onto the cobblestones. Within a few seconds, everything had descended into mayhem. Somewhere, a woman was screaming, and men were shouting. Another stone grazed his leg, and he fell to one knee. Konstantin's hand was under his arm, as he said '*mitte!*' and the tagmata fired a volley into the crowd.

'No!' Marcus shouted, but his words were swallowed by a second volley. The douloi rushed forward like a stampede of terrified deer. In an instant, they were swamped. Someone was trying to drag him back towards the convoy, but their arm loosened. He stumbled backwards, flailing about. Konstantin and the others were nowhere to be seen, just a mire of seething bodies all around him. Another gunshot rang out.

'Take the bastard!' the little man shouted, as Marcus tripped and fell onto the cobblestones. He rolled onto his side, trying to break free. Through the forest of unwashed legs, a group of slaves could be seen wrenching a rifle out of a tagma's hands. One of them raised it and shot the tagma in the face at point-blank range. Then he turned to the perimeter and began firing at one of the laser posts. Its lights flickered, then died. There was a buzzing noise, the air quivered, and the fence evaporated. The slave mass breached the gate and, scattering like a spray of pebbles, rapidly ascended the castle slope.

Against the raging Caledonian sky, the sapphire marbles of Cassian's eyes grinned down balefully at Marcus like one of the castle gargoyles. Then he felt a sharp crack on his head, and he was out.

CHAPTER 23

Agnes

Agnes stood beside the tent, nervously eyeing the corpses of the men she'd slain. She had to get through the camp somehow, and as soon as possible. She examined the black fatigues she'd pulled off the dead bandit. She might just pass unnoticed, but how to reach the camp in the first place? It was too exposed to approach from that outpost, and the other bandits might return at any moment.

There was no movement on the river, and the temple was deserted. She ran down the bank, scrambling through the papyri and dry mud. She scoured the riverbank ahead as she went, but all was still and the reeds untrammelled. There were no signs anyone had been that way, nor of any wreckage or other survivors. She pictured Strabon's corpse sinking to the riverbed. She forced the thought from her mind.

About a verst on, pitch filled the air again. She pulled her bandana over her nose. The smouldering ruin of the lookout post came into view. She was getting close. Crouching in the reeds, she unslung her rifle and loaded the magazine with the ammunition in her pockets. She had to be ready for anything now and, if they caught her, she certainly wasn't going without a fight. Not without taking the chance to avenge herself on the bastards. She stalked up to the burning wreck. There was no sign of the enemy, but for the first time, the ground was visibly disturbed. Cartridges littered the churned-up sand, which was dappled with dark streaks. Blood. The blood of her troops.

There had plainly been a skirmish there. Perhaps when the enemy first landed. She scanned the ground. Several footprints ran back up the bank, and deep grooves showed where someone had been dragged away. Whether they'd still been alive at the time was impossible to tell. *Cede.* Retreat. The disgraceful word rose to her lips. A Marian legionnaire never retreated, but she had. Her heart filled with shame and anger as she saw her women and men falling again. Had any been taken prisoner? The thought was an ignoble one, but they were her century. If any were still alive, she had to try and reach them.

Giant charcoal plumes rose from the top of the riverbank, smudging the azure of the desert sky. There was nothing for it. There was only one way through. She slung her rifle back over her shoulder and pulled the bandana up to her eyes. When she reached the summit, she didn't even stop, but walked straight into the cloud of smoke.

For a moment, her vision was completely obscured, as if someone had drawn a black veil across the narrow slit between her headscarf and bandana. The crackling grew louder, and the stench of burning plastic was overwhelming. Between the billows of smoke, the remnants of tents came fleetingly into view, many still on fire. To right and left were voices, and jarring laughter. The smoke momentarily dissolved. She was alarmingly close to a group of bandits. Her hand moved instinctively to her rifle, but she checked herself. One of them glanced in her direction. Her heart pounded, but she walked on, and the man hardly seemed to notice her.

As she moved in and out of the smoke, figures appeared and disappeared like shadows in the firelight on a cave wall. The men busied themselves with something as they stood beside the burning tents, some handling sacks. There were voices everywhere now. She had to be nearing the centre of the camp. Soon the throng was so great that she simply merged into the crowd. The muscles in her hand spasmed as she repressed the urge to reach for her gun. She just had to keep going and try not to draw attention to herself. She mustn't catch their eye.

The air cleared at last. On all sides, the bandits milled about like some infernal hive of black ants, busying themselves with the same sacks. The myrmidons were curiously disciplined, so unlike the disorderly array that had attacked them the night before. It made no sense. There were Caliphate vehicles too, and other tents she didn't recognise. Most remarkable of all, though, was their sheer number. She had been wrong that the enemy was a match for her century. There were hundreds and hundreds of them. They would have been a match for her entire legionary cohort.

All of a sudden, her eyes lit on a beret. She did a double-take. It was unmistakable. A legionnaire's beret. A Marian beret, but not the beige of the southern legions that her troops wore. Neither was it the black of the northern legions, nor the white of the military praetoria. It was grey. A cold ashen grey, like the embers of her camp. It couldn't have been taken from her troops. Her eyes darted maniacally from one beret to another, and then another. Dozens of them bobbed about like mines on the surface of that black ocean. Each group had at least one or two. The lower halves of their faces were covered too, but all were fairer-skinned, and they were giving orders to the rest.

She passed closer to one of the groups. A beret directed the others as they shovelled heaps of charred material into the sacks. A foul stench wafted into her nostrils, more overpowering than the stale sweat of her fatigues. In the midst of the bandits was a hideous pile of flesh, the unmistakable remains of bloodied, burnt and dismembered human body parts. She nearly fainted, but anger roused her. The black ants and grey berets were working as a single hive, all at the selfsame business. Removing what was left of her camp. Wiping away all trace of her century. Tents, weapons, and bodies. The bodies of her soldiers. All were being shovelled into the same sacks.

She looked more closely at the grey berets. They weren't wearing the same tired fatigues of the other bandits. Instead, all wore the same short-collar leather tunic and hose. The same uniform. Nor was it just any uniform. For it wasn't the familiar beige khakis of her century and of her legion, nor of any of the southern legions. It was a plain black uniform. The uniform of the homeland tagmata, but unmarked by the white star. A uniform without any insignia or epaulettes at all. Just a grey beret. That meant one thing. There could be no doubt. They were military intelligence.

Zradcovia, her mind screamed in her native tongue. Traitors. She had been betrayed. Her shock and rage boiled over, and she nearly threw herself on the nearest beret. He was just beside her, and she could have throttled him. It would only have taken a moment. She stood rooted to the spot as if petrified into one of the temple glyphs, but her hand flickered to her rifle. Like a battle drone, the beret rotated towards her. A pair of pale bronze eyes lit up beneath. The drone fixed her, surveying her from head to toe. She did not wait, but hastened on, cursing under her breath. She forced herself not to turn back, but could feel the baleful eyes following her as she went.

A hue and cry erupted to the north, downriver. A low siren sounded, the insistent humming of a giant beehive. A thrill ran through the camp, like wind rippling through a black sail. All was thrown into confusion as bandits and soldiers turned towards the commotion, abandoning their sacks and rushing to the riverbank.

The bastards had come back. Despite herself, she glanced over her shoulder. Her eyes met those of the grey beret. Unlike the rest, he had not turned at the siren. His malignant little eyes fixed her like a snake in the black desert of masked faces. They were Greek eyes. She began to run.

CHAPTER 24

Hypatia

Hypatia paused at the head of the garden path, looking back at the fountain. There was no sign of the mysterious blond woman. By now, she must already be ensconced in the church confessional, owning her sins to the sexless old abbess, just as she herself had half an hour earlier. But that was a ridiculous thought. There was surely no comparison between a being of such manifest radiance and a low-life such as herself. For what could such an emanation of Our Lady possibly have in common with her own besmirched life? On reflection, the very notion that she was going to Saint Sophia to confess at all seemed risible.

Surprised for the second time that day at her own strange thoughts, and no longer wholly sure the woman had been real at all, she stepped beneath the shade of the red-brick colonnade. She brushed past the tutees without acknowledging them, but could already feel a pair of resentful eyes upon her. She wasn't sure what right the little squirt had to be indignant. It was his own fault, after all. *Dea Nutrix.* Mother goddess. He had made her feel old, older than she had ever felt before, and he would pay for it.

She passed through the glass doors into the aula, leaving the tutees outside. She had completely forgotten how far they'd gotten last time with the history of heresy. Wincing slightly as she seated herself at the desk at the front, she waved her hand over its inset screen. The words '*damnosa hereditas*' projected in green letters above the desk, spelling out the title of the previous week's dialogue. The damned inheritance of the last patriarchs. That was it. Theapolitology wasn't the easiest topic for anyone, least of all the Gamma Heresy, and this lot weren't the brightest sparks.

She peered up vacantly at the quatrefoil windows of the old stone hall. On the hilltop, the castle battlements gleamed in the meridianal sun. Beneath the windows, a large portrait of the empress' sister and university patron, the Princess Amalasuntha Premyslovna, Sebastokratorissa and despotess of Morea, looked down at her unforgivingly, as if chiding her for her forgetfulness. She was sure they'd already covered the enfeeblement of state institutions by the Alpha Heresy in its final days. Still, a bit of revision wouldn't hurt the tutees. They could hardly progress to the next dialogue, on the downfall of the Osmanian tyranny, without a firm foundation. Her lips stretched into a sardonic smile.

She waved at the glass door. The tutees filed in noisily. Only when all were seated did she deign to look up. This year's intake were a mixture, but more boys than girls. About twenty in total, all were of no more than eighteen or nineteen summers. An unusually high share were also of matrician class, one or two even being from dynatorial aristocratic families, with the usual accompanying arrogance. The rest were only of equitorial rank, mainly wealthy mercantiles. Last night's lover was such a one. Her eyes narrowed as he slumped sullenly onto a bench in the back row.

'When you're quite ready,' she said. 'A reminder before we begin that the teaching of heresies is proscribed by the *Lex Iustiniana*. By the ninth imperial basilikon, however, a special dispensation is granted to the two imperial universities, to us in Mystras and to the Palace Hall of Magnaura in Mariapol, to teach their history as part of this theapolitological course.' The boy at the back stifled a yawn. She would soon wake him up.

'That with the exclusive purpose of edifying our future leaders, the better that they might guide the state away from the eros of the false prophet,' she continued, scanning the soporific and hungover eyes dully beholding her. 'So, before we move on, let us ensure that our dear future leaders have been paying attention!' She slammed her palm on the desk. Several tutees jumped up in alarm, including the boy. She smiled at him sarcastically.

'As we learned in last week's dialogue,' she said, 'the institutions of the state had become atrophied by the Alpha Heresy. Indeed, such was this degeneration that its nefarious counsels had addled the very judgement of the last patriarch king, Constantine Palaeologus. The very survival of the empire was in question.' Hypatia walked up the aisle between the tutees, trailing her hand along the benchtops.

'But even then, despite their error, in that darkest of days the Mother did not abandon the patriarchs,' she continued, reaching the end of the aula. 'For in the very hour of their doom, Our Lady gave the patriarchs a final sign, a final chance to remedy their ways. Now, I wonder, can any of our future leaders tell me what that sign was?' She paused directly in front of the boy's desk.

'I, ehm, sorry, lector, are you asking me?' he stammered. His sourness ceded to embarrassment as his face turned a delicate shade of fuchsia. Hypatia's smile broadened.

'Whom else?' she asked. 'I do believe my memory serves me right that you were here for last week's dialogue, were you not, tutee? Or were you perhaps not listening to what I had to tell you?' There was a snigger from one of the girls behind.

'As I thought,' she said, returning to the front of the hall. 'It seems that your attention spans are about that of the average wood nymph or satyr. I must say I am disappointed. I had expected more of our young scholars of Mystras.' She was beginning to enjoy herself.

'Sorry, lector, if I may?' a deep voice broke in. In her fixation with the boy, Hypatia had failed to notice the raised hand. Another youth sat on the edge of his chair, leaning across his desk eagerly. He was unusually handsome, with a cascade of strawberry-blond hair. How had she missed him before? She nodded.

'On the night of the 28th of May, *Anno Descensionis*,' he continued, 'Our Lady attempted to visit upon Palaeologus. When the enemy was at the very gates, the last king took refuge in one of the temples of his false prophet, that erroneously known as Saint Saviour, beneath the City's walls.' His pretty lips fluttered like rose petals in the breeze, straining to recount his tale before anyone else could. She looked sidelong at last night's boy, who knit his dark brows jealously, before smiling at her new boy.

'Perhaps Palaeologus realised his Error in the end, lector, for he prayed to the Mother to save him,' he chirped like a sparrow, 'and indeed, in Her kindness, Our Lady did appear to him on the eve of his doom, offering him one last chance of salvation.'

'Very good, I see we have some talent among us after all,' Hypatia said, beaming at the youth as she imagined his soft locks brushing the inside of her thighs. 'And I wonder if anyone can tell us what the Mother asked of Palaeologus, as the price of his redemption?' She skipped over the old boy as she scanned the line of vapid matrician faces.

'If I may, lector?' the blonde asked in his matrician lisp, no longer waiting for his cue. 'In Her kindness, Our Lady asked that Palaeologus return to Her his crown. That which was not rightfully his, nor any of the patriarchs' before him, for their following of the false prophet. Yet such was his pride that he refused even this clemency.'

'*Polu kale!* Very good! Very good indeed, I see you shall go far,' Hypatia said in Greek, leaning over his desk. 'You bright little boy, *stella mea.* My star,' she whispered flirtatiously, brushing his ear with her lips. Its alabaster lobe quivered as he looked up at her with a shy smile. She had him.

Yesterday's boy was positively scowling. It had done the trick. It wasn't the first time she'd had a jealous boy, but this one really deserved it. She eased herself onto the top of her desk, stretching out her bare legs as lasciviously as she could. The blonde's eyebrows raised. He was already mentally undressing her. How did he see her? His maiden huntress perhaps, caught naked in her bath? He would be her Actaeon.

'Now we've concluded our little resumption of last week's dialogue, and I can be sure you've absorbed the key points,' she said, winking at the new boy, 'let us turn to the subject of this week's dialogue, the Gamma Heresy. As we know, Palaeologus' hubris in rejecting Our Lady's Gnosis opened the way to our salvation. For in Justinia the Blessed, the immemory of the false prophet was finally destituted. After Justinia's time, we may no longer speak of the Alpha Heresy as an active force in our society.'

'But, lector,' a surly voice mumbled, 'can we truly speak of the Alpha Heresy as ending with Justinia's reign? Technically speaking, it was not until the reign of Matrona the Elect that the final revolt of the Palaeologi was ended, over a century after Our Lady's Descension. Is it not reasonable to assume that, had they succeeded, we would have fallen back into Error?' The old boy smiled stupidly. She'd soon wipe that off his face.

'Technically speaking,' she replied, 'the revolt of the Palaeologi was put down before the reign of Matrona the Elect. If anything, this only proves the resilience of Justinia's institutional reforms, and the re-classicisation admonished by the sage Plethon. For, imparted new vigour, our state was already grown too strong for the feeble dregs of the patriarchs to challenge in any serious way. As we all know, their rebellion came to naught. Moreover, it led to the proclamation of the fifth, electoral, basilikon in the one hundred and twenty-eighth year of

Our Lady's Descension, perhaps the greatest of all reforms, by which each empress chose her successor not by blood, but by the virtue of their gnosis.'

The old boy snarled.

'And let me take this opportunity as a fine reminder, tutee, that it is always good rhetorical practice to reflect before we speak,' she added. 'Might you, for example, have reflected that the holy Matrona is referred to as 'the Elect' for a reason? I do hope that when you are addressing the Council of Logothetes one day, you will bear this lesson in mind.' Some of the others giggled as the boy sank tetchily behind his desk.

'Returning to the topic of today's dialogue,' she continued, looking directly at the new boy, 'I wonder if anyone can give me a definition of the Gamma Heresy?' He looked alarmed, as if fearing she might set her dogs on him too. She smiled reassuringly. He opened his mouth, but a Numidian girl butted in.

'The Gamma Heresy is the false religious practice of the infidels,' she said, flashing her proud matrician eyes at Hypatia. She sighed. This lot really weren't the flower of the crop. Were they admitting such trash at the Palace Hall as well these days?

'Thank you,' she replied, 'but a reminder, tutee, that you aren't at the lyceum anymore, but the University of Mystras. I asked for a definition of the Gamma Heresy, not a statement of the obvious known to every common woman. I wonder, is there another bright spark among you who might offer an alternative?' There were more giggles, this time more nervous.

'If I may, lector,' the blonde began, 'the Gamma Heresy may indeed be termed the religious practice of the infidels. That is to say, the practice of the – of the unrecognised potentate of the Caliphate – and of the population dwelling in the territories under its control. While qualitatively distinguished from the Alpha Heresy, the Gamma

Heresy may also be characterised as unideist in nature, being focused on the adoration of a masculine prophet-figure.'

'*Polu kale*, very good!' Hypatia repeated, as the boy's cheeks flushed with pleasure. 'And, I wonder, can anyone tell me what the main tenets and practices of the Gamma Heresy consist of?' She did not check for any other hands.

'Yes, lector,' he answered, 'it is the contention that the teachings of their false prophet, Mazdak, must be followed in all personal and societal practices, as representing the edicts of their masculine numen. Those edicts derive from the mistaken belief that all persons are created equal in the eyes of that same god figure. The enemy therefore contends that all ownership and property must be held in common.'

'Excellent, *mea stella*,' she said, imagining his fine freckled nose nuzzling her nape. 'And can you tell me, I wonder, what the principle proof is that can be adduced to demonstrate the patent falsity of this belief, and the hostile political structures which rest upon it?'

'Yes, lector', he continued breathlessly, 'the principal proof that is adduced is that the equality of persons before their false deity is in itself a false premise. For it is predicated on the holding of all property in common by males only. In this false system, the primacy of the female principle, as revealed to us by Our Lady, is unpostulated. Indeed, so great is the error of the gamma heretic that she even believes the feminine to be subordinate to the masculine, with legal equivalence to property. Thus, *horribile dictu*, the females are also held in common by the males. This may be considered the organising political principle of the Caliphate.' He threw his head back, his locks falling across his neck like golden rivulets etched into a snowy mountainside.

'Excellent, tutee, a fine definition,' she said, her face aglow. 'You make Justinia proud.' She raised her palm to the rest. It was clear none were going to try and match him. All the same, it was never good to let them get too cocky. Her eye hovered over the sullen boy at the back.

Dea Nutrix. That mustn't happen again. She would keep the new one a better pet.

'And can you also tell me how the executive functions of the Caliphate are organised on the basis of the gamma heretic principles?' she asked with a coquettish smile. The blonde's face dropped as he stammered incoherently. The Numidian tittered, but Hypatia raised her hand.

'That is ok, a tutee is not expected to know everything,' she interrupted reassuringly. 'That is why you are here! The important thing is that you have an open mind. As Plethon reminds us, wisest is she who knows she does not know.' She looked askance at the old boy, who still glowered at her. The new one smiled shamefacedly. He was all hers.

'As we know, the Osmanian tyranny collapsed after its defeat by Justinia at the Battle of the Red Apple Tree,' Hypatia said. 'When it did so, the old Beta Heresy died with it. But alas, evil never sleeps, and from its ashes a new heresy arose, one we term the gamma. Indeed, it is perhaps incorrect to say that it was new. For its evil fruits first blossomed seventeen centuries ago, when the charlatan Mazdak claimed his false gnosis. Under Kavad the Foul, fifteen centuries ago, the enemy even marched against us under its banner, before they discovered the Beta Heresy.' Most of the tutees had already tuned out. It was like trying to roll a rock up a mountainside. Time to wrap up.

'Returning to the question at hand,' she continued, slapping the desk and making the Numidian girl jump again, 'the political structure of the Caliphate - that which emerged from the Osmanian collapse and civil war six centuries ago - describes itself as a system of *primus inter pares*, of first among equals. We know, of course, that this is a lie, where the caliph is in reality a traditional masculine tyrant. In theory at least, however, the Caliphate is a society of equals. Its sovereign politburo, the Committee of the Whole, comprises representatives of their entire demos led by their chief logothete, the shah, all supposedly of equivalent law-giving authority as the caliph. Needless to say, this false equality is meaningless in practice, demonstrating as it does the usual degeneration of the masculine principle...'

The Numidian stifled a yawn. Yesterday's boy stared pointedly out the window.

'But we get ahead of ourselves,' Hypatia said above the already scraping chairs. 'In next week's dialogue, we return to Plethon's articulation of heresy in the Justinian legal code, considering his reinstatement of pre-alpha institutions and contrasting this to the progressive enfeeblement of the Caliphate.' Her voice was barely audible over the chattering of the tutees as they filed noisily from the aula. The new boy alone did not stir.

That evening, at the appointed hour, she opened her door and the blonde slipped in. Throwing her arms around his shoulders, she kissed his shy red lips, tearing off his tunic. This one was even fresher than the last.

CHAPTER 25

Agnes

The siren swooped over the camp like some infernal vulture. Agnes pushed against the swell of black ants, trying to avoid being borne back towards the river. Grey berets and masked faces met her at every turn, but none paid her any attention. None, that was, save a single pair of bronze eyes, fixing her relentlessly amidst the crowd like laser sentinels. She raced on, breaking into a full run. She was nearly out now. She mustn't stop.

She neared the camp perimeter, leaving the crowd behind. Up ahead, not far off, were the twin statues of the patriarchs and, beyond them, the rusty hills. At the western end of the camp, a handful of tents had been erected, beside which was parked a Caliphate truck, its back piled high with sacks. A bandit leaned against its open door, speaking to another man in a beret on the far side of the vehicle. Fortunately, neither had noticed her yet. There was no one else around.

She slowly approached, pulling the bandana up to her eyes. There was no sign of the grey beret behind, only the chaos of the crowd, but he would surely be after her in no time. It was now or never. She swung her rifle off her shoulder. The bandit looked up, but he wasn't fast enough. Without awaiting his reaction, she shot him in the chest. His body slumped against the truck and fell to the ground.

The beret was faster and was already presenting. She hit the ground, diving under the truck as two bullets flew over her head. In an instant, she had discharged two more rounds, one of which took the soldier in the thigh. He fell to his knee, a grenade in his hand. She fired again, this time into his stomach, and his body fell back. The black disk rolled into the sand.

Agnes dived into the tents, clapping her hands over her ears. She lay still, but nothing happened. It hadn't detonated. She scrambled to her feet, casting about frantically like a hunted stag. The truck's door was still open. She clambered into the front, but as she did so there was a cry nearby. The grey beret with the brazen eyes was running towards her from the crowd, frenziedly brandishing his gun. She slammed the door shut.

'*Ite! Ite!*' she shouted at the dashboard, commanding the truck to go. Yet even as she spoke the words, she realised to her horror that it didn't drive itself. She turned white. The man's cries grew louder. She gripped the wheel. Its leather was rough to the touch. There was a loud crack as a bullet smashed into the glass windscreen. She looked madly at the dashboard controls. There was a button beside the wheel. She slammed her fist into it. The vehicle roared to life like a wolf.

Another bullet whizzed by. As Agnes ducked, her foot collided with something firm. The truck lurched forward. Her foot slipped and found another pedal. She depressed it and the truck halted, jolting her back upright. More cracks rent the air, glass smashed beside her, and there was a clang of metal. She looked down, panicstricken. There were two pedals. It had to be go and stop. She depressed the right one and the wolf pounded forwards.

The beret flashed by through the window, kneeling in the sand as he lowered his gun. Then she was staring wildly at the dust track ahead, only half-visible through the fractured windscreen. The beast swerved from side to side, kicking up the sand as it resisted her mastery. She gripped the wheel and pressed hard on the right pedal. The wolf roared again, submitting to her will at last. The camp disappeared. To the west, the statues of the patriarchs reared up on their colossal thrones, like giant spectres against the ochre palette of the limestone hills. If she could just get to those hills, then all she had to do was follow them north to Kaine. To Kaine and the legion. To salvation.

Something screeched behind. As the dust cleared, two trucks pulled into view in the distance. She cursed. She wasn't done with the *parchanti* yet. She pressed the pedal again, and the wolf bounded forward. The smirking faces of the stone colossi leered down at her. *Nyet!* she said in her head. She wasn't going to let the bastards win. They'd taken her entire century. They weren't going to get her too.

As if in answer, stone exploded around her. In her mirror, the headdress of one of the patriarchs slid off its mighty shoulders, the massive limestone shard narrowly missing one of the pursuing trucks as it crashed into the sand. As the vehicle swerved aside, a black shadow leant out its window, brandishing a rifle. There was a clacking noise. Dust and stone danced about her truck, like pebbles splashing on a pond. She flattened the pedal, her knuckles white beneath their coat of blood and dust, and the wolf ran for its life towards the hills.

The track bent along the mountain ridge. Her pursuers vanished. All that could be seen were the gigantic limestone cliffs overhead, riveted with enormous black fissures, as if they had been pummeled by some ancient god then left to bake for centuries in the desert sun. An instant later, the enemy skidded back into view, emerging from a cloud of sand. There was more clacking. The track veered left and right in the shadow of the hills, slowing her progress. They were gaining on her. She looked at the shabby leather dashboard with frustration. If only she had been in an imperial vehicle. She'd have long outrun them by now.

There was another crash as her left mirror exploded. She ducked as splinters of glass flew everywhere. When she raised her head again, they were nearly on her, so close she could see their faces. Two berets and two bandanas. Two officers. That was bad. She turned back to the shattered windscreen and nearly jumped out of her seat. Not a hundred passus ahead, a vehicle was parked right across the track, an automatic rifle stationed on its back. She yanked the wheel left as the sand exploded with bullets.

The truck juddered violently as it came off the road, and she was nearly thrown from her seat. She tore blindly up a side track into the hills, her enemy in hot pursuit. The truck bounced about the uneven track as it ascended a winding valley. The cliffs towered ever higher and denser, as if a choir of gilded titans had drawn an enormous veil of sand across her way. She cursed. It was a dead end.

There was a deafening crash as a grenade exploded to her right. Bullets kicked off the limestone as the valley filled with dust. The same sweet smell from the riverside rose to her nostrils, accompanied by the sound of trickling liquid. She'd been hit. She flailed about in a cloud of sand as her tyres skidded across the ivory stones and veered off the track.

The air cleared. A single peak reared up ahead in the silent valley, rising like a pyramid from the golden crown of the sandy hills, all of which inclined towards it like a thousand devotees bowing before its impossible majesty. She gasped, almost forgetting where she was, but then the engine sputtered. The wolf tired, no longer obeying its master's will. Thick fluid gushed from the vehicle, bleeding into the sand. Ahead, the track led nowhere. A truck swung into view behind. This was it. The end had come, but she wasn't going without taking down as many of them as she could. She reached for her gun.

Without warning, she spun the wheel, slamming her foot into the stop pedal. Lifting her rifle, she fired several rounds right at the oncoming vehicle. One of the ants flew off the back of the truck before she was met with an answering volley. Kicking the door open, she leapt out onto the sand. Pain shot through her leg but she ignored it, bolting for the cliff without looking back. Her heart ached with exhaustion and she had no idea where she was going, but she had to get away and warn the legion.

Renewed gunfire propelled her on, as chips of limestone flew around her like snowflakes. The path narrowed. She was right beneath the cliff face. No sooner had she sheltered behind a boulder at its foot than a hail of bullets exploded all around her. She collapsed behind the rock, completely exhausted. There was nowhere left to go.

The firing ceased. Jackboots crunched on the baked stones. She held her gun to her chest, uttering a last prayer to the Virgin for the gnosis of her soul. She steeled herself for the last stand, preparing to leap out upon the enemy.

Something glinted on the rockface above. Agnes looked up, blinded by the desert glare. Sunspots danced across her eyes like an unholy pageant of demonic faces. Then, as if stepping aside, they made way for a small figure atop the cliff. She stood alone, like a distant lighthouse on the horizon of the sea. Despite herself, Agnes let go of her gun. It was the girl from the meschita.

'*Aiteo!*' she said in Greek, forgetful of her danger. 'I ask you!' The sun flared, and the black chorus danced across her vision once more. She rubbed her eyes. When she opened them again, the girl was gone.

CHAPTER 26

Anastasia

Anastasia was back on the hilltop, beside the chapel portal. She admired the cloak of violets covering the green sward, smiling as she beheld the valley.

She started. Instead of Castel Nicolaeum, a vast medieval city lay below. In place of the plain and hills beyond was a wide channel opening to the sea. The hill sloped down to the water's edge, where hundreds of wooden ships, manned for war, were moored. Men in chainmail thronged their decks, carrying spears and cross-painted shields as they rushed about, pointing anxiously out to sea, where ships were burning. Beyond, on the far bank, was an enormous turbaned host. Some waved their curved sabres at the near bank, while others loaded giant Basilic cannons onto their ships.

She turned back to the chapel, but the little white tower was no longer there. Instead, there was a great church with a raised dome on four high pillars. Dense ranks of cavalry and tagmata massed before its portals, the grim faces beneath their steel helms all expressing the same dreadful expectation. The doors opened. An old man with a clipped white beard stepped forth. He was tall, with a handsome Greek face. On his head was a high kamelaukion crown, its band encrusted with precious gems and strung with pearled pendilia. Folded across his broad chest was a maniakion collar, richly studded with lapis and gold, but beneath his embroidered loros he wore a breastplate. A gladius hung from his belt.

The king hailed the soldiery, flanked by his patriarch and priests. As the ranks of tagmata stood to attention, he faced their commander, his domesticus, who stood before the rest. As the young man stepped forwards, he glanced back at Anastasia nervously. His face was determined, but fear was also written there. She became concerned. It was hardly the hour for hesitation.

As the king smiled stupidly at the crowd, she knew that she hated him. Was he so blind that he couldn't see how the spears trembled in the soldiers' hands? Beside her, the women stood helplessly in their white robes and bejewelled kamelaukia, holding the icons of the false prophet and Our Lady in their hands. Why couldn't he see that She wasn't coming to their aid? It was his fault, for he had rejected Her.

Pitch wafted to her nostrils. The edge of the hill had become a great battlement, the strongest walls the world had ever seen. Yet the enemy's ships were filling the Bosphorus like blood seeping from a wound. Men in turbans raised ladders to the walls as canon balls exploded all around. They were already scrambling over the castellations, even as the patriarchs paraded their false icons on the walls. Men were dying. The Sublime Port was burning. Now her uncle stood over her, smiling down at her lasciviously beneath his golden crown. He wanted to embrace her, to have her. She felt the cool steel of the knife against her palm. She looked up at him one last time, then thrust it deep into his side.

There was a deafening wailing all around. Paleologus' imbecilic smile vanished as his face turned to marble. The pained ridges of his forehead arched like the entrance to a tomb. His mouth worked horribly. Soon he would be no more than stone. She wrenched the gladius from his belt. He swayed, staggering, and tried to claw at her. He clutched his heart, gasping for breath, but instead of turning to stone his face transformed into that of the slave.

He laughed at her maniacally. She stabbed him again, but it was no use. He kept coming. The blood ran down his face into his loros, but he lurched at her with morbid vigour. Then the blood on his chin congealed into a red beard, and his eyes froze into an icy blue. The awful spectre of the Caledonian stared down at her, risen from the grave. Through his bloody beard, he berated her for her impurity and hypocrisy, trying to drag her down with him.

She screamed, but no sooner had she opened her mouth than Cassian's face morphed into that of her love. His dark Greek eyes fixed her with surprise. She looked down at his chlamys. Its white cloth was turning crimson as his blood gushed forth. She screamed again, and her love, the church, city and ships all disappeared into the smoke.

Anastasia opened her eyes, breathing hard. It was just a bad dream. She had not slain her love. No, but he had already slain her with a single look. A tear ran down her cheek. There was no life left for her worth living now. The dagger pressed against her in the pocket of her doublet. She wished that she were the king in the burning city, for whom all would soon be at an end. Her body shook with sobs.

She shut her eyes again. Bobina was whining, but something else had awoken her. There was the faint rumble of an engine and the whirring of a turbine coming from outside her window. The oak door of her bedroom opened quietly. The floorboards creaked beside the bed. Then a pair of strong arms encircled her like the feathers of a giant eagle, bearing her away. She smelt the familiar musk of leather and burnt cinnamon. Faraway, Bobina barked in welcome.

'*Otche?* Father?' she mumbled in Bohemian, still half-asleep. A large hand stroked her forehead in reply, as she floated through the air. She felt warm, as if she were wrapped in a giant cocoon. The mist dissipated from her heart, and together with it the writhing slave, heretic, and dying king. All were far away, blown away by the wind on the hilltop. Someone laid her down on something soft. Bobina's warm body was beside her. She pressed her face into her fur and yawned.

There was another muffled whirr, and it was as if she, Bobina, and the bed itself were all floating upwards into the air.

'Father?' she repeated, opening her eyes. 'Father!' she said happily, seeing her father Karel sitting nearby. She sat up, rubbing her eyes. Her eyes grew wide with surprise as they fell on the navy-white upholstery of the cabin. Through the tall glass windows the hill, castle, and town were all rapidly shrinking to the size of doll's houses. She sat on a cushioned berth, her father seated opposite at a little table.

'We're going to see your mother, Anastasia,' her father said, anticipating her question. 'Don't worry, the servants have packed all your things.' His kind emerald eyes smiled at the look of alarm on her face. The grin behind his copper beard was broad, but there was something serious in his eyes.

'But, so soon, father? I only just got here...' she said, but her voice trailed off. Despite her best attempts, she could never maintain any pretence before her father's loving gaze. She burst into tears. He was by her side at once.

'*Draha dcero*, my dear one, I know,' he said in Bohemian. 'I know all about it. I am sorry. It is all my fault. How I wish I had not left you here all alone yesterday!' He cradled her in his arms as she wept.

'No, Father, it was all my fault,' she stammered between her tears. 'I shouldn't have gone on without the tagmata, but I thought the chapel was – I thought it was safe – and now, Mother, what will she say, and what will happen – I mean – how can I still be, and after the heretic too...?' She dissolved in sobs, unable to go on.

'Listen, Anastasia,' her father said slowly, 'no one could have known that terrible man would have been there, and hiding that knife. It doesn't bear thinking about, and I would have you think no more on it. Praise be to Our Lady, it could have been much worse. I am only glad that you are safe now.' The low hum of his voice, between the drone of the turbines, calmed her. Her tears gradually dried up.

'But, Father, how can I still be sacrosanct – after – after all of this?' she asked. 'I am no longer pure, am I? I mean, I don't feel like I am anymore. I feel I have become impure, somehow. Like I am soiled! Isn't that why I sent that man to his death? Am I not just the same now, and worse, since my body is a temple of Our Lady and my offence is unpardonable?' Once more she felt the lascivious hands of her assailant against her body, and saw the Caledonian's bloody beard wagging before her as he profaned the Virgin. Finally, the enraged eyes of her love reappeared. She started crying again.

Her father cupped her face in his hands. For a long time, he looked into her eyes. She gazed back into his kind green eyes. He knew why she wept, and that it was not only because of what had happened on the hill. She could not hide anything from him, and felt guilty for burdening him so.

'Listen to me very carefully, dear child,' he said seriously. 'What happened to you was not your fault. In the eyes of Our Lady, you remain chaste, because there was no sin on your part. Besides, the tagmata have been spoken to, and no one need know what happened. Even your mother, if that is your wish. You will remain a Vestal, if that is what you desire, Anastasia.' He looked at her meaningfully.

'I, of course that is what I want, Father,' she began, but her thoughts became clouded as a pair of dark eyes rose before her. 'I am honoured to serve Our Lady. Only that...' She was struggling to maintain her composure beneath her father's gaze.

'I... what will happen to the slave, father?' she asked, changing the subject.

Her father looked at her knowingly, as if he had seen through her ruse. Yet, as she put the question, she realised that the thought really had not occurred to her once since leaving the chapel. She pictured the slave writhing on the floor, riddled with electric shocks. Her father studied his clasped hands.

'You are a Vestal, Anastasia,' he said, his face darkening, 'and not only that. You are a royal, the niece of the empress herself. You must understand, my dear, that in the eyes of the law, your personage is sacrosanct and intangible. An assault such as this upon you cannot go unpunished. It will not go unpunished. The slave will be tried for his crime, and will face the punishment that is his due.'

'But is not Our Lady clement?' Anastasia asked, her voice breaking. 'I mean, does She not forgive those who repent of their evil ways, and pray to Her for the remittance of their sins? Oh, why is it happening again, Father?' It was just the same as the heretic she had failed to save. Now, as then, it was all her fault.

'As I have said before, *draha dcero*, what happened in Caledon was not your fault, for you were only trying to help,' Karel answered. 'But not all sins are venial in the eyes of Our Lady. I will not lie to you that the man's punishment will be severe. I shall do what I can, though, if that is your wish. Still, you must understand, Anastasia, that at best he will never see the light of day again.'

Her sad eyes drooped, lingering on the white lion and golden crown on her father's collar. Did the slave have a wife or children? What would happen to them?

'Yet I sense there is something else, my child, that troubles you, is there not?' he asked. The slave faded away, replaced by a vision of dark curls tied back with golden laurel, one lock straying onto an ivory forehead. She rose, moving to the window. The dense verdure of pine forest and pasture, punctuated by little brooks, hurtled by below. She knew every valley by heart.

'You were not happy yesterday, were you, my dear?' Karel persisted. She continued pensively watching the ever-changing carousel below. Beneath the lowcraft's slender white wings the towers of Colonia rushed by, tiny beige matchsticks crowned by the black wicks of their belfries. In a few minutes they would reach Castra Praetoriana. She had nothing to hide from her father. No, but her mother was another matter.

'Anastasia, I urge you to try and put this from your mind,' he said slowly. 'I know that life can be cruel, but your sorrow will pass with time, I promise you. Our Lady heals all wounds. You do not have to see him anymore, if it has become too hard.' As ever, he could see through her. A tear ran down her cheek.

'But Father, how can you promise such a thing?' she blurted out. 'I know how it is for us. We cannot always choose. I know we must do what is required of us, and you know I will do what you and Mother wish. And yet – yet, I – it is hard, did not you yourself...?' She broke off, seeing her father's jaw quiver. She ran back to him and wrapped her arms around him.

'I am sorry, Father,' she stammered. 'I did not mean to hurt you. You know I love you very much. I don't know what is happening to me. I feel like only yesterday I was a happy child playing in the fields of Moravia, and today I am become some terrible woman. A terrible, unclean woman! A woman who's already sent one man to Gehenna, and is now sending another.'

Karel's hands clasped her cheeks again. 'You are my child, Anastasia,' he said, embracing her. 'You will always be my child, whatever happens, do you hear? And you must stop this nonsense about sending people to their deaths, and being unclean. You are nothing of the sort. Life can be cruel to us, yes, my dear, but it cannot change who we truly are. Always remember that.'

She buried her head in his chest as the comforting scent of cinnamon filled her nostrils. Bobina brushed against her leg.

Five minutes later, the cabin illuminated with golden light as the lowcraft decelerated and came about. Through the convex windowpane, the river Moldavia shone like a sapphire pendilion in the evening sun. All along its banks rose slender glass towers, and above them, on the hill, the medieval castle and church.

Soon they were descending into Pracas' citadel, the royal seat of her family. The regal retinue was already gathered in the courtyard. At the front of the serried ranks of red berets and white doublets stood a slight woman with long dark hair, wearing a ruff-necked blue kirtle, blue stockings and a tall skiadion crown. Even from afar, Princess Amalasuntha, the Sebastokratorissa, sister of the empress and youngest member of the imperial family, stood out. And even from afar, her mother was visibly displeased.

CHAPTER 27

Agnes

She looked up at the cliff face. There was no sign of the girl. Agnes had asked, but she had not come to her aid. She was not worthy. Now, only one thing awaited her. Death. The sun dimmed, then a voice rent the silence.

'*Paradinesai?* Do you surrender?' It was not the girl's voice, but a man's, speaking Greek. The Greek of the homelands. It was one of the traitors. *Nyet!* the voice inside her head answered automatically.

'Lay down your arms, centurion, and come out with your hands up!' he added more forcefully. There was no way she was going out there unarmed. They'd gun her down in seconds. Yet she had to see who the *parchanti* were. The men who had betrayed her. The men who had betrayed her century. She wanted a good last look at them, to see the fear in the whites of their eyes, before they went together to the grave. She gripped her gun tightly, hoisted it on her shoulders, and, slowly rising, emerged from behind the rock.

Their eyes met at once, each spying the other down their rifle sights. The man could not have been ten passus away. In a single glance, she took in his grey beret, unmarked black uniform, and brazen Greek eyes above his bandana. Military intelligence. The same one from the crowd. Her cheeks flushed hot with anger, but she did not fire, and neither did he. Neither retreated, but simply stood there, glaring at the other.

'Lay down your arms at once, centurion!' the man said, his voice wavering slightly. Keeping her rifle trained on him, she scanned the scene beyond. Another grey beret knelt in the sand a little way down the slope, and a bandit leant over her truck. All had their rifles trained on her, but her hand remained steady on the trigger of her gun. If she had to go, they were going with her.

'Who are you?' she bellowed back at him in Greek. Her eyes lit on his beret and unmarked lapel, where the white star should have been. He said nothing, but something flickered in his dark eyes.

'For the last time, I order you to lay down your weapon, centurion,' he shouted, his voice echoing through the silent valley. Down below, the other beret shifted in the dust. The man gestured back at him with his elbow, signalling to him to be still. Agnes hoisted her weapon higher, her finger still on the trigger.

'By whose authority, soldier? *Stellam non video!*' she answered, citing the Latin battle hymn, that she saw no star by which she might know a friend. His eyes narrowed at the words.

'Let's have done with this bitch, strategos,' the other beret shouted. His voice rattled like a snake around the fissures above. Her cheeks flushed at his words. They'd soon learn how easy it was to be done with her. A bead of sweat trickled down her enemy's face.

A black shadow passed across the crepuscular sky. A cry tore through the air, as a steppe eagle hovered above. Neither soldier looked up. It was the herald of her doom. She was ready. She would die like a soldier, here in the southern wastes. She felt a passing sadness as the vernal woods of her homeland flashed before her eyes.

Something moved behind the truck. Despite herself, Agnes' eyes left her foe. A white spectre was moving through the valley. A barefoot figure in a shawl and veil was passing noiselessly up the sandy track behind the soldiers. In its wake, a retinue of little children followed, all dressed in rags. Agnes gasped, unconsciously lowering her gun. It was the girl.

'Put your gun down, and get on your knees,' the grey cap said, but she hardly heard him. The girl had halted up the track. She turned to Agnes, slowly raising her veil. Her blue eyes burned like twin fires. Agnes stared back in wonder. The gun dropped from her hands. As it crashed into the sand, the eagle cried again.

The grey cap in the sand rose to his feet. Still training his gun on Agnes, he ran up the slope towards her. His commander took a few cautious steps forwards. She did not heed them, but kept her eyes on the girl. Although far off, her ultramarine eyes seemed right before her, nearer than her foes, speaking to her without words.

'*Aiteo!*' Agnes said without knowing why. 'I ask you!' Her voice filled the valley with an unnatural echo. The beret started, but an instant later there was another cry behind him. He turned just in time to see the other grey cap trip over a rock and fall, but instead of hitting the earth, he screamed as he disappeared beneath the sand without a trace.

His comrade stared aghast at the rock, as the bandit leapt over the truck and ran up the slope, shouting madly. Agnes awoke. She looked around her. The girl and the children were gone. The confused beret flailed about angrily as he looked for his comrade. She fled towards the cliff, abandoning her gun in the sand.

Seeing her escape, the man at once raised his gun, took aim and fired. Stone splinters exploded beside her head, but she was already back behind the rock. He cursed, dashing after her, but another cry rent the air. The man turned in surprise as the bandit too tripped, then disappeared beneath the sand.

She did not wait but ran on blindly among the crevices, desperately trying to find a way through. Her whole body was drenched in sweat and her khakis felt heavier than ever. To her right was a narrow path between two crags, just wide enough for her to fit through. She slipped in and clambered up the steep track, her boots skidding on the stones.

Jackboots crunched behind her. A whizz resounded beneath the cliff face as a bullet shot past. The grey cap was scrambling up the rock in pursuit, every so often pausing to take a pot shot at her. His furrowed brow and burning eyes became those of a furious boar of the Carpathian woodland. For the first time, she was afraid. She cowered behind a boulder as rock exploded all around her.

She kept climbing, but was growing weary now. Her leg ached terribly. Everywhere the sun beat down on the gilded rock. She grabbed frantically at a scorching boulder. No sooner had she hauled herself over than another bullet ricocheted off its surface. She collapsed into a narrow crevice on its far side. She tried to scramble to her feet, but fell forwards. As she hit the sand, her eyes came to rest on a lone fig tree growing out of the cliff face above. It was completely withered to a stalk.

There was a scuffing of rubber, and a shadow fell across her. She rolled over. The grey cap stood right over her, pointing his rifle straight at her head. Against the crimson of the vesperine sun, his face and beret were little more than a charcoal silhouette. Only the barrel of his rifle, protruding out of that black solar disk, took any definite shape. One narrow tunnel that was about to eclipse her forever. She tried to think of the Virgin, but fear put Her image to flight.

'*Poios eisai?*' Agnes cried in terror. 'Who are you?' The disk became a face, taut with a cruel smile. The soldier's bandana had fallen away, revealing features of a Phrygian cast like that of her own men. Like that of the men he'd butchered in cold blood.

'Shouldn't have meddled in what you didn't understand,' he said, 'but you couldn't help yourself. So now you must die, centurion. For the greater good. For Our Lady of Battlement.' He pressed his gun to her forehead and moved his finger to the trigger. She shrank back.

'She walketh through dry places, seeking rest,' a Greek voice suddenly rang out. It was like a whisper, yet resounded throughout the valley. Agnes wondered whether she hadn't imagined it. Then she noticed that the man was looking up, his mouth hanging open in shock. She followed his gaze. Above the rusty branches of the fig tree on the clifftop was a solitary white figure. It was the girl.

'Who are you?' the man said. 'What are you doing here, girl? Come down here at once.' There was a stirring as the other children appeared beside her.

'All of you, get down here at once,' he demanded. His voice rose with anger, but also fear. His hand trembled as he raised his gun and pointed it at the girl. Sweat ran down his black beard, and dropped onto his leather jerkin.

'She seeketh rest, but findeth none,' the girl repeated. 'Then she saith, I will return into my house from whence I came out.'

The children all watched Agnes too, and did not seem to notice the man at all.

'Get down here, damn you, or I'll shoot!' the soldier screamed, but by now his hand shook violently. His face contorted terribly. He had utterly forgotten Agnes.

'*Epistrepho*,' the girl said, 'I will return.'

The man's trembling became a frenzy. Seizing her chance, and with a will that hardly seemed her own, Agnes kicked at his knee. The man howled in pain and fell to the ground, dropping his weapon. In a flash she was back on her feet, hurtling up the rock face towards the fig tree. The man yelled with rage.

As she reached it, she saw to her horror that there was nowhere left to go. The girl was gone. She reeled about in desperation. The man was back on his feet, grabbing up his rifle. He limped towards her, his face transformed back into that of a raging boar. He raised his rifle. This was it. She was returning home.

Just as he was about to fire, he stumbled. At first, Agnes thought his leg had given way, but as he tried to steady himself, with every step his footing became less sure, as if the desert had become ice. The stones skipped beneath the soles of his feet. Panic stricken, he grasped in vain at the boulders around him. He fell to his knees, still trying to raise his gun, but immediately lost his balance and fell onto his hands. As he scrambled about, the stones fled before his fingers, giving way to sand. Then the sand itself fell away in a cascade beneath him, revealing a mighty fissure in the rock. The soldier flailed about like a drowning man, then he was gone. All that remained were his gun and beret, lying on the sand.

She looked frantically at the gaping cavern, where a second before her executioner had stood, then at the withered tree, and back up at the cliff. There was no one there. Engines roared in the valley below. Like a frightened hare, she cast about in terror for another means of escape, but there was none.

All of a sudden her feet slid from beneath her. She cried out, but it was too late. She was slipping, then falling. Her hands clawed at the sand, but it ran through her fingers like water. The sandstone sky gave way to night. She shut her eyes and let go.

CHAPTER 28

Vadim

Vadim had not stopped running since they left downtown Kremlovska. Ignoring the pleas of the tagmata, he had torn away through the streets of the city, retracing his steps homeward. No sooner had Dnilo told him about his father, than the Zaporizhzhian girl, the nightclub, the nectar and the thug had all vanished.

'*Moy gospodin,*' Dnilo called after him as he strode towards the palace's iron gates. It had been all his valet could do to keep pace with the tagmata, but Vadim barely heard him, or anything else, at all. He felt angry. Angrier than he had ever felt. As if his father had chosen to die now to spite him.

Dawn's rosy fingers were already decorating the domes of the Trinity churches with fuschia. Vadim did not see them, nor the traces of confetti from his abortive ordination with which the piazza was still strewn. Instead, his eyes were fixed on the oak door of the ancient palace emerging from the morning mist. The serrated carving of its arch, like the thousand teeth of a dragon's maw, reminded him of the prickly laurel that had cut into his temples the day before. The spectre of his father's haughty eyes rose before him.

He ripped the chlamys from his shoulders, discarding the white cloth in the portal. The crisp of air of the Novgorovian morning chilled the bare skin beneath his dalmatica. The red berets stood aside, holding open the door, but the footsteps of the other tagmata were no longer audible behind. He paused on the threshold, turning back.

'*Strategos*,' the taller one said, inclining his black beret as he stood to attention, awaiting Vadim's orders. The man clearly did not wish to intrude any further, and expected to be dismissed. His job was done.

'*Moy prints*,' Dnilo hailed him, finally arriving across the palace forecourt. 'Her Highness, Princess Eudoxia, will be glad to know that you are safely–' Vadim glowered at him. As Dnilo spoke, the tagma's eyes flitted to Vadim, before lowering demurely to the floor. Divested of his mask now, in the early morning light the soldier looked young, perhaps even younger than he was. The man clearly understood.

'*Se mnoy*,' Vadim commanded in Novgorovian that he accompany him. Dnilo raised his eyebrows, but Vadim ignored him. Instead, he nodded to the tagma, who quickly fell in behind him.

'Your name?' Vadim asked without looking at him as he rushed headlong through the doors and crossed the palace vestibule. Despite the crimson light of the Kremlovskan dawn seeping through the portal, little of the morning had penetrated the windowless hall. Its heavy red-and-gold frescoed walls were still cloaked in shade, as was Vadim's face.

'Ilya, *strategos*,' the soldier answered, stepping up beside him. The pounding of the young men's long strides on the stone floor echoed discordantly around the wooden walls, like the strumming of a rickety old kithar. The desperate patter of Dnilo's feet pursued at a distance, as his retainer again fell behind.

'*Oblast*?' Vadim continued, asking which region the tagma was from. His eyes stared dully ahead, to the end of the hall, where a flight of steps beneath a carved wooden screen led upwards to the royal chamber.

'Campus Mariae,' Ilya replied, naming the Field of Mary. A Cossack. That was good. The man had already saved him once. Such things must be important among soldiers. So it would be important to him.

'Thank you for your service,' Vadim said, not without some awkwardness. 'You will remain with me now.' The tagma inclined his head. They passed beneath the decorated screen and ascended the stairs, followed by Dnilo.

The stunted carvings of the faded mahogany screen depicted the apotheasis of Justinia and the gnosis of her soul. He had never much liked the wooden rood, always thinking it the ugliest of the many abominations of the red palace. The expression of the dying maiden, as the swirling of the divine wind assumed her into Thea the Mother, reminded him of his father's drawn face. Beholding the resplendent Mother in the eclipsing moon, crowned by the gnostic star, he realised for the first time that the day had finally come. Before long, his father's soul would be gathered to the Mother too. Freedom had come sooner than expected. Yet now it had, he felt inexplicably oppressed by it.

'Family?' Vadim questioned the soldier inattentively. He thought of his mother. After yesterday, he no longer cared what his father thought. Had his father loved him, he would have understood why he didn't want to follow in his footsteps. Instead, nothing but pride and disgust had been written on his face. Even hatred. But even now, his mother would not abandon him. He felt guilty on her account. Perhaps he oughtn't to have run away the night before.

'None, *velichestvo*,' Ilya replied as they reached the top of the stairs. Vadim tried to imagine what it must be like to have no family, but could not. No overbearing father. No overprotective mother. No spoilt cousin. The only family Ilya had were the other tagmata. No distractions or obligations. Just the palace guard.

He stepped onto the landing and marched down the corridor. The first light of the Novgorovian morning shone through the lone window at its far end. In the half-light, he could see the open door, and the two attendant deacons stood beside it like ghouls.

The nearer he drew, the more oppressive the heavy burgundy of the medieval tapestries became. Each step was onerous, as if the carpet had transformed into a thick purpureal mire. There was something inside the room, something terrible. Something perhaps not even human at all. Yet something he had to face.

He approached the door, glancing with annoyance at the deacons. They drew aside, the nearest youth scanning Vadim's bloodstained dalmatica. He was sure he detected disdain in the boy's expression. Despite being on the verge of adolescence, everything about him was morbid, from his sallow cheeks and white-blond hair to his pale and starched chlamys robe. Vadim wasn't even inside yet, and the whole place stank of death. He crossed the threshold, leaving Ilya and Dnilo outside.

It had been many years since Vadim last entered the royal chamber, but its high ceiling and slender gothic window, letting in so little of the weak Novgorovian dawn, were just as he recollected them as a child. He was filled with the same dread he had felt then, but this time Theadoric did not stand before him, extending his ringed fingers for Vadim to kiss. Instead, his emaciated figure lay outstretched upon the four-poster bed in the centre of the room. There was no one else in the bedchamber, and his father did not stir at his approach. Vadim stood paralysed in the corner, staring at the glacial sheets with foreboding. He wasn't even sure whether it was a corpse he beheld.

There was a weak exhalation, more a rattle than a breath, from amid the heavy cushions. Vadim exhaled too, unaware that he had been holding his breath. He tiptoed towards the oak bedstead, glancing up at the medieval tracery of its cross-posts. The irascible eyes of a bear, gouged into the wood, peered back at him. Theadoric lay on his back with his eyes closed, a light kamelaukion with a gold star upon his head. Beneath it, his face was so pale that it might have been his death mask, its anguished contours traced as deeply as the medieval woodwork.

He ought to have felt something. Compassion for his parent, perhaps. Or pity, at the very least. There was nothing, though. He saw only the vapid image of an icon before him, as faceless as his aunt's imperial portrait. He was on the verge of leaving when the icon unexpectedly became a face. A furrow appeared between Theadoric's brows, the same mountain cleft that had been there the day before. The storm was long since gone, but angry clouds still gathered there. Like an animal wrapping itself in its tail, Theadoric's fingers curled into a tight fist. He opened his eyes.

They rested vacantly on Vadim's face, so much so that he was unsure whether they saw him at all. Despite his initial apathy, something stirred inside him at the sight. The pathetic image of the toothless thug writhing in the air appeared before him, then the crumpled heap at Ilya's feet. He could not long bear his father's moribund gaze, and was overcome by a desperate desire to leave. Unconsciously he began to turn towards the door, but just then Theadoric raised his hand and, with the feeblest gesture Vadim had ever seen, motioned to the far side of the bed.

He moved gingerly about the oak posters, drawing closer to his father. As he did so, he caught Ilya's eye outside the door. The tagma bowed his head and hastily withdrew. Theadoric waved his hand, and Vadim lent down to his face. He coughed violently, his pallid torso shaking like an earthquake, as if his body were made of chalk and might crumble away at any moment.

'Vadim Cassimir,' Theadoric croaked. Vadim frowned. He shouldn't be surprised. He couldn't remember his father ever addressing him solely by his Marian name in life. Why did he expect that he would do so now, in death?

'You...' his father said. His eyes fired briefly, like the last-stoked embers of some god's forge, before they were extinguished by another fit of coughing. Vadim stared at his father impatiently, examining the thick purple veins of his tightly clenched fist. He wished he were somewhere, anywhere, else. He knew he should have been patient, but he still felt as if something were screaming inside. His eyes lingered on his father's crown. The diadem morphed into that of his cousin.

'You, Vadim Cassimir, are—' Theadoric resumed, but another voice from behind interrupted him.

'Thanks be to Our Lady that you are alive!' Eudoxia stood in the doorway. His mother's handsome eyes were red. Dark rings were traced below them, as if the clouds on Theadoric's brow had broken free and settled there. She clearly hadn't slept all night. Vadim felt another pang of guilt. He averted his gaze.

'Why did you run away, Vadim?' she asked, running to his side, embracing him as she kissed his forehead furiously. 'Thank the Virgin Dnilo found you, or Our Lady only knows what—'

'You, Vadim Cassimir,' Theadoric persisted, as his eyes scanned his son's soiled dalmatica and bruised face, 'are... a disgrace!'

Vadim leapt to his feet, nearly tripping backwards as he glared in horror at the pallid shade before him. All that animated the corpse were its hateful bronze eyes, glowing malignly up at him from its still tepid death shroud.

'Theadoric, I implore you,' Eudoxia said, but her husband completely ignored her. Her face contorted in horror.

'You are no son of mine.' Theadoric's voice rasped through the gloam of the bedchamber. Falling to her knees beside his deathbed, Eudoxia desperately clasped at his pale hands. Her tears ran down the translucent film of flesh that still coated his bony fingers, but he was unmoved. Vadim was disgusted. He rushed to the door. Ilya's long shadow coloured the carpet mahogany outside. He had hardly reached the threshold before his father's morbid rattle echoed in the room behind him. He gestured at the door and two deacons stepped hesitantly into the bedchamber. Eudoxia tried to press her husband's hand back down, but he resisted.

'My love, in the name of the Mother, I implore you to see reason,' Eudoxia said between her tears. 'Have mercy! Vadim is our son.'

The pontifex did not even look at her. Instead, with a momentous effort, he turned onto his side, fixing Vadim as he stood in the doorway.

'I, Theadoric Eugenianus Cassimir, Grand Protosynkellos, and Grand Prince of Novgorod,' he pronounced over Eudoxia's sobs, 'hereby disinherit you, Vadim Cassimir, as my son, and strip you of all titles, royal or otherwise, thereby conferred upon you.'

Vadim stared with hatred at the squinting brazen eyes, so rapidly extinguishing together with his father's life. He just had time to see how his body crumpled back into the pillows, like the deflating ion web of a light-craft, before he turned away.

'Vadim!' his mother called after him. 'You will always be my son!'

He paused on the threshold. Then he stepped out onto the red carpet without looking back.

He looked askance at Ilya. The tagma's head was bowed, and he did not meet Vadim's gaze. He had heard everything, though. It didn't matter. He was the only family he had now. He nodded to the soldier to fall in, and walked on.

CHAPTER 29

Zeno

Zeno stepped into his office. His feet felt unsteady, as if the floorboards were melting away beneath them like liquid glass. He stood there for several minutes with the tenebrae down, gripping his desk as he tried to steady his sea legs. He'd barely slept the night before. The truth was he could hardly even remember how he'd gotten home yesterday or back to the office this morning. For the first time in three years, he'd been last in. Without greeting anyone, he'd shut himself away in his office.

His eye rested on the greyscale of his wife's face in the hologram. It was at moments like these when he most wished she were still around. No matter how senseless the world out there became, he had always been able to turn to her and it would make sense again, every time. Now he was alone, and had only himself to turn to. That was what he had to thank the Ruthenian centurion for.

For some time yesterday, they had scoured the underground silo, but in the end had given up. It was simply too large for them to investigate alone and there had been no trace of Simeon. In the end, it had been enough trouble just getting out. There were no exits other than that by which they had come in. To Maurice's great chagrin, they'd ended by scrambling ignominiously back up the supply shaft.

His mind spun like a turbine, going around and around the subterranean dome, propelled by the mad heretic's words. Had that been the whited sepulchre? Was it some kind of code for what they were hiding? Somehow that didn't quite fit. He'd felt uncomfortable from the start, even when they were down there. He knew criminals. He knew how they thought. Always trying to stay one step ahead of the lex. Yes, and they could be cunning. Very cunning. And yet, there was always a limit to their ambition. As if it were bounded by fear of being caught. It was something they could never quite shake. This had been different. Whoever was behind it may have preferred secrecy, but they were unafraid. As if they did not fear punishment.

He did not have long to unravel the riddle. Maurice's large shadow lumbered outside the glass, like some mute totem. He appeared in the doorway, mumbling something, but before he could get the words out Zeno knew what he was going to say. The chief wanted to see him. A few minutes later, he stood outside his boss' office on the other side of the praetorium, staring at the brass plaque beneath the white star embossed on the wood. *Caput Praetorii Urbis Ravennae.* He read and re-read the words, without really knowing why. Eventually, he knocked.

'*Intrate,*' his boss called softly from behind the door, as if she had known he was standing there. Zeno stepped in mechanically, still not entirely trusting his own legs. He was dazed by the large sunlit office, with its tall glass windows overlooking the medieval city below. On its far side, a small woman with Hellenic features rose from behind a desk, smiling brightly.

Zeno crossed the grey carpeted floor to greet her, glancing up at the imperial portrait as he went. It was the same one as in his own office, Theadosia's face likewise obscured by the mandylion of the Virgin, only much larger. Beneath it was a long oak shield, its emblazon an eagle in profile accompanied by the words, '*Ravenna Caput Occidentale*'. Next to this his boss' diploma was displayed, glinting with its golden emboss of the Palace Hall University of Magnaura.

'Zeno!' she greeted him, beaming as she wrung his large hands. 'Well, you really have outdone yourself this time.' Her smile was broad, but failed to reach her eyes. Zeno smiled back politely as he stood to attention. She gestured to a suite of lounge chairs beside the windows.

'*Quanta urbs,* what a city,' she remarked with professional melancholy, waving at the cityscape below as they seated themselves. 'Indeed, as you well know, brother adjunct, our work here is never done.' Her smile was like a flashlight, and died in an instant. Her mirthless eyes lingered on Zeno's face before returning to the city below.

'Yes, alas, crime is always with us, my good Zeno,' she continued, 'and I need not tell you, who have always been a moral man, that there is no crime so heinous as *nefas*. You know your history. Immemory and irreligion and have always been with us, right from the beginning. After all, not a century after Our Lady's Descension those dregs of the patriarchs, the Palaeologi, came out of hiding in Anglia and shamefully tried to restore the heresy of the false prophet.'

'Atamana, if I may...?' Zeno asked, as soon as she paused. This breathless history lecture was so out of character for his boss, who was ordinarily so punctilious, and impatient of even the slightest digression.

'Yet, even now,' she went on, ignoring him, 'crime has not been entirely extirpated from our cities. It pains me to say this, Katepano, but acts of unkindness to Our Lady have been on the rise of late.'

Zeno bowed his head contritely, recalling their last interview about the crime statistics. May must truly have been a bad month, if the propraetorium of the Italikon had issued its mensual report on the criminal basilika even before it had actually ended. He braced himself for the reprimand that was surely coming. The image of Maurice slouching behind his crumb-covered desk appeared before him. He gritted his teeth.

'Yes, I know,' she said, as if she had read his thoughts, 'such acts of unkindness can only pain one such as yourself, who have always been so kind to Our Lady. And yet, Katepano, you should be aware – *sub rosa*, for your ears only – that so serious has the situation become in our own exarchate that measures have had to be taken. Yes, even going so far as a lustration of the Reservation itself.' Another flashlight illuminated her face.

He was astonished. The Reservation had never been raided in his living memory. Indeed, he'd never heard of such a thing. As far as he knew, it wasn't even permissible under the second basilikon that had put the prison under martial law in the first place. The Italikon must surely have had serious grounds to suspect heretical contagion, if it had gone that far. First the crypt and the silo, and now this. The world was upending itself again.

'But that is exactly why I wanted to speak to you today, brother adjunct,' she said, reverting to her usual directness. Her Greek eyes bored into him. Zeno studied his feet solemnly. The reprimand was well-deserved. Simeon had given him the slip in plain sight. The only witness to a triple homicide and, moreover, the key link to solving the mystery of the nectar silo. It was shameful.

'Such achievements must not go unmarked!' she exclaimed. 'The city – no, the whole exarchate – are indebted to you, Zeno.' Her face brightened as she beamed at him. To his surprise, there was no sarcasm in her eyes.

'Your discovery at the port yesterday was a rare victory for the cause of law and order in this city, Katepano, the like of which we have not seen for many years,' she continued. 'You have my congratulations, and not only mine. The exarch himself has asked me to pass on his personal commendation.'

His eyes widened. The nectar. Of course. An investigation by the criminal intelligence division of the Italikon must already be underway. He just hadn't been informed, as was natural. Sometimes there were reasons why these things had to be kept secret. Like the raid on the Reservation. How could he have been so obtuse?

'The discovery not only of an unauthorised slave gathering,' his boss cut into his thoughts, 'but of a criminal heretical gang as well. Heresy on such a scale has not been seen in this city for many years now, but thanks to your efforts its unholy seed has been nipped in the bud before it could put forth its poisonous shoots. You have saved countless douloi from the corruption of Error, Zeno. You should be proud.'

He stared at his boss in mute disbelief. She wasn't wrong. The slave gathering had been larger than anything he'd ever seen, and the circumstantial evidence was certainly strongly indicative of the Alpha Heresy. Indeed, Italikon intelligence would undoubtedly have applied the *confessio vi coacta*, the forced confessional, if the detainees hadn't volunteered their testimony. But could slaves really have been behind the silo? She hadn't even mentioned it, nor the crime he'd failed to solve. Besides, surely even the Italikon couldn't have concluded their investigation that swiftly?

'Atamana, I am honoured that you find me worthy of such praise...' he began, but something humourless in her eyes, concealed behind her smile, made him pause. He remembered the Reservation. The question on his lips failed to voice itself.

'Yes, indeed, and the praise is well-deserved,' she continued, as if she had not heard the objection in his voice. 'Nor shall such merit go unrewarded, as I said. I am pleased to inform you, Katepano, that the exarch not only gave his commendation. He also made a recommendation. Promotion on transfer, Zeno!' She rose, offering her hand in congratulation. He stood up automatically, hardly knowing what he was doing, smiling as she rung his hand.

'I am sure this will be glad news for you?' she asked.

He nodded, but his head spun. Promotion. It was certainly a great honour. He was still so young to make ataman of a praetorium. Especially for a man. It had long been his ambition, but only three years after his transfer from Numidia?

'Chief, I – I mean – I'm greatly honoured, of course, but is there not someone else more worthy?' he stammered. His legs felt unsteady again.

'My dear Zeno, you are so very modest,' she said with feigned incredulity. 'There is no one more deserving. In good Justinia's name, to think that you still doubt yourself so, and after exposing such heresy.' She still smiled, but the same mirthlessness was in her eyes.

'Please do not think me ungrateful, Atamana,' he said. 'I shall – of course – be most honoured to accept this promotion.' He stood to attention. The star light above the door pulsed green, before fading back to a sickly lime.

'I am very glad to hear that, very glad indeed,' she said, wringing his hands once more. Then she turned away, moving primly back to her desk. Zeno saluted, but something still nagged him.

'Atamana, if I may?' he asked despite himself, as she re-seated herself. 'The criminal heretical gang we discovered. Could they – I mean, rather – is our assessment that their capabilities encompassed an operation of such a scale?'

His boss did not look up. As she waved her hand over the holographic screen in her desk, a crease appeared between her eyebrows. Zeno turned towards the door. He felt like a fool. It was a matter for criminal intelligence. He'd overstepped the mark.

'Ataman?' she asked, her face painted with an incredulous smile. 'You haven't asked where you're being transferred to.'

Zeno was astounded. She was right. He'd been so distracted that he hadn't even remembered to ask.

'Please excuse the oversight,' he said, trying to smile. 'I was so overjoyed by the news that it completely slipped my mind. I am of course very sorry to be leaving the service of your praetorium, but I shall be delighted with transfer wherever the exarch judges I may best serve Our Lady.'

They watched one another across the room in silence. He tried to suppress the thought, but it was no use. She still hadn't answered his question. Maybe he had overstepped the mark. Maybe it was a matter for the Italikon, and not for him. But why was he being promoted for a crime he had failed to solve?

The smile disappeared from her face, its hard lines silting up like rivulets baked by the aestival sun. She looked down at her screen. Once more, Zeno had the unnerving feeling that his boss had read his mind. He shifted uncomfortably, and moved to the door.

'Cross-transfer on promotion. District station ataman. Counter-heresy division of the First Praetorium,' she said, as Zeno's mouth fell open. 'Military theme of the Opsikion.'

'I, oh, I, thank you...' he mumbled, lost for words. The desiccated fissures of his boss' cheeks slackened with amusement as she smiled naturally for the first time during their entire interview.

'Thank you will suffice,' she said, nodding to the door, then looking back at her desk. Zeno stood to attention, saluted, and turned to leave.

'And Ataman, one last thing,' she called across the room without looking up, as he stood on the threshold. 'You're taking the fat one with you.'

CHAPTER 30

Hypatia

Hypatia stepped out of the church. Yesterday's sun was gone. In its place, a heavy mist draped the Lacedamonian plain below, transforming it into a giant Stygian marsh. Wisps of watery air cloyed at the slopes of the hills, like waves splashed by the phantom greaves of some titanic hoplite.

The elation of yesterday's dialogue was gone too. Last night had ended the same way it always did, of course. If the fruit had been sweeter to the taste, the bitterer was its consumption. In the morning, she had summarily thrown the new boy out, just as she had the last. So too, once more, she'd found her way back down the garden path to the little portico of the Saint Sophia church. The inevitable confession and shriving of her sins had followed. So resumed the usual cycle of her lonely life, as she prepared her next dialogue.

As she descended the familiar stone steps, she wondered how many more times she would rehearse the same tired drama. Like some crass holospectacle whose plot had been looping for the last century, its colouration fading, growing ever dimmer as the features of its amphitheatrical actors became drawn with age. Her own ageing visage reappeared before her, as it had in the cruel verisimilitude of the mirror the morning before. *Dea Nutrix*.

Feeling a damp chill beneath her chiton, she quickened her pace. Though already the last of May, Mystras could still surprise. A few shreds of blue bunting still lingered on the fountain's proud aquiline wings. She squirmed with disgust at herself, picturing the nocturnal ravages of the feast, but her spirit buoyed at the sight of the busts of Saints Hypatia and Kassia. She was reminded of the handsome blond woman she had passed here the day before, and the naked youths vanished.

There was a smatter of raindrops against her face. It quickly grew more insistent, like a swarm of pestering flies. Before long, it was pouring. On the far side of the valley the thunder god growled, expressing his fulgent disdain. She examined her white chiton and diaphanous skirt, and started running up the path towards the nearest building. By the time she reached the red roof of the aula portal, her chiton was already soaked through. She cursed as she shoved open the glass doors, hoping no one was inside.

To her luck, the lights were off. There was no one about, just the plain ochre brickwork and dun benches, stretching out in serried ranks like the prostrate bodies of fallen soldiers. She slumped down at the end of one. The damp fabric of her chiton clung to her skin like slime. She'd doubtless be stuck here for awhile yet. She'd just have to hope none of the tutees turned up unexpectedly, especially not yesterday's boy.

It was one of the dialogue halls she rarely used. By now, the rain lashed with untold fury against its rose windows. Unlike her aula, this one had a large fresco over the doors depicting a sunlit medieval city, from whose midst rose a giant rock. Atop the rock was a temple, whose white columns and pediment gleamed in the bright Mediterranean sun. Rising above its glistening roof, looking down beneficently upon the port city as she raised her hand in blessing, was the Demiurge of the Virgin. In the foreground was a man wearing a silver kamelaukion crown. His body was girt with chainmail, and he held a drawn sword in his hand. As he faced the temple rock, he knelt in the dust, raising his hand in thanks to the Virgin. Behind him, stretching away innumerably into the distance, were thousands of blind prisoners, the hands of each placed on the shoulders of the one before. Beneath the fresco was the faded legend, '*A.U.R. 688 Basileus II Rex Virgini gratias agat.*'

Hypatia's eyes rested on the captives. The blind leading the blind. It was nothing new then, a thousand years before, as surely as it wasn't today. Her mind coiled and uncoiled over the last two days since Our Lady of Battlement. What was she pursuing, and where would it all end? The honest truth was that she didn't know. She'd been so sure Marcus wouldn't take Caledon. Since he'd left, she'd no longer been able to see any future for herself. Nothing but a long, blind march into loneliness, with no salvation at the end. That was why she'd been so angry when they'd last spoken, two days earlier. Why she always was, every time. Why did he have to leave? Her eyes grew moist.

Soles scuffed on the far side of the aula. Hypatia reeled about in surprise. A door stood ajar at the other end of the hall. A woman stood in front of it, holding a tabula in her hand and donning a pleasantly surprised smile. It was the blonde from the garden. Hypatia felt a slight frisson, though whether from the cold or her embarrassment she couldn't say. She rose, modestly crossing her arms in front of her translucent chiton, but immediately uncrossed them, realising the ridiculousness of such a gesture before another woman. Unperturbed, and without ceremony, the stranger eagerly crossed the room. Hypatia's stomach performed the same somersault it had the day before.

'So nice to meet you, the Mother's kindness be with you,' the woman said, beaming at Hypatia as she touched her palm to her chest in blessing. 'I am Cleope, the visiting lector from the Palace Hall, and you must be Hypatia, the dean of the academy of theapolitology here?

I am so sorry we have not yet been introduced. Arriving straight after the feast was perhaps inopportune.'

'Hypatia – yes, indeed – a pleasure to meet you too,' she replied with a smile, making the same gesture as Cleope. For an instant she wondered if Cleope had been implying something by her last remark, but her clear brow and honest teal eyes betrayed no unkindness.

'How fortunate I am to be here!' Cleope exclaimed. 'What a fine and good place this is. A place of such knowledge, artistry, and memory. A place where all the beauty and wisdom of the Virgin is preserved for the ages.' Her sparkling eyes rose to the fresco, resting reverently on the figure of Our Lady Parthene floating above the white city. Hypatia watched her with speechless fascination. Though she could not have been much younger than her, there was something almost childlike about her. A sort of radiantly innocent splendour. She had never seen anything like it.

'King Basil, *Boulgaroktonos*,' Cleope mused. 'The patriarch who blinded fifteen thousand of his enemies in a single day. Yet Our Lady reached even him, despite the fury and blindness of his immemory. With what grace and splendour She must have appeared to him high up on the Acropolis, amidst the ruins of that temple of the false maiden. A perfect vision of chastity and purity. A shining star amidst that ancient city of knowledge, so far fallen, guiding its people back to the light of the Trinity. Oh, to have been there, Hypatia!'

Cleope fixed her shining eyes on Hypatia. So dazzling was their ebullience that they seemed to shine right through to her core, burning her raw inside. She was struck by the simplicity of her address, as if they were old friends, and hadn't met only a moment before.

'Yes, such is Her kindness that even in the nighttime of their ignorance, Our Lady did not abandon the patriarchs, ever trying to reach those who, though they knew it not, were also trying to find their way back to Her,' Cleope continued, still staring into Hypatia's eyes. 'Oh, what a glory this bright city on the hills is, Hypatia. Truly a new

Acropolis of learning. A beacon steering us clear of the perils of the immemory of Error, dear sister. And how fortunate you are to be here. How I envy you!' Cleope fell silent, her eyes glinting with a sapphire radiance. So bright was their glare that, for the briefest moment, they almost seemed terrible. Hypatia could not disengage herself from their mesmeric glow.

Cleope lowered her delicate blond lashes, closing her pale eyelids. When she opened them again, it was as if she were seeing Hypatia for the first time. As if the unearthly inspiration that had breathed through her just before had suddenly left her. Recognition, then embarassment, entered her eyes. She smiled sheepishly at Hypatia.

'I am so sorry, Hypatia,' Cleope stammered, 'I can get rather carried away! You must forgive me. It's just such a joy to be here, but how forgetful I am. To think, here I am lecturing the dean of the theapolitological academy on religious history. What a ridiculous spectacle I must make.' A rosy tint spread over her cheeks, like dawn splaying over a frozen lake. Hypatia was stunned.

'No, no, not at all, please do not worry... I am so glad to meet you too, I, only...' Hypatia replied, but hesitated, aware of how ridiculous she surely sounded herself. 'Please, tell me, what brings you to Mystras? I confess I don't even know your discipline.' She brushed back her hair.

'Oh, what a spectacle I am indeed,' Cleope said as her blush deepened. 'I was so carried away that I did not even introduce myself properly. I am only a technician, I'm afraid. Not a philosoph like yourself.' She looked away, as if ashamed of the admission.

Hypatia was surprised. She had only met a handful of technicians in her life. There were none in Mystras. There was only one place in the entire empire where techne was researched and taught, the Palace Hall of Magnaura. Besides, she had never met one that looked and talked like Cleope did. She was fascinated.

'And, if you don't mind my asking, what is your techne?' she asked, as they sat down together on the bench nearest the door. The rain still lashed furiously against the quatrefoil windows. She was heedless of her damp chiton now, as of all else save the fluttering of Cleope's diaphanous eyelids.

'Oh, nothing interesting. The truth is I'm afraid even to admit it before a theapolitologian like yourself. I'm a technician of elementals,' Cleope stated, as if it had been the most commonplace remark in the world. She glanced distractedly at the fresco, as if she found a painting of a patriarch who had died a millenium before infinitely more interesting than her own occupation.

Hypatia stared at her in stunned silence. It was unimaginable. Not just a technician, but a technician of elemental philosophy. She had never met one, and that was no surprise. While the mechanical philosophies were open to all, the study of the elementals, the invisible and indivisible particles that made up the cosmos, was strictly prohibited, save by a select group of philosophs at Magnaura. It had been so for centuries, ever since the third basilikon of the empress Parthenodosia I against irreligious inquiries. There was no more arcane knowledge in the entire world.

'Oh, it's not what you think,' Cleope said modestly, 'and, yet, I admit it is a great honour to study the nature of the Mother's creation. For when one comes to know how intricate and heterogenous the world really is – indeed, what a wondrous thing woman herself is – how can one doubt the sublimity of the mind that created it? How beautiful, and yet how terrible, is the gnosis of Thea, sister!'

By now, Hypatia had utterly forgotten her surroundings, damp clothes and shivering skin, so completely absorbed was she by Cleope. Yet as she admired the chiselled Attic lines of her face, her intelligent eyes, and starlit golden tresses, she was overcome by a suffocating sense of inadequacy. How poor her life was beside that of this beatific creation. How mean her existence was, and how sordid all of her affairs. She looked away.

'I am sorry,' Cleope said, mistaking her aversion for boredom, 'as I said, I really am so prone to going on, even with those I've only just met. Honestly, it's so terribly rude of me, you must forgive me.'

'No, no, not at all,' Hypatia replied, almost with alarm, unconsciously seizing Cleope's hand. 'It is not that, it's just that I – I mean – you are so, so... and I, my life, I am...' Her words choked in her throat, as her eyes unexpectedly watered. She tried to gird herself with her usual wry smile, but burst into tears instead.

Before she knew what she was doing, she was in Cleope's arms. She held her close, pressing her to her soft chest as she stroked her hair soothingly. Hypatia sobbed uncontrollably. It was simply all too much in the presence of this glorious being. She wept for all her pain. For all her disappointment and disgust at her shameful life. For her lost youth. For all her bitterness at her absent husband. For all her affairs, and her uncleanness in the eyes of the Mother. For all her joyless lonely life on the Morean hill.

'There there, my dear,' Cleope's mellifluous voice sounded above her, her words hesperidean sweet. 'Do not weep. You have so much to live for here, sister. What a wondrous place this is, and what a joy it must be for you to be here. Why do you weep so, dear one?'

It was strange how this woman knew her so well. All her former self-awareness was dissolving in her warm embrace.

'I am not ungrateful – and you're right – it is a great privilege to be here,' Hypatia spluttered. 'It's just when I think of you, so, so... and there, in Mariapol, such grace and majesty... then me, here, alone, lost in my own lowly life...' Her tears came in a torrent, blemishing Cleope's spotless chiton. Seeing this, she became ashamed, and tried to pull away in embarrassment, but Cleope only held her more tightly.

'The Mother loves you and forgives all, my dear sister, always remember that,' Cleope said as Hypatia clung to her warm body. 'She will never forsake those that turn to Her with a pure and contrite heart, whatever they may have done, for we are all of us fallen from the grace of Her Gnosis.'

Cleope's lips brushed her forehead as she kissed her, continuing to stroke her hair. Only half-aware of what she was doing, Hypatia raised her head, and their lips met. Before she knew what was happening, Cleope's burning mouth was on her own, and she was immersed in the salty scent of her skin. Hypatia kissed her with a sudden furious desire, as uncontrollable as her tears. Cleope's delicate fingers touched the small of her back, and her touch was like fire.

Hypatia nearly swooned, but instead started, as if singed by Cleope's hand. She cast about confusedly, hardly knowing where she was. Hearing the rain on the rose windows, she came back rudely to her senses. She looked at Cleope with a mixture of embarrassment and disbelief.

'I am sorry, my dear, I went too far again,' Cleope said awkwardly. 'We hardly know each other, and here I am imposing my friendship upon you uninvited.'

Hypatia's embarrassment was overtaken by her curiosity. Amazingly, Cleope seemed entirely unashamed of the affection she had just shown her, worrying only whether she had been rude.

'I, no, I...' Hypatia said. 'It's just that I've never... I mean, I didn't think that it was—'

Cleope came to her aid. 'We are made in Her image, sister, and our unity returns us to Her love,' she said.

Hypatia beheld her with wonder. She had never imagined finding what she had with another woman. She had always thought such love was an aberration, an affront to the Virgin. Yet Cleope saw no shame in it.

'Have you ever prayed before Her image?' Cleope cut into her reflections, squeezing her hand. 'Before the icon of Our Lady? The first icon, I mean, the only true icon?' Her pelagic eyes glowed with rapture.

The Mandylion Icon. A gargantuan golden frame spanning the Bosphorus, thrice the height of any building to either side of the straits. An icon that was, in truth, no icon at all. For it was simply a frame containing the only true earthly image of Our Lady. An image whose likeness, like the face of the empress, the terrestrial possesion of Her Demiurge, was invisible to mortal eyes.

'No, I have never done so,' Hypatia replied, entranced by the azure of Cleope's eyes. It was not the Virgin's image that was before her, but only that of the mortal woman sat beside her, the whole of whose beautiful body pulsed with a life force purer than anything she had ever encountered. Stronger than that of any youth, be he the handsomest she had ever seen. She was more beautiful than any icon in the world. More blinding than any mandylion. The nearest mortal image of Our Lady there was.

'Then you must!' Cleope exclaimed, before pausing reflectively. 'No, you *will*.' Her eyes bored into Hypatia like lightning.

'What do you mean?' Hypatia asked. She raised her eyebrows and smiled. Her whole body was still numb from Cleope's kiss. She greedily eyed her crimson lips as they quivered with rapture. She didn't know what she meant, but she no longer cared. She was ready to believe anything she said.

'Come with me,' Cleope said. 'Come back with me to Mariapol.'

Hypatia laughed, but ceased as she realised Cleope was in earnest. For a long time, she stared into her eyes.

It was madness, of course. Dropping her whole life in the Morea and following someone she'd only just met to the capital. But when it came to it, what was really left to her in Mystras? Just longing, bitterness, and anger. Marcus wasn't coming back. Besides, another truth had already graven itself on her heart. A new truth, yes, but a truth all the same. That she could not leave this woman. It was too late for that now.

She smiled at Cleope and, without another word, took her hand.

CHAPTER 31

Marcus

Something pulled at Marcus' wrists. They felt sore, as if a rat were chewing on his skin. He tried to yank his hand back, shooing the rat away.

It was no use. The rat's teeth elongated, like great metallic strings, wrapping themselves around his arms. He tugged again, trying to pull his hands free, but he could not. Instead, his skin chafed painfully against the metal. His hands were stuck fast behind his back and would not budge. He was vaguely aware of the sound of laughter. The back of his head ached terribly, and his eyelids felt heavy. With an effort, he slowly managed to prize them open. The laughter grew louder.

At first, everything was a watery blur, as if the waves of the Bodotria had finally swept in and washed away the entire city, but as his eyes cleared, a woman came into focus. A woman in the sky, embowered in an eclipsing moon. The demiurgic Virgin, very badly painted. He was sure he had seen it somewhere before. The rest of the mural emerged, covering the entire wall. Yes, he had definitely seen it before. The image of a long room with a white marble floor appeared before him. Then a large man with a bushy red beard, standing in the dock.

The courtroom. Alarmed, he tried to sit up, but could not. The rat's teeth had not only grown around his hands, but around his chest and feet as well, fixing him fast to his chair. He tried to shake himself free, but it was no use. There was more laughter from in front of him, echoed by other voices behind. He lowered his eyes from the fresco. In the foreground, the outline of several figures gradually came into view. They were seated at a long bench facing him, jostling one another as they argued loudly. It was the tribunal. His tribunal. They were seated at his tribunal. He flushed with anger and tried to rise.

'I'd give it up if I were you, it's nay worth the bother,' came a voice from the bench, accompanied by peals of laughter. He searched the brown shades before him, desperately trying to identify the speaker. A hostile cast of gilt and russet heads stared back at him, a grim masque of anonymous faces. In their midst was a man with a ginger beard and squinty blue eyes.

'As you may have noticed, your excellency, the tables have turned a little since you were last with us,' the beard addressed him. There were cackles from the room behind, interspersed with jeering. The curia was full of people. It was a trial. His trial.

'I call this moot to order, in the name of the...' the man began, but hesitated, until a large man beside him gave him a shove. 'I call this moot to order, aye, in the name of the – in the name of – the thane!' The voices behind roared.

'What in the name of Our Lady?' Marcus exclaimed. 'How dare you? How dare you, pleb! I demand that you get down from my tribunal at once, and end this illegal gathering.'

'Your tribunal, is it now?' the ginger beard asked, to more hysterics. 'Let me bring you up to speed, your excellency. As you may have noticed, this here little bench no longer belongs to you, nor this here courtroom. In fact, if you'd care to take a look, you might notice that this here castle doesnae look to be yours anymore either, by my reckoning.' The man waved his hand at the glass windows. Marcus managed to twist towards the cityscape below. To his horror, the grey palisade of Caledon's medieval spires and insulae tenements were interspersed with scarlet icicles of fire.

'Aye, that's right, your excellency,' his judge said. 'It's nay yours any more, none of it, if it ever were. We've taken back what's rightfully ours.' There was a cry of acclamation from the back of the hall.

There were at least eight of them sitting at the bench, besides the red-beard. A mix of women and men, most were older, and one or two were wholly grey. Clustered at either end of the tribunal were a few younger people, several of whom carried clubs and some of whom had rifles. All wore the same tattered grey doublets and tunics. All glared at Marcus with abject hatred, though one or two also looked afraid. They were slaves. The same ones from the protest. What had happened to his guard? The image of a masked man being shot in the face rose before him. Marcus paled.

'That's right,' the man went on, apparently reading his thoughts, 'they're nay coming for you. Sorry to break it to you, Excellency, but I cannae say it ended all too well for them.' There were cries of assent, but a nervous-looking middle-aged woman sat to the man's other side jabbed him in the side impatiently. Her eyes were swollen. The man sat up.

'In the name of the thane, I, Justin Macleod, call this court to order!' he said. The crowd roared, then fell into mute expectation. The eyes of the whole tribunal were on Macleod. He swiped his hand over the screen in the bench, but it didn't respond. His angry little eyes darkened.

'Ex-governor, you stand accused of...' he said, swiping his hands over the screen again, vainly persisting in his pretence at due process. Finally, he lost his temper and smashed his fist into the glass. There was a loud crack. Marcus flinched, inwardly thanking the Virgin that the sonic autotranslation was still on. At least he'd know what he was being accused of. Half of that mob couldn't speak a word of Latin after all, let alone Greek. Macleod pulled a dirty parchment from his pocket and unfurled it.

'Ex-governor, you stand accused of two charges,' he said, pretending to read. 'In the first, the high moot of the thane accuses you of tyranny and perjury, for falsely accusing and murdering our good and honest thane Cassian Macleod, my brother.' The man's eyes burned like twin pools of lightning. Marcus' heart sank. The heretic had not come back to life. No, this was so much worse.

'In the second,' the miniature Cassian continued, 'you stand accused of the murder of an innocent, who hadnae done you a wit of harm.' The woman beside him burst into tears.

'Oh, what rubbish,' Marcus said, no longer able to bear the effrontery. 'How dare you accuse me of such pretend crimes? By what law am I tried here anyway? I am the lawful governor of this province. I warn you, rebel, disband this illegal assembly at once, or face the consequences.'

'He killed my bairn!' the woman howled between her sobs. 'My child, the wee thing, mercilessly cut down by him and his thugs. What did she do to deserve it, you bastard? What kind of law do you call that?' Her voice was lost in a rally of indignant cries from behind. A florid slave in a soiled tunic, who had been loitering behind the bench, resentfully watching Marcus, strode up and punched him in the jaw. He reeled, tasting blood in his mouth. The slave raised his arm for a second blow.

'Eh!' Macleod shouted, just as the man was about to strike. 'Calm down, will you? We will have order, aye, we will have order, I say! Do we really want our first act as a free people to be a shameless murder? Is that what my brother died for?'

The slave's toothless mouth hung open incomprehendingly. At last, he scuttled back to his seat.

'No, we are a free people,' Marcus' judge continued, 'so we will try the tyrant fairly for his crimes. He shall get a fair hearing, aye, and the just reward for what he has done.'

There was another cry of acclamation from the courtroom. Marcus craned his aching neck, but managed no more than to glimpse the burning skyline of Caledon. Furious black clouds gathered over the city.

'Behold the deeds of tyranny,' Macleod said. The doors crashed open. The middle-aged woman burst into tears again, covering her eyes. Furious jeering erupted behind, as if someone had opened a giant furnace. The plebs and slaves at the tribunal banged their hands on the bench. One of the greybeards touched his forehead, as if he were about to faint.

Amidst the deafening cries came the heavy tread of men's footsteps, clacking on the marble like hooves on ice. Four large Caledonian slaves appeared, girt in black and carrying a bier. A young girl lay upon it, her pale face ashen beneath her blond locks. Her tiny body was swathed in a coarse white cloth, beneath which only her feet could be seen. They were as pale as chalk. At the sight, Marcus turned the same colour. When he looked up, Macleod's eyes were fixed upon him.

'That's right, you Hromaian bastard, behold the works of your so-called justice!' he exclaimed, spittle flying from his lips. 'The girl's blood is on your head, and like your thugs, you're going to pay the price.'

The men beside the tribunal banged their clubs against the floor. An unknown assailant punched Marcus in the face again, and someone else kicked him in the side. This time, no one stopped them. He spat blood. The Mother knew he was surely done for.

'Aye, aye, lads, but due process must be followed,' Macleod shouted, raising his hand. 'How quickly you forget my brother, our martyr! Justice must be done for our thane, and this one wasnae the only one who did for him, was he? Get the other one in here. We can do them in one go.' There was another crash as the doors flew open once more.

There was rancorous laughter from all, save the weeping woman, whose daughter had now been laid at Marcus' feet. A high-pitched squealing followed. Someone was vigorously protesting their innocence. The voice caused an unpleasant taste in Marcus' mouth, besides the blood. A man in a bloodstained chlamys was flung down before his chair. The prostrate figure looked pleadingly at the pitiless faces of his judges, then peered up at Marcus.

'Governor, governor,' Solon bawled. 'In Our Lady's name, what horrors! The city – they took me – I had no choice, no, I...' His eyes fell upon the dead girl in front of him. All the colour drained from his face. He shrieked hysterically. It dawned on Marcus that he was going to die beside this coward. It was hardly the soldier's death he had been expecting his whole life.

'Solon Tzimiskes, high priest and high fornicator of Caledon,' Macleod said, to further bouts of laughter, 'you stand accused of aiding and abetting tyranny and perjury, including the false accusation and judicial murder of the martyr Cassian Macleod, the true and rightful heir. Do you have anything to say in your defence?' He looked summarily at the parchment in his hand.

'I, I – I wasn't – what do you want with me, a poor priest, for the kindness of Our Lady?' Solon stuttered, his eyes riveted on the girl. 'I didn't kill her, I wasn't there, I had no part in it. It wasn't my fault, I swear. It was all him. He was the one that was there. He ordered it. I'm innocent!' Terror-stricken, he rounded on Marcus, pointing at him accusingly. Marcus glared at the emaciated priest as if he were a little toad.

'Ah, you're nay paying attention,' Macleod said, his ginger beard wagging. 'We already know that. If I understand rightly, you may have played some little role in the treasonous accusation and wilful slaughter of my dear brother?' He was no longer smiling.

Solon squirmed, but apparently hadn't yet realised the game was up. 'I promise you, judge,' he said, in the most sycophantic tone

Marcus had ever heard, 'it was all him. He condemned your brother and put him to death. If I'd had my way, your brother would have been freed, I promise you. He had only committed moderated fornication, after all.'

'Moderated fornication, eh, is that nay a bit rich coming from you?' Macleod asked, to guffaws from the crowd. 'I'll be the first to admit that my brother was overfond of the ladies. I'm nay going to deny that. And he was certainly nay the easiest, aye. What with all his holy visions of the kingdom to come, he could even be a right royal pain. Perhaps he did want to get there sooner than the rest of us...' Grief and anger kindled in his eyes, like the last embers of a dying fire.

'I never thought he deserved death,' Solon interjected, seizing on Macleod's distraction. 'Please, I implore you, by all that is holy.'

Although pathetic to behold, Marcus was impressed by Solon's eloquence under fire. It was a shame he didn't realise it wouldn't save him.

'But my brother was a good man,' Macleod said, ignoring Solon's entreaties. 'He was our martyr, and he didnae deserve to die. As for you, high fornicator, I'm afraid we've got the court record here, and it dinnae quite square with what you're saying.' He pointed unconvincingly at the parchment.

'I, I swear, it wasn't my decision,' Solon pleaded. 'It was all him!' He pointed at Marcus again, hopping around like an overgrown stalk.

'You swear, do you?' Macleod asked, a malicious glint in his eyes. 'I wonder, priest, what are you swearing by? Let us see, lads, if he swears it true by his lady, shall we let him go? What do you reckon?' He looked around at the tribunal, as if seriously considering the idea.

'I, of course, I can swear it, yes,' he stammered, 'if that is what you wish, is it, lord? If I swear it truly, then you'll believe me, will you?' Solon's eyes skipped along the tribunal from one face to another, then back to the girl. He swallowed hard.

'By your lady,' Macleod said reassuringly, 'and we'll let you walk.' The large man beside him shot him a dark look, but Macleod gripped his wrist. The satyric glimmer had not left his eyes.

'Very well…' Solon said, clearing his throat. 'I swear it. I swear in the name of the Virgin that I had no part in it. I never accused your brother Cassian, and I did not seek his death.' Marcus stared at him in disbelief.

'You lie!' Macleod roared, leaping to his feet. 'We have the proof that you falsely accused my brother, unto the death. You perjure yourself by your very words, you scum, even by the name of your own lady.'

The furnace opened again and the room erupted. Solon turned deathly pale, looking desperately from one to another of his accusers, but all were as stern as if they were made of Caledonian stone.

'You sent my brother to his death as a heretic, but you're the only heretic here, you fornicating bastard,' Macleod said. 'Enough! We've heard enough of your lies. In my brother's name, Solon Tzimiskes, I hereby sentence you to death. Bring in the gibbet.'

The doors crashed open, wood scraping over marble. Two of the slaves with clubs seized Solon by the shoulders. He pulled away and made a break for the doors, but one of them tripped him and he crashed to the floor beside the girl. Seeing the corpse's face, he wailed piteously. The men grabbed him by the legs and dragged him kicking and screaming towards the windows.

Meanwhile, some of the other slaves had already hauled an oak scaffold into the room, depositing it beside the windows. Three nooses hung from its grim crossbeam. Marcus gritted his teeth. So this was his soldier's death. The picture of a winter's morning in the hippodrome flashed through his mind. Would Hypatia have volunteered to share his fate, had she known?

'No, I swear to you!' Solon was still crying as the mute slaves dragged him onto the platform. 'It was all him, I didn't want to…' A slave tightened the left noose around his neck. Solon still pointed at

Marcus, his panicked eyes streaming as he looked from side to side, but the crowd's blood was already up. Macleod raised his palm as he sought their approval, then nodded to the hangmen. One of them kicked the box from beneath Solon's feet. The priest screamed one last time, but an instant later his body dangled in the air, writhing about spasmodically like a fish on the shore. Then it hung limply from the gallows, like an empty sackcloth.

'Thank you for your patience, your excellency,' Macleod said. 'Now, let's see. I wonder, have you anything to say in your defence?'

Marcus considered whether there was any way to reason with the brute, but at once resolved not to give him the pleasure. He opened his mouth, determined to face his death like the soldier that he was.

'What about the other collaborator, are we nay going to do for them too, my thane?' a high-pitched voice cut in from one end of the tribunal. A pale youth with a pockmarked face and white-blond hair was staring earnestly at Macleod. Like the woman's, his eyes too were red, and blazed with a frenetic, almost manic, ire. He didn't even look to have reached his majority.

'Aye, aye, that we will,' Macleod said, but his voice was more faltering than before, as if his enthusiasm were feigned. 'That we will, quite right, Leon.' The room had fallen silent. Macleod looked sidelong at the youth, whose eyes had not left him for a single moment. Then he surveyed the room with a curious agitation. He shuffled the parchment in his hand, and cleared his throat.

'Bring in the accused,' he commanded. The doors swung open, and the loud, desperate sobbing of a woman drifted in. There were one or two shouts of 'traitor', but for the most part utter silence prevailed.

Another chair was placed next to Marcus. Then a woman in a white blouse and black skirt was thrust into it. He craned his neck towards her. His heart sank. It was Severa.

Chapter 32

Alistair

Mist rose from the river, obscuring the bridge and the walls of the city. He drew back the canvas of the tent and stepped outside. The morning air was crisp, and his lips felt dry. He looked up at the dawn sky. The sun was already beginning to burn through. It would be a hot day.

Several of his centurions were already gathered outside. They stood to attention as he approached, their gauntlets clacking against their cuirasses as they touched their armoured fists to their chests. As the mist dissipated, the rays of the rising sun flared, irradiating the entire firmament. The grey-azure of its fabric was rent in two by a blazing spear of light, crisscrossed by another. He smiled. He was not alone this day.

He felt the expectant eyes of the tribunes upon him. He eyed the far bank of the Tiber, beyond the field of Saxa Rubra. Now the mist had cleared, the ancient walls of the city were visible. Even from this distance, the feathered helms of the enemy soldiers could be seen moving between the castellations, the tips of their spears glinting in the morning light. He scoured the ancient stone for a weak point, knowing very well that there was none. The traitor had encased himself inside. Maxentius would surely not risk battle.

He shut his eyes and pictured his enemy, the false emperor. He could almost see him enthroned within the Curia, his haughty temples crowned with laurel. He imagined the ranks of togate senators lying in prostrate obeisance on the porphyry floor. Even outside the walls, he could already hear the chanting of the pagan officiants. It was a low rumbling chant, like the rolling of the ocean. Rising and falling, it grew louder, until nothing else could be heard. He pictured them raising their suppliant hands to their lord, their eyeballs rolling with ecstatic expectation.

There was a sudden scream from inside the walls. It was a heart-wrenching scream, that of a soul ripped from a body. He could imagine the corpse of the hapless victim falling back, the white linen of their toga spattered with blood. Then the priest's snowy hood leant over the body, examining it with a silver sickle. Everyone waiting in impatient silence, and most of all Maxentius.

'*Victoria!*' someone cried. The low groan of the chant resumed, wafting over the battlements towards his encampment. He opened his eyes. Beyond the camp sentinels, something stirred on the far side of the Milvian Bridge. More spears glinted on the castellations. The bronze doors of the gatehouse keep opened. The foul chanting polluted the morning air. Like a rancid smog, it fumed out of the open gates, across the Tiber towards his camp. A stench of stale incense and rotting flesh was emanating from the city.

Soon, the very stones of the bridge vibrated with the awful song. A giant man in a bear's hide stepped from the shadows of the gate, a line of soldiers in his wake. In his hands he bore a standard, the false vexillum of the enemy.

The fearful eyes of his own men were upon him, but he was unmoved. Instead, he smiled back at them. Misled by his false gods, the enemy had erred. Misled by the sacrilege of his divination, the enemy had chosen to give battle. It was a sign.

The dull thud of drums could now be heard across the river. The unholy murmur of the chant swelled like thunder. The sky was still scarred by the two intersecting rivulets of fire. Despite the smoke and incense, its blue sheen was blinding. Kneeling in the dust, he traced two crossed lines upon his shield, then added another, topped with a halo. Rising to his feet, he smiled again at his tribunes and centurions. Hoisting his shield on his back, he advanced towards the bridge. He raised his spear, and a deafening cry went up from his camp.

Across the bridge, a man in a purple robe and fur cloak stepped from the gate, a gladius hanging from his belt. Even from afar, the familiar hard lines etched into his enemy's bald head, crowned with its golden laurel, could be seen. Maxentius' dark eyes met his own, sparkling like stars on a clear summer night. One of them would die today. He touched his hand to his chest and said a silent prayer. Ever the low moan of the pagan chant rose and fell, crashing like the tides, but it would not wash him away.

Alistair woke with alarm, the chant still ringing in his ears. He looked for the man in the fur with the gladius, but he was not there. Nor were the river and the ancient walls. The Milvian Bridge was gone, and in place of the blue sky was corrugated metal. The chanting gradually resolved itself into the dull humming of the ship's engines. The pale imaginings of the night receded like the mist off the Tiber. It was just a dream.

It was dark. The storage room was empty. There was no sound from the decks above. To his relief, the sailors were not up yet. He was lucky. Another night had passed without his being discovered. His stomach moaned pitifully. The hunger was terrible, like some relentless vulture that had pinned him to a mountainside and was gnawing at his innards. He desperately wanted to eat something, anything, but the old man hadn't come yet.

He was the only one of them Alistair had seen up close. Every day, the blond sailor with the leathery skin would come to the storeroom to fiddle with something. He always seemed to be eating something, and must have been careless because he kept dropping food without noticing. Alistair was always careful to conceal himself when he came, but he'd realised after a time that the man must have been going blind. Not only did he drop his food, but he'd not noticed Alistair once. He'd stowed himself away here for two days now, but had somehow managed to escape detection.

Some instinct had told him from the moment he'd crept onto the freighter that it wouldn't do well to be found. He'd glimpsed some of the other sailors in passing, and heard them talking once or twice. Most of them looked Latin, but their Italic was strange and he could only grasp some of the words. Even so, the little he'd caught had been enough to know they were best avoided.

It was a miracle that he'd even managed to get onto the ship at all. He'd travelled by night. He'd had to steal too. The first few times he'd wondered what Father Zosim would have thought, but soon hunger had gotten the better of him. By following the sound of the magic carts, he'd eventually made it to Ostia. He'd been utterly exhausted by the time he arrived in the port, and still terrified he'd be caught. His curiosity had overmastered him, though. The buildings were all strange, and not only made of wood and stone like in the Reservation. Although some of them were old, there were also some that looked brand new, with large windows and walls made of something you could see right through. For a few hours, he'd wandered about aimlessly in the dark, wondering if he wasn't dreaming.

At last he'd found the quayside. The sight of the sea, oscillating before him like an enormous grey-green python in the first crepuscular light, had nearly made him cry. Fear had clutched his heart at the sight of the boundless expanse of water, and his eyes had ached with the endless monotony of the view. The roar and wild onrush of the waves seemed to repeat a melody of their own, gloomy and mysterious, unchanging since the world began. The only birds had been the silent white gulls, who seemed to fly mournfully about it for all eternity. Stumbling in the darkness, it had been all he could do not to tumble in.

There were ships, too. He'd heard about such things before, and read about them in the book. He'd had no idea they were so large, though. Some of them were even as big as buildings. Nor had he known they could move on their own. He'd seen one coming into port in the half-light of dawn. It had looked as if someone had upended the roof of the apostolica on the water, then dropped the rest of the building on top of it. He had watched as it floated in magically, as if drawn by a gargantuan invisible rope. He must have sat there on the quayside for hours.

At first there'd been nobody around, but as the day dawned, people had come off the ships. Soon the alleyways between the strange buildings had filled with people. He'd never seen so many of them before in his whole life. They were just like the ones in the apostolica paintings, all of different shapes and sizes and all moving about frantically in different directions. Most fantastic of all, they all wore different clothes which, unlike the friars' habits, were an opalescent patchwork of various colours and cloths. There were men in striated white-and-blue shirts and cloth caps, or else red-and-black doublets with taut hose like the Marians. There were women too, more of them than he had ever seen in his entire life, wearing long iridescent dresses with curious high collars that fanned out like a lion's mane. Once or twice, he'd even seen a few men dressed like the monks, except their habits were white, not black, and had a red star sown onto them.

It had soon made him dizzy. He'd retreated back into the buildings, and ended up hiding out in a storehouse on the wharf. He'd lain low for a few hours, wondering again whether he shouldn't just give the whole thing up. Overcome by hunger, he very nearly had, but then he'd seen something that changed his mind. There were some other slave orphans, living feral and surviving by filching food coming off the ships whenever no one was looking. The morning he was there, a young girl had been caught. He'd watched helplessly as a ruthless port official beat her to a bloody pulp.

The next day, as soon as he could, he'd snuck onto the first freighter he came across. That wasn't so difficult in itself. Fear had been a great teacher. The image of the white caps was always before his eyes. He'd learned very quickly how to move as silently as he could. To listen for the sound of footsteps. To mind who was behind him. The harder part had been surviving once he was aboard. At first, he'd had nothing at all to eat. Parched by his thirst, he'd been driven to craning his neck beneath a pipe for hours to collect the few droplets of sour water that dripped from it. He'd tried to read the book to distract himself, but half the stories in it seemed to be about hunger, and soon he could hardly focus on the page. Besides, there was only the dim light from the corridor in the storeroom where he was hiding.

Then at last, late the day before, the old sailor had appeared. The smell of the food had been overpowering. He'd been seized with a terrible desire to grab it from the man at once, but fear had overmastered his hunger. Instead, he'd cowered in the shadows, waiting for the sailor to leave. When at last he had, like a miracle he'd forgotten the leftovers of his food. So it had been again that morning. Once more, the man had fiddled with some crates on the other side of the room, singing a song in a strange language. Then he'd sat on the floor, eaten some but not all of his food, and left.

There were voices in the corridor, and shadows danced on the porthole in the storeroom door. Alistair withdrew behind a crate, curling up into a ball as he tried to compress his gangly frame into as small a space as he could. With a grating of metal, the door swung open. Raucous laughter echoed in the corridor, followed by raised voices in the strange Italic, dying away as the door closed. There were footsteps on the far side of the room, and scraping as crates were hauled about. Then came a song, this time in Italic:

'It came upon a Wednesday, Brown Robyn's men went
to sea,

But they saw neither moon nor sun, nor starlight wi'
their ee'. □
We'll cast kevels among us, see what the unhappy man
may be. □
The kevel fell on Brown Robyn, the master-man was
he. □
It is no wonder, said Brown Robyn, although I do not
thrive,
For with my mother I had two bairns, and with my
sister five. □
Tie me to a plank of wood, and throw me in the sea. □
And if I sink, you may bid me sink, but if I swim, just
let me be!'

There was a loud crash of metal, then the song continued.

'He had not been in the sea one hour but barely three,
Till by it came Our Blessed Lady, Her Holy Sophe with
She. □
Oh, will ye go to your men again, or will ye go with Me?
Will ye go to the high heavens, with My dear Sophe and
Me?
I will not go to my men again, for they'd be feared of
me,
But I will go to the heavens, with Thy dear Sophe and
Thee. □
It's not for your honour, it's for no good you did to me. □
But it is for your fair confession, you've made upon the
sea!'

The man slumped onto the floor and was soon munching through something. It sounded like bread. Overcome by curiosity, Alistair peered between a chink in the crates. The old sailor sat near the door, a hunk of bread and cheese in his hand. The crumbs spilled messily from the corners of his mouth. It was terrible. Alistair's stomach groaned loudly. The man raised his blond head at the sound. Alistair ducked. His heart thumped loudly, but after a few seconds the crunching resumed. He breathed a sigh of relief.

'*Tu veux pas me joindre, garcon?*' the sailor's strange Italic floated across the storeroom. 'Why don't you come out, boy, there's enough for two? *Tu – tu non vis – cibum – cibo?* You no want food?'

Alistair froze like a hare at the broken string of Italic and Latin. The sailor knew he was there. It was no use. Trembling, he slowly stood up.

'Come, no be shy,' he said. 'You no first stowaway we have on ship, boy.' He patted a spot on the floor beside him. Alistair stepped tentatively from the shadows and sat down. His mouth watered terribly at the smell of the bread. He eyed it with a fierce desire. The sailor smiled and, breaking off a piece, handed it to him. Alistair seized it greedily and wolfed it down at once. The man chuckled, but he hardly heard him. It was the best thing he had ever tasted.

'Where from?' the sailor asked, still smiling encouragingly. Although tanned and weatherbeaten by the sea, his skin was pale and freckled, not unlike Alistair's own. He looked into the sailor's pale blue eyes, wondering whether he could trust him. The Ostian girl rose to his mind, beaten senseless by the praetorian, then Father Zosim's anxious eyes in the firelight. No, he mustn't trust anyone.

'From the south,' Alistair replied in Latin.

The man's beady eyes fixed him unflinchingly like twin stars. There was something knowing in them.

'That ok, boy, we had many runaway slave on ship,' he said, at last looking away. 'Only, strange is. You no look from south, boy. You look like north.' He grinned and pointed at his own face and sparse blond hair. It was true. The aquamarine of the sailor's eyes was exactly like his own.

'But it best you stay hide,' the man went on, handing him another piece of bread. 'You know, *garcon*. Other crew no like runaway slave, see... But me, I no mind. You see, I leave food for slave, eh?' He slapped Alistair on the back. He had known he was there all along, and had been leaving the food for him deliberately. Despite his caution, Alistair could not help but smile in gratitude. The man beamed back at him, displaying several gold caps where his teeth should have been.

'*Quo vadimus?*' Alistair asked, starting to feel more confident. 'Where are we heading?'

The sailor looked at him, and for the first time the glint in his eyes dimmed. He shook his head and looked nervously over his shoulder at the door.

'We go Portus Ivaneus,' he said. 'Then ship go on Novgorovia. But you know, boy, no ask too many questions. You stay hide, ok?' He nodded towards the crates. Just as he did so, there was a clanging in the corridor outside, followed by voices and laughter. Alistair's eyes widened. The sailor shook his hand at the crates.

Alistair needed no further cue, but hastily concealed himself in the shadows. Something crashed down beside him. The sailor had thrown him his water flask. Alistair seized it gratefully, wondering again at the kindness of the old seaman. He lay still, listening to the shuffling of the man's feet as he resumed his work. The voices grew louder, until they were just nearby. Alistair held his breath, praying they would pass by.

'*Salut!* Where are you hiding, old man?' someone asked as the door crashed open. 'Work-shy old codger's been hiding in the storeroom again, lads.' Grating laughter filled the room. Alistair nearly leapt out of his skin. There had to be at least four or five of them.

'Am working, am working, no you worry,' the sailor protested as he dropped another crate. 'You no see am working, but am working, and more than you, cretin.'

'*Paix, paix,* old man,' the unseen speaker said. 'Calm down, no need to get angry now. And you'd do well to watch your tongue, blondie. If you were younger, I'd have half a mind to teach you a lesson.' Alistair pictured the titanic praetorian from the Reservation thrusting his finger at the Latin.

'*Bon,* well now, what do we have here?' he went on. 'What you been keeping from us this time, blondie?' There was a rustling of paper, then loud crunching. 'You forget your kindness, *toi avare.* You know you really ought to share with your brothers, you old miser. Just think, keeping all these delights down here to yourself!' the voice exclaimed between mouthfuls of bread. There was more rustling of paper as the man distributed the sailor's food to his companions. Alistair flushed, indignant at the old man's plight.

'You, you, you no can take,' the sailor protested feebly. 'You thief! You no right to come here and take food. I tell katepano.'

'Oh, I no can, eh?' the cruel voice replied. 'Well, it rather looks to me like I am, blondie. And what you going do about it, eh?' There were more guffaws and munching of bread. Then, quite abruptly, they ceased. Alistair lay mute, trying not to breathe. Had they all gone? Why had the sailor not come back for him?

There was a terrific crash as the crates were kicked aside. Alistair bawled in abject terror, but a large hand had already seized him by the collar.

CHAPTER 33

Agnes

A thick white fog hung in the air. Inside the meschita, Agnes could see nothing at all.

The fog became a heavy dust, and she began to choke. She tried to brush it away, but every time she swiped at it, it just wrapped around her arms more thickly. She couldn't breathe. She ran, trying to escape, but every way she turned, the blight just grew thicker and thicker. Soon she could smell pitch. Something was burning. She tried to find her way to the door.

Gradually, the fog lifted, and the white wall of the meschita came into focus. She ran towards it, placing her hands on its cold slabs like a blind woman, but still she couldn't find the door. She ran desperately along the inside of the wall, pushing harder and harder at the marble revettting, but it didn't budge.

She pummelled the stone with her fists, chasing the wall as it receded in an infinite circle before her. She had to get out. This was her only chance not to be imprisoned there forever. She screamed, but the air darkened as the white fog descended again. She coughed uncontrollably. The fog turned black, and became smoke.

At last, she found it. The mihrab slipped beneath her fingers. Between her choking, she cried with joy. She shoved the slab aside. Inside, the gleaming brick shone incandescent. Somewhere Strabon was calling, but she ignored him. This was their only chance. She reached out her hand.

Her fingers touched the nectar, but it was strangely hard. She withdrew her hand. The white block was gone. In its place was a small wooden frame. Inside the frame was a painting of Our Lady with a veil. Her heart filled with joy.

As she touched the frame, the painting changed. Its Hellenic eyes turned green, its olive cheeks pale and rosy. The face had become her own. Then it blurred and dissolved to a translucent white, as dense as the fog. The imperial mandylion. She scried the featureless face of the empress, trying to see through the veil. She leant closer to the wall.

All of a sudden the wooden frame burst into flames. The clouded face melted as the paint ran. In its place, a red hammer and crescent seared with fire. Horrorstruck, she stumbled backwards, tripping onto her back. Above her, the whole meschita filled with thick black smoke. Furling and unfurling like the giant canvases of overlapping sails, it swirled in angry billows towards the roof.

In the gaps between the sails, the walls of the meschita were no longer white, but golden. They were larger too, much larger. Larger than the walls of any church she had ever seen. Above them was an enormous dome studded with precious gems. On the walls were hundreds of frames, all of different sizes, but all containing the same icon of the Virgin. As she marvelled, they too burst into flames, sending more peals of smoke into the air. Terror-stricken, she covered her mouth. The icons were burning.

Somewhere in the dark, a pair of bronze eyes were watching her. They were getting closer. The curtain of smoke drew back, and a grey beret appeared. She felt for her gun, but it wasn't there. She crawled back in terror, but he was too fast. In an instant he stood over her. His cruel eyes smiled down at her. She curled up, clawing desperately at the flaming marble.

ochre and gold danced before her eyes. As the shadows moved to and fro in the flickering light, they unveiled a rich tableau of beasts and glyphs. There were oxen, dogs, and snakes, ibises and cranes, and all manner of river birds. Standing sidelong in endless lines, they crowded beside men and women with unnaturally long arms and legs, and beaks instead of noses. All donned the same crowns with the extended lapels, and some carried long staffs in their hands. All raised their arms in adulation of a strange symbol in the sky.

There was a sputtering noise. Candles. She sat up with a start. She was on the floor of a rectangular stone chamber, the entirety of whose walls were covered with the curious pictograms and painted animals. To her right, the mouth of the tunnel rose steeply into the darkness.

Feet shuffled to her left. She turned and caught her breath. In the middle of the room was a great porphyry sarcophagus. Its blood-red stone was graven with hundreds of the same white glyphs, like tiny nails hammered into the frame of an icon. Surrounding the lidless coffin were innumerable candles, littering the sandy floor. Nothing but impenetrable shadow could be seen within the sarcophagus. Something ineluctable called her towards it. She reached out and touched it. Its cold stone chilled her fingers like ice. Gripping its rim, she peered in.

She felt nauseous. Her feet were unsteady, and her vision blurred. The evil glyphs danced in the candlelight. In their midst was a young girl wrapped in a white shawl, her tiny body dwarfed by the giant coffin. She lay deathly still within, a veil drawn across her pale face.

'When the unclean spirit is gone out of a woman,' she whispered, 'she walketh through dry places, seeking rest, and, finding none, she saith, I will return unto my house whence I came out.'

Agnes tripped backwards, sending the candles flying. When she scrambled back to her feet, the pallid spectre stood in the coffin, staring directly at her. Though its face was veiled, its eyes were wide open. The terrible shade was watching her every move.

Agnes screamed, running madly back towards the tomb entrance. She ascended back into the darkness, but soon her feet slipped beneath her again. Horrorstruck, she cried out, but it was no use. Then she was lying facedown on the cold stone of the chamber floor.

CHAPTER 34

Marcus

'Siobhan Ferguson,' Justin Macleod addressed Severa. He hesitated, looking up from his parchment at the crowd.

No one stirred. All that could be heard was the creaking of the gallows crossbeam, straining with the weight of Solon's pallid corpse, and Severa's muffled sobs as she stared at the dead girl. The mascara ran in black rivulets from her tearstained eyes. Marcus could hardly bear to look, but he forced himself not to turn away.

'Siobhan Ariadna Ferguson...' he continued. 'No, on second thoughts, just Ariadna Ferguson. Seeing as you have betrayed your country, lassie, you'll forfeit your right name, and we'll use your bastardised name instead. Ariadna Ferguson, formerly known as Siobhan, you stand accused of betraying your country by assisting at the false accusation of your thane, Cassian Macleod. You were aware at the time, were you not, that the said Cassian was your right and lawful thane?' There was no joy in his eyes, but they burned with an implacable fury.

'Not just assisting at the false accusation,' the youth Leon interrupted. 'You forgot accessory to judicial murder, my thane.' The boy looked at Severa with a terrible hatred. Marcus' nose wrinkled with disgust. It was the hatred of the spurned lover.

'Silence!' Macleod said, slamming his fist into the table. 'Don't you dare tell me what I've forgotten and what I've nay, Leon, you brat. I know very well what I'm about. I'm the thane now, do you hear?' His eyes flared like twin lighthouses as they swung round and fixed upon the youth. Then they pivoted back to Severa with the same untamed fury. A tense silence reigned, as if the very strings of the air itself had been overtightened, and might snap at any moment. He surveyed the onlookers, as if daring them to speak. He dusted down his tunic.

'Aye, we will have order, aye,' he said, examining the by now completely crumpled parchment. 'I repeat my inquiry. Ariadna Macleod, were you, or were you not, aware that Cassian Macleod was your right and lawful thane at the time you wrongfully assisted at his false accusation, when you were in the service of the tyrant?'

'For Our Lady's sake, Justin, have mercy,' Severa sobbed. 'I was just doing my job, like the rest of you.' She waved accusingly at the crowd. There was an uncomfortable shuffling of feet, accompanied by some grumbling. Severa had neither mentioned nor looked at Marcus once. He was stunned by the woman's bravery under fire. He had not seen the like since his days in Hispania, and even then only among his bravest soldiers, like Agnes Radomira.

'You will address me by my right name, traitor!' Macleod shouted over the crowd. 'I remind you that, since you and your lot slaughtered my brother, I am now your right and lawful thane, and you would do well to remember that.'

Leon strode up the tribunal and whispered something in Macleod's ear. His beard wagged as his mouth stretched into a grin.

'Aye, aye, that's right, my boy,' Macleod muttered. 'The shameless wench sold herself to the tyrant, body and soul, and must answer for her perfidy.'

Severa's cheeks flushed to pomegranates. She stared at the youth in disbelief.

'No!' she screamed, as Macleod nodded to Leon. He ran down from the tribunal. Severa tried to rise, but two slaves held her back. In a moment, the youth had ripped off her blouse and yanked her skirt to her feet. There was jeering at the back of the courtroom.

'In the name of the Mother, what rubbish!' Marcus said. 'What is the meaning of this?' He had hardly finished before someone slapped him across the face. Leon threw Severa bodily to the floor. In nothing but her undergarments, she lay there spreadeagled beside the dead girl.

'You shameless wench!' Leon squealed, his white locks spinning like a flail as he turned from side to side, appealing now to the tribunal and now to the crowd. 'You sold us all out, and didn't even hold back from giving yourself to the tyrant as well.' He spat on Severa. Marcus snarled at the boy.

'And what are you looking at, old man?' he asked, rounding on him. 'Not had enough fun already?' He too slapped Marcus across the face, then backed up to kick him.

'Enough, enough,' Macleod said. 'We've heard quite enough from you, laddie! As you were, Leon.' He waved at the end of the tribunal.

Leon, whose bloodshot eyes flared like the nostrils of a bull, slowly became aware that the eyes of all were upon him. He retreated reluctantly to a corner of the curia, but his hateful gaze did not leave Severa for a single moment.

'Now the guilt of the collaborators has been duly established,' Macleod said, 'we return to the main heads of the accusation.' He no longer even bothered to look at the parchment.

'Ex-governor, I apologise again for the further interruption,' he went on sarcastically. 'Now I ask you again, have you nay anything to say in your defence? That being, namely, against the charges of perjury and judicial murder of the true and rightful heir, wilful murder of an innocent child, and the enslavement of the people of Caledon?' The gates of the furnace opened again, as the mob bellowed its approval.

Marcus looked back at the raging Caledonian. This was it. He had no choice. He would die like a soldier. Yet, as Severa squirmed on the floor, guilt and shame rose within him and, alongside them, something else. Something he hadn't felt in a long time. Honour. The soldier's honour. He was her commander. It had been his decision to storm the castle. It had been his mistake that led to her suffering. He must take responsibility. The right devotion of the legate was to die for his legion, and this was no different.

'Let her go,' Marcus commanded. 'She has done nothing wrong. All she did was serve. Many others here have done no less. Are you not above giving in to a hotheaded youth?' He looked from Macleod to Leon, his eyes resting on the boy.

Macleod was taken aback. Severa, too, watched Marcus with a mixture of shock and gratitude. A low grumbling emanated from the back of the crowd. Macleod shifted uncomfortably, then cleared his throat.

'We are not concerned with the guilt of the collaborators, which has already been clearly established, but with your own, ex-governor,' he replied, addressing the crowd more than Marcus. 'I ask you one last time, have you nay anything to say in your defence?'

'Look, you're a reasonable man,' Marcus tried again. 'What has she done to harm anyone? Why not just let her go? I didn't mean for the girl to die, but if someone must pay, then take me. But I implore you, spare her. You wouldn't let yours face punishment on your behalf, would you?'

'How dare you tell me what I would and wouldn't do, you Hromaian bastard,' Macleod said. 'I'm the thane, do you hear? I'm the thane! And the thane's heard enough of this rot. If you've nothing to say in your defence, then you can bloody well go to Gehenna. You and the traitor killed my brother, and then you killed the girl. I find you both guilty. String them up!'

'Exarch!' Severa screamed, but the roar of the crowd drowned her out. A slave grabbed her roughly by her naked calves and dragged her across the floor. Someone kicked Marcus in the back and, still bound to his chair, he crashed headfirst into the floor.

For a minute, he was out completely. When he came to, they were already on the gibbet. Someone had untied him and was hauling him by the collar to the centre of the wooden platform. They had already stood Severa on the next box and were tying one of the nooses around her neck. To his other side, Solon's corpse hung like a withered branch, swaying gently in the breeze. The crowd had gathered around the gallows, cursing as they jeered at Severa and spat at him. He was back in the stadium. The plebs and slaves transformed into a pack of wild beasts. The mother of the girl howled with rage, after his blood. She morphed into a pig, grunting terribly. The face of Leon, who was frantically punching the air, became that of a raven.

Marcus was hoisted onto his feet, and the middle noose tied around his neck. Severa's cries chafed painfully on his ears, like a Caledonian frost. How had it come to this? It was all his fault. He had led his men into the eye of the storm, against Konstantin's advice. Perhaps he deserved such a fate, but Severa did not. She had been cruelly dragged along to share in it. Nor had Cassian deserved death, not truly. He might easily have let him off with a prison sentence, after all. Then none of this would have happened. Why had he not been more merciful? It was only because the Caledonian had riled him. And why had he been so riled? Was it really Hypatia, or was it just because, in the end, he was no better himself? Yet, by insulting Cassian, he had thrown the first stone. He wished none of it had ever happened. That he had never come to Caledon. That he had stayed with the woman he loved.

Something glimmered in the corner of his eye. A white shadow moved behind the crowd, gliding like a swan towards the window. As it floated before the high glass panes, the shadow took form against the gathering storm clouds and burning cityscape without. Marcus' eyes moved in and out of focus. Then he saw it.

At first, he thought his heart was about to stop. He did a double-take, and it was still there. The dead girl. Unremarked by the crowd, she had risen to her feet and walked up to the gibbet. She stood mutely before the windowpane in her bloodstained shawl, facing Marcus. No one else seemed to have noticed her. A veil covered her face, but beneath it her eyes were wide open. She was watching him. Raising her emaciated arm, she lifted the veil. Her bright blue eyes burned into him like stars. He had seen them before, in the stadium, amidst the torrent of the crowd. The dead Cassian rose before him. Then the faces of the others, the slaves from the riot long ago. He began to weep.

'Ask, and it shall be given you,' he read on the girl's lips. Her voice came from afar, no more than a whisper. Through his tears, he beheld her sorrowful face. He turned to Severa.

'I'm sorry,' he said, moving his cracked lips as the tears ran down his face, 'forgive me.'

Severa looked back at him sadly, her handsome blue eyes smudged with mascara. Her bright hair hung to her shoulders, concealing the noose and framing her face like a halo.

Her hand reached out and clasped his own. She opened her mouth, but was interrupted by Macleod's cry. When Marcus looked up, the girl in white was gone.

CHAPTER 35

Zeno

Zeno threw his bag down and slumped onto the bench. He crossed his arms, sighing heavily as he stretched out his long limbs.

He glanced irritably at his holowatch, then at the entrance to the departure lounge. Admittedly, Maurice had only had the same notice period for his departure that he'd had himself. He hadn't initially appreciated how soon he was being transferred, but within minutes of his strange interview with the atamana, the epistle had been delivered. Only one day. He'd never heard of such a fast transfer, but assumed the First Praetorium operated differently, and got on with it. He had no commitments, nor family, and, as far as he knew, neither did Maurice. He was surely a loner like himself. How long did the Lombard need to pack his bags?

There was hardly anyone on this side of the lounge. Just a few women and men of no obvious occupation. An old sacerdote in a scruffy dalmatica loitered by the embarkation doors. He was accompanied by a young deacon, who kept hopping around him in his black gown like some ridiculous crow. The other side teemed with people, unlike the citizens' lounge. His keen eyes scanned the crowd through the grimy dividing screen. The praetorians were lazily doing the rounds, batons in hand. Why did they fail to notice everything he did? How the two male slaves at the back of the crowd nodded furtively to one another as soon as they passed. How the douloi drew closer, then how, though facing in opposite directions, their hands interlinked for the briefest moment.

The praetorians blearily surveyed the throng of slaves, noticing nothing. There was another pass elsewhere in the crowd. Then another. Zeno slammed his fist onto the bench. The young deacon skipped even higher into the air. Why on earth were the damned Osmans letting them carry on like that? He'd never have let his officers get so remiss. Then he remembered that it didn't matter. That it wasn't his business anymore. None of it was. Soon Ravenna itself would be no more than a distant memory.

The deacon eyed him nervously across the civic lounge. Zeno recalled that he wasn't in uniform today. Averting his gaze, his eyes fell on a large mosaic above the glass embarkation doors. Like the screen, it was filthy, but it was just about possible to make out the scene. A man in medieval costume stood on the prow of a ship, a jewel-studded crown on his head. The dromon was sailing eastward into the dawn. On the horizon, the golden domes of a city rose from the shore. Above the king's head, a great icon of the Virgin was nailed to the ship's mast, her unforgiving mien driving him on towards the city. Traced over the mosaic were the faded words, '*A.U.R. CCXXC Heraclius Rex ad Urbem Sanctam Virgine Reductus*'. Despite its illumination by the rising sun, the patriarch's face seemed pained. In the galley, hundreds of exhausted slaves plied the oars. Zeno glanced mistrustfully at the servile throng.

There was a flash of light out on the harbour. A hovercraft appeared on the teal sash of the horizon, decelerating as it came into port. As it moored, a gelatinous spray issued from the dockside against its stern. The liquid rapidly solidified, stabilising into a gangway. With a shrill siren, the glass doors of the servile lounge dissolved. The slaves shoved at one another as they rushed to board, and the lounge soon emptied. Only a few nervous children remained, whom the praetorians brusquely shunted onto the gangway.

The sacerdote gestured to the deacon to pick up his bags, as the handful of civilian travellers slowly moved forwards. Zeno looked at his holowatch again, then back at the entrance. He swung his bag onto his shoulders. It looked like he was on his own after all. It didn't matter though. None of it really mattered. He eyed the empty bench, where a woman and child should have been. It was just like last time, when he'd left Numidia. Now he was done with Ravenna too.

The near-side doors melted away, this time unaccompanied by any siren. With less haste, the civilian travellers mounted the gangway. The sacerdote stood back to let Zeno pass, holding his deacon by the shoulders and smiling up at him placatingly. The priest resembled the greybeard from the crypt. The one who had spewed all that rubbish about fire and war, and whited sepulchres. Like pallid shades, the old king and the lion with the red eyes rose before him. He reminded himself that it was all nonsense as, guided by his praetorian's instincts, he took a seat in one of the cabin's back rows. It was always better to have a clear view.

He looked out at the bay. It was nearly two antemeridian now, and the sun was already high over the Adriatic. His eyes followed the curve of the harbour, lighting on the port in the distance. Yes, it was all rubbish, no more than the febrile imaginings of a few worthless slaves. Perhaps the crypt itself and the madman had all just been a figment of his imagination, and maybe Simeon too. How had the slave got away, after all? Were they even still looking for him? He would never know now, and he didn't care anyway.

The last citizens took their seats in the near-unoccupied compartment. He glanced at the empty seat beside him. The sacerdote, who sat across the aisle with the deacon, pulled a book out of his satchel. The Greek words on its cover read, '*Paradigmata*

Hagie Gnosie'. The old man spread the book on his lap and pressed his eyelids, bringing his lenses into focus.

'All seek for the One whence they have come forth. All were once within Her, the Illimitable, the Inconceivable, who is beyond all thought,' he whispered loudly, pointing at the pages, but the deacon seemed more interested in Zeno than the paradigms of the Holy Gnosis. The boy kept glancing furtively across the aisle.

'But ignorance of the Mother brought terror and fear, and terror thickened like a fog, such that none could see. And so, Error waxed powerful. Yet he worked upon his worldly form in vain. Since he was ignorant of the truth, he put upon himself a false vesture and devised, with power and beauty, a substitute for truth,' the priest droned on, his rasping growing louder. Zeno grew annoyed, hoping the whole journey wouldn't be like this.

At the back of the cabin, the doors remained open and the gangway up, but there was still no sign. They'd surely close for departure in a few minutes. He pictured the warehouse shutter, and Maurice standing there gormlessly with the pendant in his hand. No, he hadn't imagined that. He wasn't going mad. It had all been real. Simeon, the crypt, and the slaves. And if they had been real, so too had been the white reservoir. That powder mountain beneath an unearthly neon sky.

'Yet terror and immemory and deception are as nothing, while established truth is immutable and unshaken, transcending worldly beauty. For this reason, despise Error, despise the eros of the deceiver,' the sacerdote recited, his voice growing faint. The heat seemed to be getting to him. Zeno was glad. With a bit of luck, the old doddard might soon shut up altogether.

A door opened at the front of the cabin and the conductor stepped in. The sacerdote stopped chanting and, as everyone else, looked up. The young woman looked anxiously at the passengers and empty seats, then raised her wrist to her mouth.

'Dear citizens, we thank you for your patience and apologise for the slight delay,' she announced. 'The Adriatic-Aegean transit will commence shortly. However, due to unforeseen demand today, cabin class restrictions are exceptionally being lifted. We thank you in advance for your understanding.' Her final words were drowned out by loud protestations from Zeno's fellow passengers.

No sooner had the woman disappeared than the stairwell to the lower cabin opened. There was a tumult below, followed by scrambling on the steps. The silence, previously disturbed only by the priest's soporific chanting, was rent asunder as the sound of crying babies filled the cabin. A few slave children ran into the civilian compartment, pursued by their mothers. A skinny Italic girl ran straight up to Zeno's seat, pointing hungrily at her toothless gums. He held up his palms to show he had no food, waving her on.

Soon, all the seats were taken. The male slaves had joined their women and children too, and an unpleasant smell filled the entire compartment. Zeno looked up irritably at the air purification vents, which were not yet on. At length, a single praetorian emerged from the stairwell. He cursed. Did they really think one was enough for this whole odoriferous lot?

'Error had no root. He was in a fog regarding the Mother, but he was there, preparing his deeds of fear and forgetfulness, thereby to attract and capture those of the middle,' the sacerdote continued, apparently unphased by the servile throng. Zeno glowered at him across the aisle, but his view was obscured by a large female slave. She slumped herself down next to him, her fat thighs spilling over onto his seat.

He pressed himself up against the window, examining her with annoyance. A thin string hung about her neck. He followed it to its end point, from which something was suspended, concealed in the folds of her ample cleavage. The slave looked up at him bashfully. Zeno turned back to the bay in disgust, but the shadowy outline of the pendant was still before him. In his mind's eye, another female slave appeared, the woman in the crypt. She had also had an amulet around her neck. He saw it falling to the ground again. Then another pendant swinging from his deputy's hands.

His eyes widened. He rounded on the slave, who started in alarm, but just then there was another announcement and everyone looked up. The conductor apologised again for the delay, before stating that the Adriatic-Aegean transit would not now commence until one antemeridian. There was a loud cry of woe, most despairingly from the citizen travellers.

'Through the hidden mystery, Our Lady enlightened those who were in the darkness of forgetfulness. She enlightened them and showed the way. And that way is the truth She taught them. For this reason, Error was angry with Her and persecuted Her. But he was restrained by Her and made powerless. For Our Lady became the fruit of the Knowledge of the Mother,' the priest's words wafted across the aisle. The slave woman still looked slightly alarmed. Why had he been so agitated before? It wasn't his problem now. What did he care what a few useless slaves were up to? He glanced at the back of the cabin again. The doors were still open.

'The fruit of that tree did not bring destruction, but made those who ate of it to come into being–' the deacon read, but was interrupted by the sacerdote correcting him on his Greek pronunciation. 'And – and – they were joyful in that discovery. For Our Lady found them within Herself, and they found Her within – within – themselves.'

Zeno scowled at the pedantic old man, then studied the red brick of the old dock-houses on the quayside, trying to tune out his words. The laser gauges danced on the stone walls of the harbour mouth. The sentinels flashed green as another hovercraft passed between them at breathtaking speed. In a few seconds, it had come to a standstill, floating downwards and landing on the waves like a deflating balloon.

The ship moored at an adjacent embarkation gate. The upper door opened first and a crowd of well-dressed citizens, mainly Greeks and Ionians, shuffled out. A handful were paler-skinned and round-headed, likely having picked up the trans-Euxeine connection from the Field of Mary or elsewhere in the Hetmannia. Their simple dress betrayed their lower civic class, mainly that of guildsmen, but there were also a few tagmata and droungoi among them, and another sacerdote.

'She is the One who set the all in order and – and – the all is with – within – Her,' the deacon struggled on. The last of the passengers entered the citizens' arrival lounge. No sooner had the liquid glass solidified behind them than the doors of the hovercraft's lower deck opened, and a throng of slaves poured out like a thick grey sludge. Zeno examined the dirty rags on their backs, scouring the necks of every one for amulets. How many heretics were there among them?

'After them came the little children, who have knowledge of the Mother. And when they gained strength and learned of the expressions of the Mother, they knew, they were known, they were glorified, they gave glory,' the deacon concluded.

The praetorians lazily boarded the other hovercraft and shooed some slave children across the gangway, which a moment later dissolved into the seawater below. One of the stragglers, a young boy, did not quite make it in time and splashed into the harbour. The praetorians laughed pitilessly as he flailed about in the waves, nearly drowning before the other slave children managed to rescue him.

Zeno scanned the embarkation doors a final time. He wasn't even sure why Maurice was being sent with him. Not that, deep down, he didn't admit that he would have been sorry to be going alone. It was just that there was no reason why the atamana would have cared about that. It was his promotion, not his deputy's. There was only one explanation that made sense. Maurice had been there in the nectar silo too. Other than Simeon, who had disappeared without a trace, he was the only other who had seen it. The only other witness to that magnificent subterranean beehive, where someone, with military precision, was offloading staggering quantities of nectar. Offloading it from freighters coming into the port, almost certainly from somewhere to the south.

The ghost of the Ruthenian centurion appeared before him again, putting fire to his village and murdering his family. He gritted his teeth. No one had ever spoken of what had happened there either. Where was she now? What if she and her legionnaires were involved in some way? No, that was madness. It was impossible. He was letting his anger get the better of him. It was leading him astray again.

Above the harbour, the cerulean dome of the sky became neon, and the still Mediterranean waters turned to white powder. The truth was that the last two days had passed like a dream. The port, the homicide, the crypt, the silo, his promotion, all seemed long ago. As if, like King Heraclius in the mosaic, the Virgin was propelling him forward with unnatural speed. After his interview with his boss, he'd of course filed his full report at the praetorium. As ever, he hadn't stinted on detail, and his razor-sharp memory had not betrayed him. There'd been no chance to question the suspects and witnesses, all of whom had immediately been handed over to Italikon intelligence, but such deficiencies were more than made up for by his own testimony. Every element of his audiovisual record had been spotless. His detailed description of the silo had even enabled the algorithm to reconstruct the precise model of carrier drone he'd observed.

Yet even before he'd finished his report, a little voice inside his head had been telling him something. Something uncomfortable, even unnerving. Something he would rather not have known: that it didn't matter. It didn't matter in how much detail he recorded what he had seen. It didn't matter what audiovisual, kinetic or emotive data he provided to the recording, because it wasn't going to make any difference. For the simple reason that, after his interview with his boss, the entire file was going to stay right where it was.

Why, after all, had he been transferred so suddenly? For urgent assignments, a week's notice wasn't unheard of, but just a single day? Besides, why did he need to be transferred so far away, not just out of the exarchate of the Italikon, but all the way to the capital? There were surely a thousand better candidates than he for counter-heresy ataman of the First Praetorium. Nor was it the only thing that was odd about the whole situation. That raid on the Reservation. He'd never heard of such a thing. No doubt there were reasons why the Italikon kept some things close, but then why was he informed about the lustration at all, and then only just before his departure to be ataman of another praetorium? If the situation were that serious, he ought to have been told sooner.

Then, for the final time that morning, he remembered that he no longer cared. It was someone else's problem now. Once more, he was getting overinvolved. He ought to have known better by now. He was making the same mistake again, the same one he'd made back in Numidia. Maybe the whole episode with the crypt and the silo, the Reservation, and all the rest of it, were another sign that the world was going mad, but what was that to him? Last time he'd got invested in trying to stop bad things from happening, he'd paid the price. Beneath her beige beret, the Ruthenian centurion's face peered back at him through the glass, its hard lines illuminated by the fire engulfing his home.

There was a sudden crash at the back of the cabin. Several of the passengers turned, chuckling to themselves. Maurice was rising from the floor. Catching Zeno's eye, he grinned, waving as he came towards him. Before he'd even reached him, there was a high-pitched beep as the glass doors solidified behind him. Zeno shook his head. The oaf had only just made it.

Half an hour later, they stood together on the panoptic deck as the hovercraft skimmed the azure waves of the northern Aegean. To east and west, the Dardanelles flashed past, like giants' fingers reaching out towards them. As they crossed the Propontine sea, the meridianal sun blazed in the stainless sky. To the right, a tower glinted high on a hilltop. Rising into the sky like a shard of silver glass, it marked Chalcedon, the home of the fleet.

At last, the Golden Horn appeared upon the horizon, threaded with mercury stars. The stars soon became ships, and the chrysoband an array of a thousand golden domes. Rising gently from the shore, each was crowned by a navy flag with a white star. Maurice gasped. Zeno's heart swelled with pride. They had arrived in Mariapol.

CHAPTER 36

Alistair

Alistair slid across the rough iron floor as the sailors dragged him into the centre of the storeroom. His whole body quaked with terror, but there was no hope of getting away now. They had already surrounded him, and in any case, where could a stowaway escape to? He was stuck on the ship. His fate was in their hands.

'*Bien*! Well, well, well, what do we have here?' a voice exclaimed in the strange Italic. 'So you've been keeping something else down here, have you, *viellard*? You naughty old miser, got yourself a runaway slave as well, have you? Keeping a boy for himself, is he?'

Terror-stricken, Alistair looked up at the man. He had a bristly coal-black beard, above which two copper eyes stared down at him malignantly. His head was shaven and on his cheek was a great scar, running nearly from mouth to ear, from which a golden earring hung. The man was short, but built like a barrel. The others, crowding behind as they tried to get a better view, towered head and shoulders over him.

'You leave boy alone now,' the blond sailor protested, but the little man took no notice. As he grinned at Alistair, his scar creased into a sort of second smile. Alistair cried out in terror at the dreadful sight, covering his face.

'Oh, now, now, my little doulos, nothing for a runaway slave to be afraid of here,' he said, his words greeted with sycophantic laughter from the others. 'We won't harm you, my stowaway, we'll soon let you go, don't you worry.' He winked at his confederates. All their faces had a like cast, their tanned skin dressed with the same trim black beard. One or two also sported the same golden earring, and all wore the same dirty blue vests. All stank of stale sweat.

'All we ask is a little entertainment for the boys before you take your leave. Now, that ain't too much to ask of a runaway slave, is it?' he asked, both his smiles ogling Alistair. He nodded to one of his companions, who grabbed a crate. Dropping onto it, he pulled a wooden tube from his pocket. In the shadows of the storeroom, it sparkled with ever-shifting opalescent lights. Despite his terror, Alistair was mesmerised by the colours. He'd had no idea such things existed.

The seaman put it to his mouth. A strange music flooded the room as the little piece of wood trilled with all the colours of the rainbow. Its high-pitched whistling notes were unlike anything Alistair had ever heard. He had no time to listen, though, as a sharp pain stung his buttocks. The short sailor had grabbed up a piece of crate fastening and was using it to whip him. There was another crack, and another bolt of pain. He leapt onto his feet, to loud guffaws from all sides.

'Come here, my little Jacky! Now I've smoked my backy, let's have a bit of cracky, till the boat comes in,' the sailor sang merrily, as the others joined in. 'Dance to thy daddy, sing to thy mammy, dance to thy daddy, to thy mammy sing!' As he sang, he lashed mercilessly at Alistair's feet. Once or twice the fastening caught painfully at his ankles, but soon he was hopping about to avoid the swinging of the metal cable. The men cried with delight at the spectacle, jeering him on.

Desperate to partake, one of the others seized another piece of fastening. He was large, even taller than Alistair, and his muscles bulged beneath his blue sailor's vest. The old man rushed up, trying to stop him. With a laugh, the sailor gave him a shove and he toppled backwards into the crates as if he had been made of straw.

'Thou shalt have a fishy on a little dishy, thou shalt have a fishy when the boat comes in,' Alistair's new assailant sang with glee, as the ringleader made way for his friend. 'Here's thy mother humming, like a canny woman. Yonder comes thy father, drunk he cannot stand.' Raising his makeshift whip, the giant brought it down with terrible force, cracking it against Alistair's backside. He squealed and leapt into the air.

'Dance to thy daddy, sing to thy mammy! Dance to thy daddy, to thy mammy sing!' the man bellowed in baritone as the sailors laughed hysterically. 'Thou shalt have a fishy on a little dishy, thou shalt have a haddock when the boat comes in.'

The pain was so great that Alistair tripped and fell, but a second later the whip cracked his ankles again and he was back on his feet, hopping about madly as he tried to avoid the flailing of a third's sailor's whip. He was exhausted and hardly knew if he was even alive anymore. The torture seemed like it would never end.

Then, quite unexpectedly, it did. The music stopped. The flute disappeared. The fastenings dropped to the floor, and the sailors stood back. A portulent man stood squarely in the open doorway, his hands on his fat hips. He had the same blue vest and clipped beard as the rest, but on his head he wore a battered tricorn hat.

'What in Gehenna's name is all this racket?' His face was white with rage. As his bloodshot eyes roved from one sailor to another, each squirmed and shrank back.

'Katepano, I can explain...' the short sailor began. The man in the hat pointed a grubby finger at him, then made a zipping motion across his lips. He opened his mouth to speak, but suddenly noticed Alistair. His mouth fell open.

'And who, in holy Anicia's name, is this?' he asked. His bulging eyes surveyed Alistair's gangly frame with amazement. He glanced around the storage room at the crates, taking in the loose fastenings on the floor and the remains of the food.

'I explain you,' the blond sailor broke in. 'He just runaway slave, Katepano. He not hurt anyone. Just put ashore when arrive and all be ok.'

The captain slowly pivoted from Alistair to the old sailor. He looked at him dumbfounded. 'Just put ashore,' he said, mimicking the sailor, 'and do you know, I wonder, where this slave came from? In two days, we arrive in Portus Ivaneus. Praetorians all over the ports, looking for runaways right now. And you want me to, what did you say, "just put ashore"?'

'He just Latian slave, no hurt anyone, no problem,' the old seaman persisted, but the captain had already turned back towards the short sailor. He stood before him, poking his nose into his face.

'*C'est toi,*' he barked at the man, sticking his finger into his scar. 'This is you, troublemaker. I'll wager this is all your business. So, *Hispaniane*, I don't care how, but you bloody well sort it out. Now. Otherwise it's you I'll be putting ashore. I don't want to hear of it again, you hear?' The captain about-turned and made for the door. When he reached it, he paused. He turned back, looking Alistair up and down.

'I don't care how, you hear?' he repeated, lowering his brows as he stared pointedly at the sailor. Then he disappeared into the corridor. The door slammed behind him.

Alistair tried to run, but he tripped over someone's leg and the floor rose up to greet him. As he tried to scramble back to his feet, two pairs of hands fastened on his ankles. He winced at the pain, but before he could struggle free he was being dragged from the room. The old sailor cried out in protest, but an instant later the door slammed again, there was another crash of crates, then someone was banging on the porthole.

The sound receded as he was blinded by the bright lights of the corridor. His whole body felt sore as it scraped painfully across the floor, so much so that he soon felt numb all over. A door kicked open ahead. Someone lifted him from the ground. He couldn't see where he was being carried, but there was a sudden howling of wind. The cold bit cruelly at his skin. With a heavy thud, he dropped to the deck. He rolled onto his back. The terrible face of the little Hispanian stared down at him. Neither of his smiles showed now. Instead, his face was grim. No one was laughing.

'Goodbye, Brown Robyn,' the man said, almost with resignation. 'Pray to the Mother now, and if you swim we'll let you be.' He gave him a violent shove. Alistair cried out, but his shout was immediately lost in the sea wind. His stomach dropped. He was falling. There was an almighty crash, then he could hear nothing at all.

A terrible chill engulfed his whole body, as if he had been embalmed in ice. He was underwater. He wanted to scream, but to open his mouth was death. He flailed about desperately, kicking wildly with his arms and legs. Somehow he reached the surface. He gasped for air as he tasted salt in his mouth. Soon he was sinking again. He kicked furiously at the water as it tried to pull him downwards.

He was vaguely aware of the ship, rapidly sailing away into the distance. He groaned in despair, as the water weighed on his legs like lead, but just then something moved on the stern. A small figure was jumping up and down on the deck, waving its arms. The sun appeared from behind a cloud, illuminating its blond head. It was the old sailor.

The man gesticulated wildly at the waves nearby. As Alistair kicked about, he spotted something bobbing atop the surf. It was some kind of giant cork, floating towards him. The ship was fast disappearing, but Alistair could just make out the sailor hammering with one of his fists on top of the other. With a flash of inspiration, he understood.

He swam madly towards the cork and, in one last act of desperation, threw himself upon it, clapping his hands around its girth. His body was thrown into the air and bounced, as lightly as if his flesh had been made of cotton. Then a liquid film surrounded him, as if he were being encased in an enormous balloon. He shut his eyes.

At first he thought he'd drowned. For a few minutes, he lay motionless on his back. He could still feel the chill of the wind on his face. A gull cried overhead. His mouth tasted of salt. He slowly opened his eyes. There was sky above. Clouds moved across it at an unnaturally fast pace. Every so often, blue patches would appear between their grey forms like the fleeting banners of a cerulean knight.

He sat up. He was in some kind of strange boat, constructed of fabric and air. The waves rocked beneath him. In the distance was a speck on the horizon. The boat. He started weeping, but the salty air immediately dried his eyelids. Something caught his eye, floating in the water nearby. It was his sack. He leant carefully over the side of the boat and paddled towards it. Splashing in the water, he grabbed it up greedily as if it were food. Falling back into the raft, he clutched it to his chest, completely exhausted. He wanted to sleep, so very much. As his eyelids drooped, the old sailor who looked like him appeared before him. He had saved him again. Then his smiling eyes became those of Father Zosim, flickering sadly in the firelight.

'Do not sleep too heavily this night!' the monk's words thundered through his mind. He sat up in alarm, opening his eyes. His heart raced, but there was nothing but the low moaning of the sea. Then he saw it.

Like a white fillet drawn across the temples of the earth, a line of cliffs rose before him on the horizon. At first, he thought they were clouds, then snow-covered mountains, but as the raft drifted closer he saw that he was wrong. The chalk cliffs reared up like the pallid shades of titans, towering ever higher as the waves bore him relentlessly on towards them.

The boat jolted beneath him. The rocking of the waves ceased. To port and starboard, a band of multicoloured stones stretched as far as his eye could see, a vast jewel-encrusted collar. He looked up at the monstrous white facade of the land, off which the mist hung heavily like a cloak, and wondered whether he hadn't died after all. Were these not the great gates which Father Zosim had spoken of to him as a child?

The clouds moved, and the mist lifted. He gasped. Atop the cliffs was an enormous citadel, its steep black walls as unforgiving as the sheer rock beneath them. A blue flag fluttered from its keep. Beneath the image of a seated woman, bearing a spear and crowned with a star, was the legend, *'PROV. BRITANNIA MAIOR'*.

CHAPTER 37

Marcus

The strange mist engulfed Caledon. Marcus took one last look at the hateful city. He shut his eyes, readying himself for the end.

Dimly, he heard Macleod roar, and the shuffling of the slaves' feet on the gallows. Soon it would all be over. The image of a hibernal morning in the hippodrome long ago appeared before him, and the smiling coal-black eyes of a young woman. He smiled through his tears. *Carbonopsina.*

He listened for the sound of the box being kicked out from beneath him, but it did not come. The wait seemed endless. A second later, it had become interminable. Yet still, nothing happened. He opened his eyes, wondering whether he hadn't already achieved gnosis, but the window was still there, and the city outside, embalmed in mist. Not just mist. Smoke too, and inside the glass. The courtroom was filling with smoke.

Macleod shouted, but his voice was drowned out by an enormous crash as the courtroom doors exploded. There was a low thud, followed by a rush of hot air nearby, as a directive calefactive pulse blew the slaves off the gibbet, like no more than autumn leaves in a storm.

The smoke was so dense that he couldn't see anything. There were loud cries from the crowd below, but these too were drowned out by the deafening sound of gunfire. He turned to Severa. Her eyes looked back at him like those of a frightened doe, then her body dropped to the platform. The air whiplashed above him, then he, too, was falling. The hard oak of the platform rose up and punched him in the face.

'Exarch?' Severa called. He rolled towards her. As if in some shadow play, the youth Leon ran through the smoke towards the gallows. In a single bound he had leapt onto the platform, but just as he grabbed Severa by the arm he began to dance to the cackling of the air. Blood poured from his punctured chest as, turning the frenzied whites of his eyes to the sky one last time, he threw out his arms and fell backwards. Another pair of hands, sheathed in black leather, caught Severa and pulled her away into a cloud of smoke. Then gloved hands wrested him from the gibbet, too.

'Exarch,' the familiar voice of his tribune addressed him. The man knelt beside him in a night visor, discharging a small automatic rifle into the smoke. There were cries beyond.

'I advise we extract from this location at once,' Konstantin continued. 'Castle is encircled and fallback location taken.'

Marcus staggered to his feet. Another masked man thrust a pistol into his hand. A light cloth fell about his shoulders, stiffening around his torso. There was gunfire from the other end of the courtroom, and a masked man collapsed nearby.

'*Iunge!*' Konstantin commanded. 'Exarch?' This time, Marcus did not gainsay his tribune. There was another volley, followed by groans from behind the veil of smoke.

'Take it down,' Konstantin commanded, waving his hand at an invisible confederate. Marcus was forced onto his knees. There was a low sonic thud, followed by an enormous crack and a spectacular crash of glass, as if a glacier had fractured. A blast of cold air followed. The smoke dissipated. Before him was a vast cavity where the courtroom windows had been. Rain lashed the floor like tears on a marble face. Where his curial bench had been was no more than a shipwreck of exploded wooden splinters. A pile of grey bodies lay beside the door.

There was shouting outside. Someone dragged him to the window. As he scrambled blindly over the wreckage of the windowsill, the curia doors crashed open. A hail of bullets flew overhead, but were lost in the storm. One of the tagmata swung his arm at the window. There was a deafening explosion, and a cry from within.

Soon he was running. Running down the hillside. His knees ached. The frozen wind caught up the shreds of his sleeves, clawing mercilessly at the bare and bruised skin of his arms like rusty nails, but he was heedless of the pain. The enemy were hard on their heels, after their blood. After his blood.

'Exfiltration point identified, Exarch,' Konstantin shouted through the wind. The black silhouette of his tribune was outlined against the grey mountain beyond. His left arm was raised as he spoke into his wrist, while with his right he waved at the sky. The outline of a wing appeared in the clouds behind him, like a giant charcoal jellyfish beneath the surface of the waves. Another followed, as the form of an armoured lowcraft crystallised against the irascible Caledonian sky. It flew over them, overtaking them in their flight, and circled overhead near the foot of the castle hill.

There was another crack of gunfire behind. Konstantin and another tagma fired several automatic rounds back up at the castle. Marcus made ready to fire his pistol, but his tribune's arm was on his back at once, steering him away. They had nearly reached the foot of the hill. The crackle of gunfire was audible ahead now too. A quarter verst below, beside the castle gatehouse, a group of tagmata were drawn up in orbital formation. On all sides, a swarm of armed rebels rushed at them. There were two main bands. A larger, more mixed, group of slaves were attacking the soldiers from below. Some of these sallied forth with hunting rifles in their hands, while others scrambled onto the surrounding buildings, from which they threw improvised explosives. On the hillside above the gatehouse, was a smaller, fast-thinning, group of Caledonians, trying to bear down on the soldiers from above.

'*Iacula!*' Konstantin said into his wrist. Like a gargantuan aerial seal, the lowcraft swung around in the air, its muzzle pointing directly at the gatehouse. A few Caledonians fired at the airship, but the bullets glanced harmlessly off its hull. There was an enormous crackling, as if someone had released a thousand firecrackers at once. The sallow mauve of the sky was slashed with twin lines of scarlet, as two rockets shot from the belly of the lowcraft. The ancient gatehouse exploded, its dun limestone flying off in all directions, as the second rocket detonated midway up the castle ascent.

When the smoke cleared, nothing remained of the upper group of Caledonians. Tagmata poured from the castle, like a hive of black ants, descending to where the gatehouse had stood moments earlier. The lowcraft reeled about in the sky. Soon joined by their comrades from the castle, the tagmata at the foot of the hill pressed forward towards the buildings, repulsing another slave sally as they cleared space for the airship to land.

Konstantin's hand was on Marcus' back again, pushing him in the direction of the tagmata below. They had very nearly reached the defensive line when there was a sudden crash in the sky. One of the lowcraft's wings had a giant hole in its side. Like a circus performer trying to regain her balance, it briefly wavered in the sky. With a second crash, one of its turbines exploded. Leaning from a window was a man in a threadbare tunic with an imperial grenade launcher in his hands. An instant later his lifeless body, peppered with bullets, fell like a puppet to the street.

The Marians were too late. Groaning like a wounded beast, the lowcraft tottered, veering to one side. At last it lost its balance completely, careering towards the buildings. On all sides, tagmata and slaves dived for cover. There was a deafening crash as metal collided with stone, followed by the roar of fire.

Soon they were running again. In the maze of smoke it was impossible to make out anything for sure. There was a bout of gunfire nearby. Konstantin fired into the haze. Somone cried out. The surface grew rougher beneath Marcus' soles as he found himself running on cobbles. As the air cleared, little stone walls and lancet windows pressed in around them. He was in a narrow alleyway.

'Alpha exfiltration point rendered unviable,' Konstantin said into his holowatch, as two more tagmata fell in behind. 'Retreat to beta exfiltration point.' Sweat poured from his blond brows. Marcus' garments were completely drenched too. Fires crackled all around them.

Marcus' heart pounded. His mind raced. The defenestrated slave appeared before him, the grenade launcher falling from his hands. If the rebels had gotten hold of imperial weaponry, the situation was dire. Surely they hadn't managed to sack one of the legionary castra?

'Severa?' he asked, panting for breath, but his tribune only shoved him aside. Marcus tumbled backwards into a stone archway, dropping his pistol. Gunfire resounded around the alleyway. His tribune knelt with his assault rifle raised.

'*Sponte!*' Konstantin told the tagmata to fire at will. All discharged their weapons. At the other end of the alleyway, someone cursed in Caledonian. One of the tagmata flew backwards, borne off his feet. Konstantin threw himself into the archway beside Marcus. With one hand he hauled him back onto his feet, as a neon green light flashed in his other. The tribune shook his arm as he and the remaining tagma took cover. There was an explosion, the alley igniting like a furnace.

They were in another narrow passageway, forced into single file. Marcus chanced to be in front, running on blindly. The passage snaked to left and right as he led the two soldiers on. The overhanging jetties of the medieval houses crowded ever denser above, as if conspiring to trap them.

The walls fell away abruptly as the artery opened onto a small cobbled square. Konstantin and the tagma ran out in front of Marcus, their rifles raised as they took the little shopfronts and pothouse entrance in their sights. There was no one there. Marcus slumped against a doorpost, completely exhausted. Fallen. The city had fallen. How had it happened? What was happening now? It was a miracle that he was even alive. But what about Severa? Had she made it out?

'Exarch, we must extract,' Konstantin interrupted his thoughts. 'Beta exfiltration location identified in near vicinity. Are you wounded?'

Bent double, Marcus raised his head. The tall Novgorovian stood over him, examining his body armour for punctures.

Marcus did not respond. As his bleary eyes focused on the forum, it felt curiously familiar. He had never been there before, of course. A governor had no occasion to visit the plebeian quarter. Yet as he beheld the high medieval gables and sickly green of the leaden roofs, something emerged from the smoke, like a half-remembered dream.

Marcus' eye rested on the hollow windowpane of a taverna. Its sill was completely covered in shards of glass, and its sign had collapsed from blast damage, but he knew he had seen it before. In the same smoky greyscale as he saw it now. In the holorecord, the record of a crime. A crime of passion. The ghost of a red-bearded man rose before him, standing before the taverna. Then the neon image of a Caledonian woman in a sash, smiling back at him.

With a rapid scuttling of feet, the shade of the woman became flesh. He did a double-take as rubber jackboots scuffed the cobbles on the far side of the forum. Konstantin swung around, raising his rifle. Two masked figures in heavy armour materialised beside the woman. They trained their rifles on Marcus and Konstantin, but immediately lowered them. The woman in the white blouse and tartan skirt had been replaced by another. She too had long blond hair, hanging loosely to her shoulders in disarray. Instead of a blouse, though, she had a shawl over her upper body, beneath which her legs were bare. Severa. Their eyes met, and without thinking he ran towards her. Konstantin tried to stay him, but he pulled away, pushing through the smoke.

'Exarch!' Konstantin said. There was another scuffing to his left and movement in a third corner of the square. A gun detonated hard by, followed by a crash of glass. He felt Severa's hand in his, then lost it again.

'*Sponte!*' his tribune bellowed, as an answering crack ran out. There was a heavy thud as a tagma fell to the ground. Konstantin pushed Marcus backwards into the entrance of the taverna. Severa lay near the doorpost. He darted towards her. His hand shook as he turned her over, but she was unharmed. He lifted her in his bruised arms. They ached terribly, and he tottered on his unsteady legs, but he didn't care. All he knew was that he had to get her away.

'Marcus?' Severa addressed him by name for the first time ever. Another crack rent the air, vibrating beside his ear. They were under attack. The city had fallen. There was no sign of Konstantin, but he had to get her out somehow. He stumbled to the right, diving into another alley. He limped along with Severa in his arms, as fast as his exhausted legs would carry him. He could feel her laboured breath on his chest as she clung to his neck. He was running for his life now. For their lives. They had to get out of Caledon.

Beneath the cacophony of gunfire and explosions was a low hum, like the rumbling of the ocean, coming from above. He glanced around desperately at the dim walls of the alleyway, and the tiny grimy windows, looking for some way out. A shadow passed overhead, colouring the buildings to ash, as the wing of a lowcraft moved against the doleful sky. They must have chanced on the right path to the beta exfiltration point.

A grey ghost dashed across their path. He just had time to look again before two Caledonians emerged from an archway fifty passus ahead. Two barrels distended from the smoke. His soldierly instincts kicked in in the nick of time, and he threw himself sideways into a gateway just as the damp air whistled. Severa screamed as they crashed into its lintel, then tumbled headlong into an old door. Its rotten wood collapsed beneath their weight like crumpled paper. Instead of the floor, nothing rose up to meet him. He was falling, then rolling downwards. He cried out in alarm, flailing about in the darkness, but he couldn't stop himself. He shielded his head as best he could as the stairs spun around him. His body performed a final somersault, and he crashed to the floor. Severa landed on top of him.

Marcus was spreadeagled on his back. The hard floor was cold and damp beneath him, but above him it was warm and, despite his soreness, he was engulfed by a familiar scent. Someone's breath was on his face. He roused, opening his eyes.

'Severa?' he whispered, feeling for his secretary's shoulders. He shook them. At first she did not respond. Alarmed, he shook them again. Finally, she stirred. Two ovals emerged above him, like sapphire stars in the night sky.

'Marcus?' Severa asked drowsily. 'Where are we?'

He remembered the rebels and tried to rise, but immediately fell backwards. Severa rolled off onto the floor beside him. He reached over and seized her arm.

'Are you hurt?' he asked, peering up at the rickety staircase and open door above. 'We must get out of here!' He again tried to rise, but only succeeded in clambering onto his knees. Something moved across the dim portal above. He rolled aside, tumbling back onto Severa.

Someone shouted in Caledonian. Severa looked up in terror. It was up to him. Even if he didn't make it, he had to get her out. Fired by a last desperate hope and ignoring the pain in his bruised limbs, he hauled himself back onto his feet, lifting her from the ground and retreating into the darkness of the cellar.

There was another cry above, nearer at hand now. A puddle splashed. The stairwell dimmed as everything went quiet. Skulking in the shadows, Marcus reached for his pistol, but it wasn't there. His blood ran cold. The stairs creaked as phantoms danced on the wall. A gaunt grey spectre descended, a rifle in its hand, creeping down to the cellar like an alley cat. The man was tall, but of only meagre build. If he could spring him, that might just give Severa enough time to escape.

The light moved again. Another ghoul appeared in the doorway. He crept onto the top of the stairs, signalling back at the street and raising a finger to its lips. The other had already reached the foot of the steps. There was no way out. Marcus readied himself to pounce, but even before he could move the man had seen him. The slave raised his gun. Marcus shrank back, covering Severa with his body.

'*Mitte!*' someone cried. Marcus reeled. Why was the slave shouting Latin? Then he saw that it was not the slave. The man looked up in terror at the top of the stairs. The air clapped, and the body of his comrade flew down the stairs.

'*Expurga!*' a second command rang out. The slave bolted for the door, howling in terror, but was not fast enough. A neon disc clanked down the stairs, glowing green like a dazed firefly. Marcus grabbed Severa, diving for cover. There was an almighty crash and a rush of hot air.

'Severa?' he called into the dark, choking on the dustcloud cloying at the air like thick cobwebs. He rolled her over and felt for her face. She stirred. He thanked the Virgin as he lifted her again, limping back towards the stairs. All that remained of the slave was a few shreds of grey cloth. Muffled Latin floated down from the street, as two black silhouettes moved away from the doorway.

'Tagmata!' he called with all the strength left him. One of his knees collapsed onto the first stair, and he nearly dropped Severa. One of the silhouettes re-emerged in the doorway. Its arms grew as its heavy body armour came into view, like a giant bat spreading its wings. Marcus cried for joy, steadying himself against the splintered balustrade.

'*Legate,*' the bat said, addressing him by his military title. '*Huc, huc, exarchus inest!*'

Another bat appeared by its side. Panting and coughing, Marcus looked up at them. The man spoke Latin with a familiar accent. The vowels were unmistakably Greek. As the men descended the stairs, white stars emerged on their black lapels, beneath which were stitched the numerals '*XX*'. As the foremost extended his arm, epaulettes appeared on his shoulder. A centurion. The twentieth had arrived.

'Are you harmed, legate?' the centurion asked, as the other legionnaire lifted Severa and carried her up the stairs. A single silver spear, affixed to the side of his black beret, glinted in the half-light.

'*Kale,*' Marcus replied in Greek. 'Just a few scratches, but the woman is exhausted.' He nodded up at the other legionnaire. The centurion pulled Marcus up the broken steps. It was all he could do not to fall between the splintered planks.

'Sitrep, Katepano?' he asked, as he stumbled out onto the cobbles. 'And what has become of the exarchal tagmata? Any sign of the tribunal strategos?'

As if in response, gunfire crackled in the distance. Beneath it came the dull hum of legionary lowcraft. There were now about ten legionnaires in the street.

'Caledon sectors east, south and west have fallen to seditious element, legate,' the katepano of the twentieth replied. '*Legio XX Theadora* has resecured sector north and is pushing into central sector, to recover sector west. Proconsular domesticus deploying reinforcements from Vindolanda. In absence of exarchal command, proconsul has ordered civilian evacuation to Anglia.'

Argyra's aquiline eyes floated before Marcus.

'We have had no further communication from tribunal strategos since initial distress signal received,' the man added. 'Intelligence suggests seditious element aided by tagmatic defectors of native ethnos. Pre-emptive detention of native tagmata underway, but indications of operational groundwork undertaken in advance. This was planned, legate.' The spear looked at Marcus significantly.

Severa stood in the street nearby. A legionnaire had wrapped a tunic over her shoulders, but she was still shivering. As Marcus beheld her pale blue eyes, those of his judge appeared before him again, ordering their execution. Then Justin Macleod's face morphed, its red beard growing into that of his heretic brother. The barbarians had had the whole thing planned from the start.

'Exfiltration point identified, legate,' the spear said. He was already steering Marcus towards the end of the alleyway, flanked by several of his legionnaires. As they passed beneath the archway, Marcus looked back at Severa. She followed, her arm tightly gripped by an Italic legionnaire, as if he did not trust her. Their eyes met again. Marcus read the silent wish expressed there. *Do not leave me behind. Never leave me again.* He knew he would not.

A pallid circus of sandstone walls, cobbles, timber doorposts and lancet windows flashed before his eyes as the legionnaires escorted them rapidly through more fora and blind alleyways. Marcus was barely aware he was on his feet anymore, but kept listening for Severa's soft patter behind, intermingling with the heavy tread of the legionnaires' jackboots. Once or twice, they passed the corpses of slaves, which had been dragged into the gutter. The hum of the turbines grew louder.

They turned a corner and a large square opened before them. In its midst were the ruins of an ancient church, the white rubble of its Doric steeple and Marian star lying in the dust nearby. Parked beside the wreck of stone was a small armoured lowcraft. The star-shaped funnel of its nose and the two rocket-launchers beneath its lower pair of wings were pointing right in their direction. Marcus started involuntarily.

'No fear, legate, they're with us,' the centurion said, scratching his olive cheeks as he surveyed his legionnaires. Snipers knelt on the cobbles, training their rifles on all corners of the forum, as if they expected a congregation of grey rags to appear at any moment. The spear signalled to them as they approached. One or two rose, looking surprised. Those who realised who Marcus was stood to attention, saluting.

There was a loud whirr, and a rush of air. A second lowcraft was rotating overhead, turning southward. First its upper rudder decoupled, like a column splitting in two, forming dual vertical wings. Next the airship's two lower wings descended, until all four pointed in different directions like a compass. For a moment, the ship floated noiselessly in the air like an elegant white starfish, as its propulsion engines mobilised. Then two streaks of particles shot from its upper wings, like translucent blue ribbons. There was a loud crackle, as if someone had lashed a giant whip through the clouds, and the airship vanished.

They stood beneath the lower wings of the parked lowcraft. Another heavily-armed legionnaire in a black uniform stepped up and, saluting, ushered Marcus onto the ramp. As he limped up its incline, Severa clutched at his arm. He smiled at her in relief, but she did not return his smile. She was still anxious. She was right. They weren't out yet.

'Exarch,' the centurion said, as he and Severa slumped into the seats lining the wall of the narrow white cabin, 'legionary flotilla will extract to first secure location south of Adrianic Line.' The soldier was already turning back towards the ramp. Marcus tried to protest, but he did not let him speak.

'Your safe exfiltration is our top priority, exarch,' he said. 'We will evacuate the remaining citizenry once central sector is secured.' As the spear finished, gunfire crackled in the distance. Severa flinched. Marcus opened his mouth, but the soldier was already touching his fingers to his beret. Like some great armoured ant, he leapt from the ascending ramp, swinging his rifle off his shoulders. Marcus felt like a coward.

The turbines hummed beneath them. The cabin's white walls vibrated as they lifted into the air. The sallow face of the old city flashed into view out the rear porthole. Thick wisps of smoke rose from its grey crown, like loose black tassels. Marcus' heart skipped a beat. Then Severa leant her head on his shoulder, and his nostrils filled with the musky scent of her hair. He thanked the Virgin. He had got her out.

The rumble of the turbines dimmed, then cut out altogether. The air clashed like giant cymbals in the sky, drowning out the gunfire. Outside, a mist came in from the sea, engulfing Caledon. It devoured everything, blotting out the hateful city. Marcus' stomach lurched as an elastic force pulled the lowcraft away.

CHAPTER 38

Agnes

Agnes resolved to face the ghost. She turned towards the sarcophagus, but there was no one there, just the candles sputtering in the darkness. With an effort, she raised her sore limbs, tottering towards the stone coffin. She peered inside, but the girl was gone.

Then she saw them. On its far side, a group of children sat in a circle. All wore the threadbare rags of slaves. In their centre sat the strange spectre, the girl in the white shawl, her face covered with a translucent mandylion.

Agnes' fear slowly receded. Driven by the same ineluctable force that made her look into the sarcophagus, she approached. The girl gave no sign that she was aware of Agnes' presence, but one of the other children looked up. Without a word, the child slowly raised her arm and pointed at Agnes.

At this the rest of the children, save the girl in white, stared at her too. Their expressionless faces, all dark or olive-skinned, unlike that of the veiled girl, reminded her of icons. Their wide hollow eyes were just like those of the Mother, as if they were gazing upon eternity. Yet, unlike Hers, all were the amber of the buffer. Those same handsome eyes that had become so familiar since she'd been sent south, they shone in the candlelight just like Strabon's. Just like those of the woman and child in the burning village, the one she had fired. A tear ran down her cheek, like a drop of wax from one of the candles.

Noticing this, the girl who was pointing at her beckoned her to come closer. Agnes moved cautiously around the sarcophagus, pausing by its corner. The girl gestured to her again. Agnes approached the ring of slave children, treading carefully between the candles. The girl shuffled aside, nodding towards the centre of the circle. The eyes of all the children lingered on her vacantly, save those of the veiled girl. Her head lowered, she instead stared at a lone candle, set before her in the middle of the ring. Driven by the same compunction she had felt in the meschita the day before, Agnes sat down beside the veiled girl.

'Who are you?' she asked, staring at the veil. The pale outline of the girl's face rose beneath the mandylion, like water beneath the frozen surface of a lake. Just as in the meschita before, she neither stirred nor spoke. The girl had not heard her.

'*Poia eisai?*' Agnes repeated her question in Greek. The candle sputtered. The girl raised her head slightly. As Agnes beheld her strange white garb, the children, and the painted walls of the burial chamber, she began to wonder how they had all got there.

'What is this place, and how did you come here?' she asked, glancing around nervously at the heavy walls of the tomb and the steep shaft of the dark tunnel. 'And were you not in the meschita with me? How did you get there, and come back here safely from the battle?' Her voice rose, almost angrily. Her questions came in one relentless tide, but still the girl did not answer. Her heart pounded. She would never be able to climb back up, and there was no other way out. She was trapped down here. It would be her tomb too.

'Seek, and ye shall find,' the girl whispered, as if she had read her thoughts. 'Knock, and it shall be opened unto you. For every one that asketh receiveth, and she that seeketh findeth, and to her that knocketh it shall be opened.'

Agnes stared at her dumbfounded. The Greek she spoke was old, unlike anything she had ever heard spoken.

'I don't understand,' she replied, trying to stay calm but her voice rising in desperation. 'Where do I have to seek to find the way out, or where must I knock? How do I get out of here?' Her eyes took in the immovable sarcophagus, impenetrable tomb walls, and shadows of the tunnel above.

'Why did you save me, little girl, only to imprison me in this tomb?' Agnes asked. 'It was you, wasn't it, in the temple and in the valley? You did save me, didn't you?' Her voice broke. The animal-headed people were dancing in the candlelight.

'In the Mother's name, I don't even know if you're real!' she cried in despair. 'Perhaps I'm just imagining you, all of you.'

All the children were watching her now, wide-eyed. They looked afraid, mirroring her terror. She reeled, then, quite suddenly, burst into tears. The children did so too.

'Whosoever will save her life, shall lose it,' the girl whispered, 'but whosoever shall lose her life, the same shall save it.'

Agnes stopped crying, and the children followed suit. The girl too faced her now and, beneath her veil, her lapis eyes burned.

'Must I die, then?' Agnes asked. She thought of her women and men, their frightened faces transfigured into those of hares. Of the terrified eyes of the Numidian woman and child in the burning village. Of Strabon. All were gone. They had trusted her, and now they were all dead. It was all her fault. She looked down at her hands contritely.

'How think ye?' the girl replied, cutting into Agnes' thoughts. 'If a woman have an hundred sheep, and one of them be gone astray, doth she not leave the ninety and nine, and goeth into the mountains, and seeketh that which is gone astray?'

'You mean,' Agnes asked, 'that you came here for me? Why did you come?' Her eyes watered, and her lip quivered. Perhaps she didn't deserve to be saved. Her eyes found the sarcophagus. Oughtn't she just to lie down there, and never arise again?

'If so be that she find it,' the girl continued, following Agnes' eyes, 'she rejoiceth more of that sheep, than of the ninety and nine which went not astray.' The girl watched her intently through her veil. Agnes could not bear her gaze. She looked back at her clasped hands.

'Whosoever shall humble herself as this little child,' the girl said, gesturing at the one who had invited Agnes into the circle, 'the same is greatest in the kingdom. But whoso shall offend one of these little ones, it were better for her that a millstone were hanged about her neck, and that she were drowned in the depth of the sea. Except ye become as little children, ye shall not enter.'

Agnes looked at the Nubian girl, then at the other children. Only now, for the first time, did she really notice how threadbare their garments were. None wore any shoes, and their legs were like stilts beneath the poor cloth. Their rags became the torn uniforms of her soldiers, clinging to the charred remains of their bodies as they lay abandoned and rotting in the desert sand. She thought of their young lives, all sacrificed because of her. Then of the smouldering ruins of the Numidian village. All had been sacrificed because of her haste. Because of her pride.

'A good tree bringeth not forth corrupt fruit,' the girl said, her blue eyes fixing Agnes once more, 'neither doth a corrupt tree bring forth good fruit. A good woman out of the good treasure of her heart bringeth forth that which is good, and an evil woman out of the evil treasure of her heart bringeth forth that which is evil.'

'It's my fault that they're dead, isn't it?' Agnes asked. 'I led my legionnaires to their deaths, even though my heart misgave me. And I burnt that village to the ground, for the sake of a few criminals. I had no right, but I went on anyway. Only I brought evil upon them!' Her tears welled up again.

'You are a woman set under authority, having under you soldiers,' the girl said. 'You say unto one, go, and she goeth, and to another, come, and she cometh, and to your servant, do this, and she doeth it.'

'Yes,' Agnes replied, 'and by doing so they followed me to their very deaths. Yet I alone survive. The centurion outlives her century. What shame! What terrible shame.' She thought of Strabon, her brave second. Her eyes returned to the sarcophagus.

'She that is faithful in that which is least,' the girl said, 'is faithful also in much. And she that is unjust in the least, is unjust also in much.'

They had not deserved death. Neither her legionnaires, nor the innocent mother and child. None of them had. Only she had. She knew that now.

'Ask, and it shall be given you,' the girl repeated. Agnes' sad eyes looked back at her searchingly. She could no longer resist the feeling that the girl had penetrated her very thoughts, as if she needn't have voiced them at all.

'But what should I ask for, or what am I to seek?' Agnes asked quietly. 'What is there left for me to ask for but death?'

For a moment, the girl was quiet. Then, slowly, she lifted her veil. Agnes was at once overwhelmed by the clarity of her opalescent eyes, which seared her like ice. The girl's pupils seemed at once to focus upon, and see right through her, as if peering into some immeasurable distance.

'How canst thou say to thy sister, sister, let me pull out the mote that is in thine eye, when thou thyself beholdest not the beam that is in thine own eye?' she asked. 'Cast out first the beam out of thine own eye, and then shalt thou see clearly to pull out the mote that is in thy sister's eye.'

As Agnes listened to her strange Greek, understanding dawned on her. Like the first rays of the morning sun on the sea foam, it touched her, then radiated through her. It was true, all true. She had been blind.

In her pride she had failed to see, or had not wanted to see, the truth. It was a truth that was still too terrible to behold, even now. Yet it was one that had stared her in the face earlier that day. One that had stared back at her across the field of battle. One that had stared back at her from the merciless bronze eyes beneath the grey beret, and from the burnt and scarred faces of her dead legionnaires.

She had been betrayed. Betrayed by the masters she had served so loyally, and so long, and then been left for dead. Once more she pictured the man in the grey beret, then another, no more than a gaunt shadow, among the enemy line. Her heart beat fearfully.

'Where are they?' Agnes asked, fear glinting in her eyes as she remembered her pursuers. 'What happened to them?' The girl's eyes moved to the candle.

'Wheresoever the carcass is, there will the eagles be gathered together,' she answered. 'Be not afraid of them that kill the body, and after that have no more that they can do.' Agnes studied the impassive lines of her cold face, and knew she would never see the grey beret again.

'What must I do?' she asked. She no longer saw the tomb, nor the dark tunnel. Instead, she beheld only the girl's freckled face. She was her only hope. She was no longer afraid.

'When the branch is yet tender, and putteth forth leaves,' the girl said, the candlelight flickering in her pale eyes, 'ye know that summer is near. So ye in like manner, when ye shall see these things come to pass, know that it is nigh, even at the doors.'

The withered fig tree from the valley rose before her.

'But what must I ask, or seek, for?' Agnes asked. 'Or at what door must I knock?' A series of entranceways opened in her mind. The temple pylon, the blind alleys of Thebes, the meschita, and the mihrab. All slammed shut in quick succession.

'Whatsoever they bid you observe, that observe and do,' the girl answered, 'but do not ye after their works. For they say, and do not.

For they bind heavy burdens and grievous to be borne, and lay them on men's shoulders, but they themselves will not move them with one of their fingers. But all their works they do for to be seen of men.'

The sea of grey berets bobbed before her eyes, clearing away the remains of her soldiers. Then the snowy block of nectar appeared, turning incandescent as it transmuted into a burning icon. It had not been the enemy. It had never been. It had been her own. It had been her own all along.

'Then shall many be offended, and shall betray one another, and shall hate one another,' the girl continued, picking up Agnes' thoughts. 'Many false prophets shall rise, and shall deceive many.'

She too had been deceived.

'And because iniquity shall abound,' the girl said, 'the love of many shall wax cold. But she that shall endure unto the end, the same shall be saved. For the stars of heaven shall fall unto the earth, even as a fig tree casteth her untimely figs, and every mountain and island shall be moved out of their places. And the queens of the earth, and the great women, and the rich women, and the chief captains, and the mighty women, and every bondwoman, and every free woman, shall hide themselves in the dens and the rocks of the mountains.'

'So am I not to remain here forever?' Agnes asked, casting around the burial chamber. It was all that she had deserved. The right devotion of the centurion was to die for her century, not to outlive it.

'See ye not all these things?' the girl asked, pointing at the far wall of the chamber. 'There shall not be left here one stone upon another, that shall not be thrown down.' She rose and stepped from the circle, moving towards the wall. Agnes followed.

'Every valley shall be filled, and every mountain and hill shall be brought low,' the girl said. 'The crooked shall be made straight, and the rough ways shall be made smooth.' As her bare feet passed, the candles eddied like wind-kissed ripples on the sea surf.

'Yet a little while is the light with you,' the girl continued. 'Walk while ye have the light, lest darkness come upon you. For she that walketh in darkness knoweth not whither she goeth.' She placed her palm against the glyph-covered limestone. It yielded to her touch at once.

Agnes gasped. A concealed door had opened before them in the tomb wall. Beyond was another tunnel, leading upward in a gentle incline to a distant spot of light. Without another word, the girl entered. Agnes followed. For some time, they ascended in silence. The air grew drier and warmer on her skin. She could smell the desert. A light breeze touched her face.

They stepped out into the desert night. All was still. They were high above the valley, atop the rockface. The stars shone clearly over the majestic pyramid of the hills. Down below, the shadow of the burnt-out camp rose from the floodplain like the encrusted shell of some giant fluvial monster. She could never return that way.

The girl did not face the river, but instead looked in the other direction. As white as the moon above, she stood there in her shawl, her tiny arm pointing into the distance. She was pointing away from the river, away from the camp. She was pointing southwards, to Nubia. To the buffer and, beyond, to the lands of the enemy.

Acknowledgements

My thanks to the Glastonbury Seven, to the priest, philosopher, teacher, barrister, and mandarins, for your encouragement, corrections and, most of all, your friendship. I thank my inspired editor too, for sharing this journey with me.

И наконец, я благодарю тех давно умерших русских писателей, которые были моими верными друзьями.

About the Author

Dr. Richard Warren is a classicist and art historian who has published on the cultures of central and eastern Europe. He draws inspiration from his mixed British-Asian heritage and time spent overseas, including during diplomatic service in Africa.